REALMS OF THE FANTASTIC

Jumpmaster Press
Birmingham, Alabama

Copyright

Cover Art copyright: Mariusz Patrzyk Image ID: 55288685

Library Cataloging Data
Names: Various
Title: *Realms of the Fantastic*, by Various Authors
5.5 in. × 8.5 in. (13.97 cm × 21.59 cm)

Description: Jumpmaster Press™ digital eBook edition | Jumpmaster Press™ paperback edition | Alabama: Jumpmaster Press™, 2018 - 2022. P.O Box 1774 Alabaster, AL 35007 info@jumpmasterpress.com

Summary: A collection of creative Fantasy stories written by talented authors affiliated with Jumpmaster Press™.

ISBN-13: 978-1-958448-68-7 (eBook) | 978-1-958448-15-1 (print)

1. Fantasy 2. Anthology 3. Realms 4. Knights 5. Authors 6. Collection 7. Writers

Printed in the United States of America

REALMS OF
THE FANTASTIC

Table of Contents

ALYSE THE INTREPID
CS Devereaux

"Come on, come on, where is it?"

Alyse sprinted through the darkened cave, an occasional red emergency light her only guide. Her staccato breath echoed against the cavern walls and fused with the slap of her tennis shoes against cool limestone. A bearded, craggy-faced creature about three feet tall, waving a nightstick, jogged after her as fast as his short legs would carry him.

"Stop!" he barked.

Way Out on an old hand-lettered sign loomed in deep vermillion shadows. She skidded inside its low, narrow hallway and crouched behind a stalagmite column. Cold sweat beaded on her brow. The odd little man trundled past the opening while a mildewy scent tickled her nose. She stifled a sneeze.

"Guess I shoulda left after the third exit warning," she murmured. A visit to Fairyland Cavern sparked her creativity, but she never imagined a chase scene.

The thwack of advancing boots interrupted her thoughts.

"Persistent bugger." Alyse hastened deeper into the corridor. She discovered a primitive wooden door and dashed towards it.

"Stop, goldurn it!" the little man shouted.

The little man's determined footsteps pounded behind her. She glanced over her shoulder—too close for comfort.

"It's a dwarf; definitely a dwarf."

She slung the door open, scooched inside, and slammed it shut. The footfalls stopped on the other side. Her pursuer thumped his stick hard, then tugged the latch.

"Get outta there, girl!"

Alyse gripped the knob with trembling hands. "Go. Away."

He yanked extra hard. She lost her grip and her sneakers slipped on the damp stone. Alyse shrieked, then hurtled backwards down, down, down an abysmal cavity, deep into the earth. She tumbled in a never-ending descent into the pitch-dark unknown. Roots protruding through tiny crevices scratched her face and hands. She clutched at them, but they slid through her fingers. She plummeted farther, faster. The roots gave way to a slippery, musty material. Wetness drizzled over walls. Beetles scuttled. Bat wings fluttered. A sour stench filled her nostrils as the channel grew warm, warmer, warmer.

Her blacker-than-black surroundings lit with a ghastly brightness, revealing knobby yellow rock formations coated in a sticky, grayish-pink fungus. An enormous blast of stale air belched her from her portal. She plopped onto a dry, brown surface, rolled, and skidded to a stop. Covered in slime, her head throbbing, she lay prone and panted.

"Yecch, me taste human! Tummy ache," a voice grumbled.

Alyse peered towards the sound, aghast, as the gray mountain from which she erupted lumbered upright, took the form of a three headed Colossus. It trundled away from her across a broad, barren plain, grumbling, rubbing its belly, and shaking the earth with every step. In the faraway distance arose a mountainous terrain, bleak as where she now sat.

Alyse squeezed her eyes shut and opened them. Still the same: a flat gray sky enveloped a cheerless landscape. Before her, the twisted timbers of a bare-branched forest flanked a cobblestone walkway that began nearby. A rugged, ebony mountain rose beyond the woodland; a fortress blacker than the rock perched near its top.

"What is this place?"

Dry-mouthed with fear, Alyse teetered to her feet. Her shoes sank into parched humus and she scrambled onto the pathway. Though she felt no breeze, the trees sighed and whispered among themselves.

"Dryads? They abandoned the Earth ages ago—This *is* Earth, isn't it?"

A dragonfly hummed by, then returned for closer inspection. At second glance, it more resembled a tiny, winged person.

"My name is Pip. Lucky for you, Lump has indigestion. He's a gordingnag. What are you?"

Alyse didn't answer right away. "I–I'm a girl," she stuttered.

"Are you a dragonfly or a fairy?"

"A *HUMAN* girl?" The fairy screeched and vanished.

"Fairies are real?" Alyse whispered. "What *is* this place?" She took a few timid steps along the cobblestone path.

The winged creature darted back in front of her face. "You don't seem scary."

"I'm the one who should be afraid. I'm lost. Can you help me?"

"Maybc. Maybe not."

"Where am I? Why is it so hot?" Alyse removed her jacket and tied it around her waist.

"This is Middengaarde; the Rhisonian Dominion, specifically. I don't know why it's hot. Until recently, it was a lush forest with beautiful gardens everywhere. Now our lakes and rivers are drying up and everything is dying. Queen Cybeli rules Rhisonia. Perhaps she can answer your other question." Pip danced around Alyse in a flurry of fairy dust. "So, you're lost. You searching for yourself or a place?"

Lightheaded from fairy dust, Alyse suppressed a giggle. "A place, of course. Home."

"The queen may help you, if you ask nicely."

"Would you take me to her?"

Pip bobbed at Alyse's eye level. "Dragonfly or fairy? I wish I were a dragon-fairy; then I'd be brave." Her first try at a roar resulted in a goose honk. She coughed and tried again, letting loose a fearsome bellow.

Alyse stumbled backwards, then repeated her question. "Would you take me? Please?"

7

"Only because I like you, strange girl."

"My name is Alyse."

"The queen's castle is through the wood, that way—Alyse." The fairy pointed left. "This path leads to Darkmore Castle. You *don't* want to go there." A shiver passed through her tiny body, then she took flight through the timbers.

Alyse paced after her through what once had been a trail, aware of eyes following her movements. Birds chattered while whispers and titters traded on every side. Alyse's fear transformed to wonderment, and she saw beauty in the woodland's desolation.

"Pip, slow down!"

A wisp of a woman stepped from within a tree trunk. Alyse started, skidded to a stop, and stared. The woman stood naked except for golden oak leaves covering her womanhood. Waist-length strawberry blonde tresses cascaded over her shoulders. Kindness filled her moss-green eyes.

"Hello, Alyse. I'm Neomiris," the nymph whispered.

Alyse stared at her, stunned. "You know my name?"

"We see and hear what the noisy ones overlook. A virtue of silence." She scowled at a pair of squirrels chittering at a sparrow.

"You're a dryad!"

Neomiris smiled. "You will meet many dangers in Rhisonia. The Green Man, Pegim, is our leader. Trust what he tells you. You are one of the good ones, Alyse. We will protect you."

Pip bobbed in Alyse's face. "We're almost at the river. Hurry!"

The tree nymph stepped back into the sapling, leaving behind a single oak leaf. Alyse slipped it into her jeans pocket.

Alyse followed Pip along the riverbank and broke into a sweat from the increased humidity. Here, a plethora of vegetation grew, some familiar, others unlike any she had ever seen.

"Look at the plant life!"

"There's plenty of water and fertile soil here. All of Rhisonia was like this."

Alyse pointed out a stand of heavy vines with pretty, bee-covered blue flowers that proliferated on the far side of the river. They sprouted anywhere with damp soil. "We call that kudzu. It's a menace where I come from."

"You mean tippitwitch? It's worse here. Keep watching."

The vines multiplied by the minute. Along the length of a young vine, a seed pod opened and spewed its contents, followed by another and another. Sticky prongs lined rosy-red pod interiors and snapped around any living thing it touched. With each meal, the stems thickened and grew another foot, strangling everything in its path.

"It loves the heat and bees love it; tippitwitch honey used to be a delicacy. Now it's everywhere."

Alyse shuddered. "That's a carnivorous plant from hell."

"It used to be too cool for it to grow. Let's get out of here."

୨৵   ৵৩

They crossed the wide River Oshun by a bridge of polished moonstone. On the far shore, the path lead around a curve. A turquoise stream flowed from the mouth of a nearby cave and mixed with the river water. It changed the direction of its flow and created an eddy.

"The palace is just ahead," Pip said, "atop that mountain." She hovered near Alyse and pointed toward the cave.

A meager waterfall trickled off the boulders above the cavern's opening. At its peak stood a crystal palace resplendent with towers and spires. It gleamed despite the drab sky.

Alyse gawked at its beauty. "It looks like Cinderella's palace!"

A girl-child waited on the river's sandy banks. Dressed in a silvery gown, her white hair featured a pointed crest atop her head. At the sides, willow vines intertwined long, thick braids. Cobwebs wrapped around her tiny feet and radiant eyes the color of a deep lagoon sparkled. She approached, bearing a rolled parchment.

"State your business here, starting with your name," she demanded. Her voice reminded Alyse of icicles in a wintery breeze.

She gaped at the silvery being, so Pip spoke for her. "Her name is Alyse. She's lost."

"Then this is for you." The childlike being handed Alyse the scroll.

She opened it and read it. "The queen accuses me of disobedience. Why?" She folded the parchment and stuck it in her jacket pocket.

The ethereal creature turned to a gnome who stood guard nearby. "Call the oarsman!"

He blew two long blasts on an elk horn. Within minutes, a second gnome paddled a rowboat from inside the cave.

A giant green dragon swelled from the water. Alyse's jaw dropped. The beast had blazing yellow eyes. Rows of sharp teeth. Scales covered its body save for a hard shell on its back that extended down most of its side and resembled that of a tortoise. The dragon roared, then overturned the rowboat with a swish of its tail. The oarsman sputtered and splashed to the riverbank.

"It's Folo! Run for your life!" the guard shouted.

The gnomes ducked behind a rock and the girl-child faded, leaving Alyse and Pip alone. The serpent set his sight on Alyse, lowered his head, and growled under his steamy breath. He expelled a blast of fishy-smelling fumes, almost knocking her off balance.

Alyse trembled, too frightened to move. The dragon sniffed her from tip to toe. "N-nice dragon," she squeaked, quaking in her shoes.

Pip peppered fairy dust over the dragon's head. He blinked, then set his chin on the ground before her and purred. He meant her no harm.

"Hello, Folo. I'm Alyse." She presented a cautious hand, then stroked his velvety snout.

The guard edged from behind the rock and righted the rowboat. "Climb in. And be quick about it."

"You don't have to be rude." Alyse tossed him a dirty look. "I'll ride Folo, thank you very much, if he'll let me. She clambered onto the dragon's shell. Folo bobbed and rocked, unused to a passenger, then settled.

The guard threw up his hands. "Suit yourself."

Alyse nudged Folo with her heels and the dragon jounced forward. "Easy, boy!" she called. He smoothed his gait and carried her under the dribble of falling water into the cave. Pip sped after them.

Inside the cavern, gemstones glittered on the ceilings and walls. A reflective light source shone on stalactites hanging from the ceiling. Stalagmites and calcified columns thrust upward from the narrow floor at the sides of an underground lake fed by waterfalls.

Deep within the cavern, the child creature waited at a dock. "Follow me."

Alyse disembarked and bid Folo farewell, patting his soft nose. Hesitantly, she trailed the girl-child down a long hallway. Pip secretly coursed after them while the dragon whined and puppy-eyed his new, departing friend.

They approached a wide stone door flanked by sentries. One of them swung it open. "Queen Cybeli awaits." The girl-child motioned for Alyse to enter.

Alyse stepped inside the expansive room, astonished at its grandeur. Golden light beams bathed the hall in radiance; flickering torches in crystalline sconces added to the ambience. She gazed in wonder at its mineral-encrusted walls and the marble floor inlaid with an intricate cut-stone design which pointed to the dais.

The queen's council, a mix of elves, dwarves, and other creatures, sat in a crescent that flanked two sovereigns. They murmured to one another at the sight of a Top Side earthling.

A tall, slender monarch sat upon an elevated throne; a gilded marvel carved from the giant gnarled trunk of a centuries-old sycamore. She held a staff of lapis lazuli in one hand, a signal that court was in session. A mane of feathered, indigo hair flowed about her shoulders, giving her tawny skin a frightening yellowish pall.

A Green Man sat to her right side. Almost as tall as the queen, greenery covered him from head to toe, and he sported a fine beard of what appeared to be English ivy. Cybeli turned to him and whispered, "Hair of burnished copper. Gilded bronze eyes. How curious, she is afraid, yet courageous. Pegim, this young human bears signs of great power. What should I do with her?"

"Test her, my Liege. Human beings can be unpredictable. If she passes with her life—then decide," the leafy guardian responded in a low tone.

"Ah, yes, a challenge." Cybeli tapped her cheek with a talon-like nail, eyeing Alyse. She struck the floor with her staff. The baton's thunderclap resounded throughout the room, and the chamber silenced save for a lingering reverberation. "Come closer."

Alyse approached her throne and curtsied. "Your Highness."

"Do you know why I summoned you?"

"Your scroll stated I disobeyed you. How can that be? I only just arrived. I want to go home. Can you help me?"

"Home? Young lady, you breached the sanctity of Middengaarde. Worse, you trespassed into my realm. My penalty for this infraction is death," Cybeli blasted.

Alyse gasped. "Please! It was an accident. I don't want to be here." A single, salty tear rolled down her cheek, and she trembled.

An angry, iridescent crest like a peacock's tail unfurled atop the queen's head, its intense green-gold color stunning.

"You violated Fairyland's gateway." Cybeli's coal-black gaze pierced Alyse to her core. "We do not tolerate humans here, you pestiferous giglet."

"Pesti—what?" Alyse caught herself. "I'll do whatever you ask. Just let me go."

Cybeli cocked her head, then turned to Pegim. "Have you anything to say?"

"Merciful Queen," he replied. "It is her first offense to the Dominion."

The monarch tapped the arm of her throne with the nail of an index finger; her raised crest smoothed as she thought. Then she leaned forward and stretched her long neck. "Come here, Earth Girl."

Alyse's knees buckled, and she crawled to a spot near the queen's silver-slippered feet.

"Perform one task for me. If you succeed, I will grant you your life and send you wherever you wish."

Encouraged, Alyse met her gaze. "I'll do anything."

"Ha! Be careful what you agree to," Cybeli snapped.

Her worried brow creased. "Three ahnns since, the sorceress Malaka stole our most precious resource, the Sacred Ruby. The Top Side sun finds its way to Middengaarde through random crevices in the Earth. When struck by it, the ruby's facets create light which nourishes all life in Middengaarde. Without it, our graying skies grow darker; woodlands, brown and dry; the temperature continues to rise. My sapien subjects go hungry without grain or vegetables and our water is giving out. We will soon die in total darkness if we do not starve first.

"Malaka hid our precious stone in her fortress, formidable Darkmore Castle. Your task—Rescue the ruby and return it to me. Mind you, it is the size of a fist. Plan ahead."

"Darkmore Castle!" Alyse swallowed hard.

"She will kill you, if she can. And I will be next." Cybeli leaned into Alyse's face. "Bring me her head."

"K—kill her?" Alyse's chest tightened. "That's two tasks."

"One cannot succeed without the other. You must protect yourself. And our ruby. Sir Thad will help you."

"Where is he?"

"I don't know!" Cybeli quaked with anger. "Thaddeus and my sister, Clotilde, were to be married. Jealous, the witch put a spell on him, a curse to ensure no female sapien will care for him. Then she kidnapped Clotilde."

"Where is she?"

The queen's voice quivered. "Dead." Regaining her composure, she added, "Sir Thad's gone. Find him."

Impatience replaced Alyse's queasy fear. "And there's number three. This is impossible!"

"So is your chance of leaving Rhisonia—unless you do as I command." Cybeli's eyes filled with hostility.

"This is insane."

Cybeli interrupted her. "You'll need proper attire. And a horse."

"I can't ride a horse."

"Learn. Fast."

"Lend me Folo. I can ride him."

"Folo?" Cybeli slackened in her seat and burst into laughter; her court followed her lead. "Folo is a dragon. He'd sooner eat you than carry you on his back."

"Folo won't hurt me."

Cybeli snorted. "As you wish. The dragon is yours, foolish Earth Girl." Cybeli scrutinized her. "You look a sight."

"So would you if a gordingnag gagged you from its gullet like a fur ball."

"Ah. Earth's mountain portals can be brutal." Cybeli stifled a smile, then summoned her lady-in-waiting. "Draw her a bath and give her proper clothing, a suit of chainmail, and a sword." She returned her gaze to Alyse. "On the morrow, Pegim will show you out." The queen motioned to her court. "This eventide, we feast!"

From her hiding place near the throne, Pip chittered, "Alyse needs help! I'll alert the dryads," and zipped from the room.

The next morning, hot and itchy in her armor, her worried brows knit, Alyse walked beside Pegim to the inner landing dock.

"Alyse, I fear for your safety. You cannot befriend a dragon. They are not reliable."

"But Folo is my friend." She put two fingers to her lips and whistled. Its echo bounced off the walls.

The creature rose from the water and waved his tail, creating waves that splashed over cavern walls. He spewed a joyful burst of steam and swam to meet them. Alyse beamed up at him. Pegim took cover behind a pillar.

"Good boy, Folo. Hey Pegim, got any marshmallows?"

Pegim peeked from his hiding spot. "*What?*" He pulled at his chin-vines. "Humans!"

"Sorry, Folo, you'll have to stick with fish." The beast rumbled contentedly while she stroked his muzzle. "Why does he have a turtle shell on his back?"

"Dragon whelps make efficient gondolas. We harness them with a shell to inhibit the use of their wings." He inched towards the girl and her dragon, eyeing Folo, "Now listen, Alyse, you must find Sir Thad. My dryads tell me they last saw him—"

Word spread that a human tamed the queen's dragon and a small crowd gathered to watch them leave for Darkmore Castle. Queen Cybeli observed from a window in her private chamber, with Pegim at her side.

"Girl and dragon are fast friends, as she said," Cybeli said. "This human is powerful but doesn't know it." She flashed wary eyes at the Green Man. "I was wise to send her alone. It may be best if she never returns."

Pegim entwined his fingers with hers. "Fear not, my queen. It is easy to see Alyse is special. But she is no threat. Rhisonia's survival depends on her now."

᠀   ᠀

Folo lowered his massive head to the shore by an inlet at the edge of Shadowland, and Alyse climbed down his neck. Behind them, islands dotted a watery landscape. Ahead, obsidian mountains and Darkmore Castle loomed in the distance beyond barren timbers. Alyse's grumbling tummy told her it was time to eat.

"Pegim told me to look for Sir Thad here. Now what?"

She left Folo to graze on minnows and wandered deeper into the brush, listening to the woodlands' whisperings and chattering wildlife. Though she found it beautiful when she arrived, today it felt menacing.

She found a small tree whose branches hung heavy with bright green, leathery-skinned fruit. "Oh, my goodness. Avocados?" She plucked one and sliced it open using the dagger Pegim gave her. "They are! Who would have guessed?"

Folo roared, and a stir of wings disturbed the air. A prehistoric bird descended upon her, its sharp tooth-lined beak agape, talons extended. Alyse dropped her meal, drew her sword, and slashed. The creature withdrew, then charged again. She screamed and dodged behind a rocky outcropping, swinging her weapon. An arrow pierced the beast's breast. It screeched and tumbled, crashing through tree branches. The avocados transformed into a flock of flaplings that scattered across the sky.

Alyse spun towards the sound of a metallic clank.

A knight armored in chainmail, tall as the sapiens at Cybeli's court, stepped from within the timbers, crossbow in one hand. A visor vent concealed his face. "Malaka's enchanted decoys discourage visitors. One must beware forbidden fruit. I've been tracking you and Folo for miles."

She raised her sword. "Tell me your name."

"I am Sir Thaddeus, a steadfast servant of Queen Cybeli. I see you've stolen the queen's dragon."

"If you're so loyal, why did you run away? She sent me to find you."

"A loathsome human? Not likely."

"She *did*. I stole nothing and I'm not loathsome. Now show yourself."

"You expect me to believe you tamed him?"

"I'm riding him."

He hesitated, then lifted his visor to reveal the face of a green, wart-covered toad.

Alyse sucked in her breath. "You're not any kind of knight I've seen."

"Ever see one with an evil spell on him? Believe me, I'm Sir Thad."

Cybeli's tale nagged; he had no reason to lie. "My name is Alyse. Queen Cybeli assigned me to rescue the Rhisonian Ruby from Malaka." She shook her head. "You must help me. I don't know what to do."

"You're smarter than you think, Dragon-tamer. But why *you*?"

"It's a long story. Short version: I fell into a hole, got belched out by a gordingnag, and here I am. I agreed to this, so she'd send me home."

His enormous eyes scrutinized her. "That's so ridiculous it must be true." He dragged the avian creature closer to the river and cast a worried glance at the darkening sky. "Time is running out. We must return the ruby to Cybeli's observatory, or we'll soon be in total darkness. Then we'll die." He hacked at the bird, grumbling. "All right, I'll help you. But we need to eat. Make yourself useful and gather firewood."

After building a small fire on the shore, Thad cooked the meaty parts over the campfire. He offered her a hunk on a stick.

She grimaced. "Try it. Roasted rapiosaur is pretty decent. Especially when you're starving."

While they ate, Alyse watched Folo romp farther out in the depths and listened to his noisy slurps as he guzzled fish and plankton. She found the knight's habit of lapping insects from the air with his tongue off-putting but endured it without complaint.

"Cybeli didn't send her troops to accompany you." Thad said. "I wonder why not."

Alyse stared at the ground. "Maybe she wanted me dead."

"Nonsense. She's desperate for the ruby. I think she counted on me helping you." He shook his head. "Clever bird, she knew I would—Pegim knew where to find me. The dryads tell him everything that happens in the forest."

Alyse forced a half-smile. Even with Sir Thad's help, this seemed an impossible mission. "The queen told me Malaka placed a curse on you. She said Clotilde is dead."

"She's *not!*" he barked. He took a breath and visibly calmed himself. "Like you, I don't know where to look. We make suitable partners, eh?" He stared into the campfire, his bulging golden eyes blinking from bottom up. "I'm sure she's alive, with a spell on her as well. Not knowing what kind makes her harder to locate.

"Clotilde and I grew up together; I've loved her all my life," he continued. "When Malaka learned of our pending marriage, she flew into a rage and turned me into this. Then, she kidnapped my fiancé."

"Would Malaka hold her prisoner in Darkmore Castle?" Alyse took a last bite of rapiosaur.

He shook his head. "Too easy. No, she's hidden somewhere far away. As for the stone, we know where to find it." He stretched. "That's enough for tonight. You sleep while I devise a plan to steal it back."

Her stifling armor prevented slumber. The events of the past forty-eight hours and too many unanswered questions buzzed through her brain. "Sir Thad?"

"Yes."

"What is this place, Middengaarde? I've talked to a fairy, a Green Man, and a dryad. They only exist in children's tales, so how can that be?"

"Oh no, they're real." He scratched his cheek in thought with a finger-like toe. "We all roamed the Top Side once until the fifteenth century. Humans, fearful of our differences, hunted us almost to extinction. We could not coexist with mankind, so we moved underground and created this beautiful world for ourselves. Once we were gone from the Top Side, men turned us into myths. We created our own legends about humans' cruelty— the only species to murder its own kind without cause." He leveled accusatory yellow eyes on her.

"You can't judge everyone by the actions of a few. We're not all bad. I keep hearing about witches, curses, and magic spells; they're not real either."

"There's no evil on the Top Side?"

"Sure, there is."

"You have good and bad. So do we. Bad hunts down good, hoping to annihilate it. But that will never happen. Try to sleep; I need to think."

The sharp crack of a stick woke her, followed by the whinny of Sir Thad's horse. Alyse jolted upright. In the glowing coals of their campfire, she saw Thad on his feet, sword drawn. She heard Folo across the river, harassing night fishermen.

"Folo!" she called, then whistled. He seemed not to hear her.

From the darkness, a lariat swooped over Sir Thad's head and lassoed his arms to his sides. A band of sapien thieves leapt from behind trees and dropped from the branches above.

"Hand over your valuables!" their leader demanded.

"We have none," Thad declared. "Be on your way."

"Think again. Two suits of armor and a horse are worth plenty. You're coming with us."

The robbers tied their hands and shoved them into the woods.

"Folo, Folo!" Alyse screamed.

Too late, the dragon swam to the riverbank, roaring, then toddled ashore, unable to travel fast or far on legs unused to dry land. He wailed and struggled until the sides of his tortoise shell snapped. It cracked again and fell away. One bound wing slipped beneath its encumbrance, then the other. Like a fledgling, he bounced and flopped, shaking the ground, but could not rescue his friend.

ℒ   ℛ

After miles of prods from their captors, Alyse and Thad stumbled into the thieves' camp, a primitive village deep within a forest with smithies, armorers, builders, weavers, and minstrels. A rabble of beings, male and female, baked bread, fed children, and watered horses. Sapiens mingled with dwarves and elves. Purple and gray ogres in chains carried heavy stones or uprooted trees for lumber at the command of their masters.

Their abductors hustled them to a large hut. A tail of smoke rose from a central hole in the roof.

"Wait here," commanded a bandit. He parted the rawhide flap and entered. He soon returned, shoved them through the opening, and gestured towards an odd creature sitting before a fire pit. "Our leader, Drogo Tusk." He cut their bindings and left them.

A part sapien, part warthog, sat before them in the haze of campfire smoke. Four sharp fangs protruded from his hairy snout and a spiky bristle topped his knobby skull. His armored breastplate bore a distinctive gold crested eagle.

Thaddeus slowly removed his helmet to show his speckled toad head. "You're under Malaka's spell also?"

The leader nodded once. They eyed each other; the experience of shared misery dissolved the barriers between them. Alyse looked on, pitying them. She felt the freak among them.

Drogo motioned to Thad. "Sit. I see you and I are not enemies. Join me for a meal. We'll talk."

Thad removed his knee plates and knelt beside him. Alyse held back, intimidated.

"You too, human," the warthog being said. "We're friends here."

Over a breakfast of porridge and roasted rodent, the two warriors exchanged pleasantries, then turned to important matters. "After Malaka swiped the ruby," Drogo explained, "she wreaked havoc on the peasants who occupied Rhisonia and neighboring dominions. She forced them into the Shadowlands. I organized them, formed a small army, and fought back. She won, as my current revolting state attests.

"The ruby sustains us. Without it, our fields won't grow, leaving us with no bread, no medicine. She stole our source of life! We must restore it to the observatory, post haste. I won't stop trying. Our numbers multiply daily and soon we will launch another attack. Everyone here wants the witch dead." He took a sip of brown liquid from a gourd. "Tell me, what is your business, you and this human, alone in the Shadowland?"

"I'm searching for my true love, who is also under one of Malaka's evil spells." Thad related his sad tale, then told of his and Alyse's mission to retrieve the gem. "Drogo Tusk, your reputation as a warrior precedes you. Will you help us? Together, we can beat her."

The leader shook his gigantic head. "If you had an army, then yes. Otherwise, we are but a trifling force." He stroked his chin stubble. "Your unhappy plight recalls an occurrence that's nagged at me since your arrival.

"Two ahnns past, my scouts found a beautiful female sapien in the deepest, most barren part of the timberland, high on a desolate hilltop, apparently dead. Someone left her for scavengers. A wolf pack protected her. By some miracle, the beasts allowed my soldiers closer inspection—she was alive. When my men brought her to our camp, the wolves accompanied them. They guard her still."

Alyse and Thad exchanged glances. His three eyelids expanded wide, and his eyes lit with hope. "May I see her?" he asked.

Drogo led them to a modest hut, set apart from the others. Wolves surrounded the dwelling, and they snarled warnings at their approach.

"The tip of the alpha's ear is missing—Zounds, I know these animals," Thad said. "They're Clotilde's."

"Then why don't they know you?" Alyse flashed him the side-eye.

"I didn't use to smell like a toad. And our warthog friend smells like dinner."

Alyse wrinkled her nose. "I get your point. But how will we gain their trust?" The alpha male flattened his ears and snarled. She backed away. "Drogo?"

He shrugged and shook his head. "No one dares go near them."

Tree branches rustled, and the woodlands erupted in a flutter of whispers. The canines' ears perked, and their grumblings ceased.

"The dryads," Alyse thought, and cautiously extended her hand. This time, the alpha whimpered. "Good wolfie. We won't hurt her, I promise."

He sniffed her hand and stepped aside, opening the way for them. The other wolves followed his lead and stood aside.

The hut appeared empty in the morning gloom. A shaft of gauzy light broke through a crack in the ceiling and cast its beam on a comatose body laid on a dais, chalky hands folded over her midsection. Someone had arranged the skirts of her sky-blue dress. Her beautiful face was ashen and dull, feathery green hair fanned about her shoulders.

Thad drew in his breath. "Clotilde!" He rushed to her side, then fell to his knees. Tears trailed down his cheeks while he stared at her, red eyed, gasping with grief.

Alyse ventured closer. "Speak to her. Maybe she can hear you."

He wrapped his four rough toad fingers around Clotilde's delicate hands and gazed into her lifeless face. "My darling," he whispered, "Can you understand me?"

He kissed her palms, wetting them with his tears. Wherever they landed, her natural caramel color blossomed, and her pale hair deepened to an emerald hue. Her chest heaved, and she inhaled a deep breath.

He leaned near her. "My dearest Clotilde, I love you. Always have, always will."

"I love you, too, Thadpole," she whispered, using her childhood name for him.

He bolted upright. "You're alive!"

She opened her coal-black eyes—and yelped. Struggling to sit up, she backed away from him. "Egads, what trick is this? Where's Thaddeus?"

"You don't understand," Alyse pleaded. "This is Thad— Don't play Malaka's game. Kiss him!"

"Who are you?" Clotilde gaped at her, then noticed Drogo, misty-eyed and standing in the shadows. "And who, or what, is that?"

Two wolves burst through the door, saw her awake and padded to her. They bared their teeth at Thad. He backed away. Clothilde stroked their furry ears and smiled. "My faithful servants."

"That's Drogo Tusk; he owns the place. I'm Alyse," she replied. "Thad and I are going to kill Malaka and steal back the Sacred Ruby. Now you're supposed to kiss him and break the witch's magic spell. —Don't you love him? He sure loves you!"

Clotilde burst into laughter. "Of course, I do! I was just— surprised." She brushed tears from her cheeks. "I've been asleep a long time; give me a minute." She stood, wobbled on shaky legs, and threw her arms around Thad's neck. "My sweet Thaddeus, I don't care if you're a toad. I will love you forever." She kissed him, first on his lumpy green skull, next on the lids of his bulging eyes, and on his nose. Finally, she kissed his lips.

At her touch, his toadness vanished. His features transformed to those of a sapien, with an aquiline nose, a magnificent golden crest, and shoulder-length, feathered locks. They hugged each other as if they had been apart forever.

Drogo stood in a corner and observed, his loathsome visage filled with sad yearning.

Clothilde strode to him and took his hooves in her hands. "Kind-hearted Drogo, we meet at last. Your valor precedes you. Thank you for giving my wolves and me sanctuary." She kissed him once on each brown, hairy cheek. "In return for your generosity, I shall lead my command with yours to Darkmore Castle and kill the sorceress, Malaka. The moment she dies, her hold on you will vanish. All her spells will shatter."

A glimmer of hope sparkled in his tiny black eyes. "You have an army?"

"I am Clotilde, Queen Cybeli's sister. Whatever you need to fight this evil witch, ask; you shall have it."

He dropped to one knee. "Princess, I am your loyal servant."

"I am honored. As of this day, I knight you, Sir Drogo." She tapped his shoulders with her right hand. "Fight hard and well, Drogo Tusk. That is all I demand of you and your soldiers. I will meet you here the morning of the seventh sun, with my troops. In the meantime, ready your men." She glanced at Alyse. "Bring the human; I've heard tales of their savagery. She could prove useful."

"Seriously?" Alyse scowled.

Clotilde crossed the room and placed her hands on Thad's cheeks. "We will be together again soon, my love." She strode from the room, accompanied by her canines.

Thad motioned to Alyse and smiled. "Come along, my slandered human accomplice. Show her you are above the lies." Clothilde returned to her palace to assemble her troops. Sir Thaddeus departed for Cybeli's castle to muster his sapien soldiers while Alyse remained in Drogo's camp. For the next week, Drogo and his warriors completed battle preparations while she target practiced with her dagger. With his careful guidance, she learned to defend herself using her broad sword. Though cumbersome, properly wielded, it could slice through a sapien's neck.

One morning, she awoke with a start. Queen Cybeli hovered over her.

"Your Highness!"

"Congratulations, Alyse, you did far better than expected. You found Sir Thad. And my sister is alive! This is more than I believed possible. With them reunited, my realm's power doubled. My army is ready. Led by Sir Thad, they will join Clotilde and Drogo in battle against Malaka. Together, we are unbreakable. But time is of the essence—our light is disappearing, and the Sacred Ruby awaits."

The monarch faded into the half-light until only her crown remained.

A week after her departure, Clotilde arrived with her army. A fearsome sight, her once-long green locks, now shorn close on sides and back, culminated in a striking Mohawk crest. Her burnished bronze chainmail featured a black armored breastplate etched with lime-colored scrollwork. Her plate armor collar, pointed like Folo's wings, stood high to protect her neck from an unsuspected blade-slice. A pair of emerald-eyed bird heads with sharp open beaks adorned her helmet. Armed with an ax, a rope with a grappling hook, three daggers, and a sword on each side of her belt, she stood ready for battle.

Primed for war, Drogo and Thaddeus waited. Altogether, their unified armies were a frightful force.

Sir Thad selected a small mare for Alyse. "Old Reliable will carry you up the mountain. You won't need a horse after we arrive."

The commands marched through the Shadowlands and up the elevation to Darkmore Castle. Alyse's adrenaline soared at the sound of marching feet, the clatter of metal on metal, the thunk and clunk of shields and wooden wheels. Ogres struggled to maneuver the catapult-like onager and other heavy war machines through the timbers and up the steep climb. Soldiers carried battering rams and crossbows. Drogo's warriors, fortified by both liquid and inner courage, brandished axes and spears.

They camped on a modest hillside near the castle and prepared to siege at the first hint of light. From her vantage, she observed Malaka's soldiers. Odd creatures with long pointy noses scurried along the battlements. Their shrill shouts echoed through the night as they primed their weapons, filled cauldrons with sticky black oil, and lit fires under them.

Half of her wished she could just watch from the safety of the hillside; her other half expected the fight and wanted to help. But what could she do? She studied the fortress—while Malaka's army prepared for war, servants emptied chamber pots into the few inches of foul muck that served as a moat. Kitchen staff added a spoiled carcass and table scraps to the fetid sludge. A wry smile curled Alyse's lips when an idea formed in her mind.

"Pip, are you here?" she said aloud. In a blink, the fairy appeared.

"I've been here," she tittered.

"Remember the day we walked along the riverbank?" Pip nodded. "Bring me all the tippitwitch seeds you can find. Hundreds of them. Put them in drawstring bags—I need two. A jar of tippi honey would be nice, too," Alyse added. "Tonight, I want you to plant the seeds next to the moat around the bottom of the castle."

"Do you know what you're asking? A pod could snap me up!"

"Please, Pip. Do your best. This is important." Pip nodded and disappeared.

In the deepening darkness, Alyse saw a rosy glow in the keep's highest windows. "The ruby," she whispered. "I better tell Sir Thad my plan."

She spotted him strolling hand in hand with Clotilde into the woodland and smiled. They had other things on their mind besides war; she'd inform him of her idea in the morning.

"May I join you?"

She recognized Drogo's voice without turning. "Have a seat."

He offered her a hunk of roasted stag on a forked stick. "Take it. You need your strength." He eased himself to the ground.

"Thanks." She pinched off a bit of meat and popped it into her mouth, nodding towards Thad and Clotilde. "They truly love each other, don't they?"

"I think so. Theirs is the real thing."

She swallowed and gestured towards Darkmore. "It looks smaller than I imagined."

"Small? You're looking at the barbican. We must fight our way past that to enter the main buildings inside the curtain walls. The keep is in the far corner. It won't be easy to reach. The morrow will be a challenge."

Alyse grimaced.

Drogo patted her shoulder. "Think positive, my friend. Our fighting force is the toughest this old castle has seen. Our chance of success is good."

The sky shimmered with a Borealis, both fascinating and eerie. An iridescent radiance lit distant mountain peaks.

"What are those ridges?"

"They're called the Accursed Mountains; they say a river of fire accounts for the peculiar light. No one ever travels there, but tales abound of other kingdoms beyond it."

"Maybe you should check it out."

Drogo chuckled but did not respond.

She opened a new thread of conversation. "No stars, no moon. It's odd."

"What's a moon?" he asked.

"On the Top Side, as you call it, billions of twinkling stars fill the night sky. And one beautiful moon; sometimes so bright you can see everything around you."

A rapid succession of chartreuse surges flittered.

"Beautiful, yes?" Drogo replied. "Legend is our ancestors built a fire bridge to the sky. When we leave this life, we cross it into the afterlife."

"They're caused by the clash between molecules in the Earth's atmosphere and super-charged solar particles from the sun." Alyse frowned. "Except there's no sun here. I think your legend is the better explanation."

Drogo wrinkled his muzzle. "I don't understand. But I'd like to learn more; tell me about your moon."

"Let's begin with the sun. Ours is golden and on a sunny day, it lifts the spirit. I miss it the most." Their conversation lasted into the night. They shared stories of life. Laughed together. She slowly realized she was having fun.

"Drogo, there's something I've been wanting to ask you. When we met, you didn't judge me for being human. Why not?"

"Look at me. Who am I to judge anyone? Besides, I prefer to know one's heart before I decide who they are." The Borealis' display faded, and he got to his feet. "We'd better turn in. Big day ahead."

"I enjoyed talking to you."

"I should thank you. Few women would spend their precious time with an ugly beast like me. Truly, none."

Alyse gazed up at him, surprised at his words. A last green volley flared behind him, and she perceived an individual far different from whom she met a week ago.

"Drogo Tusk, you are the handsomest man I have ever known. Kind and generous, you possess a beautiful soul."

His gigantic head bobbled; her words touched him.

"Good luck, Drogo."

"Anon, fair Alyse. May good fortune favor us."

Before settling onto her mat, she glanced at Darkmore and gasped. Hundreds of tiny lights flickered at its base. "It's Pip! She brought a fairy army." The fairies tapped soil over top of the seeds. Afterward they floated on the air and wandered in and out of the castle's open windows. It reminded Alyse of a summer night, and she thought of home. It occurred to her she may never see her mother again. She forced herself to be positive, but then remembered Folo and saddened at the memory of his plaintive wails. Saying a prayer, she rolled over, and slept a few uneasy hours.

She awoke and found two large velvet bags folded next to her.

At first light, bowmen assumed formation behind them higher on the hillside while mounted soldiers waited right and left. Atop the hill, ogres secured and readied the war machines. The infantry surrounded the fortress; standards, spears, and halberds raised. Alyse's heart pounded while she listened to Sir Thad give the forces a rousing pep talk outside the barbican. Clotilde and Drogo matched his action farther around the bulwarks.

Across the stronghold's ramparts, cauldron fires blazed. Helmeted warriors lined the crenellations while archers occupied arrow slits.

The horizon lightened, revealing the first rays of light. Sir Thad's army stood ready. A light breeze ruffled the plume on his chief commander's helmet. At Sir Thad's signal, he lowered his standard. Drummers drummed. Horns blasted. Fighters pounded their shields. Their voices pierced the morning air in a nerve-shattering bellow that galvanized their hatred of the evil Malaka.

The Commandant gave the order, "Charge!"

Drogo dropped to all fours and plowed ahead, leading his motley array of warriors in the assault, his tusks skewering any fighter of Malaka's that crossed his path.

Thad galloped to Alyse's side. "Stay with me while I seek an entry point. I don't know what we'll find, so follow my lead."

She nodded, too nervous to speak, then trailed him out of the way of battle. Inside her armor, sweat rolled between her shoulder blades and her hair plastered to her skull under her helmet.

Clotilde joined Thad and Alyse and together, the three observed the fracas hidden from sight. Under the cover of ever-shadowy light, made hazy by billowing black smoke, they approached the castle on foot and waited for an opportune moment to sneak into the castle.

"Thad, I need to tell you, er, both of you, about my plan," Alyse began.

"What plan?" they replied together.

"Last night, I was thinking, what would ensure a win in case Malaka's army is like, you know, too strong? Then it came to me." She blurted her last words. "I asked Pip to plant tippitwitch seeds around the base of the fortress."

"Tippitwitch?" he replied. "What good will that do?"

"Are you insane?" Clotilde's expression morphed into shock and concern. "You did that without consulting us first? That vine could take over everything! It would eat our armies alive, as well as hers."

"Only if it grows, my love."

Alyse hung her head. "I just wanted to help."

"Next time, go through the proper channels of command. Thank you for trying, Alyse," Thad soothed.

She offered him a grateful half-smile but felt like throwing up. Pointing to a lancet high on the keep wall, she said, "That's where she keeps the ruby. I saw its glow last night."

Sir Thad absently nodded and scanned the battlefield. The broken bodies of his soldiers littered the field. Blood-saturated, stabbed, limbs lost, they lay moaning, dying, or dead. Droog mercenaries—huge, hairy, battle-bred forces who threatened with mean-eyed slits—were Malaka's commissioned warriors. They hacked at those sapiens still standing, invincible against their efforts to stop them. The bulk of the witch's army, amalgamations of rats or weasels, continued to fight after injury. Thad frowned and narrowed his eyes.

"Look, Clo. Though we outnumber Malaka's troops three to one, our soldiers die while hers live. If a leg is severed, it regrows; their wounds heal within minutes. They only stop moving if strangled or crushed."

"Egads, you're right!" Clotilde bit her lip. "No one would fight for her except the droogs. Their numbers are few, but they're invincible." She snapped her fingers. "Of course! Her army's enchanted. There, a dead rat snapped back to life, transformed into a soldier, and rejoined the action. Weasels, the same. What can we do?"

"She will defeat us unless we act fast. We need to get inside, grab the stone, and retreat. Let's go!"

Attacking forces breached the barbican and lowered the drawbridge. They balanced ladders on the curtain wall and scaled them. Fiery oil met a few on the climb, while many more penetrated the battlement.

Alyse followed Thad over the bridge and chanced a glance at the castle's foundation. There, encompassing its base, tiny tippitwitch shoots had sprouted overnight and inched higher every second, nourished by rich soil and foul moat water. The first pods had formed already. It would not be long before they became deadly. "That was fast," she murmured, concerned at the plants' rapid maturation.

Concealed by chaos, the trio snuck inside via a narrow door next to the drawbridge and slipped into an anteroom off the central courtyard.

"Drogo told me the fastest route. He's been here before, remember?" Alyse said. "The stairs to the right lead to the main galleries. They finish in a T-shaped hallway lined with chambers. Turn left. At the long end of the hall is another set of steps. The ruby's on the top floor. No telling who or what we'll meet; we've got to be careful."

Thad and Clotilde gazed at her with increased respect.

Drogo and his men burst into the anteroom from outside. Malaka's fighters dashed in from the courtyard. Thad turned and defended the women against an attacker, a weasel that refused to die. "You two go ahead. I'll catch up!" Thad shouted over the maelstrom.

The fight edged closer to the inner yard as Drogo's soldiers pushed forward. Clothilde and Alyse darted up a spiral staircase leading to the galleries.

They crept through a covered gallery, alert for attackers. Alyse heard Folo's roar and rushed to an arched opening. "He's here—and flying!"

Clotilde grabbed her and clapped her hand over Alyse's mouth before she could call out. "Don't you dare give away our position!" she hissed.

In the hallway beyond the galleries, a chamber door flew open. A trio of animated corpses lurched, one wielding a battle ax, the other two swords. Their death stench was unbearable. They attacked, separating Alyse from Clotilde.

"Go, go, go!" Clotilde shouted. "I can handle these foul death-devils."

At the far end of the passage, tippitwitch vines ascended onto the second-floor windowsill. A stem slunk across the floor. Another continued upward outside the castle wall. Along the way, its flowers blossomed, spewed seeds, then changed into deadly pods.

Alyse gasped. "They're out of control! This is a disaster!" She sprinted away from the vines towards a staircase at the end of the hallway and leapt up the first few treads.

Four of Malaka's weasel-guards dashed into the hall. Pods devoured them before they reached Clotilde. More guards followed. They retreated from the vines except for one who pursued Alyse. Clotilde threw a dagger into his exposed neck. He fell at the foot of the steps.

Alyse, sword in hand, scurried farther up the staircase. The clash of armies, screams of warriors in pain, howls of the dying ebbed as she ran deeper into the castle. Fireballs from Drogo's onagers exploded into the walls of Darkmore. The din of Folo's roar assured her she was not alone.

On the third floor, she found a single closed door. Heart pounding, she stood before it. "Where is Malaka?" she whispered. She took a deep breath and kicked it open.

Heat swept over her. Burning torches and ancient tapestries with images of odd creatures in woodland settings adorned the outer walls. Lit candles rested on every solid surface. Dried vermin and strange herbs hung from the crossbeams overhead. Old wooden chests, several stacked with smaller boxes, lined one wall; a bookcase filled with vintage volumes leaned against another. A tall cabinet with ornate doors dominated the room, across its top set a colorful array of bottles.

A carved wooden table and chair stood before a narrow window—Malaka's desk. A corked earthenware pot rested near a corner of the desk. In the center sat a simple box. A telltale crimson radiance pulsed from a crevice between its lid and the bottom half.

"The Sacred Ruby!" She dashed to the table, fumbled with the ribbons on one of Pip's sacks, and slipped the box into it.

"Help me!" a voice squeaked.

Her eyes scanned the room. A dim glow emitted from a corked glass jar atop the cabinet.

Again, it cried, "Alyse, help me!" The plea came from within the bottle.

"Pip! What happened?" Leaving bag and box on the table, she shoved a chest to the cabinet's side and topped it with a smaller box.

"The witch caught me. My air is almost gone."

Alyse climbed onto the trunk, stood on tiptoe on the second box, and reached as high as she could. Her fingertips brushed the glass; it tipped, then righted itself. "I need another box."

"Hurry!" Pip whimpered.

She placed a second on top of the first, climbed, and wrapped her fingers around Pip's urn. An unseen force swept her legs from beneath her. Alyse and the boxes tumbled. Pip's prison turned on its side, rolled to the edge of the cabinet, and stopped.

Alyse scrambled to grab her sword. She gazed upward amid archaic maps and broken vials of potions spilled from the two now-open boxes. Before her stood a stunning sight—Malaka!

The witch hovered a few feet off the wood floor, small in stature, and unexpectedly attractive. Pale, flawless skin enhanced her delicate-featured face. A simple black dress enhanced the creamy smoothness of her neck and hands. Malaka's rosy-red lips wore a sneer and evil radiated from her bright blue eyes. Thick, chestnut hair flowed from beneath a poison-green ebony-horned headdress. Long, red phoenix feathers arched from its peak, writhing as if alive.

"Why are you in my private sanctuary, you beslubbering, pigeon-livered geck?" She fired lightning from boney fingers. "I hate humans!"

Alyse sidestepped the attack and defensively raised her sword in trembling hands. "I'm here for the Sacred Ruby."

"Apish horn-beast. That beautiful stone is mine. You have no inkling of the power it holds."

More lightning bolts followed. They struck tapestries, overturned candles, ignited the strewn maps. Liquid from spilled potions burst into flames. Alyse dodged the growing inferno, lunged forward, and sliced with her sword. She missed Malaka's feet by inches.

"What will you do when you've finished here? Work your witch's evil in my world?"

"Excellent idea! —Alyse. Maybe I'll keep you for an impish pet instead of killing you right away."

Alyse shuddered upon hearing her name uttered from the witch's lips. Cackling, Malaka soared throughout the room and threw a series of fiery bolts. She swung at the witch, shredding her dress.

A fire-bolt nicked Alyse's arm, and she yelped.

Pip struggled to roll her confinement on the cabinet and succeeded. It smashed, and she bolted into the air.

A tippitwitch vine writhed through a window and slithered towards the frenzy. Another snaked through a second opening.

The sorceress, unaware of the creepers, chortled and tossed an armload of rats at her intruder.

Pip pointed her finger; a stream of fairy dust changed rats to mice, and the rodents scattered. Furious, the witch wailed and slung a hornet's nest at Alyse.

Alyse swung her sword like a baseball bat and hurled the nest back to Malaka. Stinging insects exploded from the hive.

Pip let loose a spirited roar and Folo answered from a distance. She focused on the earthenware jar on Malaka's desk. It sailed across the room in a flurry of fairy dust, smashing against the witch's horned headpiece. Tippitwitch honey oozed over her, top to toe.

Malaka shrieked. Her headdress toppled, exposing her true identity—a grizzled old hag. Her face grew hoary and haggard, with deep-set white irises and narrow red slits for pupils. Lips wrinkled and thinned, pointy teeth yellowed, and the gray, shriveled skin of her stooped, misshapen body peeked from the neck and sleeves of her torn dress. Once lustrous, her locks hung gray and stringy below a bald skull. She sank to the floor, inundated by swarming hornets. Howling, she clambered to her feet, spun, slapped, and waved her toothpick arms. She stumbled into a mass of vines.

Tippitwitch encircled one leg and then the other. Its pods nipped at her, growing larger with each nibble. A mature pod raised its ghastly head and stretched wide its rosy, snakelike carpels. It clamped them around her body with a snap as loud as an animal trap, severing her legs and head. It devoured her.

Alyse screamed and backed away from the horrific sight. "Folo, help!" Her ragged wail hardly carried beyond the tower walls. She coughed and bellowed, "Folo!"

The dragon roared outside the keep. A sweep of his tail ripped the top of the spire from its beam. Flames and smoke billowed into the air.

Alyse dashed to the table, dodged a vine inching up its legs, and grabbed the bag containing the ruby.

"Wait! Malaka's head," Pip reminded.

The witch's severed head, scalded with bubbling brown tippi honey, lay near the now-complacent pod, which had settled on the floor to digest the witch's body. A neighboring pod capsule threatened to explode. Breathless, Alyse prodded the cranium away from the tippitwitch with her sword and dropped it into the mouth of her open sack. "Eeeww!" she exhaled. "I can't believe I just did that."

Folo lowered his neck into the inferno. She leapt onto his snout and dashed on board, gripping the sacks which held her precious cargo—the ruby and head.

Pip fluttered next to her. "The honey pot on Malaka's desk was supposed to be for you. Sorry."

"No worries, you used it well. Thank you, Pip, you're awesome."

The fairy blushed with pleasure and vanished. Folo torched the rest of the keep, roared with all his might, and winged his friend from danger.

Alyse peered into the darkness with the flaming fortress as her only light. A horror of mangled and disfigured bodies littered the field, many garroted or crushed by tippitwitch vines. Even now, they fed on those closest to the moat. She felt ill at the sight, but grateful to those who dragged the wounded from the jaws of danger.

"My God, the carnage. Clotilde was right. I am to blame!" She called out to Folo. "Find Thaddeus and Clotilde. Hurry, before the castle collapses." They searched the battlefield, the courtyard, and balconies. "There they are, down there!"

Folo swung low over an open parapet. A pack of attacking droogs surrounded the trapped couple. Folo shot fire at their aggressors and circled back, legs lowered. Clotilde slung her rope around one of his enormous, hooked talons and climbed. She pitched a leg over the claw, then guided the tether for Thad. He grasped it. His hands injured and oozing, he lost his grip and fell. On his second try, he ascended to safety.

The fortress, now engulfed in flames and shivering under the weight of massive tippitwitch vines, collapsed. Folo spirited them from the danger and made a sweep of the battleground.

"Where's Drogo?" Alyse called. "We won't recognize him without the witch's curse."

"I see a crested breastplate," Thad shouted. "Alyse, get us closer." Folo descended towards the chaos. "It's him! A soldier pulled him to the edge of the battlefield."

Drogo lay among a profusion of wounded warriors. The dragon landed close by, and his passengers rushed to the side of a wounded young man with shoulder-length brown hair. He was shorter than most sapiens, though taller than Alyse.

Clotilde reached him first. "That's his family crest. A pod got to his leg."

"No, no, no!" Alyse cried. "Drogo, don't be dead. Please, God, don't let him die."

Drogo's eyelids fluttered, then opened.

"You're alive!" She jerked off her helmet. "Oh, Drogo, I should've told you about the tippitwitch. It was my idea to plant it around the castle walls. I wanted to destroy Malaka's army. It's my fault it spread. My fault it hurt you—" she sobbed, unable to finish.

He clasped her arm with a bloodstained hand. Alyse leaned in to hear his slow, soft-spoken words. "Don't cry. Vine didn't harm us."

"But your leg."

"Not bad. Looks worse. Saw fairy lights. Investigated." He took a gasping breath. "I know tippi seed when I see it—warned commanders." He wheezed and gazed into Alyse's red, swollen eyes. "You are remarkable." He found her hand, gave it a weak squeeze, then passed out.

"He's unconscious." She peered at Clotilde through her tears. The warrior princess barely masked her anger. "If Drogo dies, the blame is yours. Let's get him to the palace. Thad, will you carry him?"

He hoisted the fallen knight over his shoulder and placed him in the middle of the dragon's back. The women seated themselves on either side of him. Thad sat at the rear. Alyse brushed Drogo's mane from his face. "He looks like Ryan Reynolds with long hair."

"Who?" Thaddeus asked.

"A famous human on the Top Side."

"Drogo's father was human," Clotilde replied.

"Wait, what? He never mentioned it. I thought you first met him at his camp in the forest."

"I did. Drogo's well known, respected despite his humanness—"

Alyse glowered. "Stuff the human jibes, sapien stork-woman. I've had enough of it."

"Leave her alone, Clo," Thad scolded.

Clotilde raised an eyebrow at her betrothed, then gestured towards the two bags. "May I?"

Alyse shrugged.

The warrior woman gazed at Malaka's blackened visage. Her eyes narrowed. "Where's her headpiece? I want it!"

Tremors shook the earth, and Lump appeared, his three gruesome faces lit by the burning fortress. "Mmm, droog and tippi." Flashing an absurd, yellow-toothed grin, he extinguished the flames with his hand. He scooped up screaming droogs with one tremendous mitt, tippitwitch with the other, and stuffed his two voracious mouths at once. His third head kicked up a fuss. "Hey, me left out!" They argued, and their ire escalated.

"Let's get out of here!" Sir Thad shouted.

"Folo, to Cybeli's castle."

Darkness fell upon the Dominion, blacker than any night before it. Sporadic Borealis shimmers provided fleeting light into the observatory atop the palace. A small, spherical room, it featured a domed ceiling, opened for a planned ceremony. A chest-high stone pedestal stood in the center, a dim glow within its base.

Pegim, bearing a torch, lit the way up the steps and placed his torch in a wall sconce. Behind him, Queen Cybeli carried the cherished ruby on a velvet cushion. Alyse trailed them, holding her long dress above the toes of her slippers. Cybeli handed him the pillow, reached for the ruby, then hesitated.

"You earned the privilege of sharing this moment with me, my young friend. Place your hands near mine."

Alyse approached. The gem's raw vitality coursed through her. Startled, she jerked her palms away. Its pulse thrummed and reminded her of a family trip to Sedona, Arizona, where she stumbled into one of Sedona's energy vortexes. While the vortex elevated her senses with a mild vibration, the stone's power overwhelmed her. She replaced her hands and traced an indentation near its base as she sought a firm hold.

Cybeli recited the incantation. "I call on you Mother Earth, element of the physical, to cleanse and purify the Sacred Ruby. Blessed Mother, purge Malaka's evil from this precious stone forever."

The stone awakened and hummed with mounting energy. Together, Queen Cybeli and Alyse placed it on the pedestal. The ruby ignited with brilliant beams. Pink lightning shot forth and flickered throughout the sky. Dawn broke, illuminating the shadows with every shade of coral and peach, and settled to a delicate blush that shined upon the entire kingdom. Thin light shafts morphed into a dazzling sun.

Joyous cries broke out as Rhisonians celebrated a new day.

A soft spring shower, one that allowed the sunshine through, cooled the atmosphere, nourished the earth, and created rainbows that stretched as far as Alyse could see. From the tower, she watched sapiens embrace in the rain, taste its pure sweetness on their tongues, and sniff the wet fresh air. Some fell to their knees and kissed the dampening soil.

Tippitwitch vines, which had breached the moonstone bridge, shriveled in the cool air, and retreated across the River Oshun.

Alyse shared in the sapiens' happiness and beamed with joy—She had saved Rhisonia!

♀   ♂

"...I now pronounce you husband and wife," Queen Cybeli proclaimed from the base of the dais. After a gentle nuptial kiss, the newlyweds faced the congregants in the queen's Great Hall. "Ladies and Gentlemen, I introduce to you the wedded couple, Princess Clotilde and Prince Consort, Sir Thaddeus." Cybeli caught Alyse's eye, nodded at the handsome war hero beside her, and smiled.

In the front row, Drogo leaned on a crutch beside Alyse. He took her hand in his. She gazed up at him, neither speaking a word. The look in their eyes spoke volumes. Her cheeks flushed, and she looked away. In the background, the waterfall's cascade punctuated the air. In the distance, Folo roared and splashed in the river.

Clotilde and Thad strolled to the balcony to address the waiting crowd. Cheers erupted as they lifted their joined hands.

"Alyse, come here," Queen Cybeli beckoned.

She stepped before her and curtsied. "Your Highness."

Pegim winked at Alyse, then passed the ruler a small box from which she removed a gold encased amulet on a purple silk ribbon. Her peacock-feathered crest unfurled, its iridescent green suns enhancing her regal appearance. She placed the talisman around Alyse's neck.

"Alyse, you accomplished what no other before you has done. You saved Rhisonia. We are indebted to you." The monarch stepped from the dais. "Come with me, dear. You, too, Sir Drogo."

Cybeli took Alyse's hand in hers and they joined the newlyweds. Thad and Clotilde stood on one side of the queen, Alyse and Drogo on the other. Pegim, holding a draped object, placed himself behind Alyse.

"All of Rhisonia, hear me well," the queen announced. "We share a day like none other. First, we honor the marriage of my sister, Clotilde, and Sir Thaddeus." Cheers lifted. "There is another cause for celebration. The young human, Alyse, with help from Sir Thaddeus, Clotilde, and Sir Drogo, rescued our precious gem from evil hands—and delivered the beautiful life-giving light we all now enjoy."

Pip popped into view. "Hey! What about me?"

"Let's not forget our courageous little fairy," Cybeli added.

Pip scowled. "Dragon-fairy! I'm a dragon-fairy, Your Highness."

"Oh my! Our brave dragon-fairy, Pip, played an important role in its return."

Pip took a bow.

"Together, they saved our land. Our guest, fearless Alyse, valiant Alyse," Cybeli beamed at her, "Alyse, the dragon-tamer, killed the sorceress, Malaka, who stole our Sacred Ruby."

Pegim handed the monarch the item he carried from the Great Hall; she removed the cloth, then held Malaka's deteriorated head aloft to mixed gasps and hoorays.

Alyse stammered, "But I–I didn't kill her. The tippi—"

"Shhh, they don't care," Drogo whispered. "You're famous. Go with it."

"Rhisonia is free!" the queen exclaimed. "I declare this day— Alyse the Intrepid Day."

"Huzza! To Alyse," her subjects clamored.

Cybeli turned to her. "Alyse, what is your wish? You have but to ask. A title, perhaps? A grand manor house? I know a knight who would be a good lord." Her black eyes twinkled.

Alyse examined Drogo's face, caressed his firm jaw and soft lips, and committed every inch to memory. The tears in his dark eyes tugged at her heart. She could no longer bear it and kissed him.

He wrapped her in his arms. "Please stay." His soft words brushed her ear. "Or I could come—"

"Drogo, I care for you; I do. But we would never work together. Our worlds are too different. Many beautiful sapien women would gladly give their heart to a good-looking guy like you."

She faced the queen and spoke quickly before she changed her mind. "You know my answer."

ç♥ ♥ç

Ms. Johnson handed back the Creative Writing assignments, her unmistakable scrawl in red pencil on Alyse's paper: 'A+'.

"Good work, Alyse! Your imagination is impressive. My science-minded students often fall short on expressiveness. Where did you get your idea?"

Alyse fingered her pendant, felt it throbbing, and smiled. "Thank you. It was just something I dreamed up."

After the instructor moved on, Alyse turned over the case and read the inscription:

To Alyse the Intrepid,
Pursue Your Passion.
With Gratitude,
Cybeli R,
Queen, Rhisonian Dominion

She gazed out the classroom window. Students sat in small groups on the grass under ancient trees. Memories flooded her mind: the sapiens' strange elegance. The incredible Rhisonian beauty. The harsh realities of war. The horrible droogs.

"No dryads will glide from within these oaks," she mused. Above them, the deep blue October sky seemed endless. "No rosy tint here unless sunset rewards us with one. No Pip, no Folo." She sighed. "Most of all, no Drogo." Alyse brushed a tear from her eye.

The ruby pulsed in her hand.

"Did I make the right decision?"

Curmudgeon Quest
Art Lasky

Dishes done—well, added to the towering pile in the sink—Crispoff settled into his comfy chair. A second cup of coffee sat within easy reach on the end table. *Routine, that's the key, have a daily routine and stick to it,* he thought. He picked up a well-worn copy of *The White Dragon.*

It was another sparkling Tuesday morning, and the city busily hummed along outside his open window. By 8:30, the balance between early-morning fresh air and rush hour noise reached its tipping point. He rose and rushed to the window. "Stop blowing your damn horns. The guy in front of you can't move because the guy in front of him can't move because the guy in front of him—morons, all of them!"

He slammed the window shut. "Why is the whole damn world in such a rush?"

Crispoff no longer missed having a job and someplace to be busily rushing off to. At eighty-five, rushing was not high on his agenda. With a last muttered curse aimed at humanity in general, he settled back into his seat and opened the book. Within moments, he was back on Pern awaiting threadfall.

A high-pitched crackling sound caught his attention. He reached behind his ear, groping for the control on his hearing aid. "Cheap, foreign piece of crap—"

The words trailed off as he looked up to see a bright spot slowly growing in the middle of the room.

"Damn cataracts, damn bifocals, damn—"

The spot took on a humanoid shape and, once again, his words trailed off. The glow faded and he beheld a tall, slender figure. Seven decades of reading fantasy stories paid off; *Fairy, she's a fairy,* he thought. The elf had a lush pile of auburn hair that did not quite conceal the tips of her pointed ears. She wore form-fitting silver armor, deadly and alluring at the same time.

"I am Faye, a knight of the Silver Court—" she said in rich, husky voice that could ignite a fire in a young man's heart.

"Knight? You look like a beautiful Princess."

"A girl can be both."

"Are you sure your name isn't Arya?"

"Who?"

"Never mind. What do you want from me?"

"You are summoned on a quest."

Crispoff studied the beautiful fairy standing in his living room. "A quest? A quest isn't exactly what I've got in mind," he said, wiggling his eyebrows.

Faye stood quietly, unimpressed and unresponsive to his advance.

Crispoff shrugged and changed his focus. "Well, if it's a-questing you want to go, you're seventy years too late."

"It's never too late, if you are true of heart."

"Ha, did you read that in a fortune cookie?" Crispoff sneered.

Wistfully shaking his head, he continued. "When I was a teenager I'd have jumped at the chance to go questing with an elven knight. When I was in my twenties, I would've followed you and that Kathleen Turner voice of yours on a quest to steal Satan's ice bucket from his throne room in Hell. Nowadays, Girlie, that just ain't gonna happen."

"But you must; we—"

"I am not going with you," Crispoff interrupted, folding his arms over his narrow chest. He defiantly stuck his jaw out.

Faye shook her head and snorted, mildly frustrated. "How can you refuse? The high council has chosen you to recover the enchanted Rod of Redemption. They always choose the right champion. You are hereby summoned on this quest—"

"You said that already," he interrupted again. "I'm old, too old to be running off on an adventure." He sat down and tried to return to his book.

"But you must. The enchanted Rod of Redemption—"

"Could you just call it the Rod?" Crispoff scoffed. "It'll save a lot of time; trust me I won't confuse it with any other rod."

"Since the Rod was stolen by Fearfang the Black, the kingdom is in grave danger," she explained. "Sea Trolls are rampaging deeply into the northern fishing grounds, destroying our boats, and killing the crews. The Pirates of Perdition are raiding the coast of Coney, not even the rabbits are safe. Worst of all, a plague of singing locusts swept through the romantic Crystal Groves of Diamandia."

"Singing locusts don't sound so bad; unless they're singing show tunes, tell me they're not singing show tunes."

"Worse, they sing off-key, and all the crystal has shattered. The romantic Crystal Groves are now the Glass Shard Dunes of Diamandia—not so romantic."

"Listen," Crispoff replied, "I've always been partial to redheads, and even twenty-one years ago if you'd batted those smoky green eyes at me I would've signed up. But I'm old O-L-D. Old!" He shook his head. "You don't need me, I'm an old man. Get a great warrior or a wizard. That's it, go find a wizard."

"The High Council chose you. They always pick the right—"

"I can't, I won't. Bother someone who cares."

"But—"

"Tell it to the Marines, why don't you?"

"But—"

"Listen kid, I just don't have that kind of time. I've got all these dishes piled up in the sink. They're not gonna do themselves, you know."

Faye triumphantly smiled and snapped her fingers. The dishes clattered and clanged, the silverware rattled and flashed. Crispoff watched, mouth open wide in surprise, as everything was magically cleaned and stacked away. The scent of fresh brewed coffee drew his attention to the cup at his side, where his coffee was suddenly topped off.

"Ready to go?" She asked.

"Just because you did a few dishes? Ha!"

Faye whimpered, then sobbed, then cried. There is a certain compelling magic in crying. The tears of a human can be ignored, the tears of a fairy—not.

"Stop crying, it's not gonna work."

The waterworks cranked up to full cascade. Crispoff surrendered.

"Please stop, please. Alright, stop! I'll do it, I'm in. But I want a reward."

The crying instantly stopped, and a glorious smile bloomed on Faye's lovely face. "Well, what do you want?"

Crispoff waggled his eyebrows, again.

"Not gonna happen, how about some treasure?"

"How much?"

"Lots and lots."

"I'm in— wait, when you say treasure you're not talking bitcoin or that NFT nonsense, are you?"

"I don't know what that is," said Faye. "Gold and silver; your weight in gold and silver."

"Count me in," said Crispoff.

ও   ৫

Transporting to Faye's world was a non-event. Faye took his hand in hers and gestured with the other hand. A glittering ring on her index finger rapidly grew brighter. Crispoff was blinded by an intense flash of light; when his vision returned he stood in a small glade. It was night, and the light of two full moons filtered thru the slender birch trees. Faye efficiently set about making camp, pulling a surprising amount of gear from her backpack.

Crispoff stood and slowly turned in a circle. "Say, who are you trying to kid? This is Central Park. That extra moon is just a streetlight. I can hear Bethesda Fountain splashing over there through the trees." He pointed toward the sound.

Faye shook her head. "No, you are on my world; trust me."

48

Before Crispoff could continue the argument he was distracted by a rustling and snapping in the undergrowth. He turned toward the new sounds in time to see a lizard the size of a Saint Bernard push its way into the clearing.

He jumped in surprise, his eyes widening. "H-h-holy sh-sh-sh-smokes!"

"Don't worry." Faye laughed as she reached out to pat the creature's head. "It's a grendel, they're harmless and friendly, unless you're a rodent. They eat nuts, berries, and rats— mostly."

Crispoff took a few calming breaths. "I guess we're not in Central Park."

"We're not far from the Elven Enclave."

"Does Fearfang live with the elves?" asked Crispoff.

"Of course not, but they're the only ones who know where to find him."

A mixture of doubt and anger filled Crispoff's face. "You said this quest wouldn't take too long."

Faye paused in her work. "I did."

"You lied."

She cocked her head and a mischievous smile played on her lips. "Maybe, maybe not. Time will tell."

"Damn. Just damn."

He stifled a yawn, and then another. *Hmm, I don't know if the darkness is triggering some kind of reflex, or maybe it's the aftereffect of travel to this world, but I am tired,* Crispoff thought. He did not argue when Faye suggested they turn in.

Despite the finely crafted fairy bedroll, the ground felt hard. The smoke from the campfire made his throat ache. *Hell,* thought Crispoff, *the side of my body facing the fire is too hot, and the other side is freezing.*

He tried to fall asleep by counting sheep but ended up counting aches and pains instead. He periodically turned his freezing side toward the fire and his scorching side away. *I feel like a slab of beef turning on a spit, damn. I'm too old for this nonsense.*

His thoughts wandered toward his beautiful companion, Faye, sleeping within easy reach. Being an old man trying to sleep on the cold hard ground, his thoughts quickly moved from trying his luck to whether she'd prepare a hot breakfast. *Coffee, I hope she makes lots of fresh hot coffee, not that instant crap or, god forbid, decaf.*

Crispoff finally slept, fitfully. He woke to the sound of Faye moving about the camp. She saw him stir and greeted him. "Good Morning, did you sleep wel—"

He interrupted. *No! It was too cold and too hot. The ground was too hard and everything from my throat to my toes hurts too much!* That was what he planned to say; all that came out of his sore, smoke-ravaged throat was an unintelligible croak, followed by a coughing jag.

"Coffee," he finally managed.

Faye reached into her pack and pulled out a steaming mug. "Here, drink this." She pushed the cup into his hands.

He sipped; it was warm and peppery. His throat stopped hurting. He drank it down. Everything else stopped hurting, and all was well.

"Wow, good stuff! I feel great, you should bottle this, maybe call it *Redder Bull*. Now, how about you reach into that pack of yours for some breakfast? Nothing elaborate, a few hot croissants with Irish butter and strawberry-rhubarb preserve, maybe a cup or two of Jamaican Blue Mountain coffee, just a dash of cream, no sugar."

Faye, reached into her pack offering him a thick slice of something that looked like pound cake. "This is all I've got, it's a loaf of journey-ration. You know, my backpack's not a cornucopia."

Crispoff stared at the loaf for a long moment. "Are you kidding me? I'm helping save your world and all you offer me is some stale sponge cake? That's not right; that's not fair. You can magic up something better than that."

"You know this type of magic's not easy," the fairy replied. "It requires energy and focus, and just like any other discipline it has its rules and limits."

He remained sitting on the ground, arms folded, shaking his head in silent protest of the elf's failure to meet his dietary demands. Faye took the ration back and set about breaking camp.

"Well?" growled Crispoff.

"Well, what?"

"Hot croissants with Irish butter and strawberry-rhubarb preserve, maybe a cup or two of Jamaican Blue Mountain coffee, just a dash of cream, no sugar."

"No problem." Faye, reached back into her pack, once again holding the thick slice of journey-ration. She handed it to Crispoff. "Use your imagination."

Faye finished packing up the camp. "Are you ready?"

Crispoff rose, brushing the journey-ration crumbs from his pants. "I'm ready, as I'll ever be."

"Then let's go find some elves."

She spoke as they walked along. "Do you think you could walk a bit faster; I'd like to find the elves sometime in this century."

"Don't rush me girlie. If you want a hero who can walk fast, take me home and find someone forty years younger," snapped Crispoff.

Nonetheless, he picked up the pace. They continued along in companionable silence for the next few minutes.

"Our first problem is going to be communicating with the elves. They don't much care for fairy kind," said Faye, thinking out loud.

"That is a problem. Maybe we should quit. You can just give me my treasure and take me home. I'll try not to be disappointed."

Faye did not bother replying. They traveled for an hour along a cheerful forest path. They both enjoyed the quiet and the scenery. The trees of the forest began giving way to grass and shrubs with little violet flowers.

"What's that tapping noise? It sounds like dozens tiny hammers tap, tap, tapping," said Crispoff.

"It's dozens of tiny hammers tap, tap, tapping," said Faye. "The elves are shoemakers; in fact, they make most of the shoes worn on this world."

"You know I used to sell shoes," said Crispoff.

"Good to know."

"Yes. I managed the entire shoe department at—"

"We're here," Faye cut off his reminiscence.

The tapping noise abruptly stopped as they emerged from the tree line. A sparkling lake lay ahead of them across a flowered meadow. Scattered widely through the meadow were dozens of diminutive workbenches with shoes in varying states of completeness. There was not an elf in sight.

"Hello, I come in peace," Faye called out. "I mean no harm. We just need a bit of help and we'll be on our way."

Silence was the only response.

While Faye tried to convince the elves to show themselves, Crispoff wandered over to the nearest bench. He picked up a nearly finished shoe,

"Hmm, what a nice work boot. It's got a sturdy but supple upper, and an impressive toe box. On the outside the toe box feels like it could withstand a sledgehammer, yet from inside it is soft and snug — remarkable."

He set the boot down and walked to the next bench, letting out a low whistle of admiration as he picked up the shoe, it was a T-strap. He reverently lifted it. "This is not a shoe, it's a work of art. Move over Dolce and Gabbana, Givenchy, don't move over, just give up."

"You like my work? You really like my work?" a high-pitched voice asked.

He looked toward the source of the voice and beheld a two-foot-tall humanoid, brown curly hair, fine features, though curious conch shell-looking ears.

"Y-you're an elf," Crispoff replied, surprised. "You're a real elf, of course, what else would I expect, I mean— Forgive my babbling. Yes, this is the most magnificent shoe that I've ever seen. And I sold shoes for nearly fifty years. I was the manager of the shoe department, at Sears. I —"

"Hey, human come see my shoe."

"No, over here, look at this one."

"Forget them, here look at this slingback."

Elves surrounded him, demanding his attention. He happily obliged, going from table to table, admiring shoes and discussing the finer points of shoemaking. The air grew warm, as the sun crept toward noon in a cloudless sky.

Faye, could not stand hearing another word about shoes. "Enough! We've got a mission. No more shoe talk, we need your—"

All but one of the elves disappeared in a panicked rush. The lone, bravest of elves hid behind Crispoff. She tugged on his pant leg,

"Is that thing—that fairy—with you?"

"Yes, she is my guide and my friend," he replied.

"Is she dangerous?"

"Don't worry, she is harmless. I will vouch for her peaceful intentions," he assured. *And that's why they named me salesman of the year in 1963.*

"In fact," Crispoff added, "she is as much a shoe lover as I am."

"Is that true?" said a second elf, as he appeared between Faye and Crispoff, looking warily from one to the other.

Crispoff caught Faye's eye and whispered. "Ell-tay em-thay ow-hay uch-may ou-yay ove-lay eir-thay oes-shay."

It took a moment for the fairy to catch on. "Uhm, yes. I just love your shoes. I can't believe how beautiful the workmanship is. It has me speechless."

Faye continued to praise the shoes as more and more elves re-appeared. Faye and Crispoff began to move from workbench to workbench, admiring the shoes. Faye fell silent, smiling to herself, *I am glad to let Crispoff talk and talk and talk.*

By the time each and every shoe had been adequately admired, it was dinnertime.

The elves set out a dinner of bread, honey, nuts, and berries. There were pitchers of sweet-tasting water and dandelion wine. Crispoff and the elves sat up way into the night talking about shoes. Faye excused herself, though it was well before full dark, and let the drone of their voices lull her to sleep.

Dawn arrived in a vivid display of pink and orange, which the snoring Crispoff missed. He finally woke up with a snort as the tap, tap, tapping of dozens of tiny hammers started. Before he could begin complaining, Faye shoved a cup into his hands. "Drink, don't talk; and here's some journey-ration. Do me a favor, eat it without complaining."

Crispoff was about to complain, but it was a fresh glorious morning, and he decided to let it go. While he ate, Faye packed up their gear.

"The elves gave me directions to Fearfang's lair," she explained. "It is in a place called Murkfen. There, atop a hill, sits the ruins of a mysterious castle. In the vaults deep beneath the castle is where Fearfang is said to abide."

"Murkfen? Sounds delightful. What is so mysterious about this castle?"

"Nobody knows who built it, and all that the elves could tell me about the previous occupants is that they were giants who disappeared one day in a mighty explosion that left the castle in ruins, and to this day—" Faye stopped talking suddenly.

"What?" said Crispoff.

"Never mind," said Faye.

"No. What, tell me what you were going to say."

"And to this day, it is haunted by the giants' ghosts."

"You didn't hesitate to ask me to face a fearsome dragon, living deep within a ruined castle," Crispoff scoffed. "I'm eighty-five, I live with ghosts. My photo albums are full of them—family, friends, enemies all gone. My memory is filled with their spirits, so are my dreams. Do you think a few ghosts are a showstopper?"

"No, I guess not." Faye smiled, "I've finished packing let's get going."

Their path led around the shore of the lake. They waved goodbye to the elves and headed toward the water's edge.

"How far are we from castle Murkfen?"

"It's several hundred miles away, just beyond the Greater Spine Mountains."

"Whew, I was worried it would be too far away," Crispoff wryly said.

His companion did not respond, and he spoke again. "Hey Red! I meant that sarcastically. It will take me ten years to walk that far."

A hint of a smile tugged at the corners of her mouth. "You asked the wrong question."

"And what should I have asked?"

"You should ask, *how will we get there?*"

"Okay, Princess Literal. How will we get there?"

"Now that's a good question, Crispoff. There is a hollow tree on the other side of the lake. If we stand within the tree and say the magic words that I learned from the elves, we will be transported to a hollow tree at the foot of the castle's hill."

"Right. The trouble with you is that you are so slow to use your magic, I forget that you can."

"And the trouble with you is that you think magic works like, well magic. You don't understand there are things it does, things it can't, and other things you can use it for only with great preparation and effort."

"Faye, there's an old saying—"

"Ha, everything you say is an old saying, grandpa."

"—there's an old saying. *A poor craftsman blames his tools.*"

"Well, Crispoff, here's a new saying, shuffle faster or we won't get around the lake until tomorrow."

They both lapsed into silence. Crispoff concentrated on the scenery and Faye concentrated on slowly picking up the pace without him noticing. They found the hollow tree shortly after the sun passed its zenith.

"Here's the tree; are you ready?" said Faye.

"Lunch!" demanded Crispoff.

"Finish quest first, lunch later," said Faye.

Crispoff sat down on a log, crossed his arms, and slowly shook his head. "Lunch. I'm thinking a cheeseburger, fries, coleslaw, and some coffee."

Faye, reached back into her pack, removed a slice of journey-ration and handed it to Crispoff. "Use your imagination."

He snatched it from her hand and grumbled in between chews. Lunch finished, Crispoff rose with an impressive creaking and crackling of stiff joints. "Let's go, chop-chop, we're burning daylight here."

He made his way to the hollow tree. Faye joined him and spoke the incantation she had learned from the elves:

> *There are holes,*
> *in my soles.*
> *So, I can't use,*
> *my best shoes.*
> *To Mirkfen let's go,*
> *It's no time to be slow.*

"Worst rhyming ev—"

The tree started to spin, cutting off Crispoff's remark.

Long moments later, the motion stopped, and they stumbled out of a different tree.

Crispoff was so dizzy he had to hold onto the tree to keep from falling.

Faye quickly recovered and looked around. Dark, threatening clouds concealed the sun, and a sharp breeze put a chill in the air. The grass and sparse undergrowth were a sickly yellow, and most of the trees were stunted, twisted, lifeless things.

Atop a low hill sat Mirkfen castle; a dark, jagged silhouette in the dismal light. An ancient, cobbled road curved past where they stood and ran up between two ebony standing stones, climbing the hill toward the castle.

"You're on, Crispoff," said Faye pointing toward the castle.

"Wait, how do you expect me to recover this Rod of Redemption if I don't know what it looks like?"

"All you have to do is distract the dragon, I'll sneak in and find the Rod."

"How would you suggest I distract a dragon?"

"You'll think of something; remember, the High Council chose you. They always pick the right—"

"Yeah, yeah, yeah. They always pick the right champion."

Faye kissed Crispoff on both cheeks. "The dragon Fearfang is up in the castle. Remember the hopes and blessings of my people go with you."

Crispoff shook his head, stepped onto the road, and walked up the hill. He passed between the standing stones, they loomed over him in dark, silent threat. The wind picked up, whistling around the stones. He could almost make out words in the wind. He paused, adjusted his hearing aid, and listened,

"Fee fie fu fam, I smell the blood of a human."

Crispoff snorted. "Another bad rhyme, that's all you've got?"

A swirl of haze resolved itself into a gigantic spectral figure barring his path.

"Fee fie fu fam, I smell the blood of a human," it thundered.

Crispoff gasped. Fear washed over him, quickly replaced by anger.

"Give me a break, a ghost, a talking ghost; that's supposed to scare me. At my age, I know more ghosts than living people. Every trip to the cemetery feels like a family reunion. I go to funerals so often, I'm on a first-name basis with the undertaker."

"Fee fie fu fam, I smell the blood of a human?" suggested the specter.

"Right, got it," said Crispoff and continued on his way. He sensed nothing more than musty dampness when he walked through the ghost.

The hill wasn't much of a hill, so the climb wasn't much of a climb. At the top was a broad and flat area covering, perhaps, two acres of ground in front of the shattered and rusted castle gate. Crispoff paused. The ground was blasted and burned into a hard glassy surface. It had a greasy color, dark brown almost black with the rainbow highlights one would see in an oil slick.

What kind of horrific inferno could do this to so much ground? he thought, and immediately answered his own question. *A fire breathing dragon, the grandfather of all fire breathing dragons.*

Unlike the giant ghost, the thought of facing the dragon filled him with big fear and bigger misgivings. Crispoff found himself having second, third, and fourth thoughts. He forced his uncooperative legs to wobble their way across the tortured ground. His pace slowed and meandered as he drew closer to his ominous destination. To bolster his resolve, he began to chant.

"I'm not scared, I'm a friggin' hero on a friggin' quest. I'm not scared, I'm a friggin' hero on a——"

The quaver in his voice begged to differ with the brave words. He halted outside the main gate and before he could summon the resolve to enter, he heard a deep voice from within.

"Come, enter my castle, o great hero."

The dragon!

The dragon's voice was beautiful, its rich tone and complex harmonics rendered it hypnotic. Crispoff's hearing aid distorted both the high and low end of the register; the dragon's voice had little effect on him. Nonetheless, despite his misgivings, he entered. The castle's interior was dark, but as his eyes adjusted he could make out shapes that could only be piles of treasure, and heaps of plunder.

"In all my long centuries of life, I've never seen a human quite so old and feeble. You should be at home on your deathbed, surrounded by your family," said Fearfang.

"They never visit. Never! Besides, I've always wanted an adventure and—"

"And?" prompted Fearfang.

"—and, the fairy was so convincing."

"They always are," said the dragon. "And now you are here to do their dirty work. How sad and pathetic. A decrepit old sack of man-bones doing the cowardly bidding of some fairies."

Anger, lack of sleep, and no coffee made Crispoff forget his fear. "Hey! Ease up on the insults, Snake Face."

Surprise etched Fearfang's long face. The man should have been subjugated by the power of his voice. Crispoff's impudence should have angered him; instead, he was amused and curious. The life of a terrifying dragon is lonely, and boring at times. He decided to let things play out, until he got hungry.

"Ah, a brave sack of man-bones," he smiled, allowing a few flames to flicker in the gaps between his dagger-sized, serrated teeth. "Do not push your luck too far."

Proximity to a very big and very fiery dragon convinced Crispoff to hold his temper.

"O mighty worm, I come before you seeking a boon."

"I don't like being called a worm, ape-thing."

"But all the books say—"

"All the books are wrong. Tell me what is your name? And where are you from?"

Crispoff knew, from his reading, that you never give your real name to a dragon. "Bilbo Baggins, from the Shire."

"Delighted to make your acquaintance, Mr. Baggins."

Crispoff, pleased with himself over the little subterfuge, said, "Why don't you call me Bilbo? All my friends do."

"Very well, Bilbo. Just so you know, if we get to playing at riddles, do not ask me what you have in your pocketses, my precious, or I will burn you where you stand!"

"Oops—So, you've read *The Hobbit*?"

"Of course, I read *The Hobbit*, everybody's read *The Hobbit*. Now, my friend, we are friends, aren't we? What shall we do?"

Crispoff managed a nod and a sickly smile. "Riddles, you mentioned riddles, shall we play a game of rid—"

"No! I hate riddles. They're a stupid waste of time. Why don't you just tell me about yourself, starting with your real name."

"Crispoff's the name. I'm retired twenty years and widowed eighteen. I have three kids, a boy and two girls. I have seven grandchildren, two great-grandchildren. I don't remember their names or ages. Why should I? They never visit, never call, the momzers never even write. But, I get ahead of myself, my story starts on the morning of August 27, 1933—"

Everybody has a talent. More often than not it is for something trivial; sometimes the talent, as in Crispoff's case, goes undiscovered. His talent was a world-class one, of which he was completely unaware. He was an Olympic-level bore, he was so boring that acquaintances walked the other way when they saw him coming. He was so boring that both the Mormons and Jehovah's Witnesses refused to ring his bell. He was so boring that his family never visited. Several hours passed—

"Which brings us to 1957, that's when I started working in the shoe department at Sears. You know the job didn't pay very much, but the *wingtips* were great. Ha-ha. Get it? Wing-Tips?"

Crispoff did not notice that Fearfang did not laugh. He also did not notice, despite the thunderous sound of dragon snores, that he had bored the dragon to sleep almost an hour earlier. The man droned on, completely unaware of anything until Faye poked him in the ribs.

"Okay, good work. I found the Rod and some treasure, let's get out of here before the dragon wakes up."

"But I'm just getting to the good part. You know, in 1961 I was made manager of the entire shoe department, both men and women."

"Crispoff, you are a great hero. Generations of my people will be composing songs to honor your name. Epic poems will be written to tell of your great achievement. But for now, please shut up, before you put me to sleep as well."

Hurrying out of the castle, Crispoff spotted a little niche in which sat a very dusty crystal. It reminded him of one of those old-time glass-crystal doorknobs, without much thought he grabbed it and stuffed it into his pocket.

The trip home was another non-event. Faye left Crispoff with a far from sisterly kiss, several sacks of gold and silver, and the thanks of a grateful people.

"Hey wait! You're saying that the dragon found me boring. I've never been called boring. How could you say such a thing, why in 1963 I—" The elf vanished, returning to her world in mid-sentence.

"Oh well," Crispoff shrugged. He tottered into the kitchen to fix himself a long-anticipated cup of coffee. He remembered the crystal in his pocket. He cleaned it with some dish soap and water. "Son of a gun! A ruby as big as my fist."

Curmudgeon Guest

62

Riches of the Stone

Jeanne Hardt

Chapter 1
Blind

Every quest had its quirks, but…

"Ugh." Caden rubbed his pounding temples. "Are you certain about this, Fen?"

"Yes, sir. Once we cross the bridge, we cannot look upon the castle."

His loyal servant had never failed him, and since Fen had studied every aspect of this venture, Caden needed to trust him. Still, walking blindfolded to one's destination was *not* appealing.

He glanced about. A murky river flowed before him; its tainted water traveled from east to west for miles. Fortunately, he and Fen had recently drunk deeply from a pure, crystal stream that satiated their thirst.

A simple, crudely cut wood bridge crossed over the fast-moving river, and it seemed harmless enough, but that was not his worry. They currently stood upon earth alive with growth. Grassy sprigs popped up everywhere, and bright-green, leaf-covered trees lined the road. Some of the fruit trees even had spring blooms—a promise of eventual abundant fruit. Once they went beyond the river, the terrain morphed into ugliness.

The trees on the opposite side of the bridge bore no leaves, and virtually no color. Their bare branches stretched high into the sky like long fingers that reached out and begged for aid. The gray limbs of the dense trees twisted and contorted. Each tree intertwined with the next and created a sinister-looking wall.

Beyond the questionable forest, they would have to endure the dubious bog, and in many ways, their covered eyes would render them helpless. Serpents were known predators of the mire. Never before had he feared snakes, and under normal circumstances—if he were to come upon one—he would slice off its head before it could strike. His sword never failed him. Yet, if he could not see the reptile, the blow of his weapon would have no aim.

"I need to cast aside all my doubts, Fen." Caden looked down at the man and narrowed his eyes. "Wait here."

"Very well." His servant gave a slight bow.

Caden peered far beyond the ground that sloped into the presumed bog. The castle—their ultimate destination—could easily be seen in the distance. Aside from the low grayish-green mist that hovered over the tallest towers, it seemed *normal*. The finer details were too far away to discern, but one thing was certain, even from where he stood. The rumor of enchantment was no myth. He sensed it all the way to his slow-beating heart.

Every day he grew weaker, and he had come to accept another truth. This would be his last quest. Because of his curse, he would not live to see another full moon.

"Why fear snakes?" he mumbled and stepped onto the bridge. "Death will soon take me regardless of what I do."

He kept his eyes affixed to the castle as he crossed the river. The moment he set foot on solid ground again, the castle vanished. He gasped and moved backward, while keeping his gaze forward. As soon as both of his feet rested on the bridge, the distant structure rematerialized.

He hastened to Fen. "Did you see that?"

"Did I see *what*, sir?"

Caden pointed. "The castle. It was there, then gone, and back again."

"From my vantage, it never left. I spoke truthfully. This bridge marks the beginning of the enchantment. If you look upon the castle once you cross, it will forever slip from your sight *and* your grasp. You will never reach it."

"Then do what you must. I will not fail King Lorin. I must finish this quest." He only hoped the coveted gemstone—the very purpose of his mission—had not been taken elsewhere and still remained somewhere within the castle.

"As you wish." Fen removed the pack he had slung over his shoulder and withdrew two long strips of dark cloth. "If you kneel, it will make this easier."

Caden did as he suggested. His servant had not been blessed with height or exceptional strength, for that matter. Nevertheless, he had been a loyal aide for as long as Caden could remember. He could not recall a time when Fen was not at his side.

Fen tied the long band around Caden's head, securely covering his eyes. "Can you see, sir?"

"*No.*" The entire world had become as black as night.

"I am now fastening my own cover." Fen's breathing grew more rapid. "I trust you, sir, but I fear we may stumble about."

"Grasp my arm. Even in the dark, I will lead the way. The trees on both sides of the path will keep us from veering in the wrong direction, and the castle lies straight ahead. If we walk at a reasonable rate, we should reach it within the hour." Caden jiggled the hilt of his sword, sheathed at his waist. It comforted him to know it lay within reach, even if he could not see to strike a blow.

Fen also had a sword, but rarely wielded it. The man was no coward, yet Caden always led any necessary charge, and Fen had little need to fight. He tightly grabbed Caden's forearm, and they stepped onto the bridge.

They crossed to the other side and put their feet on solid ground once more, and with every step, Caden fought the urge to lift the bottom of the cloth that covered his eyes. He despised feeling helpless. More than once, they both tripped over roots of trees, rocks, or ruts in the dirt path. Fen had said that long ago this had been a well-traveled road, but not anymore.

Once stories emerged of those who had gone missing after venturing to the castle, people began to fear it—and for very good reason. The evil enchantment emanating from it hovered in the air and spun around Caden like an invisible force. Strangely, it drew him nearer. In his current state, he could easily lose his sense of direction, yet the castle's magic kept pulling him in.

"Are you growing weary, sir?" Fen's voice held genuine concern, with a hefty amount of underlying sympathy. "Your breathing is shallow."

"My time is short, but I *will* finish this."

The way Fen held his arm changed. It felt more like an offer of support, rather than a reliance of guidance.

Caden stood a little taller. "Do not pity me, Fen. This curse was cast upon me at my infancy, and I have accepted it." They kept walking, step by slow step.

"The very reason you chose not to marry, is that not so?"

"That it is. I would not allow myself to love a woman, when I knew I would die before our union took root."

"Instead, you devoted yourself to the service of the king. Your actions have always been commendable, but I fear they have not brought you happiness."

"My happiness is not as vital as the prosperity and safety of the realm, and I have no reason to complain. My life has been satisfactory." Had their eyes not have been shielded, he would have offered Fen a smile. "I have had my share of joy. Likely, more than I deserve."

"But—"

"Oh, bother!" Caden's foot sunk into mud. "The bog."

Fen shuddered so hard that Caden felt it through their connected arms.

"Please, do not have snakes," his servant muttered.

Perhaps Fen *did* possess a scant amount of cowardice. Then again, he could not fault the man for fearing the wretched creatures when he himself dreaded a possible encounter.

They advanced deeper into swampy ground. Thick mud sucked against the bottoms of Caden's boots as he painstakingly moved his feet. A sickening stench surrounded them, and they both coughed through the fumes.

"It smells like death," Fen choked out.

"Yes. Rotted flesh. It is probably best we cannot see what we are traversing." Caden coughed so hard it sent a jolt of pain through his sluggish heart, yet he did not have time to dwell on his discomforts. "I suppose we can look at this in a positive light."

"How?"

"The smell might keep the snakes away." The moment he said it, something wrapped around his ankle and tightened. "Hold, Fen."

Fen froze and fearfully hissed air through his nostrils.

Caden eased his sword from its sheath. He could not *strike* at the creature. The abrupt action would likely cause it to sink its probable fangs into Caden's flesh. Instead, he ever so slowly lowered the tip of his blade to his ankle and drove it through whatever had encircled it. The creature instantly loosened. True to its enchantment, the sword accomplished its deadly purpose. Time and again, Caden owed a debt of gratitude to the kind wizard who had enchanted his weapon. The spell he cast upon it ensured it would not fail in any dire circumstance.

"You see, Fen. Even blind, I am able."

They continued onward.

The mud turned to thick, warm water that smelled no less foul. They plodded through it, and it rose higher and higher until it reached Caden's chest.

"It is rising up my neck," Fen squeaked out. "I cannot swim, sir. If it grows deeper, I fear I shall drown."

"Climb upon my back."

Fen wasted no time scrambling onto Caden's back. "Thank you, sir."

More than once, Caden had been chided for keeping Fen as a servant. The king had offered him stronger—more capable—manservants, but Caden had refused them. Trustworthiness was not guaranteed from someone new, and Fen had proven his loyalty. In addition, the man had great intellect that Caden valued more than strength, especially since Caden fought all their battles. If only he was as strong as he used to be. If he indeed found the stone, he was sure to face one last encounter with whomever guarded it, and he hoped he could see it through.

In his weakened state, he appreciated Fen's small stature. Above all else, Caden valued his companionship. One day soon, however, *Fen* would face being alone.

Caden cast aside all ill thoughts and kept going. The castle continued its mystical pull.

He pushed away what seemed to be floating pieces of rotted wood. Other, slimier things, slid along his fingers as he waded through the water. Flies buzzed around his head, and he swatted at mosquitos. For all he knew, he plodded through a graveyard. The odor certainly warranted it.

The ground beneath his feet slowly rose upward, and the level of the water subsided.

Fen jumped down from his back and latched onto Caden's arm once more.

"We are getting near," Caden whispered.

"How do you know?"

"I *feel* it." Caden swallowed hard. His slow heart grew heavier, yet he kept on going.

They stepped onto completely dry land and shook off as much water as possible. Caden sniffed the arm of his tunic. "I reek."

"As do I," Fen added with a grunt.

Caden agreed but did not voice it. They both needed a good bath and somewhere they could actually relax and maybe even enjoy a tankard of ale. He doubted they would be greeted at the castle with such things. "Let's finish this. If death awaits us, then so be it."

"I honestly prefer not to die, sir." Fen gripped Caden's arm more fiercely than before.

On every other quest, Caden always offered words of assurance, but in this instance, he had none to give. He doubted either of them would live to see another sunrise.

Silently, he moved onto what felt like a large, flat stone. He eased forward and touched the toe of his boot into another *raised* stone. "I believe we have come upon the castle steps."

Inch by slow inch, they eased onward. They stepped up again and again. He cautiously took each step, all the while guiding Fen, until finally, Caden butted his foot into another hard surface.

A strange pulsing sensation encased him, stronger than anything he had felt before. Almost as if a heart beat around him and enclosed him inside it. He abruptly stopped and slowly extended his hand, palm raised and flattened. He pressed it to a cold, stone wall.

The castle.

"You should not have come!"

What?

The harried voice was not that of Fen.

"Who are—"

Caden collapsed to the ground.

Chapter 2
The Castle

Fen shook Caden's shoulders. "Wake up, sir!"

Caden slowly opened his eyes. A dull throb emanated from the back of his head. He reached up to touch it and discovered a small trace of blood on his fingertips. The truth of his situation rushed in, and he recalled where he had been.

He stared at Fen. "I can see you."

"It pleases me to hear it. That guard hit us both with the butt of his sword, yet I believe he pommeled you much harder. As you have become aware, the impact gouged deep and rendered you unconscious. I, however, fought the man as he dragged me here to this wretched cell. He had the gall to laugh at me."

Caden carefully pushed himself into a seated position and took in his surroundings. Light seeped into the chamber through a little, barred window and revealed slimy, moss-covered stone walls. The damp air was not as pungent as the swamp, but it still smelled rank.

He pointed to the door at the front of the cell. It, too, had only a single small opening, barely large enough to look through. "Has anyone come to check in on us since our arrival?"

"I thought I saw an eyeball in the peep hole, but I cannot swear to it."

"What do you remember of the man who brought us here?" Caden hugged his knees to his chest and tried to dismiss the pain pounding in his head.

"He was large. Bearded. *Smelly.*" Fen moved beside him and leaned against the wall. "I failed you, sir. When he uncovered my eyes and I saw you lying on the ground, I tried so hard to fight. I am worthless."

"Never say that again. I have no truer friend."

"I feel the same, but I wish I could have done more."

"Think no longer of it. Together, we will find a way out of here." Caden groaned as he got to his feet. Fully upright, he swooned and braced a hand to the wet wall to keep from falling over. The blow to his head—along with his already failing heart—made *him* useless.

After several deep breaths, he regained his composure. Out of habit, he reached for the hilt of his sword, then grunted in astonishment, finding his weapon in place. His head had taken a brutal whack, and he chided himself for not immediately comprehending the availability of his weapon. "Why was my sword not stripped from me?"

"I have mine as well. Perhaps they expect us to take our own lives and save them the trouble," Fen grumbled.

Caden unsheathed his faithful sword and held it aloft. It glimmered in the streaming light. "They are certainly senseless."

"Press yourselves to the far wall!" a voice bellowed through the small opening in the door.

"I am armed!" Caden boldly replied. "You will not harm us further!"

"I have no intention of harming you, you fool! I, too, am a prisoner!"

Caden exchanged confused glances with Fen, then curiosity prompted him to do as the man requested. "We are standing at the wall. You may enter!" Regardless of the man's assurance, Caden kept his weapon at the ready.

The door creaked open, and the man walked in.

"That is he," Fen whispered from the side of his mouth. "The one who brought us here."

The large, bearded man remained near the door. "The Lady wishes to see you. She is not to be harmed. Do you understand?"

"No." Caden narrowed his eyes. "I have more questions than you can imagine. First and foremost, how is it that you are a prisoner, yet you roam free?"

"I have nowhere to go. Neither do you. You touched the walls of Arburon, and therefore, you cannot leave."

"Arburon?"

"The castle. You both touched it, and therefore, you are its prisoner. *Forever*. If you go outside and venture off the front steps, you will turn to dust."

Hmm.

Caden's list of questions rapidly grew, and he studied the man, wishing he could give him a truth potion.

Has anyone actually seen someone turn to dust, or is he merely making a threat to keep everyone bound in servitude to this mysterious Lady?

If Caden asked that particular question, the man would likely lie, so why bother asking it at all?

At least Caden was not troubled by the idea of being there *forever*. His forever would be short-lived. Fen, however, would have to endure the horrid place for years on end. He glanced at Fen and frowned, pained by the thought of his friend's dismal future.

Caden took a single step closer to the questionable *guard*. "Do you not fear that I will use my sword and strike you down?"

The man shrugged. "Truthfully, I would welcome it." He pushed the door wide and gestured for them to exit. "Please. If kept waiting, The Lady becomes irritable."

"Does she not have a name?"

"Yes. *The Lady*."

"Original," Fen mumbled.

Caden held in a chuckle. Now was not the time for humor, yet in many ways, he appreciated Fen's newly acquired ease.

Fen laid a hand on Caden's arm. "Are you *able* to walk, sir? Your wound concerns me." He glared at the man who had inflicted the damage.

"Worry not over me," Caden said with utmost confidence. "My head aches, but my good senses have returned. I will not be bested again." He faced their captor. "Do *you* have a name? *Man*, perhaps?"

"Bing," he coldly replied.

"Oh. Well, then, *Bing*, lead us to *The Lady*."

Bing held up a single finger. "Know this. I *saved* you by bringing you inside. You would have died out there. I had to strike you down, so you would not fight me and force me from the front steps."

"You could have simply opened the door and bade us in. Would that not have been easier?"

Bing puffed out his chest. "You looked dangerous."

Caden grunted. "Our eyes were covered."

"Yes, but you had weapons." Bing shook his finger. "And *you* allowed us to keep them. You lack reasoning, but I will not judge you entirely until I come to know you better. However, I do forgive you for knocking me unconscious."

Fen groaned. Obviously, he did not approve of Caden's mercy, yet something had compelled him to grant it.

"So many things have piqued my curiosity," Caden went on. "If you cannot leave the castle, how do you eat?"

"Food is not an issue. An enchantment provides our daily sustenance. Food. Wine. Even sweets. Meals are the only joy I find in my days."

"Sweets?" Fen asked. "Such as cakes?"

"Yes. My favorite is strawberry." Bing smiled, but it quickly vanished. He popped his eyes wide and fluttered his hands in the air. "We have wasted too much time talking! The Lady will not be pleased." He waved them out of the cell more vigorously this time and briskly led them away.

"Sir," Fen whispered as they walked, "do you suppose they might offer us cakes *today*? I am incredibly hungry."

"I do not know *what* to expect." Caden smiled at his servant. "I am hungry as well."

They walked along a candlelit corridor, rounded a corner, and ascended a line of narrow stairs. Randomly spaced candles flickered from their wall sconces and cast eerie shadows on the steps.

Like before, a strange magnetic pull encased Caden and drew him forward. Even if he wanted to flee, he feared the magic of Arburon would never allow it. Besides, if what Bing had said was true, Caden did not want to end his life as a heap of dust.

They reached the top of the stairwell and entered an enormous, high-ceilinged room. Sunlight streamed from half-a-dozen large open windows that surrounded them. The floors changed from cut, gray stone to dark-green, swirled marble, and the air had a sweetness to it. A welcome change.

A tall, ebony pedestal at the center of the room caught his gaze and took away his remaining breath.

The stone!

Fen butted his shoulder and pointed. "It actually exists, sir."

Caden could not find a word to utter. He managed to keep breathing as he stared at the giant ruby that literally floated above the pedestal. It spun in circles and glistened, radiating its own light. Its heavy magic beckoned him closer.

The nearer he got to the gem; his heart beat a little stronger.

His hand shook as he reached to fulfill his quest. King Lorin wanted the ruby in Shanavar because he claimed it held the kingdom's future. With no one guarding it, Caden could easily accomplish his task.

"Stop!"

He yanked his hand away and snapped his head in the direction of the female who had barked the order. A lady dressed in blue silk strode toward him. Her long, blond hair flowed around her shoulders like a cape and framed her perfectly formed face. Her lovely lips were as red as the ripest berry. Never had he seen anyone so beautiful.

She gracefully glided toward him. "If you touch the stone, you will die," she said in a much softer and enticing voice. She tipped her head and studied him, and her crystal-blue eyes sparkled. "I am The Lady of Arburon, and who might you be?"

Caden could have sworn Fen groaned.

"Sir Caden of Shanavar," he said and bowed. "Sent by orders from the king."

"A knight." She pursed her lips. "And a Shanavarian one at that. I am honored to have you here. I presume Bing told you that you cannot leave."

"He did." Caden widened his stance and folded his arms. "I came for the stone, yet you tell me that if I touch it, I will die. Shall I assume I would turn to dust?"

"Indeed. It is Zeborah's preferred method." She leaned close. "Easy to clean up after."

Caden took a step back. "Zeborah?"

"The sorceress who created Arburon. The one who is responsible for all of this." The Lady smiled and opened her arms wide, revealing her perfect, female form.

She was the epitome of the fairer sex, and Caden admired her exquisiteness.

Stop!

He shook his head. He had a task to perform, and it did not include her. "Where is Zeborah now? I must speak with her."

"That is impossible. She is dead."

Fen moved closer. "Dead? If the witch is dead, why does her enchantment linger?"

The Lady bent over and peered into Fen's face. "You are a little one to be accompanying such a strong and able-bodied knight." She waved at him in dismissal, stood fully upright, and faced Caden again. "In answer to your servant's question, Arburon became its own entity. The castle itself wields the magic, and Zeborah is no longer needed."

Caden easily accepted her explanation. The castle practically *breathed.*

He returned his attention to what truly mattered and walked slowly around the pedestal, mesmerized by the swirling orb above it. "How do you know I will die if I touch the stone?"

"I have seen it happen more than once. Trust me when I say that the ruby renders nothing but death. Greed has brought many here. They believed that a gem of this size would bring them good fortune—wealth beyond measure. Is that not why your king sent *you*?"

"King Lorin told me that the stone held our kingdom's future. Yet, if greed enticed men to risk their lives in coming here, if I happened to gain possession of such a rare thing, men with the same motive would fall upon Shanavar in order to attain it." Caden held his hand near the spinning stone. The ruby was the size of his fist. "It would *destroy* Shanavar's future by bringing war. More lives would be lost."

He sighed and faced The Lady. "I find wisdom in your words. Something of this value would indeed assure more death." He rubbed his bearded jaw. "Can *you* touch the stone?"

Her eyes opened wide, and she pressed a hand to her breast. "*No*." Her features softened. "Only the one who is true of heart will possess the riches of the stone and be allowed to leave this place unharmed. My heart is anything but true."

"Are you saying you are untrustworthy? If so, why should I believe anything you tell me?"

"Yes," Fen interjected. "Why should we trust you? Obviously, you served the dead sorceress."

She glared at Fen. "I am not addressing you, little man. This matter concerns your master and no one else. Have you not learned to be quiet and speak only when spoken to?"

Fen returned her scowl, then gazed up at Caden. "Forgive me, sir, if I have spoken out of turn. This situation troubles me, and I am only looking out for your best interest."

"As you always do." Caden faced The Lady. "My man has just as much at stake here as I. I ask that you treat him with respect."

"Respect?" she scoffed. "You are a knight, Sir Caden, and you have earned esteem. Your man does not warrant it."

"And what of you? Why should I show you any semblance of reverence? You had your man, Bing, beat us down and throw us into your dungeon." Caden peered about. "And now, he is nowhere to be seen. He claims to be your prisoner, just as we are. Fen spoke truly. If you serve the dead witch, you cannot be trusted."

"I serve no one." She crossed to a throne-like, high-back chair and daintily sat. "I, too, am a prisoner."

Caden turned to Fen and received the same questioning gaze that he himself had cast.

Her unexpected words prompted another line of questions.

Chapter 3
The Stone

Fen jerked his head to the side and widened his eyes.

Caden knew that look. He crossed to his servant and they both ventured farther across the room and out of The Lady's hearing.

"You need to ask her where she came from and how long she has been here," Fen said.

"I was just about to do that very thing. Worry not, Fen. I may be dying, but my mind is still sharp." He tapped a finger to his temple and turned to walk back to The Lady.

Fen grabbed his arm and stopped him. "Do not let her beauty sway you, sir. I do not trust her."

"Nor do I. Nonetheless, only she can answer my questions."

Fen's brows wove. "Can you believe her answers?"

"What choice do I have?"

"That is a valid point, sir." Fen released him.

Caden squared his shoulders and strode to The Lady's side. "How is it you are a prisoner? You seem to be the authority here."

She smiled, making her even lovelier. "Before Zeborah died, she entrusted Arburon to me. She cast a spell, giving me beauty and long life. I am bound to the castle *and* the stone, and my sole purpose is to protect the sanctity of this place and warn those who try to bring it to ruin."

"Where did the stone come from? I have heard stories about it since I was child, but no one ever spoke of its origin, only that it existed."

The Lady gazed at him in a *motherly* fashion. Almost to the point of being somewhat disturbing. "I am certain you were told many stories in your youth." She shook her head as if waking from a stupor and cast a more regal expression. "It is said that the stone is actually a crystallized dragon's heart and *not* a ruby, and the power of dragons still lies within it, making it even more valuable than a gemstone. The tale states that the last two dragons in existence fought to the death, and the victor ripped its claws into the chest of the other, extracted its heart and covered it with its fiery breath. The heart turned to the shining red stone you see here. I firmly believe the stories, because sometimes, if I listen closely, I can hear it beating."

She stared deeply into Caden's eyes. "You have heard it, too. Have you not?"

He swallowed hard and nodded. "At least, I have heard *something*." Whether or not her story was true, it held his interest. One thing he did know—the beautiful and desirable gem possessed strong magic and *needed* to be feared.

"So," he said, pressing onward, "when anyone comes to take the stone, you simply allow them to turn to dust?"

"I give everyone a choice, just as I am giving you now. Touch the stone and die, or remain here in servitude for the rest of your days. If you choose the latter, you will not be harmed, and you will be well-fed and at peace."

"Like dogs in a cage," Fen muttered.

"Silence!" The Lady spat and shot from her chair. "Say another word, and I will place your hand to the stone myself!" She took a long, drawn-out breath, then sat again. "Forgive me, Sir Caden, but ill-mannered servants grate on my nerves."

"Fen is loyal and true. It is possible that if you indeed put his hand to the stone, he would not die. Never has there been a truer heart."

She slyly smiled. "Then have him touch it. See if his goodness is genuine."

"No. I will not endanger his life. Mine, however, is worth the risk of sacrifice. I have but days to live."

"What do you mean, days? You look to be but two and twenty. I had hoped you would choose to stay and offer me company. I have lacked decent conversation."

Caden glanced at Fen—who rolled his eyes—and gave his full attention to The Lady once more. "From infancy, I, too, have suffered under the incantation of a sorceress. She came to my cradle and cast her wicked spell, condemning me to death on the first full moon after the day of my birth in my twentieth year. That happens in two days."

The Lady's face fell. "I cannot efficiently express my disappointment. Still…" She thrummed her fingers on the arm of her chair. "Perhaps you can fulfill your king's quest before you die."

"How?"

She pointed at Fen. "Have him touch the stone and take it into his care. If he is as true-hearted as you say, perhaps he will break the spell and you can both go free. Although…" She pursed her lips, gazed upward, and released a long sigh. "The stone's enchantment is unrelated to that of Arburon, so I fear the power of the castle will still remain. I honestly have no idea what will happen if the one true of heart grasps the stone."

Fen nervously licked his lips and approached the pedestal. "I am willing to take the risk and will proudly do it and finish our quest. I do not fear the silly stone." His quaking voice said otherwise. "I cannot bear the thought of living out my life here. Strawberry cakes or not."

The Lady grinned and sat perfectly straight with her hands folded on her lap. "Bing! Bring the broom! We may need it!"

"No!" Caden unsheathed his sword and leapt in front of Fen. "It is too dangerous." The sword vibrated in his grasp. It pulsed in a manner he had never experienced before—as if it called out to him.

"I know what I must do," he muttered.

He swung the sword toward the stone, using every ounce of his remaining strength. True to the blade's enchantment, it hit its mark. The ruby broke into thousands of particles and scattered red dust across the marble floor. A flash of light threw him backward into a wall, and thick, smoky fog filled the room.

He moaned, once again unable to see a thing.

Chapter 4
Transformation

"Fen!"

No answer.

Caden twisted sideways to work out the wrench in his back. He would be bruised from the impact of hitting the wall, but at least the new pain helped him forget his aching head. He carefully stood, still surrounded by the strange mist. "Fen!"

Someone moaned.

"Fen?" Caden followed the sound and cautiously made his way through the fog. "Say something, so I can find you."

"I am here."

Whoever spoke did not sound like Fen, and when Caden reached him, he found an old man sitting in the chair where The Lady had been. He wore dirty, tattered clothes, and his hair and long beard were as white as the strange mist. Deep wrinkles circled his eyes and mouth.

Caden stared at him. "Where did *you* come from?"

"I have been sitting here all this time."

"No, The Lady was here."

The old man appeared as if he might cry. "I *am* The Lady."

"You? But how?" Caden shut his eyes and the answer struck him. "I understand." He looked at her—*him*—again with pity. "The enchantment of which you spoke. The one that gave you beauty and long life. You said you had been given the task of overseeing the stone, so by destroying it, I also broke *your* spell, did I not?"

He frowned and nodded. "Dear, Caden. There is so much to tell you."

"Dear? Why do you speak to me with such familiarity?"

The man stretched out his wrinkled hand and touched Caden's cheek. "I served your father. I am Deagon."

"*Deagon*?" Caden's heart wrenched. He dropped to his knees in front of the man. "You left with my father fifteen years ago. I was so young, and I scarcely remember you being in my life. But my uncle often told me stories about you and your loyalty to my father."

"Your uncle, the *king*." Deagon sighed. "I am so weary." He lowered his head.

"Please do not sleep! What happened to my father? Surely, you know."

Deagon sluggishly lifted his head. "I know *everything*, yet it tires me to speak. The broken enchantment has taken much from me."

"*Try*." Caden firmly gripped the man's hand.

"Very well." He moaned and arched his back, then slumped down again. "Your father came here seeking Zeborah *and* the stone. He hoped it would break your enchantment."

"*My* enchantment? How?"

"They were cast by the same sorceress. Zeborah was in love with your father, but he married your mother. When you were born, Zeborah cursed you with a death spell. Because of it, your mother's grief put her in an early grave. Your father vowed to find Zeborah and seek vengeance." Deagon breathed harder and harder, and all the while he spoke, the truth of Caden's past stabbed painfully deep.

"If you and The Lady are one in the same, why did you— *she*—seem to have no knowledge of my enchantment?"

"My mind was muddied as The Lady. I sometimes sensed things from my past, but I was fully transformed and set to the task put upon me by Zeborah. The Lady completely overtook me, but when you broke the spell, all of my memories returned."

Caden nodded his understanding, although the entire ordeal overwhelmed him. "So," he went on with urgency, "you and my father ventured *here* to attain revenge against Zeborah."

"Yes. He begged her to undo your curse, but she said only you, Caden, could end the enchantment and that the stone held the spell's reversal. Your father said he would take it to you and reached for it, and she tried to stop him. Yet, he touched it and..." Deagon sniffled and wiped at his eyes.

"He turned to dust," Caden whispered.

"Yes. Right before my eyes. I watched it all happen like a helpless fool."

"What did Zeborah do?"

Deagon's fist tightened. "She wailed and threw things, behaving very much like a spoiled child. I believe she actually loved your father—as much as anyone so evil was capable of loving. It was then that she cast her spell on me. I became The Lady, and Zeborah told me the truth of the stone before her grief overtook her and she drove a dagger through her own heart."

Deagon sobbed.

Caden patted the man's back. "You still grieve for my father."

"Yes, but it is more than that."

"You do not care to be old and weary, do you?"

"My age is inconvenient, but that is not why I am so upset." He looked Caden in the eyes. "Try to imagine being hopelessly in love with yourself. I spent hours on end gazing into the mirror in my chamber. And now, The Lady is gone forever."

Caden cocked his head. He could not fathom such a thing. "I am sorry for your loss, truly, I am. However, I must decide what should be done next. I need—" He gasped, struck by panic. He had been so focused on the old man that he had forgotten Fen. "Deagon, do you know what happened to my servant?"

"That *poor excuse for a servant*, if you ask my opinion. He is much too outspoken."

"So, there *was* a trace of you that came out in The Lady. Not only in the way you reacted to Fen, but there was also one time when you studied me with affection—as if you knew me in my youth, which you did. But please, do not ridicule Fen. I assure you that he is irreplaceable. I rely on him for counsel."

"Very well." Deagon sighed, then yawned. "So, so weary…" His eyes drooped. "I will try to be kind to the man. I can hear in your voice that you revere him, and I trust your judgement." He clicked his tongue. "This fog is so thick." The man squinted. "Perhaps the blow from the broken enchantment hurled him into the wall and knocked him senseless. Or better said, knocked some much-needed restraint into the man." He slapped a hand to his mouth. "Forgive me. I will try to do better."

"Fen!" Caden cried out. "Please answer me!"

"Sir Caden?" The meekest of voices rose from another corner of the room. It did not sound like Fen in the slightest.

Caden guardedly crept through the dense mist, only to find a woman slumped on the floor. He knelt at her side. "Are you hurt, m'lady?"

She was dressed in a blue silk gown similar to the one The Lady had worn, and when she lifted her head, he discovered the kindest of faces. Although not as stunning as The Lady, this woman was fair with golden-brown curly locks, rosy cheeks, and a lovely smile.

"Caden," she repeated. "I am fine, but I feared *you* had been killed."

"How do you know me?"

"Do not jest with me, sir. Do you not recognize your faithful servant? I am Fen."

Caden dropped hard onto his bottom. "Fen?" he squeaked out. "But you…" He wiggled his fingers at Fen's unfamiliar form. "You have—*female* parts."

"Have I not always?"

"*No.* You were a man. Short and somewhat weak, but definitely male. Do you not remember?"

"I know I have served you for many years, and I recall every venture, but I have no memory of being a man. My form feels as it always has."

Caden gulped. "This is quite strange. Come with me." He scrambled onto his feet again and reached out to *her*.

She took his hand and a tingling sensation cascaded along his arm. Their eyes locked, and his stomach flipped. If things became any stranger, he feared he would go mad, yet this turn of events seemed incredibly beneficial. If only he had more time to appreciate it.

The fog cleared from the uppermost part of the room and hovered low at their feet. Fen gazed at him with complete devotion, and his heart constricted. It would not beat much longer.

He kept hold of her hand and led her to Deagon. "I found Fen, but he—*she*—was also changed by the broken enchantment."

Deagon rubbed his temples and shook his head. "Zeborah had a dark sense of humor. She loved to toy with people. I imagine she somehow manipulated him—*her*—into your service."

Fen stared at the old man. "If I was enchanted, will I remain the way I am now?"

"Yes. You are as you were meant to be, just as I am." Deagon sorrowfully sighed.

Caden realized his fingers were still linked with Fen's and released her. Even though he felt a deep sense of affection for her, if he showed it, it would only make his absence harder to bear. "Deagon, I know not what to do. The stone is destroyed, and I cannot fulfill my quest. *If* I am able to leave here, I have no horse—mine bolted when we neared the enchanted lands—and I only have two days to return home. I will die before I reach King Lorin to tell him of my failure."

"Oh, Caden…" Deagon perked up and patted his hand. "You did not fail."

"Of course, I did. I was to return the stone to the king, and I shattered it."

Deagon sat taller. "Did you find the *black* stone?"

"Black stone?" *The man is deranged.*

"Yes. As I told you, before her death, Zeborah revealed to me the truth of the gemstone and the black stone within it. When you sliced through the red dragonstone with your blade, the smaller stone likely attached itself to it." He pointed at Caden's empty sheath. "Where is your sword?"

Bing approached out of nowhere. "I have it." He dropped to one knee in front of Caden and held up the blade. "I am forever in your debt, Sir Caden. No more will I fear those who come to Arburon. With the stone destroyed, I can find peace living here."

Caden took his sword from the man. "Rise, Bing. I am no king, and I am not worthy of your devotion."

Bing slowly stood. "You are a royal by blood, and I am indebted to you." He glanced at Fen, curiously drew his head back, then stood beside Deagon. Oddly, he showed no surprise to *Deagon's* new form.

"What is that on your blade, sir?" Fen gestured to it.

Deagon chuckled. "The black stone."

Caden stared at the thing. The dark, round object—slightly bigger than a snail—stuck to his sword as if it had been glued there. He reached for it, then stopped. "If I touch it, will I turn to dust?"

Deagon laughed harder. "You *have* to touch it. Truthfully, you must swallow it."

"*Swallow* it?"

The old man's laughter subsided, replaced with solemnness. "You are the true of heart, and you can still possess the riches of the stone. When Zeborah cast the death spell on you, she took a piece of your heart and magically placed it within the dragonstone. She then spread rumors about the ruby, its worth, and its healing powers. She specifically aimed them at your father in hopes of bringing him here. As I told you before, her plan went horribly awry."

Deagon's breathing grew heavier, and his weariness seemed to be taking a stronger hold. "That missing portion of your heart is why you are dying. Swallow the stone and your heart will be made whole again."

Caden was afraid to believe it. Something so outlandish could not be real—yet he had seen more than one magnificent transformation. Magic provided many possibilities. "I would live?"

Deagon answered with a warm smile and nod, and his assurance gave Caden the courage he needed. He grasped the small stone and pulled. The sword would not release it. "It is stuck."

"Pull harder. The magic coming from both has bound them together."

Caden put his entire fist around the black stone, forcefully yanked it free, then popped it into his mouth and swallowed. He assumed it would get lodged in his throat, but it glided down easily as if it knew its destination. Warmth flooded over his entire body, and with each second that passed, his heart beat stronger.

Deagon had spoken truly.

Chapter 5
Who Will Go?

Along with renewed strength, Caden's appetite returned. To everyone's good fortune, the destruction of the red stone had no effect on the daily food provisions. Arburon's enchanted power remained. A feast appeared in the early afternoon, and they all ate their fill.

"You were right about these strawberry cakes," Fen said to Bing. "They are delicious." She licked a glob of sticky icing off her delicate fingers.

Caden's attraction to Fen had grown, and seeing such actions tormented him. He had come to learn that she was still the same friend he had always known, yet now that she was female, she piqued deep desires that he had long suppressed, having never taken a wife. The realization only amplified his frustration. They enjoyed the fine food, but he knew their happiness would be short-lived. Since Arburon retained all its power, he assumed all the castle's spells still held. Only *he* could leave unharmed. He doubted Fen had come to the realization that she could not leave with him, and he dreaded their shared sorrow once the truth came to light.

He decided to keep smiling and allow their bliss to continue a while longer. "I assumed there would be others here. Are there not more people in the castle who will partake of this meal?"

Deagon's head bobbled and lowered, and it looked as if he might fall asleep in his mound of mashed potatoes.

Bing butted the man's shoulder. "You can sleep *after* the meal."

"Huh?" Deagon jerked his head up. "Oh. Yes. *Others*. I am afraid not. For years, it has only been Bing and me. Did I not tell you that I lacked decent conversation?"

Caden grinned at the scowl Bing cast in Deagon's direction. "*The Lady* mentioned it. Shall I presume you have retained all of her memories?"

"Sadly, yes. I wish I could dismiss the images of the abundant deaths I have witnessed. The seekers of the stone never took the second option. They were always compelled to touch it."

"Except me," Bing said. "I did not want to die, and I was hungry. When The Lady mentioned food and peace, I chose them. And when others came and I saw how they died, I was thankful I chose wisely."

"I must know," Caden said. "Why were you not surprised when The Lady became an old man?"

Deagon grunted and resumed eating.

"I always knew she was enchanted," Bing said. "I often saw the temperament of a man in her, and one day, I discovered her admiring herself in the mirror. The way she was—" His nose wrinkled. "Well, I just knew something about her was unusual." He shrugged. "Her transformation made sense."

Bing reached for another slice of strawberry cake. "I actually prefer her this way. I truly can live out my life in peace. Once you spread the word that the ruby has been destroyed, wayward thieves will no longer trouble me, and *he* will likely sleep all the time." He inclined his head toward Deagon. "And hopefully, not complain nearly as much."

Fen softly laughed, then cast the loveliest smile. "Perhaps he will come to find that you are a better conversationalist now." She, too, took a second piece of cake. "I cannot resist these incredible sweets. The cake is likely the most wonderful thing I have ever eaten."

Caden grinned at her. Like before, their eyes locked, and he gulped. He had to look away.

The meal and the day waned, and night came. After several glasses of wine, Caden needed sleep. "I pray you have available chambers with beds," he said to Deagon.

"Indeed. Arburon has many. I will gladly escort you to one, so that I may retire to mine."

Fen daintily dabbed a napkin to her mouth, then stood. "It will serve us well to rest."

The moment they all left the table, it cleared itself. The remaining food vanished, and the dishes cleaned themselves and sparkled. Caden wished he could take that particular spell with him. Like everything and everyone else, it would have to be left behind.

Bing bade them goodnight and headed down a long corridor. Caden and Fen followed Deagon in another direction. They ascended a rounded stairway and came to another hallway.

Deagon gestured to an open door. "You may have this chamber."

"Very good." Caden gave the man a single nod and headed for the room.

Fen followed.

Caden froze and spun to face her. "You cannot come into my bedchamber."

"Why not, sir? I always sleep close by. I must look after you."

"You *used* *to* lie nearby, but not anymore. It would be inappropriate."

"I do not understand. Why has everything changed?"

He placed a hand to her soft cheek. "I know this is difficult for you to comprehend, but in my eyes *you* have changed."

She blinked ever so slowly and leaned into his touch.

Her action and close proximity set his regenerated heart wildly thumping. "I must bid you goodnight, Fen." He took her hand, lifted it to his lips, and gave it a gentlemanly kiss.

Her head tipped up, and he swore she silently begged for a *real* kiss. He could not. It would only compound their already difficult upcoming separation.

He bowed low, backed into the room, and shut the door.

❧   ❧

Morning brought a different kind of heaviness to Caden's heart. Although it beat strongly, the thought of leaving Fen broke it.

He had a long road ahead of him, so he ate a large, enchanted breakfast, and after, everything cleared just as it had the night before. The meal brought him little enjoyment. His looming departure soured everything.

The four of them returned to the main area with its high ceiling and empty ebony pedestal. The enormous room seemed void without the spinning red stone. No longer did the air pulse around Caden; the strong pulsation rested deep within him.

He could not prolong leaving any further, but before he departed, he had one more question for Deagon. "Do you know why my uncle believed the stone held the future of our kingdom? Yes, it kept me from dying, but Shanavar would have gone on without me."

"You truly do not know?"

Caden shook his head.

"Your cousin, Lang, has a rare illness. King Lorin held onto hope—like that of your father—that the stone could heal. It indeed had the capability, yet only for you. The king will be distraught that Lang will not benefit from the ruby's powers, but he will still have an heir. You, Caden."

Caden gaped at him in disbelief. "He never spoke of Lang's difficulties." He rubbed across his aching heart. "Am I to be king?"

"Yes. Lang will not live long enough to take the throne, and from what I have seen of you in these short days, you will wear the crown well." Deagon turned and smiled at Fen. "And I believe you will have a very *loyal* queen at your side."

A rosy hue filled Fen's cheeks, and she shyly bent her head.

Caden's awe turned to fury, and he tightened his fists. "Why do you torture her so? Shame to you for speaking so boldly of something that can never be! You know she cannot leave here!"

"What?" Fen's entire body deflated, and tears glistened in her eyes. "I am to remain at Arburon?"

Bing moved beside her and placed a hand on her shoulder. "Destroying the stone did not end the castle's enchantment. Only the one who is true of heart can leave without dying."

Fen lurched forward and flung her arms around Caden. "I will die here without you!" Her tears streamed.

Caden held her close and stroked her silky hair. An essence of lilacs emanated from her, so unlike the stench from the bog. "You are strong, Fen. You always have been. Here you will live and be well, but I cannot stay. If my cousin is truly ill, I have a duty to the realm. I must serve the people." He took her face in his hands. "But know this. A part of my heart will remain here with you, for I have come to know that I love you."

Her chin quivered. "I have *always* loved you, sir."

He thought back to their many years together, and finally, everything made sense. "We belong with one another, Fen."

Deagon cleared his throat. "I was by no means trying to be cruel in Fen's regard. I recognized the love you bore for one another. If she genuinely holds a piece of your heart, then I believe she may be able to go with you. Did you not say that your heart is not whole without her?"

"But she *could* die. How would I go on if she turned to dust in my grasp?"

Fen sniffled and wiped her eyes. "I have to try. I would prefer dying in your arms than living out my days here in your absence." Determination and devotion filled her gaze.

How could he deny her when every part of him wanted this endeavor to succeed?

"Very well."

He lifted her from the floor and cradled her small form against him. He had always been compelled to protect her, and he prayed he could see this through. No quest had ever been this important or meaningful.

Deagon and Bing accompanied them to the front door, opened it, and followed them out onto the stoop.

"Tell your uncle that your father died bravely," Deagon said.

"I will, and I thank you for your guidance on this venture." Caden gave the man a respectful nod and moved toward the first step.

Overwhelmed with a different kind of fear his heart pounded as he descended.

Fen's grasp tightened. "I only hope it will not hurt to become dust," she whispered. She let out several shuddered breaths and buried her face into his shoulder.

"I have you, Fen, and no matter what happens, I will not let go."

He reached the final step, shut his eyes, and took it.

Fen trembled in his arms, and his heart leapt.

He made another leery step forward. She lifted her head, stared into his eyes, and softly smiled. "I can see you."

He chuckled. "And I, you." The love of his life had not turned to dust.

Although tempted to dance in elation, that was not in his character. Instead, he pressed his lips to hers in a gentle reminder of his deep devotion.

Fen let out the most pleasant sigh, then her eyes widened, and she craned her neck. "It is gone, sir."

Caden spun around with Fen still in his hold. The castle was nowhere to be seen.

"The enchantment indeed remains," he said and gazed at the beautiful woman in his arms. "I may not have what most men would consider the riches of the stone, but I bear the greatest treasure. You, Fen."

Her smile lit up the gray hue of their surroundings. They would soon have to traverse the bog and endure other hardships on their way home, but they would do it together.

As they *always* had.

The Dragon Knight
J. L. Lawrence

Chapter 1

Alyssa popped into her twin brother's sleeping area. Adam had just returned from another dangerous mission, and she needed to see that he was okay. His snoring confirmed he'd once again survived. They'd been fighting against evil for decades now. With her latest visions, she didn't see a light at the end of the tunnel. Instead, a new war had begun to brew, and they'd be stuck in the middle of the battle once again. Since misery loved company, she decided Adam should join her. She leapt on top of him.

"Ow. What the…?" Adam snarled at her. She placed a finger over his lips and smiled. His pale blue eyes glared into her identical ones. She ruffled his short reddish-brown hair to irritate him further. "Alyssa, what are you doing in my tent? I needed some space tonight, and who knows what could have been going on in here."

"Oh, please." Alyssa snorted. "You mean a girl?" She chuckled. "Not likely. I'm your twin and can read all your thoughts and emotions, dummy. I knew you were just sleeping."

"Just?" Adam pushed her into the floor. "I returned from a three-week mission in South America late last night. I haven't had decent sleep in forever. Dad doesn't travel much anymore, so it's up to me. You know this." He paused the tirade and looked at her. "Which is why you're really here. You're worried. Something spooked you."

"I'm sorry for disturbing your beauty sleep." Alyssa slyly smiled, showing no actual remorse. "Is it the missions keeping you awake at night? Or memories of *her*?" She knew exactly how to put him back on the defensive.

He growled and tried to turn away from her, but Alyssa caught his shoulder. "You still dream about Kate. I see it and feel it. It's been twenty-five years since we graduated."

"What if I do?" His voice turned to steel. "I can't control my dreams."

Alyssa hated to watch Adam suffer so much after all those years. Kate had been his high school sweetheart, his soulmate, or so they thought. Together the three of them had saved a lot of lives, but Kate had feared the power within her. She had been raised with an intense desire to be normal. Alyssa and Adam had been born into a family of witches and warriors. Kate wanted no part of that life. In a moment of desperation, Kate had used her power to delete all her memories and connections to them.

Adam lost the love of his life, and Alyssa had lost her best friend. Despite the passage of time, the betrayal still stung. Their bonds ran deep, and Alyssa thought about her every day. She missed having that one person she could talk to about anything. She'd never found that type of friendship again.

She controlled her wayward thoughts and brought her focus back to Adam. "You still love her. It isn't healthy."

"Not like you think." Adam sighed and gave up on the notion of sleep. "It feels like unfinished business and hangs over me like a dark cloud. She deleted her memories but ours remain. Our bond remains. I think if I could see her and know she found whatever she was looking for, I could let it go. I need to know why. On the other hand, I look at the life I chose to lead, and I know the answer."

"She would have made a brilliant witch, but I see your point." Alyssa couldn't take away the pain that had chased them for over fifteen years, but she could give him a new mission. "Speaking of dreams, I've had a lot of new ones lately."

Adam's head snapped up. "What kind?"

"Big evil coming. What else is new?" She sighed. "A few weeks ago, the visions began with a girl crying out for help. She'd been attacked by demons, I think. The whole scene felt orchestrated by something evil. Powerful. Based on her condition, I'd say they took advantage of the poor girl." Alyssa struggled to wipe the horrid images from her mind, but visions didn't work that way.

"Then what?" Adam asked through gritted teeth.

Alyssa treaded with caution. Adam had a heavy temper when it came to physical assaults. His skills in battle and proficiency in martial arts made that anger a deadly weapon.

"The next dream showed the same girl huddled next to the fireplace. Her mother begged her to get rid of the evil baby inside her. The girl refused. She said it would be our saving grace, or the key to our destruction. She had seen things. I could tell. This baby is important to the upcoming war. Her mom asked her to stay in the protection of the house, but the girl said she had to hide. That the baby must be born into the hands of pure light. The hands of the Mystic."

"The Mystic?" Adam scratched his facial stubble. "The real one?"

"No, the pretend one." Alyssa narrowed her eyes. "Camilla spoke about the Mystic and her powers. She won the last Rising. Camilla often called her pure light."

Adam drummed his fingers on the tiny tray next to him He grabbed his canteen and poured some water on his face. "Maybe I'm still tired, but if this all-powerful Mystic has it handled, why on earth am I awake at four a.m.?"

"My latest dreams have shown me that we must play a part." Alyssa whispered, even though she couldn't explain why. "The girl's name is Sarah. She's in trouble and needs our protection until the Mystic arrives to deliver the baby. If we fail, the child will be taken by demons and raised to destroy our entire world."

"Could be a nightmare, Sis." Adam tilted his head. "It seems far-fetched even for us."

"You're wrong." Alyssa grabbed his arm and forced him to meet her eyes. "The last message came from a young girl in another realm. She showed me glimpses of what could be. I have to find her and obtain some type of medallion with a dragon on it. She said it would guide us to the girl. If I don't complete the mission, we all plunge into darkness. I can go by portal."

"I don't think so," Adam snapped. "You know better than to jump into crazy situations."

"It's destined," Alyssa argued. "I can't explain it." She paused, briefly revisiting what she'd seen. "And I swear I felt Kate's presence in the vision. I didn't see her, but I'd recognize her energy anywhere."

"Weren't you just telling me to let her go?" He raked his finger through his hair.

Alyssa snorted. "Have you ever listened?"

Their mother lifted the flap of the tent and walked in. "What are you two arguing about this early in the morning?" She stared at them in total disapproval. "Alyssa, I didn't know you'd returned."

"I've only been here a few minutes." She cut her eyes toward Adam. "We were reminiscing about Kate and some new visions." Since she also shared a link with her mother, she transferred the knowledge instead of repeating herself.

Alyssa expected to hear the same argument from her mom, but she sat down on the edge of the cot and simply said, "I see."

"What do you see, Mom?" Adam pressed. "You haven't told us something. I see the guilt."

"It's about Kate." Their mom soundly exhaled. "She called me the night she decided to erase her memories of us. She wanted me to help both of you understand her choice. I never imagined our lives would remain intertwined. What I didn't tell you is that the whole thing was my idea. I showed Kate how to delete the memories. She made a memory box of items her senior year of college that she couldn't bear to destroy and asked me to keep it for her. I locked it away.

"Anyway, about eight years later, I felt an overwhelming urge to connect to Kate and decided to check it. When I opened it, all of Kate's belongings had disappeared. In their place was a silver locket." Their mom reached into her pocket and held it up for Alyssa to see. "It had a note attached in Kate's handwriting that read, *for Alyssa when the time is right.* I can't explain it."

Alyssa gasped. She recognized the locket from her visions with the strange, blue-haired girl. Her destiny began to take shape. "How do we know the exact time?" She took the necklace. On the back, it had two small figures. A dragon and a phoenix.

"I'd say the time is now." Her mom nodded toward the box. "When I opened my eyes this morning, the box sat beside my head. It should be locked in our family vault very far away. But it's not. Alyssa, I think your visions are real and you must go to another time and place to retrieve the rest of this locket. It won't be easy, but I believe in you. Without the guide, we won't find the girl, Sarah, in time."

Her mother grasped her hands. "You alone must complete this quest."

"Wait." Adam reached for the necklace. "Fifteen years ago, you were doing all that casting and high-level witchcraft with Camilla. That's when we stopped aging because of something you did. What if this makes it worse?"

"Grow up, Adam. What if we start to age again?" Alyssa fired back. "Everything isn't about you. Maybe we were held in place for this moment. I can do this."

Alyssa knew the arguments would never end. She steadied her thoughts on the mysterious blue-haired girl and the silver locket. A portal began to take shape. She tried not to worry about what awaited on the other side. She ignored Adam's protests and jumped inside before she could change her mind.

Chapter 2

Alyssa hit the ground hard and rolled to her left. She came face to face with a young girl with gray eyes that had thick sapphire rings circling the smoky color. The teenager's hair had half black and half the same blue from her eyes. "Who are you?" Alyssa recognized her from the visions but still had no clue where she'd landed.

"I'm Princess Maggie." The intriguing girl watched her. "And you're the Witch Warrior. Took you long enough to get here. I've been waiting forever."

"What are you talking about?" Alyssa had a bad feeling that she'd just jumped down a rabbit hole into crazy town. "Why would you be waiting for me or know so much about me? My name is Alyssa by the way."

"Why do you recognize me?" Maggie thoughtfully eyed her. "I sent you a vision and told you to come. Not sure how that's a shock."

"How old are you?" "Alyssa demanded. "How is it we speak such a similar dialect?"

"I'm fifteen but in human years much older." Maggie scoffed. "And I can speak any language and dialect." She pointed at a tattoo on her upper arm. "I earned that ability in a previous quest."

"Where am I? What quests?" Alyssa's patience level hit an all new low. She didn't have time to play around. "Just tell me what I need to know."

"Very well." Maggie took a breath. "You are in the world of Draconia, specifically the Dragon Realm. My quests are of no importance for your purpose. However, we must begin yours soon. You've only been granted a limited time in my realm."

"Did you say dragons and a quest?" Alyssa couldn't hide her shock. She must have hit her head or landed in some sort of weird fairytale land. She took note of her surroundings. A lot of the vegetation looked similar but some of the trees were different and had purple and pink leaves. She didn't know Draconia, but she definitely wasn't in her own realm.

"Yes, we must hurry." Maggie stopped and turned her attention to the hiss coming from a tiny, funky looking lizard on her shoulder.

Alyssa squinted to get a better view of the odd creature. "Okay, I get the urgency, but I'm still confused. And what kind of lizard is that?"

"It's a dragon, silly." Maggie laughed. "You act like you've never seen one before."

"Dragons aren't real." Alyssa shook her head. "They're myths. I must have taken a wrong turn with my portal."

"Not real, huh?" Maggie nodded to the pet on her shoulder. "Meet Firespark."

The lizard-like animal jumped down and grew larger until it stood close to eight feet tall. The dragon lowered its head to meet Alyssa's eyes. She took a small step back. Blazing blue eyes—the same color as Maggie's—met hers. She gasped. Even its smooth polished black scales were tipped in the sapphire color. Alyssa sensed a strong bond between the two of them. She pinched herself to make sure she wasn't dreaming.

"This can't be. They aren't real." Alyssa stammered. "I don't understand what's happening to me."

Maggie reached for her shoulder and affectionately squeezed. She motioned for Firespark to return to her shoulder. He bowed to Alyssa, and then returned to his perch on Maggie. "Let me explain a little." She motioned for Alyssa to sit on a nearby boulder.

"Since I was a very young child, my mother told me of a powerful Witch Warrior who would one day need my help to save both of our worlds. Now, I have my own visions and have also seen the destruction to both our realms and many others if you are not successful. I visited your dreams because I had begun to fear you'd never come. I'm not sure how time works between our worlds, but I couldn't deny the urgency I felt to contact you."

"How long have you looked for me?" Alyssa took the opportunity to ask a question. The whole thing sounded more like a movie plot than reality. And she'd seen some strange things in her life. If she was honest with herself, she had hoped the portal would take her to Kate, not this strange place.

"My mother provided details about the time of year, what you'd look like, and your required quest. But she couldn't pinpoint the exact time because we are from very different places." Maggie sighed. "So, I've been coming here year after year to this spot to wait for you. It's a relief to finally meet the ghost that haunts my dreams."

Alyssa tried not to take offense at being called a ghost. "I wish I could say the same," Alyssa grumbled. "I guess you need to tell me about this quest and help me get started. As you said time is a factor."

Maggie stood and motioned Alyssa to follow. "If my visions are correct, you only have one day in my realm. You arrived as the sun rises and must leave before it sets. I wish we had more time to compare our worlds. I'll tell you what I can as we walk. It's just a short distance to my home."

Maggie walked at a brisk pace, and Alyssa trudged behind her. At least they were outside and not in some dark dungeon. Alyssa stretched out her senses to connect to the world around her. Thankfully, she could still access her powers in this realm. Maggie spoke of her country and her parents as they walked. She mentioned a best friend named, Egan, and talked about her amazing dragon, Firespark. Alyssa felt further and further away from reality. She'd defeated demons, dark curses, evil wizards, and spent years learning the art of witchcraft. She had nothing to fear, right?

"Welcome." Maggie interrupted her thoughts.

"Whoa." Alyssa stumbled as they exited the forest. "This isn't a home. It's a freaking castle. A really big, shiny one."

Alyssa couldn't possibly take in all the grandeur and mystique surrounding the entire kingdom.

"Do you not have castles, either?" Maggie's wide eyes met hers.

"Yes, but only in the movies are they ever this grand." Alyssa stared at the magnificence of the sight before her. A small stream encircled the outer edges of the palace with several bridges providing walkways. Astonishing gardens were on either side of the main entrance path that led to massive golden palace doors. Alyssa couldn't take it all in. She'd watched fairytales her whole life but never imagined actually being in one.

The grandeur continued as they entered the main hallway. "Wait here. I'm afraid I don't have time for a tour. I'll grab a few supplies and we'll be on our way." Two armed guards opened the door for her.

Alyssa entered and gasped. They had an actual throne room. With massive royal chairs made entirely from gold or a similar substance. Several jewels had been placed in a design of a dragon above each. Windows overlooked the kingdom showing a community of houses, businesses, and farms.

Alyssa rubbed her eyes. Maybe she had experienced head trauma and landed in a white padded room. It simply couldn't be real. She walked to the windows and leaned against a wooden table. The solid furniture provided some relief that the mysterious castle was real. Speechless couldn't describe her current frame of mind. Nothing could.

She turned from the windows and saw a massive flag hung across the wall behind the thrones. It held the symbol of the dragon in the center and was surrounded by four other symbols. She peered closer. A mermaid, a phoenix, a pegasus, and maybe a sphinx. All mythical creatures, and yet she'd already met one in this world. *Could they all exist?*

Alyssa moved back toward the main hallway. Castles like this didn't exist and neither did dragons. Seeing them went against everything she thought she knew. Yet, she was standing inside the castle and had met a dragon. *What did it all mean?*

She tried to reach out for her mother or Adam but couldn't connect. Fear built in the pit of her stomach. What would be asked of her? Could she do it alone? She'd always had Adam in her corner. Beads of sweat broke out across her forehead.

"Witch Warrior." Maggie startled her and she jumped. "You think very loudly."

"My name is Alyssa. Why do you call me Witch Warrior?" Alyssa narrowed her eyes. "Can you read my thoughts?"

"To ease your mind, I cannot read your thoughts. I am an empath and can feel your emotional turmoil. There's a lot." Maggie grinned. "For your other question, my mother never knew your name in the visions. All we could see is that you were a trained warrior and taught the art of sorcery. We decided to call you that to give your face a name. It stuck after all these years."

"I'll admit I'm a little terrified." Alyssa tried to rein in her panic.

"That's unfortunate." Maggie sighed.

Dread filled Alyssa's body. "Why?"

"I haven't even explained your tasks yet. You've been given a rare opportunity to possess a jewel that protects and destroys. Very few finish the challenge." Maggie grimaced when Alyssa released a small growl. "Follow me. It's best to show you."

Alyssa bit her tongue to avoid asking the next question in her mind but finally relented. "Where are we going?"

"To the Cave of the Dragon Soul. You must become a Dragon Knight to obtain what you seek." Maggie's innocent blue gray eyes met hers. She wasn't kidding.

Alyssa's heart plummeted. What did she know about becoming a knight?

Chapter 3

"What are you talking about?" Alyssa didn't recognize the high pitch in her own voice. "I'm not becoming some fabled knight. That's so archaic."

"I don't follow your logic." Maggie looked at her in confusion. "It's a great honor only bestowed upon the most worthy."

"Sounds impossible to me," Alyssa muttered.

"Not impossible," Maggie countered. "I completed the challenge when I was twelve."

"Twelve?" Alyssa stared at her. "So, you're a knight?"

"Not exactly." Maggie tried to hide her smile. "I'm a Dragon Trainer and next in line to become a Dragon Master for all of Draconia."

Alyssa started to ask what that meant but decided it might be best not to know. She didn't have enough time to figure out all the quirks of their world. She did have a mission to accomplish and limited time. Maggie held the keys to her success.

"Tell me what I need to do for this challenge." Alyssa straightened her back and accepted the inevitable.

Maggie nodded. "We go to the caves."

"Anything but caves." Alyssa's resolve waivered. "I don't like being underground. It's makes me extremely nervous."

"You'll adjust." Maggie rushed past a massive training facility. "The entrance is just past the nesting area."

Not even gonna ask about that one either. Alyssa followed Maggie until they reached a stone entrance.

"This is as far as I can take you, my friend." Maggie pointed inside. "Once you enter, follow the corridor. It will lead to a large room that offers your challenges. Each potential knight must complete three tasks to prove they are worthy of the title."

"What type of tasks will I face?" Alyssa refused to enter without more information, considering where her last leap of faith had landed her.

"Hard to say. For me, I had to prove my bond with Firespark and choose my people above all else." Maggie smiled as she spoke about the memories. "I defeated some goblins and a couple other creatures. And I created some spells to escape a maze. But you should know all the challenges are different. To become a knight is a rare gift. It's the only way to fill the locket you hold so tight in your grasp."

"How do you know about the locket?" It had been hidden under Alyssa's shirt the entire time.

"May I?" Maggie held out her hand for the necklace.

Alyssa lifted it from her neck. "Of course."

"This locket is made from crushed dragon scales and a few other creatures from my realm." Maggie inspected it. "These designs also represent Draconia, and I suspect your world as well. I'm not sure how it found its way to you, but it proves this challenge is your destiny."

"Any other words of wisdom?" Alyssa turned to face the entryway.

"Don't die." Maggie grinned. "One important reminder. You must complete all three tasks before the sun sets on this day."

"Just out of curiosity, what happens if I don't?"

"It will destroy us all." The youth had disappeared from Maggie's haunted eyes. She'd seen too much in her short years.

No pressure there. A shiver ran down Alyssa's spine.

"If you fail," Maggie continued, "the portal will take you back to your world, and you will not be able to find the missing witch or complete the prophecy. All of our realms hang in the balance. I wish I could do more, but it's not my time. This next part is only for you, Witch Warrior. I believe in you."

She stepped back and bowed toward Alyssa. "Many blessings upon you. I'll see you on the other side." Maggie waved her hands in a complicated pattern and disappeared into a portal.

Guess it's just me. Alyssa stared at the entrance and took a deep breath. Time to face her greatest fear. Dark, enclosed spaces.

She followed the path, and it ended in front of a massive door. She searched for a handle but found none. *What am I supposed to do now?*

Tiny script appeared on the door at her eye level:

To obtain the soul of a dragon
You must pass three tests
Your enemy awaits but who will it be
In the first task you must open your eyes to see
Spells are cast and chaos reigns
With the second task you will bring the flames
Love is the strongest bond in the mortal world
But can you survive in a realm not your own
Finish these tasks and you will find the key
Good luck Witch Warrior, so mote it be

Alyssa read the words many times to commit them to memory. They didn't make a whole lot of sense, but she'd learned the importance of cryptic prophecies many years ago. She wouldn't let her loved ones down. She could do this.

The door vanished. She stepped through the open stone arch. A dimly lit area surrounded her. Shapes skittered around the edges in the shadows, but she couldn't determine who or what they were.

She moved to the center of the ring, and the doorway sealed behind her. *I'll have to fight my way out of this one.* She wished she had taken Adam up on all his offers to practice her martial arts skills. She'd learned the basics and enough to get by in past battles. Would it be enough today?

Gray blobs took shape. Not human, but she still didn't know what exactly she'd have to face. Different creatures required different types of attacks. Where did she start with a new evil entity? One rushed in and swung a sword at her. She ducked and backed up.

More would attack soon. They were testing her. She created a shield around herself to prevent surprise attacks and hold them at bay. At least she'd learned that much over the years. She thought back over the words etched into the door. They meant something about this challenge.

Open my eyes to see. What the heck did that mean? She stewed over her options. Each one seemed worse than the last. Her mind went back to a memory with her mentor, Camilla. A lesson on Chakras and reaching the level of true knowledge. She needed to open her Third Eye.

Alyssa sighed as understanding dawned. She'd never been very good with that level. It took total sacrifice of one's being and connection to the spirit world. Alyssa didn't like the loss of control and rarely achieved it. Camilla's stern voice echoed in her head, reminding her that she'd need that skill one day. That day had come.

She enforced her shield and closed her eyes. One by one she pulled energy up through each chakra level until she reached the highest one. She pushed but couldn't break through the barrier. She dug deep and let go of her fear. Her mind shifted, and her vision changed. She could see so much of the world. More importantly, her enemies had a name and a way to be eliminated.

Ugly creatures with beady eyes and pointy teeth battered away at her shield. *Goblins.* She searched for more knowledge of their weaknesses. They weren't too bright, but when attacking in mass, they could be dangerous. Weapons would be essential to defeat them. She hadn't brought any. Maybe she could connect to her own realm. She visualized her favorite sword and reached for it through time and space. It dropped into her hands. Loaded with all the information she needed, she cut the connection to her third eye.

Part of her wanted to stay hidden behind the shield, but she had no way of knowing how much time had passed. The ticking clock in her mind had no mercy.

Alyssa lifted her sword and dropped the shield. Several nasty little goblins ran toward her. She punched one in the nose, then used her elbow to hit another behind her. She swung around and sliced through a third with her sword. They threw a few weak spells that she easily deflected.

Her sword spun so fast it whistled in the air. She removed the heads from two and chopped an arm off the third due to a miss on her part. She didn't give up. A few more entered the circle. Her arm ached and sweat burned her eyes. She decided to add a little magic to the party. She pulled energy to her and released it in the form of small energy blasts.

The drain weighed heavily, but she refused to be defeated by sheer numbers of creatures. Her skills were superior. She brought her shield back into place to gather all the energy she could build. The goblins continued to attack her barrier, but she paid them no mind. She had a plan.

Light emanated from her fingertips. She waited until her body reached max capacity. She dropped the shields and released the energy. It hit the goblins like an explosion, destroying all that remained.

Alyssa glanced around the empty cavern and yelled, "What's next?"

Her voice bounced around. She fought back tears and weariness. She jerked forward and the room shifted. She spun out of control and had no idea how to stop it.

Chapter 4

Alyssa's stomach heaved as the spinning stopped. The smell of incense and chemicals burned her nose, yet felt oddly comforting. One large table was stationed in the center of the small cavern.

She crept closer. The tabletop had a variety of ingredients displayed and a large mortar and pestle in the center. A set of labels stood on the far right with the vials on the left. Apparently, the first part of the test involved potions and her knowledge base. She picked them up carefully to examine each element. There were a few ingredients she didn't recognize but used other clues to determine their purpose.

After double checking her work, she put the last card into place. Everything on the table disappeared except for a key. A string holding a piece of paper had been attached. It read: *Open the door to find the treasure you seek.*

Alyssa dropped her head and banged her fist on the table. "This is so stupid." The cryptic instructions and clues brought back memories of when she'd once saved an entire town. Kate's town. Why did everything keep pointing back to the past?

She picked up the key, and a door came into view. She couldn't imagine having to complete this task at the age of twelve. The key clicked into place, and the door opened. Two smaller tables stood in the center of the room. Each had a large empty bowl. The next task had something to do with flames, but Alyssa knew how deadly it could be to introduce fire into a potion. So, what exactly did she need to accomplish?

She studied the first potion card reading all of the ingredients multiple times. All of them were spread across the workspace. Many she recognized from her studies over the years like juniper, ivy, rosemary, scorpion tail, and demon flesh. The rest she knew little to nothing about. How hard could it be? She had the instructions.

The second table appeared similar, so she decided to see what it involved. It contained the exact same formula and items. *Weird.* Alyssa considered the test in front of her. Why have two exact potions? Then, it dawned on her. She'd been given two chances to create the challenge correctly. Not much room for error.

Alyssa closed her eyes and focused on all the memories of her training. Her mother had taught her the basics of spells and potions her whole life. Camilla had trained her for ten years on the higher levels of magic. Precision played an important role as did understanding the ingredients. She'd have to do a little guesswork on the new ones, and that made her nervous.

Her bottom lip cracked from her continual chewing. A habit she'd developed during her childhood. It became worse when she and Adam joined the family business of defeating evil. She read over the card again and picked up each new vial to study its consistency. *Goblin blood. Yuck.* Dragon scales and diamond dust sounded a little more familiar.

Each new item provided a unique texture or smell. After she gained more confidence, she reached for the mortar and pestle to begin. She followed the provided formula precisely. The last step simply said combine with the flame of life.

What the hell does that mean?

She picked up each container, but nothing represented fire or life. Many years ago, she had used pure energy that she'd learned to control in order to contain a curse. The tree at the center of the curse had represented the life of the town. Maybe her own inner light could complete the mysterious potion.

The air crackled as she gathered the positive energy surrounding her. She directed the electricity into her right hand and pointed at the bowl. She only allowed a small amount to release. Better to be cautious.

Alyssa felt elation that she'd mastered the task until the fire continued to spread beyond the large bowl. It destroyed everything on the table and continued to expand.

Energy still pulsed inside her, so she erected a shield around the table to contain the wayward flames. She struggled to hold the now-raging inferno inside the containment box she'd created. Sweat dripped down her back, and her arms shook from the exertion. She focused all her effort on smothering the flames. She shrunk the shield until she deprived if of all oxygen.

All that remained of her failed, first attempt was a thick, black substance oozing on the floor. Alyssa turned to the second table. She couldn't fail again. She'd never be able to face Maggie or anyone else if she didn't find the answer. It gave her doubts about her own training. How much did she really know about this world?

"You can do this, Witch Warrior." Maggie's voice echoed in the cave. "Have faith."

"So, you're watching me fail," Alyssa grumbled. "Figures. Like I needed more pressure."

Maggie's laughter calmed her nerves. She didn't seem concerned by the failed attempt. "From the time I could walk, I've trained. I believe in you. I've seen your success. In my realm, many things are possible. The unbelievable is real." Her voice cut off, and Alyssa felt alone again.

She leaned on the table to contemplate her mistakes. Everything had worked except the flame. She had added something from her own realm not this one. She sorted through the ingredients and simultaneously reviewed the information she'd learned about Draconia. They had dragons. Dragons breathed fire.

The only ingredient for dragons on the table said scales. That didn't scream fire to her. *The flame of life.* The words had to be important. A giant clock kept ticking in her head, taunting her. If she didn't pass the second challenge soon, she wouldn't have time for the last one.

Alyssa added all of the other ingredients and searched for the last piece. Her eyes stopped on phoenix ash. Could it be that simple? She tried to remember the myths about a phoenix. They could regenerate and be reborn from the ashes. To get ashes, you need a flame. She decided to add a very small amount just in case they were potent.

The ashes felt weird between her fingers as she dropped them into the cauldron. Sparks flew. She stepped back and prepared to create another shield. Tears burned the backs of her eyes. She waited. The fire subsided, and the large bowl revealed a bright green light from its center.

She leaned over for a closer look. A beautiful emerald liquid remained. She exhaled and closed her eyes, allowing some of the stress to release. A perfect potion. She had mastered the second challenge.

Before she could revel in her success, the room spun once more. She dropped into a cold, dark pit. She liked the goblins and potions better. A wisp of smoke encircled her waist and drew her farther into the cavern. She tried to push her fears aside and focus on the challenge. The strange mist beckoned her forward.

"Ouch!" She ran straight into a glass wall. Or a mirror. The surface appeared reflective, yet she didn't see herself.

A painful moan caught her attention. She moved along the corridor until she found an injured animal on the other side of the glass. The dragon's snout had been wrapped in some type of wire and his legs were bound in chains. Several gashes covered its sides, and there was a deep gash in the wings like someone had tried to cut them off.

The horrible sight made her turn away. She couldn't bear the brutality. She'd been taught to revere all creatures and harm none. The dragon raised its head. "Help me."

She met his eyes. "I don't know how to get to you."

"Free me. Please," the incredible creature begged.

Alyssa pressed her head against the barrier. "I don't know how, and I can't cast a portal to you."

"I'm in the Shadow Realm." He spoke into her mind. *"You can free me if you have the courage to enter the unknown."*

Camilla had told many stories about the Shadow Realm and its dangers. Many didn't return once they entered. The world had very little color or emotion, like something had sucked all the feelings out if it. Alyssa didn't care to jump into another realm she knew very little about. Her last attempt had landed her in this challenge.

The dragon groaned. Alyssa sighed. She'd once risked her life for a cat. She wouldn't ignore this magnificent beast no matter what the cost. Plus, it had to be the final challenge, so did she really have a choice?

Once she made up her mind, a small vial of the emerald liquid appeared in her hand. She remembered where she'd seen a similar potion. Camilla had created it once to free the warriors trapped in the shadows, but it only allowed entry, not exit. Camilla never spoke of it again.

Alyssa opened it and tossed the bitter liquid into her mouth before she had time to talk herself out of it. Her body shifted and she stepped into the shadow world.

A man's soothing voice startled her. He appeared to be calming the dragon, but he *could* be the one torturing it. Alyssa crept closer to better understand what she was up against.

"What are you doing here?" His gruff, deep voice caused her to jump, taking away any chance to stay hidden.

"I'm here to save the dragon." Her voice shook. "I won't let you hurt him."

"Brave words for one so young." He smiled. "Unlikely story. Humans aren't allowed in this realm. And very few others would have the power." He stepped closer and took a deep breath. "Ah. A witch."

"Camilla trained me." Alyssa hoped a little name-dropping might help.

"A wonderful lady." His golden eyes dimmed. "She did a lot for my brothers and I. A real shame she passed in the big battle."

He held out his arm. "I'm Blaze."

"Alyssa." She shook his hand, then stepped back. She wasn't ready to trust this stranger yet felt a fierce draw to him. He had to be nearly seven feet tall and built like some kind of Greek god. His facial features were perfectly sculpted. His skin seemed a little grayish, but so did everything else in the realm.

"Why are you really here?" Blaze asked. He spoke with little emotion, but she could see his aura below the surface, and it was filled with colors. She sensed his need to escape the dark.

Alarm skittered down her spine as she realized her own emotions were growing weaker except her connection to him. "Short story. I was sent into a dragon realm to gain a tool or weapon to find a girl in my own realm that's in big trouble from demons. I landed in Draconia and have to master three challenges. I've passed the first two, and freeing the dragon is my third. Then, I can go back home and save the day." She gasped to catch her breath.

"And that's the short version?" He gave a humorless laugh. "Glad I didn't ask for the long one."

She scowled, but he ignored her. "My opinion is that this dragon is not your challenge," he continued. "He's from a different realm, and I'm already freeing him. He'd been trapped and tortured by demons that I disposed of before you arrived."

"What else would it be?" Alyssa demanded.

"Probably, you were tricked into coming into the shadows to figure out how to leave them." Blaze's sly grin lit up his face and added to his handsome features.

Despite the drain in her emotions, she felt an intense attraction to this tall stranger. She'd avoided romantic entanglements her whole life and had no intention of that changing. She gathered her wits to ask an important question.

"What's the big deal about leaving?"

"Do you have the return potion or a guide that walks between worlds?" His smug demeanor irked her.

"No." She sighed. "Guess I should have thought about that. What are my other options? Can you return me?"

He visibly flinched like she'd hurt him. "I'm afraid not. My people are bound to this realm by a curse. I can't leave, but I can guide you. Do you have a possession from Draconia?"

"Only this." Alyssa pulled out the locket. "It's actually from my realm but it's tied to the quest. Will it work?"

The moment it touched his fingers, he gasped and leaned down for a closer look. "I recognize the power that formed this. You've been given a rare gift made by the Mystic herself. A great destiny must await you. I believe this locket contains the power to send you home."

"How does it work?" Alyssa stared at the necklace with a million questions in her mind.

"One of my abilities is to surf through the unconscious minds of the realms. It's our only escape from the darkness. I can open a portal door, and the power will guide you. Hold it close and think about where you want to be or who you want to see most." He paused and his eyebrows scrunched. "But be aware, sometimes our hearts and minds can pull us in two different directions. Or we can become addicted to all the knowledge in the world around us. Choose wisely."

He lifted her hand and kissed the top. "I hope we meet again someday. I can't shake the feeling this was all destined. Our wonderful Mystic does love to meddle. But always with a purpose."

Butterflies ran rampant in her stomach at his touch. For the sake of her heart, she hoped he wasn't correct about their future. "I guess we'll see. Thank you for your guidance today."

He bowed and waved behind him. A shimmering silver door appeared. "I'll return the dragon. You be careful, Alyssa."

Alyssa forced thoughts of Blaze aside. She lifted the locket and placed it against her heart. She tried to keep her mind focused on Maggie and her dragons. Her body felt like a feather, and she felt the pull to enter the portal. Instead of arriving back in the dark cavern, she arrived in a solid white hallway with two windows.

Chapter 5

Instinctively, Alyssa understood that she'd arrived at a crossroads. She glanced in the first one, and her heart leapt into her throat. She saw visions of herself, Adam, and Kate on their last day together. She wanted to reach inside and change their decisions that fateful day. Tears trickled down her cheeks as the memories flowed. It ended on the day Kate severed all ties. Alyssa screamed for her to stop. Of course, Kate couldn't hear her. But could she change the past? If she chose this option, would she be able to change fate's design? She'd be back with her best friend and probably have a better life.

It took everything she had not to take the first option. She had to at least consider the second. That window showed a young woman huddled in a dark alley. Scared and alone. She had no one to protect her. In the distance, she saw herself and Adam following the glowing object around her neck. The locket. If she made that choice, she would save the girl and potentially the world.

Why was it her responsibility? Why did she always have to sacrifice her own happiness for the greater good. What if this time she didn't? Her eyes went back and forth between the two options. For a moment, Alyssa wanted to be selfish. But in the end, she had to make the choice she could live with.

She reached out for the window with the terrified woman. The girl looked up and smiled at her. Alyssa couldn't stop herself from looking over her shoulder one more time before fully entering her chosen path. The scene changed. She barely recognized the blond woman staring back at her, but she knew those eyes. Kate smiled and nodded at her. Then, she disappeared.

In that moment, Alyssa understood that Kate had found her destiny, and now, she and Adam had to fulfill theirs. The circle of life. *Time always moves forward.*

The window surrounded her, and she let go of the past to embrace her future.

≈   ≈

"You did it!" Maggie ran to Alyssa and lifted her from the cold, stone floor. "It wasn't that bad, right?"

"Are you insane?" Alyssa dusted herself off. "I battled ugly creatures, nearly fried myself, and almost got trapped in a world of shadows. What about that wasn't bad?"

"You lived." Maggie's direct answer made Alyssa laugh.

"I guess you have a point." Alyssa motioned toward the exit. "Can we get out of here?"

"Not yet." Maggie shook her head.

"What do you mean?" Alyssa grated her teeth.

"You've earned the right to visit the inner sanctum," Maggie explained. "We refer to it as the Dragon's Soul. If you're found worthy, you will receive the jewel from your visions to complete the locket."

Alyssa glanced down at the necklace. "Fine. But it better not take long. Sunset has to be getting close."

"Not as close as you think." Maggie shrugged and opened a strange mirror case. The golden object projected a portal. "After you, Witch Warrior, or should I say, fellow Dragon Knight."

Alyssa glared. "Of course, I'd have to go first." She entered the inner sanctum.

In the center stood the largest ruby-red jewel Alyssa had ever beheld. It reminded her of a giant egg shape. "This can't be real." She muttered to herself.

"Maggie, what do I do?"

"Hold your hands under the jewel. It evaluates the energy within you." Maggie pushed her toward the massive ruby.

Alyssa did as instructed and held out her arms. Part of her didn't want to watch in case it chopped off a valuable appendage as a price tag. She held as still as she could. The jewel sparkled and lit the cavern up in multiple shades of red.

It released a shudder and a small red ruby dropped into the palm of Alyssa's hand. Of all the things she'd seen in her life, this had to be the strangest.

"So, this big jewel ruby egg just laid a baby ruby egg?" Alyssa stared at Maggie. "I mean it just pooped it right on out. I have no words for the emotions circling my mind right now. Except this is really freaking weird. Is this thing solid or can I expect it to hatch?"

"You are very odd, Witch Warrior." Maggie burst into laughter. "You've been given a piece of the Dragon Soul. It provides protection and guidance. Very few Dragon Knights are rewarded with a piece of the actual jewel. The ancestral dragons must see something great in you.

"We must return to the castle. My parents have returned." Maggie pulled her down the path. "My father bestows official knighthood, and my mother can bind the jewel to your locket. The sun has begun to dip so we must hurry."

Alyssa had no intention of bringing about the end of the world, so she chased after Maggie. The grandeur and mystery of the castle still stole Alyssa's breath as they approached. The throne room had become quite crowded with many citizens wanting to meet the new Dragon Knight.

A man and woman stood to greet Alyssa. She had no doubt they were Maggie's parents. She took after both of them, especially her mother. Both had kind eyes and a warm smile.

"Witch Warrior Alyssa." Maggie smiled. "Meet my parents. King Ausland, High Mage and ruler of the Dragon Realm and Queen Natalia, Dragon Master of Draconia."

Alyssa wasn't sure what to do, so she gave a slight bow. "It's an honor to meet you both."

"Likewise." King Ausland stepped forward and grabbed his sword. "Maggie tells us we are short on time. We will make this quick. Please kneel."

Alyssa hesitated but complied. The king raised his sword. "To all of Draconia, Witch Warrior Alyssa, you have proven your worth and wisdom. I grant you the title of a Dragon Knight. May you carry this honor with dignity always. You have the gratitude of my people. We wish you well with your future endeavors." He placed the sword on one shoulder then the other. "Rise, Dragon Knight of Draconia."

Alyssa's heart pounded with mixed emotions. The citizens cheered and clapped. She hoped to save them all one day.

Queen Natalia walked forward next. "May I hold your locket and jewel?" Alyssa gave them to her.

She held them high. "Witness the binding of powers as we join two realms into one. With this you will have a constant shield against those who seek you and a way to track the one whom you seek. Blessed journey, Witch Warrior. I trust you will do mighty things. I see the dragon within you."

The queen released a stream of dragon flame from her mouth and coated the two pieces. They forged into one without any damage to either.

The cryptic comments and weird fire caused goosebumps on Alyssa's arms. This lady possessed a depth of power that only existed in myths and legends.

"Thank you both." Alyssa bowed. "I will do my best to honor the gifts your land has bestowed upon me."

Maggie excused them and led Alyssa out into the great hall. "We need to get you home." She opened the door. "But I thought you'd like to have some fun first."

Alyssa saw Firespark waiting on the steps. He lowered his body. "No way. I can ride him?"

"Yep, I'll ride with you for safety." Maggie jumped up and held out her arm.

Alyssa mounted the dragon, and he took off into the sky. He flew them back to the place in the forest where Alyssa had landed just that morning. She laughed and hugged him as she climbed down. "Thank you, Firespark."

He nodded and stepped to the side while Maggie opened a portal. Alyssa moved toward it with a fresh resolve and new purpose.

"Witch Warrior!" Maggie called out before she could step inside. "Good luck, my friend. We shall meet again."

Before Alyssa could ask what she meant, the portal pulled her inside. She hit the ground hard in the exact same spot she'd left her own world to enter the strange new world.

"About time, Sis." Adam helped her to her feet. "Did you find what you needed?"

"Sure did, and so much more." Alyssa beamed and showed him the locket with the ruby mounted inside. "I can already feel her presence. We can track her and save her."

Adam smiled and bumped her shoulder. "So, we're saving the world?"

"Again." Alyssa sighed.

"Yep." Adam smirked and held out his hand. "What else do we have to do with our time?"

Alyssa grasped hold of him and opened a new portal into their next adventure.

Sacrifice for the Sake of a Friend
Donna Patton

Elena stood across from Damien, sword in hand. A gentle breeze swept through her long red hair tied back with a ribbon as she waited for him to make the first move.

Damien cried out and rushed forward with his sword.

Elena blocked and parried with her own blade.

Damien attempted to catch her off-guard by trying to knock the sword from her hand.

Elena's eyes caught this as she thrusted forward with her sword and knocked Damien's sword out of his hand.

Damien rushed to grab it, but Elena stopped him and stood in his way. She pointed the tip of her sword at his throat. "I don't think so."

Damien sighed. "All right. You win."

Elena laughed and sheathed her sword. "Only because you let me."

Damien laughed in return and wiped the sweat from his brow. "I didn't want to make you feel bad or ruin our friendship." He picked up his sword and sheathed it. "I think you're more than ready to join King Hubert's army."

Elena brushed a stray strand of hair out of her face. "Are you sure, Damien?"

Damien placed a hand on her shoulder. "Trust me, I'm your best friend. I wouldn't try to steer you wrong. You have what it takes to do this. You could be seen as one of the best soldiers in the kingdom of Salem."

Elena smiled. "I appreciate your faith in me, but I wouldn't have gotten this far without your help."

Damien smiled in return. "I know. God gave you a great gift, Elena. Don't let it go to waste."

Elena hugged him. "Thank you for everything you've done for me. You never gave up on me."

Damien hugged her back. "You never gave up on me when you took me off the streets. Anyone else would have turned me away for being a thief, but you gave me something better: your patience and your friendship. You helped me find my faith in God again. If it hadn't been for you, I'd be rotting away in King Hubert's dungeon right now or possibly, dead."

Elena stepped back. "Well, I should get going. I just wanted to stop by and practice with you one more time to make sure that I'm ready to face the king and ask to be in his army."

Damien's blue eyes sparkled. "I wish you all the best, Elena. Be confident in the woman God made you to be. Don't let anyone tell you otherwise. I know your parents will be so proud of you."

Elena smiled again. "You're right." She walked toward her horse and climbed into the saddle. "Goodbye, Damien. I'll see you soon."

Damien nodded. "Goodbye, Elena. Safe journey."

Elena nodded, dug her heels into the horse's sides, and rode toward the castle of King Hubert. Her heart pounded in time to the horse's hooves against the ground.

The sun sank over the horizon, bathing the sky in vibrant reds and oranges. Elena arrived before the castle's drawbridge.

One of the guards stepped forward. "What business do you have here, young woman?"

Elena tightened her grip on the reins. "I'm here to see King Hubert. I have an important request to ask of him."

The guard looked at his companion. They nodded in unison. The guard turned back to Elena. "Very well. We shall let you in. Stand back."

Elena pulled on the reins, and the horse backed away. The drawbridge lowered and hit the ground with a thud. Elena clicked her tongue and rode inside. She dismounted her horse and retrieved her satchel of belongings.

A young boy of about eight years of age came toward her. "Good morrow, Miss. I can take your horse to the stables and see that he's well taken care of."

Elena smiled at him and handed him the reins. "Many thanks." She reached into a small bag tied to her waist, took out two coins, and placed them in his hand. "Here's a little something for your trouble."

The boy's eyes lit up upon seeing the coins in his hand. "Oh, thank you so much, Miss!" He led Elena's horse away, a spring in his step.

Elena walked toward the castle and found two more guards stationed at the front doors. "I'm here to see King Hubert."

One of the guards remained stern and cocked an eyebrow. "What's your business here, young woman?"

Elena tightened her grip on her satchel bag. "I'm here to ask a favor of the king. It's about being a soldier in his army."

The guard scowled. "Absolutely not. Women aren't allowed to serve in the king's army."

Before Elena could retaliate, the other guard firmly placed a hand on his companion's shoulder. "That's enough, Gerald. We won't turn this young woman away. She has clearly come here for a reason." He smiled at her. "Come along, Miss. I'll take you to His Majesty."

Gerald folded his arms over his chest and harrumphed.

Elena smiled at the other guard in return. "Many thanks..." Her voice trailed off.

The other guard opened the door. "You can call me Nigel." He walked down the vast hallway.

Elena followed Nigel while she marveled at the various tapestries and portraits on the walls. He led her into a grand throne room. He bowed before the throne, and Elena did the same.

King Hubert sat upon his white, marble throne with red velvet cushions. His white hair came down to his neck, and a white beard hung about his chin. He wore robes of fine royal blue silk, his royal blue cloak trimmed with white fur. His dark brown eyes intently stared at the two people before him. "Arise and speak."

Nigel stood up. "Your Highness, this young woman has come to speak with you."

King Hubert nodded. "Very well." He waved his hand in a dismissive manner. "You may leave us now."

Nigel bowed again and left the room.

King Hubert raised an eyebrow. "What's your name, young woman?"

Elena stood up. "Elena, Your Majesty."

King Hubert impatiently drummed his fingers against the wooden arm of his throne. "I see. Tell me why you have come to me."

Elena swallowed the nervous lump in her throat. "I came to ask you if I could be a knight in your army. You see, I've always wanted to be a knight ever since I was a little girl. My father is the blacksmith who provides the army with their swords and shields. I helped him as much as I could, but I often dreamed of wielding one of those swords myself one day. So, I humbly request to be a member of your army."

King Hubert sat in thoughtful silence for a moment. He eventually stopped drumming his fingers and stroked his beard. "I can see how determined you are, young Elena. Before I make you a knight, you must first pass a test to prove your skills to me. For tonight, you'll be given a warm meal and a bed to sleep in. Tomorrow, I shall test you. I hope that these terms are agreeable to you."

Elena bowed before him. "I'm thankful for your kindness, Your Majesty."

King Hubert smiled. "Good." He clapped his hands together.

A servant entered the throne room and bowed.

King Hubert folded his hands together. "Please, show Elena to her room. After that, I would like her to join me in the dining hall."

The servant stood. "Of course, Your Highness. Follow me, Miss."

Elena followed the servant out of the throne room and up the stairs to a bedroom that made her room back in her family's cottage seem so small by comparison. A large bed stood against one wall, big enough for a family of four to sleep in. The walls were decorated with red, yellow, pink, and white roses. Red and orange rays of a glorious sunset streamed through the window. Across from the bed, there was a dressing table and mirror. On the other side of the room, there was a wardrobe made of cherry wood. Two doors led to a balcony that overlooked the land.

Elena marveled at the majesty of the room.

The servant cleared his throat. "Will there be anything else you require, Miss?"

Elena shook her head. "No, thank you."

The servant nodded. "All right. I shall leave you to get settled. I shall return and show you to the dining room." He turned on his heel and left the room as he closed the door behind him.

Elena set down her satchel and walked toward the window. She gazed at the lingering colors of the setting sun. Red and orange dissolved into blue and black. Elena left the window and unpacked her belongings. *I should go on and get settled in. It's going to be a long day tomorrow*, she thought.

Golden, morning sunlight streamed through the large glass windows of the dining room. Elena silently munched on her bread and fruit that the servants had served for her breakfast. She sat beside King Hubert who also ate in silence.

Elena sipped at her glass of water. *Today's the day that I show the king what I can do. I only hope that I don't disappoint him.* She set down her glass and finished the last of her breakfast.

King Hubert wiped his mouth with a cloth, laid it aside, and stood. "Let's go outside and join my soldiers. I want all of them to see what you can do. Come."

Elena's stomach nervously churned, but she ignored it. She nodded, slowly rose from her chair, and followed King Hubert outside to the courtyard.

King Hubert's soldiers stood in perfect lines. A few snickered at Elena, but no one spoke.

Captain Alexander bowed before the king. "Good morrow, Your Majesty."

King Hubert smiled. "Good morrow, Captain. I would like to introduce you and your soldiers to Elena. She wishes to become a soldier in my army. I told her that she could if she passed the test."

Captain Alexander nodded. "Of course, Your Majesty. I shall choose someone as a volunteer to fight Elena." His eyes scanned the soldiers until his gaze settled upon one particular young man. "Richard, step forward."

Richard timidly stepped forward. He appeared to be a few years older than Elena, and a few inches taller. Black, straight hair cascaded to the middle of his neck and curled around his ears. His brown eyes held a glimmer of foreboding.

Captain Alexander paced in front of him. "Richard, you're going to fight Elena in a test to see if she's worthy to join the king's army. King Hubert, the army, and I shall observe. Is that understood?"

"A woman defeating a man at sword fighting? How absurd!" A soldier snickered and muttered under his breath. The other soldiers laughed.

Captain Alexander sharply turned, and everyone fell silent. He barked at the soldier in question, "Julius! You may be the second-in-command, but you know better than to speak out of turn! I don't want to hear one more word from you!"

Julius snapped to attention. "My apologies, Captain. It won't happen again."

Captain Alexander nodded. "Very good. Now, I want everyone to step back."

The soldiers, King Hubert, and the captain stepped back to give Elena and Richard room.

Elena drew out her sword and took her fighting stance. Richard did the same despite his obvious apprehension.

Captain Alexander looked at both of them. "Begin!"

Richard thrusted forward with his sword.

Elena blocked and parried each attack, but was still forced back. She maneuvered from the circle of soldiers with great agility. She eventually found her footing again and launched an attack of her own.

Richard blocked and parried, his turn to be forced back. He dug his heels into the ground and swung his sword at Elena's head.

Elena ducked, took a step back, and hooked Richard's ankle, tripping him. He landed hard, his sword clattering out of his reach. Elena stared at him; her blade pointed at his throat. She gulped in a breath, sheathed her sword, and offered him her hand.

Richard smiled, took her hand, and shakily rose to his feet. He brushed himself off before retrieving and sheathing his own sword.

Shock flooded Captain Alexander's face. "I must say that I'm impressed by your skills, Miss Elena. I've never seen a woman fight so valiantly before."

Elena smiled. "Thank you, Captain."

Captain Alexander turned to Richard. "You also did well, Richard."

Richard's face flushed red. "Thank you, Sir. If I may confess, I was holding back to give Elena a chance."

Captain Alexander nodded. "I see." He cleared his throat. "In that case, King Hubert and I must go and discuss our decision. Julius, you're in charge until I return."

Julius saluted him.

King Hubert and Captain Alexander left the courtyard.

Elena turned to face the other soldiers. Shock filled their faces, except for Lieutenant Julius. He gritted his teeth together and strode toward Elena. He towered over her, his icy blue eyes boring into her soul. His blonde hair shone in the morning sunlight. "I don't know where you learned how to fight, but no woman is capable of fighting as good as a man."

Elena kept her composure and brushed her hair out of her face. "Perhaps, it's because you've never met a woman like me until now, Lieutenant."

Lieutenant Julius scowled. "I don't care. Captain Alexander wouldn't be foolish enough to allow you to be a soldier in the king's army. The battlefield is no place for a woman. If I were you, I'd pack up my belongings and go home right now."

Elena folded her arms across her chest. "Until King Hubert and Captain Alexander say otherwise, I'm not going anywhere. I've worked too hard and too long to turn around and give up now. I won't be stopped by the likes of anyone, not even you."

Lieutenant Julius growled like an angry dog. "Fine. But I won't make this easy for you, not by a long shot. You'll have to earn my respect, and you're a long way from that." He spat at Elena's feet, stepped back, and joined the other soldiers.

Richard gazed at Elena with an apologetic expression on his face but said nothing. He joined the other soldiers as King Hubert and Captain Alexander returned to the courtyard.

Elena's heartbeat quickened with anticipation.

Captain Alexander approached her and held out his hand. "We have made our choice. You're more than worthy to join this army. Why, I'd be proud to have a soldier like yourself in our ranks."

Elena took his hand and heartily shook it. "Many thanks, Captain Alexander. You won't regret this. I promise you."

Captain Alexander released her hand. "I'm glad to hear it. Now, we have much training to do. In the meantime, I would like for you to go and be fitted for your armor, Elena. You may join us when you're ready."

Elena nodded.

King Hubert clapped his hands together.

The same servant whom Elena met the day before stepped forward. "If you'll follow me, I'll show you where the royal seamstress is."

Elena followed.

The day lingered on at a snail's pace. The sun sank behind the horizon, and all of the soldiers joined King Hubert at the dining room table.

On her way to her room following the meal, Elena passed by two large doors with two soldiers standing there. *I don't remember King Hubert telling me about this room. I wonder what's inside.*

"Being too curious can cause trouble, you know," said a voice behind her.

Elena whirled and saw King Hubert standing in the passage. She breathed a sigh of relief and bowed. "Forgive me, Your Highness. I didn't know that you were standing there."

King Hubert chuckled. "Oh, that's quite all right."

Elena stood up straight. "If I may ask, what's behind those doors?"

King Hubert furrowed his brow. "I usually don't allow anyone to see this room."

Elena's shoulders slumped in disappointment.

King Hubert's face softened. "However, since you're a part of my army now, I suppose it's only fair that I show you what you're protecting, besides me, of course." He turned and lowered his voice to address the soldiers, "Make sure that no one sees this."

The soldiers nodded.

King Hubert brandished a golden key and slipped it into the lock. He turned it, opened the doors, and revealed a large room with torches lining the walls.

Elena's eyes lit up at the sight of the gold and jewels that sparkled in the light of the room.

King Hubert led her to the center of the room where a small, black-and-gold box rested on a table. He took out a smaller key and unlocked it. Inside, a large ruby sat upon a pillow of velvet.

Elena gasped in shock. She noted that the ruby was as large as her fist. "What is this, Your Highness?"

King Hubert gingerly took the ruby from the box and held it up to the light. "This is the Krimson Stone. It wields great power to anyone who uses it. This ruby is what has helped my kingdom maintain such good fortune throughout the years. My grandfather was the one who discovered it, and it was passed down to my father who then passed it down to me. However, given this stone's great power, it could fall into the wrong hands, the hands of someone truly evil. That is why I keep it locked away in this room, and I always have two soldiers to guard the doors. If this stone is ever stolen, my kingdom will fall into ruin."

Elena stared at the ruby in awe. "All of that turmoil over a simple, sparkling stone?"

King Hubert solemnly nodded. "Indeed. There have been many lives lost, especially those who have sought out this stone and wanted to use it for evil." He returned the ruby to the box and locked it. "Now, you must promise not to tell a single soul about this unless I tell you otherwise. Is that clear?"

Elena nodded. "I promise."

King Hubert smiled. "Good. Now, let's turn in. The hour is late, and I need my rest. You should get some rest, too."

Elena smiled in return and bowed. "Good night, Your Highness." She turned and walked from the room. She stopped and waited while King Hubert locked the doors behind him and sauntered down the hall. The soldiers kept their post in front of the doors. Elena turned and made her way to her room. She closed the door, changed into her nightgown, and settled in for the night.

ℳ   ℳ

Elena woke up to hurried footsteps and people shouting. She jumped out of bed, changed, and ran from her room. She hurried down the hallway and found a crowd standing before the doors to the room that King Hubert showed her the night before.

"What's happening?" asked one of the servants.

"It appears that something has been stolen from this room," said another.

King Hubert emerged from the room with his face as white as chalk. "The Krimson Stone has been stolen. I have sent my soldiers to search the village for the thief. Julius came to check on the soldiers and found them unconscious. He also saw the thief escaping and pursued him. He's with the other soldiers as we speak." He fell to his knees. "The stone is gone. All is lost."

Elena's heart constricted. *I was the last person to see The Krimson Stone when King Hubert showed it to me. Surely, someone won't accuse me of stealing it.* She slowly backed away and ran toward her room. Tears brimmed in her eyes. "What will happen now?"

ℳ   ℳ

Elena ate in silence at the dining room table. She watched King Hubert picking at the food on his plate.

The doors burst open, and Julius strode in with the other soldiers. Elena's stomach churned at the sight of who they escorted into the room: Damien. His wrists and ankles were bound in chains, and he shuffled before the soldiers.

Julius bowed before King Hubert. "Your Highness, we found this young man in the village. It appears that he was once a thief."

King Hubert stood up. "Is this the man you saw running away with the box containing The Krimson Stone?"

Julius stood up straight and nodded. "Yes, Your Highness."

Damien struggled against his bonds. "That's the most ridiculous thing I've ever heard. I never heard of The Krimson Stone. I wouldn't steal anything that I didn't know about, and besides, I'm not a thief anymore. Elena is the one who helped me to turn my life around."

King Hubert turned to face Elena. "You know this young man, Elena?"

Elena nodded. "Yes, he's my best friend. He's a kind-hearted person who would never steal anything from you, Your Highness."

Julius interjected, "Your Highness," Julius interjected, "the law requires that thieves should pay for their crimes. I saw this man running away with The Krimson Stone."

Damien glared at him. "If I did steal it, why didn't you find it in my cottage?"

Julius frowned. "You could have hidden it somewhere before we caught you."

King Hubert held up his hand. "Enough! Take him to the dungeon! I must consider my decision in peace!"

A mischievous grin graced Julius's lips before he and the other soldiers escorted Damien out of the dining room.

Elena stood and stepped before King Hubert. "Your Highness, please don't execute Damien. He has done nothing wrong."

King Hubert's eyes flashed with angry fire. "You must have told him about The Krimson Stone, and the temptation was too much for him. That's why he stole the ruby. You promised me that you wouldn't tell a soul."

Elena's stomach dropped. "No, Your Highness. I didn't tell Damien anything. You must believe me."

King Hubert slammed his fists down on the table. "Get out of my sight!"

Elena ran out of the dining room and down the hallway toward her room. Her footsteps echoed against the marble floor, and tears stung her vision. Elena fell to her knees beside her bed and buried her face in her arms. Tears streamed down her face. Uncontrollable sobs escaped from her throat and shook her entire body. Elena's thoughts whirled around in her mind like a swarm of angry bees. *God, please help me. I know that Damien isn't guilty of stealing The Krimson Stone, and I didn't tell him about it. I feel so helpless. Show me what I can do to save Damien from being executed.*

"Elena, is something wrong?" a voice addressed her from the doorway. "Are you all right?"

Elena slowly stopped sobbing, lifted her head, and turned around to see Richard standing there. She quickly wiped her eyes and rose to her feet. "I'm all right, Richard."

He stepped forward. "I don't believe that. Something's bothering you. I know it."

A lump formed in Elena's throat. "Richard, it's awful. My best friend, Damien has been accused of stealing The Krimson Stone. King Hubert ordered him to be placed in the dungeon, and he's blaming me for what has happened."

Richard's brow furrowed in confusion. "I'm afraid I don't understand."

Elena turned away from him. "I made a promise to King Hubert, and he thinks that I broke it. I want to help Damien, but I feel so helpless, so trapped."

Richard gently placed a hand on Elena's shoulder. "Let's go for a walk in the royal garden. We can talk about everything there, and the fresh air will do you some good."

Elena smoothed her clothes and turned around. "All right. I'd love to."

Richard offered his arm. "Shall we?" Elena looped her arm through his and walked with him outside to the royal garden.

The royal garden could have been mistaken for the Garden of Eden or perhaps, a garden found in the kingdom of Israel during

King David's reign. Trees with white flowers glowed in the morning sunlight along with trees bearing peaches, apples, plums, and pomegranates. A gentle breeze stirred up the sweet scent of the various flowers like roses, lilies, violets, daisies, bluebells, forget-me-nots, and carnations.

Elena gazed at the beauty that surrounded her.

Richard smiled. "That's better. You look more content now."

Elena smiled in return. "Thank you for suggesting this walk." She let out a heavy sigh. "I suppose that I should tell you about what has happened this morning."

Richard nodded. "I'm listening."

Elena cleared her throat. "Before I do that, I should explain something about Damien and myself. We're best friends. Damien used to be a thief, but I knew that his family had fallen on hard times. I did what I could to help him. We grew very close and became friends. Damien even helped me learn how to use a sword. It's because of him that I came to be a knight in King Hubert's army. Before I continue with my explanation, I want you to promise me that you won't tell anyone what I'm about to tell you."

Richard's face turned serious. "I give you my word, Elena. I won't tell anyone."

Elena nodded and continued. "Last night, King Hubert showed me into the room where he kept all of his treasures, including The Krimson Stone. I promised him that I wouldn't tell a soul about it. This morning, I woke up to a commotion. I came running and found out that the Krimson Stone was stolen. It wasn't until later when Julius and the other soldiers entered the dining room with Damien in chains, he accused my best friend of stealing the Krimson Stone. I didn't tell Damien about the ruby, and he would never steal something from King Hubert. Something doesn't feel right about any of this."

Elena and Richard continued to walk in the garden. They stopped under the shade of a tree with white flowers hanging from the branches.

Richard plucked a flower and handed it to Elena. "I can see why you're so distraught. Damien means a lot to you, and you want to help him in any way you can."

Elena took the flower in her hand and inhaled its sweet scent. "You're right. If only I could figure out what that—" Her eyes lit up. "That's it! I know what I must do! Richard, thank you for your help!" She hurried off.

"Wait! Where are you going?" Richard called after her.

"I must speak with the king!" Elena hurried inside and made her way to the throne room. She bowed before King Hubert. "Your Highness, I know that you are greatly disturbed by the loss of The Krimson Stone, but I know of a way that I can help. Surely, there must be an enemy who wanted to steal the ruby for himself."

King Hubert sat up straight. "There is one man who would be capable of such a thing. His name is King Ravencroft, and he resides in Ravencroft Castle deep within the forest." He stroked his beard in a thoughtful manner. "Do you suppose that someone else stole the ruby and delivered it to him?"

Elena stood. "It's possible, Your Highness. I can prove to you that Damien didn't steal the stone. Please, give me a chance to do so."

King Hubert continued to stroke his beard. "Give me time to think about this."

Elena nodded. "Yes, of course. There's one more request I want to ask of you."

King Hubert raised an eyebrow. "And what would that be?"

Elena fumbled with the hem of her white shirt. "I wish to see Damien and talk with him. He needs a friend right now. I want to make sure that he's all right."

King Hubert nodded. "Very well. I shall grant your request." He snapped his fingers, and Gerald stepped forward. "Take Elena to the dungeon to see her friend."

Gerald bowed. "Yes, Your Majesty. Follow me, Miss."

Elena followed Gerald out of the throne room and down a flight of stone steps, the walls lined with torches. They paused at the bottom step while he took a torch from the wall. "This way." He led the way down a long tunnel. She walked behind him and shivered from the cold. *I would hate to be a prisoner down here, waiting for punishment from King Hubert. This must be an awful place to spend your last days.*

Gerald stopped in front of a large wooden door with two other guards stationed on either side. He took out a key, slipped it into the lock, and turned it. The door opened with a loud creak. "Go on in. I'll be right outside."

Elena nodded and entered the dungeon. The door closed behind her with a loud thud. Elena looked around. A single torch hung high on the wall, barely giving enough light to see. Sunlight shined through a window on the opposite side.

Elena saw Damien sitting on the stone floor, his wrists and ankles bound in chains against the wall. She walked toward him and sat before him.

Damien looked up, surprise on his face. "Elena, what are you doing here?"

Elena folded her hands in her lap. "I asked King Hubert if I could see you. I want to help you out of here."

Damien let out a dry laugh. "You can't help me. No one believes that I didn't steal the Krimson Stone."

Elena gently placed her hand on Damien's knee and found it cold to the touch. "That's not true. I believe you. I know you, Damien."

Damien bowed his head in defeat. "It doesn't matter. I'm going to die, anyway. There's nothing that can be done."

Elena drew her hand away as though it had been burned. "Damien, don't talk like that. You can't give up. I know that you would never steal like you used to. I think that someone stole the Krimson Stone, delivered it to King Hubert's mortal enemy, King Ravencroft, and framed you for the crime. If the king agrees to it, I'm going to make the journey and get the ruby back as well as find out who did this to you."

Damien's head snapped up, and his eyes narrowed. "Are you crazy?! You'd never get anywhere near Ravencroft Castle! Anyone who does never comes back! It's too dangerous!"

Elena clenched her fists to keep from slapping Damien across the face. "I'm not going to let you die for a crime you didn't commit! You're my best friend! If I was in your shoes, I know that you would do the same for me!" Her anger disappeared, and tears welled up in her eyes. "Please, Damien. Let me help you. Your family would never forgive me if I let you die." She leaned forward, wrapped her arms around Damien's shoulders, and buried her face in his shoulder.

The room grew deadly silent, save for their breathing. Elena leaned back and wiped her eyes.

Damien sighed in defeat. "I know how determined you are, and you won't give up on this idea of yours. Promise me that you'll be careful. I can't bear the thought of losing my best friend."

Elena smiled and placed her hand against Damien's cheek. "I will. God will look after me. I pray that He'll look after you, too."

Damien smiled back. "He will."

The dungeon door opened with a creak. The guard stepped into the room. "It's time for you to go, Miss."

Elena stood up. "Goodbye, Damien. I'll do everything I can to prove you innocent."

Damien nodded.

Elena stepped out of the dungeon and watched the guard lock the door again. She followed him back upstairs and returned to her room. She lay upon her bed to rest and closed her eyes.

A knock echoed in Elena's dream, rousing her from a fitful sleep. She opened her eyes, got up, and walked to her bedroom door.

A guard stood before her. "King Hubert would like to see you in the throne room."

Elena smoothed out her clothes and followed him to the throne room. She bowed before the king. "You wished to see me, Your Highness?"

King Hubert nodded. "Yes, I've given some thought to your request to ride off and get the ruby back from King Ravencroft. However, I should warn you about one thing. King Ravencroft isn't just a wicked king. He's also a master of evil magic. He uses visions to confuse and discourage those who come into his territory. You must beware of such visions on your journey. Since I would hate to see anything happen to you, I'm going to send Julius and Richard with you for protection."

Elena wanted to protest, but she knew better than to argue with King Hubert. "I'm grateful to you, Your Highness. When do Julius, Richard, and I leave?"

King Hubert thoughtfully sipped on a goblet of wine before he answered, "As soon as possible. You have one month to retrieve the Krimson Stone and defeat King Ravencroft. If you don't return with the ruby within that time, my kingdom will fall into ruins, and my enemies will overthrow me."

Elena's chest tightened with fear. She rose to her feet. "I'll start packing at once. I won't let you down, King Hubert. I promise."

King Hubert nodded again. "Be on your way. May God go with you on your journey."

Elena bowed and left the room. She packed her satchel with clothes, a sharpening stone for her sword, a blanket, some food, and a canteen full of water. She tied her sword around her waist and looked around. "I hope that this will prove to King Hubert how I can serve him in his army."

Elena left her room, walked outside, and found Julius and Richard already on horseback. Julius had a quiver of arrows and a bow on his back along with his sword hanging at his side.

Elena climbed onto her horse. "Let's be off. We don't have much time."

Julius scowled. "Hold it. I know my way around the forest, so I'll lead the way. You're going to follow me. A woman like you wouldn't know which way to go." He let out a cruel laugh and rode off.

Elena bowed her head.

Richard's voice drifted to her. "Don't listen to Julius. He only wants to be the one to get all of the credit for retrieving the Krimson Stone. Let's go."

Elena nodded and rode beside him, the two of them trailing behind Julius. The trio rode into the forest.

Elena looked around at the tall trees that towered over them. *Father in Heaven, please protect us and keep us safe on this journey. I pray that we'll find the Krimson Stone and bring it back to King Hubert. Give us the strength to defeat King Ravencroft. Show us how to stop him from overtaking the land and all of the people. We mustn't fail King Hubert. He's counting on us to keep his kingdom from falling into ruin. Amen.*

The birds sang a sweet song as though to give the trio courage. A squirrel chattered noisily and scampered up a tree in search of nuts. The sunlight peeked its way through the multiple branches.

"This forest looks so calming, so peaceful," Elena stated.

Julius scoffed. "Don't be deceived. This forest is a dangerous place. No one comes out of here alive."

Elena frowned. "That might be true, but we must have faith that we'll survive."

Richard nervously laughed. "I don't know. Something about this place seems off. It's like we're walking right into a trap."

Julius laughed. "Don't be such a scaredy cat, Richard. You've got King Hubert's second-in-command for protection. If you're so afraid of this place, you should turn around and go back."

Elena added a touch of annoyance to her voice. "Enough. This isn't getting us anywhere. Let's focus on finding King

Ravenscroft's castle and come up with a plan to get the Krimson Stone back."

Silence fell upon them, and they continued to ride along the path.

The sun slowly descended, casting long shadows over the trees.

Julius stopped riding. "It's getting dark. We should stop for the night. I see a clearing off the path. We'll camp there." He pulled on the reins, and his horse trotted forward.

Richard and Elena followed him until they entered a flat, grassy clearing.

Julius remained on the saddle and looked around. "I'm going to find something for us to eat before it gets too dark. You two should stay here and gather some firewood. I won't be gone long." He rode off, deeper into the forest before Elena or Richard could respond.

Elena sighed and dismounted. She led him to a tree and tied his reins to a branch. Elena opened her canteen, poured some water into her hand, and gave it to her horse.

Richard did the same. He found some stones not far from the clearing and placed them in a circle. Elena and Richard made their way through the trees, found various fallen branches that they could use for firewood, and arranged them in the circle.

Richard picked up two smaller stones and struck one against the other over the branches. It created a spark, and soon, a fire crackled. Richard set the stones aside and sat down before the fire.

Elena sat beside him and sharpened her sword in silence. She slowly stopped sharpening her sword and sheathed it. "Richard, there's something I'm curious about. I want to know why you chose to be in King Hubert's army."

Richard remained silent and stared at the flames of the fire.

Elena realized her mistake and tried again. "Richard, I won't make fun of you like Julius would. I trusted you with my secret. You can trust me with yours."

Richard turned to face her. An apprehensive expression passed over his face. "Promise you won't laugh?"

Elena nodded. "I promise."

Richard let out a heavy sigh and bowed his head in shame. "The truth is that I don't like to fight. I'm no warrior. The reason I joined the king's army is a ridiculous one. You see, many years ago, my father served in the king's army and performed a miraculous deed that saved all of Salem. He was hailed as a hero. Ever since I could remember, I grew up in my father's shadow, hearing everyone praise him for the great work he had done. When he grew too old to serve, I made a promise to him that I would join the king's army in his stead. I did it to live up to my father's expectations and to protect my family. Even so, it's true what Julius says. I'm a coward."

Elena intently listened to Richard's tale. *Poor Richard, I can't believe that he would do such a thing to himself. And the way Julius treats him and me is preposterous.*

The fire crackled, filling the silence between them.

Elena laid her hand on Richard's. "Richard, I'm sorry that you've had to suffer so much. Your father was a brave man, it's true. However, I think you're brave, too. When we met yesterday, you could have refused to sword fight with me, but you chose to do it anyway. You wanted to show me how strong you were, even though you held back to give me a chance."

Richard lifted his head, still not convinced. "But Julius—"

"Julius is wrong," Elena interrupted. "You are no coward, Richard. You're a soldier in the king's army because you want to protect your family and to some extension, your home. No one can fault you for that. When I look at you, I don't see a coward. I see a man who is willing to do what he can to protect those he loves, even if his courage isn't like his father's. I'm grateful to have you with me on this journey." She frowned. *I can't say the same for Julius. There's something about him that doesn't seem right.*

Richard smiled and wrapped his fingers around Elena's hand. "Many thanks, Elena. You're a remarkable woman." He lifted her hand to his lips and kissed it.

Elena blushed. "You're welcome."

Hooves thundered against the ground. Richard immediately let go of Elena's hand.

Julius dismounted from his horse with two dead rabbits in his hand. He tossed them at Elena's feet. "Skin those and put them on the fire." He removed his canteen from his satchel and took a drink of water.

Elena frowned again, but she did what Julius asked of her. Once the meat had been cooked, she distributed it evenly among the three of them, and they ate. They finished their meal and turned in for the night.

Elena lay on the hard ground with the blanket spread over her and stared at the star-filled sky. Her body ached from exhaustion, but her mind restlessly wandered. Elena took a deep breath and whispered a prayer, "God, help me to sleep tonight. While I'm worried about the road ahead, I know that You will protect me. Forgive me for what I've done wrong. Amen." Her eyelids closed, and she drifted off to sleep.

Four days passed in the same manner; the trio traveled through the forest. The trees and branches gradually grew denser like long wooden hands wrapping around them. Undaunted, the trio continued.

The fifth morning greeted them with overcast skies that threatened rain. The trio still mounted their horses and continued their journey. They had not gone far when Julius froze and pulled on the reins. Elena and Richard did the same. They paused and listened.

Elena whispered, "What is it, Julius?"

Julius held a finger to his lips and continued to listen. A loud snarl echoed through the trees. A pack of wild cats, all standing on two legs, emerged from the shadows. Their muscular, lion-like bodies mixed the stripes and spots of tigers and leopards. The leader of the pack moved to block their path. Its golden eyes glowed in the dim light. The cat licked its lips.

Elena's blood ran cold with fear.

Richard trembled. "What do we do, Julius?"

Julius calmly drew out his sword. "We fight back."

Elena looked at the wild cats arching their backs, ready to attack at any moment. *Something isn't right here. Wild cats like this wouldn't attack humans unless they were protecting their pack or if they had wandered into their territory. Besides, I've never seen wild cats like these before. I've heard of mountain lions or the occasional bobcat, but not these creatures. Father in Heaven, what should I do? Wait, if Jesus can tell the wind and the rain to be still, I could tell these wild cats to seek a meal elsewhere.* She rode forward toward the leader of the pack.

"Elena," Julius snarled and grabbed her arm, "what are you doing? You'll be torn to shreds."

Elena wrenched herself free from his grasp. "Keep your hands off of me. I know what I'm doing."

Richard's trembling increased. "You're crazy!"

Elena rolled her shoulders back. "They're only an illusion. I'll prove it to you." She stared at the leader of the wild cat pack. "We're not frightened of you. Seek a meal for yourselves elsewhere. We mean no harm."

The wild cat leader let out a loud growl, turned, and disappeared like a fog on a clear, sunny day. The pack followed.

Shock filled Richard's face as he rode beside her. "How did you know that they weren't real?"

Elena stared at the road ahead. "King Hubert warned me at one time that King Ravencroft used visions like that to scare people off. I knew they weren't real because we don't have that kind of animal around here. Let's get going before we lose daylight."

Julius rode in front of her, blocking her way. "Fine. We're going to continue from here, but for now on, I'll call the shots."

He scowled. "You were crazy for what you did. You could have gotten yourself and both of us killed."

Elena tightly gripped the reins in her hands. "I told you before. I know what I'm doing."

Julius reached out and grabbed her arm again. "You will do exactly what I tell you."

Elena's blood boiled hot with anger, and she slapped him across the face. "And I told you to take your hands off me. I won't be treated like a slave, constantly following your orders just because you say so. Now, get out of my way."

Julius stared at her in shock, but he backed his horse up.

Elena rode forward with Richard beside her and Julius following behind. She looked back at him for a moment. Guilt settled in her chest like a heavy stone.

Richard smiled. "Don't worry about him. All you did was hurt his pride. Honestly, you were brave to do what you did back there with those wild cats. I never would have guessed that they were only a vision."

Elena weakly smiled back. "Thanks."

They continued the rest of the journey in silence.

Darkness fell across the land, and the trio stopped to make camp. They made a fire and ate what little food they had left. Richard made himself comfortable and went to sleep. Elena sat in front of the fire and sighed.

Julius stood beside her. "Mind if I join you?"

Elena shook her head.

Julius sat down. "Listen, I want to apologize for my behavior today. I was only trying to keep you safe."

Elena swallowed the lump in her throat and turned to face him. "I forgive you, Julius. I must apologize for slapping you. I was angry, and I let my anger get the best of me."

Julius tentatively rubbed his cheek. "Don't worry about it. I had no right to place a hand on you." He lowered his hand and looked into Elena's eyes. "You know, you're a lot braver than I thought you were. I've never seen that kind of strength in a woman. I actually like it. The only reason I didn't before is because I was jealous of you. I'm sorry."

Elena bit her lower lip before she answered, "I understand. I would feel the same way if I was in your place."

Julius laughed, a true genuine laugh for the first time since Elena met him. "How have you not found a husband yet?"

Elena's cheeks turned hot. "Well, I—I—I haven't found the right man yet," she stammered.

Julius smiled and leaned closer to her. "He could be closer than you think." He closed the gap between them and kissed her.

Elena sat there, stunned and unsure what to do. She had never been kissed before. Her body tensed up for a moment, but it relaxed with the sensation of Julius's arms wrapped around her. Elena closed her eyes and tasted the sweetness of his lips.

Julius leaned back. "Elena, I wasn't going to say anything about this before, but I think now is as good a time as any. Over these last few days, I've fallen in love with you. I've never felt this way before about anyone the way I feel about you. You're so beautiful and strong, a combination that isn't often found in women."

Elena's cheeks grew even hotter. She glanced at her shaking hands. "Julius, I wish I could tell you that I love you as well, but I can't. I don't know if I do share your feelings."

Julius placed his hand under Elena's chin and gently lifted it up to gaze into her eyes once more. "Just one more kiss and we'll find out."

Elena looked into the depths of his blue eyes. She found them mesmerizing and warm. Her throat ran dry, and she slowly nodded.

Julius took Elena's face in his hands and kissed her again, deeper than before. He ran his fingers through her hair.

Elena wrapped her arms around Julius's neck and returned the kiss without hesitation.

Julius released Elena from his embrace. "It's late. We should get some rest. We're not far from our destination now. Good night, Elena." He stood up and walked to the other side of the fire. He laid down and turned onto his side.

Elena ran her fingers over her lips, replaying the sensation of Julius's lips against hers. *I still don't know if I love him or not. Perhaps, I'll change my mind when we get the ruby back and return to Salem. For now, I'm so tired. I should turn in.* She lay down, spread the blanket over her body, and closed her eyes.

తా   ತಾ

The sun rose over the horizon, and the trio ate breakfast in silence. They fed their horses, put out the fire, and went on their journey again.

Julius pointed to a small hill. "There, King Ravencroft's castle lies just beyond that hill. We're so close. I can feel it."

Richard and Elena followed him over the hill.

Another clearing appeared before them. The grass grew brown and crunched under the horses' hooves. Large black crows cawed and circled overhead.

Richard looked around, and he frowned. "Does this look like a trap to anyone else but me?"

Elena's stomach twisted into nervous knots, but she tried not to show it. "If this is where King Ravencroft's castle should be, where is it?"

Julius dismounted his horse. "We must have taken a wrong turn."

Elena dismounted, too. "How could we? We've gone in a straight line since we started this journey. We couldn't be so far off."

Richard joined them. "I'm telling you, Elena. We've stepped into a trap of some kind."

Julius drew his sword and put a finger to his lips. "Shhh. Listen."

Elena tilted her head and listened. Multiple footsteps rushed toward them.

Soldiers in black armor emerged from the trees, each with a sword in hand.

Elena drew her sword. She took a step to charge the soldiers and gasped when her sword was knocked out of her hand. Julius held his sword high, pointing at her. "Julius, what are you doing?"

A mischievous grin spread across Julius's lips. "I'm keeping you and your little friend from taking back The Krimson Stone."

Two soldiers stepped forward and grabbed Elena's arms. Two more soldiers did the same with Richard.

Julius walked toward Richard and pointed his sword at his neck. "You should've turned around and run away when you had the chance. However, I think this worked out in my favor. Now, I can have my revenge on the man who almost killed me: your father."

Richard struggled to free himself. "I don't understand. My father has done nothing to you."

Julius let out a wicked laugh. "Foolish boy. I'm not Julius." Dark magic surrounded his body and transformed him into a man with long white hair. Black robes billowed in the soft breeze. "I am King Ravencroft. Your father was the one who defeated me in battle and left me close to death."

Elena's eyes widened at the sight before her. "It was you! You stole the Krimson Stone!"

King Ravencroft turned to face her and slowly walked toward her. "You would be correct, Elena. I stole the ruby to gain power over King Hubert and to destroy Richard's father. I took his keys while he slept and got into the room without being detected. I used my magic to keep the guards in deep sleep."

Elena scowled at him. "But why frame Damien for stealing it?"

King Ravencroft laughed again. "Well, I needed someone to blame. As for you, you were never a part of my plan, just someone who got in my way."

Sorrow welled in Elena's chest. "Then, you never loved me, did you?"

King Ravencroft pointed his sword at her throat. "Of course not, you naïve girl. I only sought to use you. I knew that you had never been in love before, and I took advantage of the situation. It's a pity, though. You were so sweet and kind to me, even after I made fun of you. Now that you've outlived your usefulness to me, I'm going to leave you here, all alone. Once I kill Richard and combine my magic with The Krimson Stone, no one will be able to stop me."

One of the soldiers tied Elena's wrists and ankles together with rope. She struggled against her bonds. "You won't get away with this."

King Ravencroft removed a small bottle from his robe and popped the cork off. "You're wrong. I will. Now, open wide." He tightly gripped Elena's chin and forced a liquid down her throat.

The liquid tasted awful and bitter, but Elena could not stop King Ravencroft from pouring it down her throat. He closed her mouth and stepped back. Elena tried to open her mouth to speak, but she could not. A wave of exhaustion swept over her, and she lost consciousness.

Elena coughed and opened her eyes. She tried to sit up, but the ropes tied around her wrists and ankles prevented movement. She looked around and found herself alone in the forest. A groan escaped her lips. Her stomach ached, not from hunger but pain. She struggled against her bonds but could not free herself. Elena turned onto her back and stared at the canopy of trees. Tears welled in her eyes. "God, I have failed You, and I have failed King Hubert. I was so foolish not to see how wicked Julius was and who he turned out to be. Now, Richard will die, and our land will be destroyed, all because of me. Please, forgive me. I need to find a way to stop King Ravencroft and save Richard. Help me, Father." Her voice choked with emotion, and tears streamed down her cheeks. Elena shut her eyes. "It's no use. All hope is lost."

"Nothing is ever lost when you have faith, dear girl," a gentle voice whispered.

Elena opened her eyes and gasped in surprise.

A beautiful woman stood by her side, dressed in a gown of white. Her long golden hair cascaded down her back, and her skin was as white as snow. A heavenly glow surrounded her.

Elena tried to sit up a second time to get a better look at this woman. "Who are you?"

The woman smiled. "I'm your guardian angel, Elena. God has sent me to free you from your bonds." She helped Elena sit up and untied the ropes from her wrists and ankles.

Elena slowly rose to her feet, winced, and lifted her shirt. A large black and blue bruise had formed on her stomach. "One of the soldiers must have kicked me when I was unconscious."

The woman picked up Elena's sword and handed it to her. "Here, you'll need this."

Elena took the sword and sheathed it. "I'm not going to fight King Ravencroft. I've failed. I'm going home."

The woman gently placed a hand on her shoulder. "No, you mustn't give up now. You asked God to help you find a way to stop King Ravencroft and save Richard. If you don't do it now, everyone will be doomed."

Elena gritted her teeth together in frustration. "Don't you get it?! I let King Hubert down! I'm not fit to be a soldier in his army! What kind of a soldier walks into a trap like I did?!"

The woman smoothed back Elena's hair. "Even soldiers make mistakes, Elena. But you must take what you've learned and use it to save those whom you care about. King Ravencroft will only win if you let him. He might have dark magic on his side, but you have God on yours. You have the strength to do this." She placed a gentle kiss on her forehead. "Carry His love with you and He will give you strength. Remember King David's words in Psalm 23."

Elena looked into the woman's eyes, and the words flooded her memory. "The Lord is my Shepherd. I shall not want. He makes me to lie down in green pasture. He leads me beside still waters. He restores my soul. He leads me in the paths of righteousness for His name's sake. Yea, though I walk through the valley of the shadow of death, I will fear no evil; for You are with me. Your rod and Your staff, they comfort me. You prepare a table before me in the presence of my enemies. You anoint my head with oil. My cup runs over. Surely, goodness and mercy shall follow me all the days of my life; And I will dwell in the house of the Lord forever. Amen."

The woman smiled again. "You see, you had the faith and courage within you all along. Now, it's time to fight evil with good." She disappeared.

Elena looked around, but she did not see her horse anywhere. "King Ravencroft must have taken him. I guess I'll have to go on foot."

A screech resounded above Elena's head. A large eagle flew down and landed before her.

Elena stared in awe at this magnificent bird. She had heard stories about the large eagles who would come to the aid of anyone who became lost. She climbed onto its back and gently gripped its feathers. "Take me to King Ravencroft's castle."

The eagle screeched again and took to the sky with a flap of its huge wings. Elena gazed at the land below, trees and a river as far as the eye could see. She spotted a large castle in the center of the forest. The eagle flew toward the back of the castle and landed there.

Elena jumped off its back and gently patted its neck. "Many thanks." The eagle inclined its head and took off.

Elena found a wooden door, grabbed the handle, and, to her surprise, it opened with a creak. She ran through the halls and searched. Black and purple tapestries lined the walls, and torches reflected their orange light off them, giving them a strange glow. An ominous chill hung in the air. Elena quietly opened the door to the throne room and ducked behind a marble pillar. She peeked her head around and found Richard tied to an altar.

King Ravencroft stood above him, The Krimson Stone in one hand and a spell book in the other.

Elena quietly unsheathed her sword and stepped out behind the pillar. "Ravencroft! I don't care what you think of me! I'm going to defeat you, here and now!"

King Ravencroft laughed and tossed his spell book aside. He stepped down and drew his sword. "Very well. Humor me with your skills."

Elena scowled. "With pleasure."

King Ravencroft swiped his blade at Elena's head. She ducked and blocked his attack. Each parried the attack and blocked. Her sword slid down his in a firework of sparks and entangled in his handguard. She gritted her teeth and forced him back.

King Ravencroft fell to the floor, the Krimson Stone and his sword knocked out of his hands. He stretched his fingers for the ruby.

Elena quickly grabbed the ruby and pointed her sword at his throat. "Give up, King Ravencroft. Your wicked reign over this land has ended. I'll give you a choice. I can kill you now, or I can take you and your soldiers back to King Hubert as prisoners and let him decide what to do with you. It's up to you."

King Ravencroft bowed his head in defeat. "I give up. Do with me what you will."

Elena scowled at him. "Don't move. If you do, I'll kill you." She ran toward Richard and untied him.

Richard stood up. "Thank you for saving me, Elena."

Elena nodded. "You're welcome." She looked at King Ravencroft and stood in deep thought for a moment. She returned to him and tied his wrists and ankles together with the rope formally used on Richard. "I'll take you and your soldiers back to King Hubert as prisoners. It will give you a chance to change your ways if you choose. After all, even the most wicked villains like you deserve mercy, and before you say anything, mercy isn't a weakness. It's a strength."

King Ravencroft grumbled under his breath, but he did not speak another word.

Richard walked over to Elena. "You were amazing, Elena."

Elena smiled. "Thank you, Richard. Let's go home."

Richard nodded in agreement.

17 Dead

Jason Houghton

Chapter 1

The hunger pangs crept into Asha's sleep. The cravings of survival interrupted the dreams of peaceful meadows. They taunted her gnawing at her thoughts until she gave them her undivided attention. Cold weather seeped into every joint and muscle but failed to pull a second of thought away from her growling stomach.

She snapped her jaw as the last bit of slumber escaped in a yawn. A look around her cave helped orient her. Night lacked even a hint of warmth that her body could pull in. She silently prayed for just a little ray of light piercing from the openings overhead. The first rotting carcass of an animal showed her prayers had not gone answered.

The darkness required her to use her hypersensitive vision to find what her stomach craved, a mid-hibernation snack. Asha knew she would have to feed during this cold season, it was part of the knowledge trapped in her genetic memory. Hunting during this time proved to be problematic. To battle starvation, she created pits for her food, supplied with the provisions to keep them alive until their services were needed.

Her size had diminished in the time she had been asleep, and she found it easier to move through the tunnel. Something seemed off with the aroma in the air. A new smell occupied the cave proving to be more prevalent than the usual musty scent a damp dwelling held. The deathly decay finished off any sense of hope in the back of Asha's mind.

Panic urged her forward, the stench nurturing her fear, the moment she peeked into the pit despair wrapped around her. None of her kind possessed precognition, but the overwhelming feeling of dread crept from her nostrils to her brain. The scent of death came from the cattle stored for her hibernation period. She sniffed at the air trying to sort out the cacophony of different aromas. The decomposing meat was one thing, but there was the tinge of something else more troubling.

Rot.

The breakdown of the food source either starved or poisoned the cattle to death. Asha frantically searched the next compartment. The results did not change. The thought of her future ignited her panic. None of the food stores were left untainted. Though it was the end of the season, a chance still existed that she could starve. Seventeen rotting carcasses may lead to her own death.

The humans always had and were food, albeit a poor tasting piece of meat. *The heartburn they left never equaled the meal.* Desperate times called for desperate measures but, she was not to that point yet. They remained a last resort.

Cleaning out the spoiled meat became the priority. *No point in bringing in more food when it would be doomed to the same fate.* She resisted getting started. The procrastination was not due to laziness, but an avoidance to admit defeat. Delaying the inevitability of the task would not likely change the outcome.

Asha knew there would be a solution to her current quandary, too much of her species' fate depended on her survival. The pressure felt immense at times, especially moments like this but the stress motivated her brain to solve her problems.

The Divine for some reason had written off her entire bloodline allowing humans to take dominance. While it may be sacrilegious, something told her to fight. Dragons had been stewards of the land until human beings were brought up from scavengers to their current role. The lack of any of her kind near her proved her side was losing the war for survival.

Asha dug further into the pits, despite her hatred of dirt under her claws. Burning the carcasses would have been an option, if she did not fear the smoke drawing hunters. She was in no shape to fight whatever armed group the humans sent. She placed a thick layer of dirt and rocks over the mess to keep it from causing further harm.

The task took the entirety of the evening. The morning light crept through the cracks in the walls. She patted down the fresh mound and yawned. The morning grew warmer.

Perhaps the cold season is coming to an end. If only I can be that lucky.

The weather teased the shift to warmer days. Asha knew it but that did not dissuade her hope. Hope was the last thing that remained for her kind.

She defeated her procrastination and thrust her head out of the loose gravel that served as the door to her home. Pebbles and debris fell in visible streams as she crested above the treetops. The clear day guaranteed her visibility for miles around, but her growing hunger stifled that fear. Safety was not a priority.

Large leathery wings snapped cracking the air like distant thunder to those who may be working in the woods below. The lack of clouds limited any possible hiding places the excursion would have to be quick.

Her stomach grumbled, almost distracting her from the rising smoke in the distance. Swooping down toward the trees, Asha tried to limit the reaction of those that most likely sat at the source of the fire.

Asha flashed a look of disdain and worry at the branches below. Despite the occasional small green bud of new growth, the branches were bare, and she was exposed; worry implanted in her thoughts. *It's too early to be out here, I will be discovered.*

Spring sprinkled the smell of growth in the air, but nothing obscured the vision. The sounds of birds chirping in a distance filled her ears attempting to distract but did nothing for her stomach.

She stayed as low to the trees below as possible along a creek. The thin strip of waterway expanded into a full river with every bit of ground gained. She contracted her body as the trees disappeared below her with the stream emptying into a large lake. She discovered the source of the smoke when breaking cover. A wooden dock temporarily housed a fishing boat with the crew of about seven men unloading today's fresh catch.

Asha broke the tree line. The men scattered in all directions. Two of them dove into the lake water. A drop of the splash hit Asha's leathery wing, she shivered from the chill. The dragon lowered her head and dove straight for the partially unloaded net. Her rear talons grabbed the netting.

Her wings snapped sending a gush of air downward. The boat rocked. Ripples spread across the lake in all directions. *How convenient of the humans to have a few days food already bundled for me*, she thought. A smile flashed across her face.

A few bites of fish slid off the deck and back into the lake's comfort. *I hope I still have enough not to make another trip.*

The boats motion sent cascading waves to pummel the men on the docks. Asha watched as they failed to gain their footing. By the time the men were able to throw a single javelin she few out of their range.

Asha circled the area several times, occasionally diving below the tree line. The fish, still alive, flopped in her net with a few more escaping to the forest floor. Certain death a reward for their vigorous fight.

When it became apparent, she had eluded any possible pursuer, she returned to her home in the cave. She set the fish aside and pushed as much dirt and gravel to patch her door. When no light penetrated through, she sat back on her rear legs and used her claws to clear the dirt from under her front talons. She hated dirt on her hands especially before she ate.

Throwing the first fish in the air, her mighty maw seized it before it began its descent. Her claws went back into the netting to grab the next bite. She paused and lifted the rope to her eye level. The frayed ends of a tear faced her, she picked at it with her other forelimb. It was the width of her claw at the base. Not large enough to dump her entire score but big enough to inspire wonder about how much she lost. The doubt that her bounty would last the remaining cold season leapt to the forefront with a growl in her stomach.

Chapter 2

"I was told this was an urgent manner." The knight's dark eyes met the raggedly dressed delegation. His voice lightly echoed against the stone walls of the outpost's meeting hall. Old maps gave off the smell the last remaining aromas of the dried plants they had been made from. That smell was pushed aside by the pungent fish aroma from the visitors. He awaited their response with a raised eyebrow.

"Sir Thane," Darkened wrinkled skin with a sea of gray hair indicated the speaker as the eldest of the fishermen. "I don't know how to explain my panic without looking like a fool."

Thane's expression quickly changed. His raised eyebrow dropped flat in line parallel with his mouth. His words didn't suppress any of his disappointment. "What is it?"

The fisherman gulped hard, "A dragon lord." Shrinking back, he then fell silent all eyes fixed on the knight.

"A dragon?" Thane's brow raised slightly, and a smile formed on his face. "Are you sure that is what you want to go with? A myth?"

"It could not possibly be anything else." The fisherman looked directly at the knight. "I know there hasn't been any sighted in generations, but the characteristics and appearance are just like those described in the texts."

"You do know my scholars question the validity of those writings and dismiss them only as pure fiction." Thane rubbed his chin; the whiskers pulled to a point.

"By the Divine, they are wrong." The fisherman stood defiantly, "my readings investigate the evidence in a more scientific manner."

"Are you a fisherman or a scholar?" one of the knight's advisors chimed in.

"Any skill can be improved with knowledge." The fisherman snapped. "I'm successful at my craft because I stay educated."

Thane chuckled, "The fisherman's point is valid, and he more than doubles most other's bounty. That is why I was eager to grant his audience."

"I pledge to The Divine; the creature has returned, and it appears not to be to our benefit." The fisherman's hand shook for the first time as it went to his mouth, the moment the sentence left.

Thane turned to the admonished advisor, "Personally inform the duke what is being reported and see his intent. I will organize a hunt." The smile erupted on his face. "If this is true my name will be spoken for generations to come, like the knights of old."

An advisor in green turned to his lord. "Shall I make a list of our strongest and most skilled peasantry? According to old custom, we need eight strongmen to hold down the wings, four skilled men-at-arms to assist you in laying the killing blow, a scribe to record for posterity, and four fools to provide distraction."

"The duke will probably want to claim your role on this quest for himself if you inform him." The admonished advisor offered. "If this is more than a fairy tale there will be much glory for him. And by the look of his Duchy, he needs it. You are the panther after all, a title earned by your ability to stalk and kill your prey. Backing down from this hunt mocks the moniker."

"Valid point. I will assemble my hunt and depart to investigate. When I have been gone a day begin the journey to his stronghold."

"If it pleases Sir Thane, I would like to provide nets and the services of my sons and I to your quest." The fisherman offered.

"Of course," Thane acknowledged with a nod. "a little vengeance is good for the spirit."

His own military force had provided the bulk of the eighteen. Pure curiosity fueled a rush of volunteers, a dragon hadn't been seen by any living townsfolk ever. It would be a tale to pass on for generations.

They will forever remember my name from all this.

His small detachment of his Duke's army provided most of the strongmen as well as men-at-arms, though he wondered if this would provide a way to dispense some of the more undesirables as the roles of fools.

It became hard for him to suppress his giddiness to be the one to kill a creature that hadn't been seen for generations. The immortality of his name could be gained with a swing of a sword.

Chapter 3

Asha threw one of the brownish-green fish into her mouth. *I wish this was beef.* The morsel slid down her throat providing a bit of badly needed nourishment. Survival became the only thing that mattered anymore, perhaps it had always been that way.

Memories of her ancestors ingrained themselves into the genetic code of each dragon. Asha thanked whatever ancestor had experienced something similar and give her the knowledge to deal with the quests. She added another piece of knowledge when she conquered the obstacle of a mid-hibernation poisoning of the food supply. Hopefully her children will not have to face that task. She chortled at the thought of her offspring.

You cannot have babies without a mate! No males of her generation had been spotted by any of her ancestors.

A thought slipped in from her subconscious. *I had exposed my existence to the hamlet of humans nearby. In the past that never ended well for her kind.* It did not bother her as much as she thought it would, to be honest she doubted there was any truth to humans being able to kill a dragon. Yet that brought up a different question, *why was her kind forced into hiding by such a squishy race?*

Yes, they seemed to be adaptable and able to construct tools to overcome many challenges, but their lives were so short. How could they really be expected to accomplish so much when they expired before even one century? Yes, they were warm blooded and had the ability to function even in the cold climates but that isn't a weapon, if it were she would have to fear most of her other food in equal measure.

Right now, I am too young to do anything about the power dynamic but perhaps when I get a bit older and stronger the dynasty of man would come to an abrupt end.

The fish relieved some of the hunger, her stomach grumbled in dismay when she pondered keeping this diet long term. Going back to sleep was out of the question, as well as going outside, so the real torture would now begin in full force boredom.

The world would be different if Dragons were once again the stewards. She grabbed two large rocks; their rough surface seemed perfect for the task she had in mind. Her fingers spread wide to grip one of each object in her front claws. The crack echoed throughout her hovel as she smacked the two light grey stones together.

The rubbing of the two rocks sent a few sparks flying. A thin slice of light penetrated from above catching the sprinkles of dirt and dust in the air. Asha enjoyed the bit of heat produced by the friction of the stones as the face of both became smooth. While they were still warm, she pressed them to the side of her face along her jawline. A soft sigh escaped her lips as she took in the moment.

When the now smooth rock cooled, she dropped the one in her left hand down and cradled the one in her right. A sharp claw dug into the stone down the middle. She repeated the action as she etched a cross bar dividing the slab into four sections. She scratched in little stick figures representing humans in the top left panel. The figures appeared to be sitting for a meal.

The second panel she drew a very crude looking dragon coming to join the meal. She imprinted evidence of a smile into the creature's face. Asha looked pleased as she ran a claw over the artwork.

Mother

Her smile faded on the third panel. She depicted the humans with swords and other weapons. Her claws too large to get the angry details on their faces right. When she finished the depiction, Asha ground her teeth.

Her scowl cast hatred as she worked on the fourth panel. An outline of her mother being chased by the stick figures. Each pass of her finger dug into the stone deeper until it began to pierce through the other side.

She set the stone down before grabbing a handful of fish from the net. With ease she tossed the trout in her mouth. A snap of her jaw caught the food midair sending an echo down the underground cavern. The rumbling gave her pause to once again ponder why she, as powerful as she was, had been hiding from the humans.

With that thought in mind she secured the second slab and got to work.

Chapter 4

Thane led the men toward the lake, the last known sighting. The question lingered in the back of his mind.

Am I up for the task?

Of course I am! The thought triggered the knight to stick out his chest. He did not earn the nickname the panther by allowing his prey to escape. Thane could see the glint of adventure in the eyes of the other seventeen in the party their thoughts must be similar, he was the man for the task!

The fisherman and his sons were different though, their faces flashed the anger from the encounter that sparked this adventure. They toiled with their hands to bring in the bounty from the lake, then watched helplessly as the beast stole the payoff of their efforts. Thane wondered what that would feel like, all he could imagine was frustration and anger.

They reached the lake just as the sun began to head home for the night, its duties done for the day. The fisherman's family greeted the party upon their arrival. The children huddled around a frumpy matron. Their young faces still held the horror of what they had witnessed. Red puffy eyes stayed locked open, contrasting against the drained pale faces. They embraced their mother tighter as the group approached staying as hidden as possible until the fisherman made his way toward the house.

"We will make camp for the night." Thane looked away from the children.

"We do not have a lot of room Sir Thane but if everyone can find a spot in my home they will stay warm for the night." The fisherman offered. "Of course, you may have our bed for the night. I am sure the children will want us in their room anyways."

"That is kind of you, but I would not even consider taking a man's bed from him. The children will be fine." He got to one knee in front of the largest and nudged his chin. "They have one of the kingdom's best knights guarding them."

The house smelled of unwashed work clothes that carried the odor from the bounty of the lake on them. The hearth of the fireplace was kept clear, but every other portion of the wood floor was covered with a bed roll. Side conversations saturated the room but slowly died down. Thane and the fisherman moved close to the fireplace.

"How do you think we will be able to find the beast?" The fisherman opened the dialogue.

"Honestly, I'm still praying the Divine gives me a way." Thane forced out a chuckle. "Never hunted a dragon before."

"I don't think anyone in the kingdom has," He tilted his head as he shrugged his shoulders toward the knight. "I still am left to wonder how the behemoth flew, as large as it was."

"Do you remember which way it headed out, at least?"

"Yes sir, I will show you in the morning light."

Thane leaned back, "And we will make the lake safe once more."

"And our names will live on forever in glory?" The fisherman jested.

"Get some sleep now. Glory will be here soon enough."

Thane barely slept, too big of an opportunity laid in front of him. His roommate did not seem to mind the knight's insomnia, the snoring told Thane the young man probably slept better having soldiers keeping the monsters at bay.

One of the older boys entered the room with a plate of bacon. Thane's mouth watered and his nose was thankful the salty delight drowned out the fish smell that lingered all night.

"Are all the men ready?" Thane did not offer thanks, he remained too focused on the task at hand.

"I believe so, lord." The young man must be unaware of proper protocol when a house guest was of noble birth.

Thane noticed he failed to bow out of respect. The chastisement would wait for another day. "Make sure, or today will be a long day for those who slack." Thane's words were curt.

"Yes, sir" The boy meekly slipped away.

When the boy left, Thane could not help but dwell on the fact that today would be the day he reached immortality. At least his name would. Perhaps the hunt would also move him past his own Duke in the king's eyes and he would surpass his current station. More importantly no history could be recorded without a text having his name on at least one page.

When Thane exited the home, his men were all accounted for and ready to move. He noticed the same hunger in their eyes as he held within his own.

"We are ready Sir Thane," The fisherman took the spot next to the knight. "Shall I show you where the beast fled?"

"Begin," Thane's voice hinted of a boom of command suppressing the excitement.

A taste of bloodthirst mixed with the scent of encroaching spring. The green of the season not quite present but buds on the plants heralded it would be approaching soon. The trees still a skeleton of their summer glory did not provide too much obstruction of the view, they swayed slightly whenever the wind gusted but not enough to disturb the attempt to find traces of the dragon.

"This is pointless, the sky holds no tracks," a murmur from the back of the group, where the jesters moved, slinked its way up front.

Thane ignored the comment, determined to find a way, the Divine would not let him down.

Before there could be another dissenting word, one of the soldiers raised a hand to warn the group of fools of impending consequences.

The silence proved the dissenter received the message.

One of the guards on the flank called a halt. "Sir Thane," unable to withhold his excitement.

"What do you have?" Unable to quell his own anxious energy, Thane ran to the guard's spot.

"I have not seen another lake or stream since we departed this morning, yet that." He used the halberd to indicate a direction. Within an arm's length a trout leaned against a branch at eye level in a tree. "That surely doesn't belong here."

"Fisherman," Thane motioned for his story's originator to come forward. When he made his way to Thane, the knight did not waste any time speaking. "Was this your stolen bounty?"

The fisherman looked for a moment. "Most of our catch was trout! Lord, yes."

"Spread out and see if you can find any more fish in the trees." He barked out to the entire party. His eyes narrowed on the fools. "Apparently we found a way to track these flying creatures."

The formation spread out and no other commentary was provided. It did not take long for a second awkwardly perched fish to be located.

"Keep looking, we are on the path."

After a few more fish were found, the group came to what appeared to be a pit of gravel dug into the ground. The last fish laid almost pointing to the center of the mass. Thane sent a jester into the gravel to retrieve the clue. Two steps into his trek the fool sunk down to his knees before his companions stopped his descent. The sound of the stones falling down an unseen hole in the pit did not stop when the fool was saved.

The group pulled the jester out just as the gravel started to build up in the center. The shifting pebbles turned into a mound. A stench of sulfur and fish broke out of the pit.

"To arms" Thane drew his sword, ordering his companions to follow suit. "Destiny is here!"

Chapter 5

The perfume of death always oozed off human bodies, even while they were still alive. She wondered if they could smell the decomposing cells on themselves as easily as other species could. Asha knew company was sitting just outside her door, and though she assumed the Divine would help her through her recent food problems she did not expect him to deliver the food to her door. Humans were so predictable; they sent eighteen snacks for her gullet.

Now was time to feed.

With little effort she burst through the gravel portal. A malicious roar greeted her human visitors. Two of the members stumbled as the entirety of her green scaled neck made it out into the cold air. Their fear became palatable, which meant the meat probably spoiled.

Before the first bit of gravel fell back to the ground Asha captured the one whose foot still occupied her gravel door. Her jaws sliced through the meat of his waist dividing his body in half. The juices of his life rolled out of her mouth and rolled down her chin.

The irony hit her; *The jester tasted funny.*

Panic struck the closest companions of her first target. It added to the humor of the situation as their legs moving in the gravel did not gain any ground. It seemed cruel to continue to watch the duo struggle. She opted for the humane option and flicked her finger. The claw separated their heads causing their bodies to crumple.

A new terror sparked, spreading throughout the hunting party. With only one of the more ridiculously dressed individuals left, she quickly dispatched him.

She turned her attention to the one yelling. *He had to be the one in charge, or at least he acted like it.*

She lunged her entire body from the pit, knowing if she did not eliminate the human menace she could never go back to her hole. Loose stones and dirt flew in all directions when Asha erupted completely from her home. The knowledge that she had just repacked the stones at her entrance enraged her further. They were all going to pay for the disturbance, and her current level of anger from being taken away from her solace demanded a high price.

When her body landed, some of the men wasted no time in charging to protect the loud human. Their pikes and halberds lowered as they screamed with their last breaths, and she expunged the acidic contents of her stomach on her attackers. Their skin boiled on their bodies after the protective garments fell away. The blisters began to pop on the men with a tiny whistling as the flesh beneath evaporated.

It sickened Asha for a moment. Their pain creating new volumes and pitches in their bellowing. Part of her soul shuttered at the thought of their torment, the other part did not waste the effort on worrying about intruders. *If they had left her alone, they would still be alive.*

She had killed six of the hunting party already, another two were wailing loudly as they lay dying against a tree. Humans can be so dramatic at the end. Unfortunately for Asha the loudmouth still lived. He was the next priority.

Two men produced bows and lit the rags on their ammo ablaze. Asha shook her head in pity. *Do they not know my kind are fireproof?*

The snap of her wings sent the dragoness skyward, but it only lasted a moment. She plunged toward the archers, all of her weight crunching the would-be attackers. Every one of the men's bones crushed to powder as their forms became completely unrecognizable as human.

Her head raised up to find the loudmouth had used the archers as a ruse. He had dashed away.

Fortunately for Asha the scent of death that followed every human left a very pungent trail.

Chapter 6

Anticipation of glory fled many steps ago. Desperation for survival propelled Thane deeper into the woods. He was not sure who was behind him and honestly did not care.

He tripped over a branch falling against the ground. A quick turning of his head revealed the dragon noticed his absence. It closed the distance in a few bounds. The longer he stayed prone the easier it was to become prey.

Dropping his father's sword Thane crawled with his elbows while fighting to get to his feet. He almost tripped again when he extended into his first step. Every part of him panicked, he probably did not even realize he was screaming.

His men surely did, heading in opposing directions from the very vocal leader. Now all but the fisherman ran amok through the trees.

The dragon did not break stride as she dealt with hunters on the flank. A piercing claw and whipping tail dealt killing blows while she closed on Thane. The beast was too quick for their legs to clear a decent space between its deadly tools and their bodies.

Thane could do nothing but watch his men die. He should have felt the loss, but his safety was more pressing. He never imagined the creature being so deadly. Reality shattered his most generous imagination of the myth.

An acrid scent overtook him as the sun was blotted from the sky. Had the creature already caught him? *No this is not how my saga was going to end!*

Chapter 7

A dozen snacks did not satiate her appetite as she drooled looking down at the knight. *This would be a very karmic kill. How many of her kind had men like him killed while they were asleep in their homes? How many were mothers like her own?*

This loudmouth would be the one to represent all those missed chances at vengeance, or perhaps just a beginning.

So far everything she feared dissipated by her own abilities. She wondered how the squishy beings were even capable of nearly wiping out her race, but she was going to ensure that human bullying came to an end.

Catching the left arm of the loudmouthed man in her jaw, she clamped down severing it from his body. It was perfect other than the metal armor, just the right mix of muscle and fat.

He just kept yammering and squealing as she chewed the severed limb. His eyes stayed shut as her forward arm held him down. But an onslaught of words continued to interrupt her enjoyment of the moment. Her snakelike neck moved down to remove his leg, which proved to be just as tasty of the arm.

After it was clear of the body, she flipped it into the air allowing it to spin twice before catching it in her gaping maw. It satisfied her more than the fish.

The growing night amplified his bellows, which moved from annoyance to sweet delight in her ears. She pondered what it meant that she found a bit of happiness tormenting this poor creature, surely the Divine would have issue with it. Or perhaps this was how he granted a bit of justice to what they had endured in generations past.

Shifting her weight to her hindquarters, Asha observed the human. At first, he laid there groaning and writhing in pain. The amusement value stayed at a minimum with this, not even the hint of cosmic justice made it enjoyable. Her head tilted back and forth pondering his dilemma.

Losing patience she nudged him a bit with a flicking of her claw, urging him to move. His face widened in shock. She was thankful that he finally became relatively quiet. His remaining arm secured the stump of where its twin had once been, but no other movement happened.

This time she lowered her head using the beak of her nose to push him a short distance away.

Compared to what his species had done to hers, she granted a lot of mercy to him up to this point. Her once proud race had taught humans how to cultivate and survive and were then rewarded with full scale genocide. Those, like her mother, that survived were forced into hiding and eventually hunted down. Starvation or the blade became the only options fate had provided her kind. Yet she was giving this human a fighting chance, which was more than her mother ever received.

Asha was perfectly willing to leave the humans alone, but they had disturbed her hibernation. They always barged in and inconvenienced dragons, so she questioned why had she shown mercy for this long already?

The loud-mouthed human tried to crawl on the forest floor using an arm to pull his deformed body. His remaining leg kicked the ground, propelling him forward. She admired his will to live, no matter how futile his future would be.

His kind stole her dreams, and that theft stung more than the sharpest dagger. She pushed her claw and sliced through his pulling arm. The hope draining from his eyes fascinated Asha. Despite its absence he still tried to gain ground, perhaps he did not weigh the true gravity of the situation.

After some time, he managed to get just outside of her neck reach. She still sat there watching. The struggle leaving a crimson trail on the ground adding to the musk of death that already lingered in the air. The metallic aroma of his blood provided a sweet, if not tantalizing, teasingly small taste of revenge.

The game grew old, and she had other things to do.

With a pounce and a piercing tooth, she ended the loudmouth. One gulp swallowed his head. A dire look etched for eternity on it, or at least until her stomach acid wiped it away. If she had not been discovered before his scream, surely every human and beast was aware of her existence now.

Chapter 8

The fisherman hid out of sight as he had advised his sons to do. Instead, they panicked and ran. They were lost now.

The rest of the family counted on him to provide for them. After he had calmed down from the initial shock and he recovered from the sight of the creature leaving the pages of a fairy tale jumping to life, his thirst for vengeance took a back seat to living.

He realized it was too late as he approached the headless body of one of his sons. The fact that after seventeen harvests he would not face another, smacked the fisherman into a fugue where the air and ground were as sticky as molasses. Time refused to go forward at a natural pace leaving more time to suffer the horrific state of affairs presented to him.

Skulking around, no head could be found. He collapsed to his knees next to the body. Wrapping his arms around the lifeless frame he curled the form against his chest. "I'm sorry my boy, this is not the natural order of things." He screamed to the Divine, "No father should have to bury his sons."

It took some time, but all three of his children were finally collected near the mouth of the dragon's cave. The fisherman counted thirteen dead bodies to include the knight who began this expedition. He was sure he witnessed the death of the other four, swallowed whole by the beast.

Life still moved slowly. He used torchlight to find a way into the pit the dragon had emerged from and ended most of their lives. Every bit of his psyche told him to abandon the adventure and go take his sons' bodies home. However, his morbid curiosity overruled his common sense, and he slowly descended into the pit. The sulfuric smell punctured into his nostrils the deeper he investigated. He pondered if it were safe to keep the torch lit.

When he finally found a large mat made of sheep wool, apparently ripped from the creatures, and leaves, he knew he found the creature's bed. It did not take long for him to locate the remains of his earlier catch. None of it salvageable for market.

Not that it really mattered at this point.

Taking the torch and shining it around the beast's home he found several pits, filled with the remains of herd animals. It would explain the constant missing inventory from area farmers.

Finally, he made his way to two large smooth slabs. On closer inspection he saw the picture telling of dragons being hunted. He wondered who the artist may be who spent the time to chisel in the saga. Each of the four panels on the first one was full of detail, except for the humans. They were just stick figures.

The sky on the single paned slab depicted an army of the winged behemoths scorching the grounds below. Stick figures appeared to either be running or burning. The small map etched in the corner displayed the lake and his Duchy, as well as Arborwick to the east.

When he gazed upon the second panel he muttered, "This is a warning of things to come!"

HAVEN

Caroline Warren

Prologue

Eluned knew he was done for. His arms burned, always wanting to fail, but still forced his body upwards. His lungs ached, and his eyes stung from the debris-filled water. *I just need a branch or something.* He pleaded. *Something to grasp.* The waters of The Grey River coursed strong and violent around him. He stretched his fingers as far as he could to pierce the surface, but to no avail. As he was slammed against a rock, the arrows in his chest and stomach were stabbed deeper into his body. It felt like someone was taking white hot knives and twisting them inside him. A gasp of pain escaped his pursed lips and the bit of air he had managed to salvage escaped.

This is it, he realized. *I'm better off dead, anyway.*

He shut his eyes and let his body go where the water willed. Memories of ash and sulphur of his burning homeland flooded his mind. He stood, defending the kingdom with his fellow soldiers, while the evil warriors of men stormed into his palace. The terrified screams of women and children echoed in his mind; the cries of the fallen Elves loud and clear. He had been the brother of the king, and his personal bodyguard.

Eluned Daysalioth, he scoffed. *A name of shame and failure that will bleed into the pages of history.* He had failed as a knight and a general, but most importantly as a brother.

Water engulfed his lungs, and his consciousness slipped away. If he did not drown, the two arrows sticking out of his torso would finish him off. He had been warding off the soldiers that invaded Rinon and trying to get his younger brother to safety. His memories of the violent battle he had just endured took control.

Fleeing the kingdom with his younger brother, Thorsten in tow, he had been warding off the enemy. He and Thorsten were vastly outmatched, but still they ran, desperate for freedom. It was so close, Eluned could almost see it. Then an arrow had plunged into his abdomen. He turned around to face the enemy, shouting to his brother to leave. Eluned had never felt the searing pain of the second arrow. Thorsten had toppled over, dead, with an arrow lodged in his heart. Eluned's overwhelmed emotions churned into strength, and he slew many a wicked man. Always when his physical strength failed, Thorsten's dead body sent new passion through his veins. But then the arrow's excruciating pain kicked in, and Eluned stumbled back on the ridge he fought on. The last Eluned saw of the sun, was its holy rays piercing the waves of the Grey River as he fell into its dire embrace.

Rinon had been a kingdom of Elves; the most glorious and powerful of the Four Realms. Eluned was one of the royal princes. His eldest brother, Loraniss, was the king. The King of Men, Morem Xarathior, had been a childhood friend of Loraniss. Morem had marched on their kingdom after murdering Loraniss and destroyed the Elven palace. Eluned knew he would never go home. Home was no more.

Chapter I

Eluned woke with a start. Subtle pain throbbed from the wound in his chest. Sunlight spilled through a window next to him. He lay on a small bed and saw a nightstand next to it. He tried to sit up, but shaky arms forced him back down. He looked at his hands. They were wrapped in a clean, white linen.

"You should eat something before trying to walk around," a female voice huffed.

Eluned's eyes widened, and he reached for the sword he always carried. He fumbled for his weapon but found nothing. He scanned the small room for the person the voice belonged to.

"I'm over here, you big oaf," she snickered. A woman emerged from a shadowy corner of the room and into the sunlight. She was tall and fair skinned, with a rounded jaw and a pointed chin. A slender nose was perched upon her face, placed in-between two dark blue eyes. She had light blond hair that was in a long braid down her back.

"Who are you?" Eluned grunted, trying to sound dignified. "And where am I?"

The woman rolled her shoulders back and held her head high.

"I am Adeena Brìghid. My friends call me Addy. You are in Haven," she crisply informed.

Eluned's hand sought the back of his head and scratched it. "You—You're not an Elf."

Adeena walked to the nightstand, picked up a jug of water, and poured some into a cup. "Right you are. What of it?" She offered him the cup, and he greedily drank.

Eluned rubbed his blurry eyes, and his thoughts ran smoother as he blinked.

"But you're not human either." He observed, slowly.

"Correct."

"So, what are you?"

Adeena snickered and stood at the foot of his bed. "You really are daft, aren't you? I'm a Half-Elf." She shrugged as if it meant nothing to her.

Eluned's stomach growled, and he flushed pink. "S—Sorry." He sheepishly smiled.

Adeena cocked a confident eyebrow. "Hungry, aren't we?" Eluned nodded and Adeena jabbed a finger to the hallway outside the door. "This way," she instructed. Eluned turned and dangled his legs off the side of the bed. Holding his breath, he looked down at his torso. He raised his eyebrows and let out a small gasp. His wounds had been diligently bandaged in clean linens. In a daze, he slid out of bed, and walked at a slow pace out of the room and into the hallway. There was another bedroom to his right, and a wide-open space straight ahead. He decided that must have been where Adeena had gone.

"Ugh, my aching head," he murmured, and rubbed his temples. He could not comprehend what had happened. All he could recall was owning some kind of ruby and falling into a river.

"Hey! You coming back there?" Adeena called from outside.

"Yes," Eluned groaned. He walked to the doorframe which had a long red curtain instead of a door. He heard children laughing and splashing around in water. He drew back the curtain and held his hand in front of his eyes to shield them from the bright sun. He blinked a few times to let his eyes adjust, and what he saw took his breath away.

A thriving village, surrounded by towering mountains, lay before him. Giant oak trees swayed in the gentle breeze, and the long grass danced. Dark wood-made houses were scattered across the hills; some bearing fields of crops, and others had windmills. The sun filled everything with a hazy light from the towering trees to the stacks of firewood. A small waterfall descended one of the grey mountains and splashed into a clear pool of water where children scampered and played.

Eluned looked harder at their ears. *Half-Elves,* he realized. *An entire village of them!*

The men tended their crops or worked on various substances in their shops. The women fondly talked to one another and called out to their children not to wander too far.

A ball rolled across the grass and tapped Eluned's foot. A crooked grin crossed his face. He stood, slightly confused, looking for the owner.

Not far from him, was a small group of children. They spoke in hushed voices amongst each other. A little girl with flaming red locks of hair was pushed out from their group. She couldn't have been more than eight. She stuck her tongue out to her companions and rubbed her hands together when she caught sight of Eluned.

He chuckled and held out the ball to her. "Is this yours, little one?" he softly inquired.

The girl's green eyes got wide. She held her head low.

"Come on, it's alright," Eluned offered her another smile. The girl cautiously looked about and tiptoed over to him. She slowly reached out, her tiny hands grasped the ball, and she giggled in childish glee. Stepping closer, she raised an eyebrow and stared at him. She shifted the ball under her arm and reached her free hand up to touch his face. Eluned wanted to melt upon feeling her gentle caress.

"Sad," the girl mumbled. "You are sad." Her little brow furrowed, and she took her hand down.

Eluned froze. He was sad. What's worse, he *knew* he was sad. He felt soul crushing pain; he couldn't remember why.

"I'm Twyla Delroy. I live in the big house on the hill, there." She pointed up the path. It led up a hill to a house much bigger than the rest.

"Ah, I see. It's a pleasure to meet you, Twyla. I'm Eluned," he introduced.

The girl bounced up and down. "Well—see you, Mister!" She cried and happily ran off with her ball. She scampered away with her laughing friends and vanished behind one of the hills.

"Enjoying the view?" Adeena interrupted his tranquility. Eluned immediately stood, but instantly regretted the decision, as his wounds burned and throbbed. Having a desire to look dignified, he tried to straighten his posture.

"Yes. Haven is beautiful…" he trailed off.

Adeena tilted her head to the left. "Come on, even Elves need to eat." She puffed some of her hair out of her face and led him up the dirt path. Passing all the joy-filled houses made Eluned want to dig through his mind and find some memory that he could only touch; never hold. He slumped his shoulders and sighed.

"Addy—"

"Adeena," she corrected.

"Right, sorry. It's just—I'm certain I don't belong here! Where did you find me? Why am I here?"

Adeena stopped, turned on her heel, and faced him. He towered over her, but he felt a twinge of fear whenever he looked into her dark eyes.

"Alright, *your Highness,*" she snorted. "You *really* mean to tell me you don't remember the mess that got you washed up here? Give me a break." She waved her hand and kept walking.

Eluned's breathing quickened, and beads of sweat trickled down his forehead. "No, please! You have to tell me why I'm here and what happened!"

Adeena looked up at the afternoon sky and sighed. "If you really can't remember, then you've got a lot of catching up to do, General Eluned. You've been unconscious for a week."

Chapter II

"Well don't just stand there with your mouth hanging open! You look like an idiot." Adeena scoffed. She seized his hand and marched up the path. Eluned became dizzy as all things around him blurred. Adeena dragged him into the big house that Twyla had pointed out.

A week? How was that possible? He was certain he'd only been out for a day or two. Adeena waved him ahead of her and shooed him into the doorway of the house. The inside was warm and elegantly decorated. Paintings on the walls and carpets on the floors jogged glimpses of memories of an old home for Eluned. He stood there feeling lost, helpless, and empty.

"Chief Àlkimos! It's Adeena," she called up a stairwell. "I'm here with that bonehead of a prince that we found last week."

Bonehead? He did not know what to think of this woman, always calling him names—but he knew there must be a reason for her dislike of him.

"Ah," a deep voice called. "I'll be right down. Take him to the dining room."

Adeena glanced at Eluned. "I'm sure this will pale in comparison to the lavish dinners you're used to but considering the times, it will be the best that Haven has to offer. We're not used to having royalty, you know."

Eluned ran his fingers through his hair and grunted. "Hang on, now! Why do you keep calling me royalty? *Considering the times?* What's *that* supposed to mean?" he asked.

Adeena's face contorted and she opened her mouth to say something. Small, running feet interrupted her.

"Hey, Mister Eluned!" Twyla exclaimed, dancing around the hallway. She wrapped her arms around his calves and giggled. Adeena cocked her head. Eluned helplessly shrugged.

A slender woman with raven-black hair and bright eyes rounded the corner. She had a small infant in her arms. She let out a small yelp of surprise upon seeing Eluned and fell to her knees. "My lord, Eluned!" she gasped, bowing her head. "I had no idea I was hosting the brother of the king!" She looked up with a softened expression. "I am so sorry for what happened."

Eluned did not respond; he had no words to meet the woman's sympathy.

Adeena cordially smiled. "You can stand up, Lady Zuriñe. This—" she slowly looked Eluned over, as if searching for an insult she had not used yet, "—hunk of muscle doesn't remember what got him here, or so he says; so, your condolences are of no use." She finished, walked past Zuriñe, and shoved Eluned into the dining room. She sat him at a long, oak table with engravings of wheat and bountiful harvests on the legs. Eluned immediately felt at home.

Twyla walked into the dining room, holding her brother. She laid him in a crib in the far end of the room and plopped down beside Eluned. "Hi! Hi!" she laughed. "Mommy made her special soup tonight because you're here. Thanks!" She wiggled around in her seat and licked her lips in anticipation.

Zuriñe emerged from the kitchen carrying a platter of hot bread rolls, trailing steam. One maid servant followed, carrying a large silver bowl of soup. Two more emerged carrying wild-green salads. They placed them in a long row down the center of the table and lit candles placed in silver holders.

"Ha, ha, ha! There he is!" Chief Àlkimos entered the room. Eluned jumped at his boisterous voice, and his abdominal muscles screamed at him. The Chief came around the table and playfully slapped his shoulder.

"Ow," Eluned winced.

"O-o-oh, you're a muscly fellow, aren't you?" he squeezed Eluned's arm.

Eluned flushed.

Adeena snickered.

"Well, we'll make sure you stay that way—after you enjoy my wife's wonderful meal!" Àlkimos bellowed.

Zuriñe blushed and curtsied.

"Th—thank you for your hospitality," Eluned stated, messaging his sore bicep. He smiled, rather awkwardly, to establish that there were no hard feelings. Àlkimos grinned and took his place at the head of the table.

He was a merry looking fellow with a larger figure and bright red hair like Twyla's. He wore it pulled into a bun on the back of his head. It seamlessly melded to a closely trimmed beard. He wore furs and adornments that suggested he was a hunter. Scars that resembled claw marks raked along the right side of his face. He had a large, pointed nose and sparkling eyes. Zuriñe sat down at his right side and Eluned happily found he had been placed at Àlkimos's left.

Àlkimos lifted his jug of ale and all at the table raised their glasses. Twyla, too young to know the significance of a toast, raised up her cup of goat's milk as well.

"Hail to family, The Daysalioths, and the fallen Elven realms!" He cried with passion.

"Hail!" Everyone cried and drank.

Eluned stared down at the rippling red wine in his glass. *My realms have fallen?* he pondered. The name—Daysalioths— triggered something. *A twinge of familiarity, perhaps?* He knew that name, he was certain he did.

The soup, bread, and salads were passed around, and Àlkimos fondly spoke with his wife. Eluned noticed Adeena peering at him from across the table with a hawk-like glare.

"Talk to him," she mouthed.

Eluned grumbled and turned to his host. "Chief Àlkimos?" he meekly began. *After all, this is a powerfully built man of nobility; one must be careful when speaking to such people.*

Àlkimos turned to him and flashed his white teeth. The laugh lines grew long in his face when he looked upon Eluned. The Prince instantly trusted him "What is it, son? Is the food to your liking?"

"Oh yes—yes, My Lord. I—"

"Yes?"

"Well, what you said about the Daysalioths—what *did* happen exactly?"

Àlkimos choked on his soup, balled his fist, and punched his sternum to regain his composure. Zuriñe's eyebrows rose, and she whispered something to Adeena.

"Son—" Àlkimos's brows came together in a sad expression. "How could you *not* know? You were there when the Kingdom of Rinon fell." Eluned's expression remained saddened and blank. "It was a mighty kingdom with light that felt no darkness. The Elven race dwelling there lived in peace under the rule of Lord Loraniss Daysalioth, Maker bless him."

Zuriñe sadly shook her head. Eluned gripped the arms of his chair with white knuckles and leaned closer.

Àlkimos's smile vanished and he sat his hand on Eluned's shoulder. "King Morem of Men invaded your homeland, lad. He lured Loraniss into his clutches and murdered him. He burned the city to ash and killed its people or took them hostage." He stopped to observe Eluned's reaction.

Images flashed before his eyes. Fires. Crumbling buildings. Corpses. *I was there*, Eluned realized.

Àlkimos sighed and continued. "The battle raged like nothing this world has ever known. Your people fought mightily, Eluned. Princess Ayleth, second to Loraniss was banished or killed, no one knows which. The second in line after Ayleth was the knight to the king and a leader of his armies. Thorsten, the youngest son was killed. And Milla, poor little thing, has been dead these five years." Àlkimos tightened his jaw and bowed his head. "You were *powerful,* Eluned. No one could defeat your family so long as you had each other."

"So, the kingdom was divided and overrun." Eluned breathed.

Àlkimos solemnly nodded.

"Not even a week ago," Zuriñe added.

Everyone stared heavily at Eluned, awaiting to hear what he would say. "I—" His words caught in his throat and tears welled in his eyes. He balled his fists, and his fingernails stabbed his palms. "So, I have abandoned my people. I can't remember my family." He mumbled. He turned to Adeena. "Where did you find me?" Eluned managed, through clenched teeth.

Àlkimos adjusted his belt and glanced at Adeena. "Care to tell him how you saved him from drowning, Addy?"

"No."

"Why ever not! It *was* you that did it, or do you have some twin running about that I don't know of?"

"You know I'm not much of a talker, sir. You also are aware of how I feel about *his* kind."

Her tone made Eluned boil inside. His home had been ransacked and burned to the ground and she had the audacity to dislike him for the species?

Àlkimos shifted in his seat and smiled. "Fine then. You can either tell him yourself, or I'll make you go sit beside him and whisper it to him. Whichever you prefer."

Adeena choked and looked like she had smelled something rotten. "Okay, okay, fine! Look, Prince BoneHead; Chief Àlkimos and I were scouting the Grey River like we do every day. I saw something adrift in the water, and upon further investigation it was you. I stitched you up and brought you back here. End of story." She slumped back in her seat and crossed her arms as she puffed her hair out of her face.

Chief Àlkimos erupted in cheery laughter. "You didn't mention how fast you dismounted your horse, leapt into that freezing water, and swam out to the middle of the river all to save his skin!"

Chapter III

Chief Àlkimos wanted Eluned to stay awhile after supper, especially after Adeena stormed out of the house. "She'll come around," he assured Eluned, but the Prince was not so sure. Zuriñe walked Adeena home while Àlkimos and Twyla showed him around their house. It was filled with artwork and treasures from the worlds of Men and Elves.

Eluned was both intrigued and impressed.

Twyla squealed and grabbed Eluned's hand when they came to Zuriñe's tapestry room. It was a large room with oak floors and many windows. A fire flickered in a hearth, flanked by a rocking chair and a spinning wheel. Many of her works hung on the walls, and Eluned recognized the style in tapestries hanging throughout the house.

"Beautiful," he breathed, rubbing the smooth threads in-between his fingers. He gazed at a tapestry of a castle nestled in-between two mountains. "Where is this?" A shimmering river ran through it, and the castle gleamed white as pearl with golden gates.

"That was Trigon's Palace in Rinon, named for Loraniss's great, great, great, grandfather. It was a sight." Àlkimos tilted his head as he looked at it.

His eyes reflect a sad sort of nostalgia, Eluned thought. He gazed at it and ran his fingers along the silver yarn that brought the river to life. "It looks—alive," he muttered.

Twyla bounced in place and tugged on Eluned's tunic. "Doesn't it! Sometimes I just sit in front of one for hours, and hours imagining that I live there." She drew a long sigh.

Àlkimos laughed and scooped her up. "Alright, Miss Daydream, it's past your bedtime."

"Awww," she moaned.

Zuriñe returned and Àlkimos handed Twyla over to her. He gave Twyla a kiss on the forehead. "I'll come tuck you in later," he promised. Zuriñe left and Àlkimos scratched his head.

"Well—I had hoped that seeing this tapestry would jog your memory. Guess not." He bit down on his knuckles, and silently contemplated.

Eluned rubbed his right ring finger and his gold signet ring. He fidgeted with it, earnestly praying that he could remember more. "Listen, I do appreciate your help, but I have to get back home, Àlkimos. If Ayleth was banished then I need to find her."

"What home, Son?" he asked, placing his hands firmly on his shoulders. "*Home*, for you, doesn't exist anymore. Besides you're in no state to travel. Two arrows were sticking out of your gut and chest when we found you, Mate. You've got a long road of healing ahead of you."

He turned to leave the room and motioned for Eluned to follow him.

"You're right." Eluned sighed, staring at his bandaged hands. "I can't walk without feeling pain."

He followed Àlkimos down a corridor and into a generously sized bedroom. "We'll start on some therapy tomorrow, but in the meantime, you'll be staying with us for a while, If you see fit."

Eluned's heart leapt, but he kept it suppressed. "Yes," he nodded. "I can't pass up your wife's cooking."

Àlkimos put his hands on his stomach and laughed. "This is the truth, my friend!" He rested his hands on his belt. "Are you in need of anything else before I bid you goodnight?"

Eluned furrowed his brow and looked into his new bedroom. The canopied bed was three times larger than the one back in Adeena's hut. The wooden floors were adorned with rugs spun with the vivid colors of Zuriñe's tapestries. There was a bookcase on the wall opposite the bed, and a large window parallel to it.

"I would like a book about the Daysalioths—If you have one?" he asked.

Àlkimos sympathetically smiled. "Yes, lad. I'll go grab it for you, along with some nightclothes."

Eluned smiled as Àlkimos walked away. He turned and went into his room. He lit a candle and sat it on his nightstand. He looked vacantly at its dancing flame and brought his fingertips as close to its heat as he could stand. He sat hunched over on the side of his bed, contemplating what Àlkimos had told him.

That would explain why I was adrift in the river. But why would Adeena bother risking her hide to help me? She's made it clear she hates Elves. This thought jogged memories. He was speaking with a beautiful Elven woman; robed in white with eyes like two sapphires.

"They are shunned," she explained. "Half Elves are shamed by humans for their Elven blood and by Elves for their mortal blood. They're outcasts. They have no ancestral home like we do, my son." She spoke gently to the young Eluned; like the cool breeze that kisses the spring grass. Eluned flopped back on his bed, relaxing his tensed abdominal muscles.

It can go either way, he thought. *The Half Elves will either love or hate their blood.*

He knew he had a long way to go, but the sight of his mother in his mind boosted his morale. Àlkimos came in with some folded nightclothes in his arms, forcing Eluned out of his thoughts.

"Here you are." He sat them at the foot of the bed. "Your book is folded up in the clothes. Sleep well." He bade and left as quickly as he had come. Eluned lunged forward and unraveled the book from within the folds of the white linen.

Its cover was leather, and the title was inscribed in golden lettering: *The Complete Histories and Family of the Daysalioths.* His eyes roamed the by like and Eluned felt a stab to the heart. *Written and Collected By Milla Estienne Daysalioth.*

Eluned's heart rate accelerated, and his stomach somersaulted. A new grief pulsed through his body. He gritted his teeth and clawed his fingers into his shoulders. He dripped with cold sweat and squeezed his eyes shut. He *finally* remembered something, and he longed to die rather than re-live Milla's death.

Chapter IV

Be sure you keep this safe, Eluned—that's all I ask." Milla slipped her pale hand out of Eluned's. She left in his open palm a fist-sized ruby. It glinted faintly in the candlelight; mirroring Milla's fading life.

"Hmmm," she smiled weakly. "It used to be so much brighter than this." She tilted her head back, and drew a long, shaky breath. Eluned defiantly shook his head. He eased himself down beside his sister on her deathbed. She used to be so blooming, so youthful, so full of life; now she lay cold and pale, hardly strong enough to sit up. Her long, brown waves of hair spread out across her pillow, perfectly framing her thin face. He took her hand, folded it between his, and pressed it to his heart.

"I need you to stay with me, stay with us. I can't lose you, Milla," Eluned croaked. Milla pursed her lips and strained as she reached out her arms. Eluned pulled her into him and stroked her hair. She weighed nothing, but even if she hadn't been so sick, Eluned would have carried her from east to west if he had to. He sobbed and buried his face in her hair.

"There is no place you can go where I will not still be with you," she whispered, and rubbed the back of his neck. "But I had so hoped—I would become a mother before I became a corpse."

"No!" Eluned cried as he shot up. Sunlight spilled through his window and bathed his bed in warm light. He was drenched in sweat. His heart raced and his exhales were sharp. Tears blurred his vision.

Àlkimos burst into the room and swiftly looked about. "What happened? Who ambushed you?" He exclaimed. Eluned wiped his face with his hand and gripped the sheets as he tried to collect himself.

Àlkimos slapped his forehead. "Well, I am an idiot." He sighed and walked to Eluned's bedside. "Night-terrors?" he gently asked. Eluned turned his head away and nodded. Àlkimos' face softened. "Ah, I see. Well, son—" he started, stopped, stood, and stretched. "Breakfast is ready when you are and—Oh! I almost forgot. Today you'll start earning your belongings back."

Eluned gaped at him. "So, I didn't lose my armor in the river?"

"No."

"My sword? Bow, quiver, and arrows—you have them?"

Àlkimos nodded.

Eluned leapt out of bed. "These things are inherently mine. I need them back!"

Àlkimos shook his head. "I'm sorry, Eluned. But it's customary for all men here to earn their weapons. As the chief, I can't play favorites. Surely you understand." He turned on his heel to leave. "Oh—And if you could put a shirt on before coming down to breakfast that'd be appreciated." He finished and left the room.

Eluned stumbled back like he had just been punched. "What am I going to do?" he moaned. He thought about the ruby he had seen in the memory. He felt like it had something to do with why his memories were vague. He slid on his tunic and went downstairs for breakfast. One thing was for certain, Zuriñe's cooking had no equals. She asked him how he slept and said she had been worried when she heard him cry out. Eluned assured her he was fine; but that was a lie. She was so full of kindness, and Eluned knew he would hold her in the highest honors for years to come.

After eating, Eluned went outside to meet with Adeena. One look at her scowl and he knew it was not optional for her to be there. She huffed; her face contorted in anger. She wore a black outfit, with silver armlets and shoulder armor. She bore only one sword, and it glinted a faint light. Àlkimos deemed that the village's terrain was not physically challenging enough although

Eluned begged to differ. He led them up to the mountains surrounding Haven.

They went every morning and stayed late into the night for several days. Eluned was determined and fiercely loyal to regaining his strength. Àlkimos was encouraging and bragged about him. Although, whenever Eluned would beat him, he seemed fiercely concerned. Adeena never spoke much. If Eluned happened to beat her she'd mumble "Take it easy." And left it at that. Eluned, despite his injuries, soon found he could handle a blade with all his previous skill.

He constantly thought about his sister's ruby and knew that he had always carried it on him, so it would be with his restrained possessions. Every day he remembered more and more, some good things and some loathsome. He had hoped that once he could remember everything and had his personality back, Adeena would respect him.

He was wrong.

It seemed quite the opposite. She avoided him unless they trained. One day, Adeena had refused to speak to Eluned, until he swung his sword the wrong way during training.

"You're doing it wrong," Adeena grunted, returning to her starting position.

Eluned slid his sword back into its scabbard and glared at her. "No—I'm not."

Adeena tossed her hair and rolled her eyes as she turned away. "You Elves are so insistent on your ways."

Eluned squeezed his eyes shut and tried to contain himself, but his rage boiled over. He grabbed her arm. "What's wrong with you?" he yelled. "It's like you saved me just to shame me later on—I'm sick of it! Tell me why!"

Adeena looked up at him, a twinge of fear in her eye. He was a tall, powerfully built Elf; with the height, skills, and strength of a god. Defiance replaced her fear. She sneered and tried to rip her arm out of his grasp.

"If you're as smart as you think you'll figure it out," she snapped.

Eluned grabbed her by both her shoulders and looked her in the eye. "No! I've let you push me around for too long, Bríghid. You're going to tell me why." He lifted her off the ground with ease and held her up to eye-level. He glared into her dark eyes, and he almost felt sorry for her. The fear in her eyes was of him. *He* was the one frightening her. Adeena looked away, shrugging off the fact that her feet weren't even touching the ground.

"Fine. You want to know, I'll tell you." She sucked in a deep breath. "I have your ruby. I thought if I kept it, you wouldn't remember who I was. I guess it must have worked, because among many things you can't seem to remember me. You know me Eluned. You almost killed me—twice."

Eluned's heart plummeted to his stomach. "What?"

Adeena rolled her eyes. "I'm only going to explain this once, so try and follow. That ruby your sister gave you possesses magical powers. All of your memories concerning her are attached to it, or I thought they were. I don't know how you were able to retrieve your memories of her, because I still possess that gem."

Eluned placed her down and stumbled back. He strained to remember Adeena but could not. "Why did I try to kill you?" he asked.

Adeena fidgeted with a piece of her hair. "Think about Milla, Eluned. What did she die of—what was going around at that time?"

Adrenaline surged through his veins as images flashed before his eyes. "The Plague." He breathed in realization. Adeena nodded and continued combing her fingers through her hair. "What does that have to do with me almost killing you?" he cried.

Adeena grunted in exasperation. "Look, not everybody in Haven had a nice, warm upbringing like the Chief, alright? Some of us had to do wicked, dirty jobs just to put food on the table!"

She slapped her palm against the side of her head. "*Think,* you Meathead!" She screamed.

Eluned's breathing became empty and desperate. Vague echoes of him roaring in hatred and a woman screaming for mercy clouded his thoughts. "You did something to me—to my family." Eluned managed.

Adeena coiled back and rested her hand on the hilt of her sword.

"Who were you before coming to Haven?" he growled.

Adeena tensed. "I followed no king's orders but worked for whichever offered the most pay," she uttered.

"Adeena Bríghid—"

"Y—Yes?"

"What were you?"

She shut her eyes and her breathing grew weak, shaky.

"It doesn't mean I'm proud of what I did—I just happened to know how to do what they asked me to."

Eluned grabbed her hand and stared at her. "I don't care. I *have* to know, and you need to tell me."

Adeena looked away. "I—I can't tell you."

Eluned took on a gentler tone and exhaled. "Yes, you can, Adeena."

"Eluned."

"Adeena, you can tell me."

She drew a long breath and looked him in the eye. She drew her sword, leapt into the air, and pinned Eluned to the ground. He laid in the long grass in amazement but refused to fight back.

"What's this supposed to mean?"

"Fight me like the knight you are and find out!" She spun her weapon around in her hands, daring him.

Eluned stood and drew his sword. It gleamed and reflected the sunlight. "If what you say is true, then I cannot fight you." He cast down his sword and glared at her.

Adeena braced her feet, expecting him to charge.

"If I tried to kill you twice, I have lost my honor, and there is no honor in unnecessary bloodshed."

Adeena's eyes widened. "N—No. This—This isn't how things should be." Her legs quivered and she fell to the ground.

Eluned raised an eyebrow. "So, you do have feelings?"

Adeena snorted. "Just shut up and take the ruby." She pulled the glowing gem out of a pocket in her cloak and tossed it to Eluned. He caught it and she squeezed her eyes shut. "Have mercy," she whispered under her breath.

Eluned rubbed his fingers across the smooth surface of the ruby. He blinked and was borne away by a flood of memories not his own.

Chapter V

"Are your orders quite clear, my devoted assassin?"

King Morem sat on his throne of obsidian with a golden crown atop his head. His thick black hair fell neatly across his shoulders, framing his pale, sunken face. A woman, cloaked in black with a mask pulled up over her face, clutched a bottle filled with a glowing, red liquid.

"Yes, My Lord."

"Will it take long to end her?"

"Yes, Sire."

"Will she suffer?"

"Indeed."

Morem leaned back and exhaled through pursed lips. "Good," he whispered. "The Elves shall pay at last. Our score will be settled. Is your hatred for them still strong?"

"Surely it is, Sire. What if anyone spots me doing the deed?"

Morem snickered and fingered his gold signet ring. "This is a stealth mission; try not to be seen. Kill anyone who interferes." He waved his hand and the woman stood up. "Show no mercy, Adeena Rowan."

Adeena slid the potion into a small pouch in her black leather belt and bowed her head. She turned and ran out of the throne room. Her feet made no sound as she made her way out of the palace, and mounted her horse to ride to Rinon, the Woodland Realm. A malicious smile pricked at the corners of her mouth envisioning the heavy payload,

She would be set for life.

The wind brushed against her face as she rode through the night, but it didn't bother her. Nothing did. She was empty and numb. She felt nothing, sad or joyful. A small voice inside her still begged and pleaded for her to think again, but she refused. Thinking had been what had gotten her life messed up in the first place. Her older sister, Claire had been sweet, kind, beautiful, and gullible. She had been foolish enough to think there were good people in the world. Her naivete would make Adeena think twice before trusting anyone—or anything.

The road to Rinon was long and winding—a three-day ride, but her horse was swift and she was light. She reviewed this plan over and over again. All she had to do was slip inside the royal palace, pour the poison in the Princess's cup, and return to collect her bounty.

Why Morem wanted a fourteen-year-old girl dead, she had no idea—nor did she care. She assumed it was personal, or political. Soon, the castle gates of Rinon loomed over the horizon, she tied her horse's bonds to a nearby oak tree. She ran through the thickets as swift and silent as a shadow. The ivory gates that lead into the city were heavily guarded by well-trained soldiers. Adeena decided to avoid the bother of checking in by going under them, by way of the Grey River. She walked with the cover of darkness like a cloak around her in the woods surrounding the walls, until she found the barred gap in it where the Grey River ran through the city.

She stood at the bank, debating on the merits of entering via the river. *What other way was there?*

She held her breath and dove into the cold water. Her slender frame easily slid in between the widely positioned bars and into the city. She pierced the surface silently and gasped in air. She swam to the shore and crawled up onto dry land. The flourishing city of light and peace was asleep, and Adeena sighed in relief. She darted about the outskirts of the city, avoiding the guards, and found one of the towers connected to the palace. Scanning the tower, she noticed a window that was open. Crawling up to it, she calculated she'd be able to slide right through. She leapt up and wriggled inside. She grinned with success when her feet hit the carpeted floor.

The Palace of Trigon was enormous, but Adeena had studied detailed drawings of every hall and corridor. She knew the way. She avoided all of the guards and made her way up winding stairways that lead to the royal chambers. Her heart stopped and she whipped out a dagger when she saw one of the bedroom doors open. She stealthily flattened herself against the wall and listened to a hushed voice echoing from the room.

Curiosity overtook her and she moved to the doorframe.

The King's Chambers. King Loraniss knelt in front of an open window with his hands folded, fervently praying. Adeena leaned in to hear.

"I know not what ails him, nor how to help him. Dear Maker, Morem has been overtaken by something greater than what lies in the world of mortal men. I—I want so much to save him. Not even a fortnight ago, I saw him and the wretched state in which he now lies. I believe it's because of his wife's recent death, but he has a son! Oh, Mighty, Ancient One, he cannot see the monster he has become." He sighed and covered his head with his hands.

Adeena rolled her eyes and darted across the hallway where her victim lay peacefully sleeping. She slowly slid the door open. Gossip said that whenever the princess awoke in the morning, she drank a glass of water. She saw the glass on a small nightstand by her bed.

Once in the water, my poison will become odorless, tasteless, and colorless, Adeena thought. She crept through Milla's room. *It will mimic symptoms of the Plague.*

Adeena paused, standing over the prone form like a wraith. Milla was young, flourishing in beauty. Her long, brown hair lay across her pillow in waves. Adeena peered at her sweet face, calm and slack in sleep. She breathed peacefully and comfortably, unaware of the demon preparing to strike.

I'm sorry, Princess, Adeena thought as she poured the poison, *but fifty-thousand Royal Pounds, is fifty-thousand Royal Pounds.*

She replaced the vial in her pouch and, for a moment, felt a twinge of regret. She resembled her sister, Clair. Adeena shook her head and hardened her face.

The job is done, there's no turning back. She turned her back on Milla and left.

჻჻჻჻჻჻჻჻

Princess Milla died of the Plague a month later. Her older brothers and sister fell into a great state of mourning, except Eluned. Eluned turned bitter. His world narrowed down to revenge. Eluned found a cork on the floor of Milla's bedroom the day she fell ill and immediately knew it was not the Plague. He sought out the finest poison makers in the Elven Realms, but none of them were capable of making something to mimic the Plague's symptoms. Eluned searched for months, tracking down the finest poison makers on the black market. None of them were capable of mimicking the plague...but all knew someone who could. They all pointed to Adeena Rowland. Eluned chased her down to kill her, to seek revenge for what she did to him and his family. Loraniss found him first and stopped him. He said there was no honor in blood. Adeena went free and Eluned went home, ashamed.

჻჻჻჻჻჻჻჻

Eluned's knees buckled, and Adeena continued to crawl away. He heaved and pressed his hand to his forehead. "It was you," he croaked. He turned to face her, fury burning in his eyes. "You killed her!"

Adeena bowed with her face to the ground. "Please!" she pleaded. "I know it was wrong! I know now what an awful person I was!"

Eluned's hands grew hot and closed around the hilt of his sword. "After what you did you expect me to let you live?"

Adeena trembled. "I—I—I was just trying to live!"

Eluned reached down, grabbed her by the collar of her tunic, and lifted her up. She yelped in surprise and tried to rip his hands away. Eluned raised his sword and gritted his teeth.

"You almost drove me mad with grief and helped Morem tear my family apart. For what? Fifty-thousand pounds?"

"Loraniss should never have stopped me from giving you what you deserve!" he screamed. "She was a child!"

Adeena gasped in air. "I know," she sniveled. She looked at him, and the cover that had been veiling her eyes collapsed. Eluned saw past her darkness. Adeena transformed into a small, lonely, terrified girl.

His hands shook and he forced his anger to be fuel to strike down his enemy, but he could not. His sword clanged to the ground.

Adeena rubbed her neck and groveled at his feet. "I—I—I never wanted to keep the ruby. Not after I found out you could remember things anyway. I promise it was nothing personal, it was just—"

"*Business*!" Eluned yelled. His voice echoed, and he felt a surge of power.

Adeena shrank back.

He sank to the ground and covered his face with his hand. "You took my sister away from me. If it had been money, a sword, or even if you had wounded me that would be fine! Money can be recollected, swords can be reforged, wounds can heal, But Milla! You took away something I could never get back." He bit his lip. Tears stung his eyes. He saw everything clearly, and it made life even harder.

He saw the kind face of Loraniss, who had never failed to guide him, and be gentle in his strength. He remembered Ayleth, who was so wise and offered him council that he often rejected. Thorsten had always been a sweet soul, never afraid to do what was right. He could vividly recall Milla's sweet grace, which had never failed to comfort him.

Adeena hugged herself and let her head fall against her chest.

Eluned let the tears silently descend his cheeks, no longer caring that she was present.

"Adeena Rowland? What else are you not telling me?"

Chapter VI

Eluned and Adeena did not speak for three weeks. Adeena spent the time in the mountains, keeping watch over the growing threat of the black castle. Eluned confined himself to his bedroom, refusing to see anyone or be comforted. He felt numb and distant from reality. He ran his fingers over the smooth, gold lettering of his family history and traced them over, and over again. He was a coward. He had abandoned his people and his family. Eluned had two nephews and a niece out there somewhere. He feared they suffered. He pulled his knees up to his chest and drew a long breath. He did not hate Adeena, no matter how hard he tried to convince himself he did. He did not blame anybody for what had happened besides himself.

"Adeena was just lost," He dismally murmured. "I was out for blood."

A soft knock sounded at the door. "Eluned? Are you in there, son?"

Eluned wanted to be with Àlkimos and Zuriñe more than ever; they were the closest thing he had to family now. He sighed and Àlkimos took that as permission to enter. He and Zuriñe walked in and sat with him on his bed. Zuriñe's dark hair was pulled into a braided bun in the back of her head, and her bright eyes reflected a sad kind of light.

"I'm so sorry, Eluned. That doesn't seem like enough to say about something like this," she sympathized. Àlkimos clapped Eluned's shoulder and looked him in the eyes. Eluned lifted his head up.

"Do you want to perform the traditional Elvish custom for grief? It might help provide some closure." Àlkimos kindly offered.

Eluned bit his lip and swallowed back a sob. "Maybe— maybe sometime soon. I still just—" His voice cracked with held back emotion. "I can't believe they're gone," he finished, barely above a whisper.

Àlkimos looked at him with sympathy. "Whenever you're ready, lad. But—Adeena wants to talk to you."

He cringed at the sound of her name. "Really," he scoffed. "Why on earth would she want to talk to me?"

Zuriñe and Àlkimos exchanged sad glances. "You never wondered why she became an assassin?" Àlkimos prodded.

Eluned chewed his lip and shook his head.

"She knows your story, Eluned, it's about time you knew hers," he said.

Eluned straightened his back and pursed his lips. "You're right, per usual," he admitted. He slid off the bed, put on his tunic and donned his armor. Àlkimos and Zuriñe smiled and got off the bed. They headed for the door, but Eluned stopped them.

"Thank you for everything." He said and smiled. Zuriñe caressed his cheek, and Àlkimos squeezed his shoulder. They were so much like his parents; that was the only reason he had not run-away weeks ago. He finished strapping his scabbard to his belt and sighed. He knew exactly where to find Adeena.

He walked out into the crisp morning air and noticed everything was quiet. *Too quiet.* No children ran about outside, and all the houses were shuttered. Eluned eased his hand down and rested it by his sword. He steadily walked up the hills and around the creeping mountain passes. He followed the trail that led to the mountain face where they always stood guard. He came around the corner entering the area, and heard a low, soft voice carried on the breeze. Eluned crouched down and stained to hear it better.

It was Adeena.

She sat, curled up with her hair hanging loose, blowing in the mountain breeze. Her eyes were fixed straight ahead on the dark castle. Her face was fair, but solemn. Eluned felt a twinge of compassion and curiosity at the tears in her eyes. He realized he was staring, and blushed.

"Adeena," he called, clearing his throat. "Are you up here?" Adeena quickly stood.

"Um, yes," she sniffed, and wiped her face with the end of her sleeve.

Eluned emerged from his hiding place. *She looks more distraught than I thought.* "I was told you wanted to speak with me?" He cleared his throat again and shook off the fact that he found her attractive with her hair down. Adeena bit her thumbnail and motioned for him to sit on the ledge with her. He eased himself down in the grass, watching the grey clouds roll across the sky.

"I'm sorry, Adeena," Eluned sighed. "I let my anger take control of me. I—I want you to know that—" He gritted his teeth with the force of the words he knew he had to say. "I want you to know that I forgive you."

Adeena's eyes widened. "Oh." Her lower lip trembled. "You shouldn't forgive me. I don't deserve it."

"Do any of us?"

"You don't know what an awful person I am!"

Eluned softened his face. "Hey, I've done some bad things, too. You're not the only one who—"

"Why do you have to be this way!" she yelled. "Every time I see you, you just make me feel more alone!" She shut her eyes and cried. Eluned's shocked mind raced for words to say... but found nothing. He merely rubbed her shoulders out of instinct, not knowing what else to do. She choked and grabbed his hand. Eluned blushed but did not jerk away.

"I—I saved you, because my sister told me to," she said.

"Your dead sister told you to save me?" he asked, confused.

Adeena struggled to speak. Her words tumbled between sobs. "My older sister, Clair and I were orphaned when we were younger. We were taken in by my grandmother, not as children but as slaves. I couldn't keep living that way, so I told Clair to pack one day, and we left. We went to the capitol of Mordrien—

Kazgül Varen—to try and find work. Oh, Clair was beautiful, and outgoing. She could sing and dance really well, too. She made lots of money dancing on street corners and started to work her way up in society. We eventually had a house, and she got paid a fair amount. I didn't care what she did as long as she was safe and happy. Meanwhile I fell in with—with a bad group of people. They were like a dark armored force that controlled the underside of the capitol. They needed me as bait for a mission to break into Morem's palace, take the recipe for a poison, and bring it to them. They didn't tell me I was going to be the bait; I overheard them."

She paused and Eluned furrowed his brow in sympathy.

"I stole the poison," she continued. "We started to make it and sell it on the black market. I got paid well, and Clair never asked any questions. I wish now that she had. She got to the point where the new king—Morem—wanted her to come sing for him on his coronation day. He kept asking and asking; until it was merely visits for them to socialize. While they courted, I became an assassin. Soon, Morem and Clair were married, but Morem only ever talked to me when he was asking about my job. No one was supposed to know, but he did. Clair died in childbirth with her first son, my nephew, Marlōs. I—I fled the castle after he was born. I didn't want more attachment that would just kill me later on. I didn't ever feel anything besides bitterness. I let it grow and fester, like the poisons I made." She shook her head. "I heard her voice out on the banks of The Grey River one day, urging me to save you." She let out a long sigh. "So here we are. I, too, abandoned my family."

Eluned squeezed her hand to comfort her.

"Utterly unworthy of love." She scorned and took her hand away. Eluned shook his head and his eyes wondered to the distant horizon. A knew passion kindled inside of him.

"That's it." Eluned declared, jumping to his feet. "This snake must be destroyed." Adeena gaped at him. "You don't mean—"

"Yes, I do, Adeena! Morem's hurt too many people. I will no longer stand by and watch while he makes people suffer!" He turned his back on Adeena and took off down the pass.

Chapter VII

Alkimos refused to aid Eluned in killing Morem. "Two wrongs don't make a right." He had cautioned Eluned. He said as long as Morem never found out the Eluned was in Haven, his fury would never be unleashed. Eluned knew better and confessed this to the men of Haven. If word got out that his body had never been found, he would send scouts into the farthest reaches of the world. Morem would march his troops on the village and burn it to the ground...just like Rinon.

Eluned felt guilty.

He had brought the news of doom on his heels to these kind people. He knew who he was now. He knew of his past, his family, and his city...perhaps he should leave. He knew Morem was ruthless and cold. He would kill everyone. Eluned refused to let this happen...he would not let more innocent lives be taken on his watch. He made up his mind one night, after long hours of discussion with the village Elders, to go and confront Morem himself.

Yes. He thought. *And this way, no innocent blood will be shed.*

After what he thought was his last dinner in the presence of Zuriñe, Àlkimos, and Twyla, he thanked them dearly. He pulled them into his armor-clad arms and hugged them tightly. Àlkimos looked confused and sad...but said nothing. Eluned gathered his few belongings, once night had fallen, and made sure his ruby was secure. He slipped out of the house, and quietly shut the door. He tightened his jaw and began to head down the trails to the exit out of the mountains.

He trod lightly, and as he came to where the exiting path rose over Haven, his heart longed to stay. He knew he could not. He turned around and came face-to-face with Adeena.

"I—" He found himself unable to speak. Adeena shook her head and folded her arms.

"You can't fight him alone."

"I have to."

"No, you don't."

"I must avenge my family."

"Being angry will get you nowhere."

Eluned huffed. "What right have you to say these things?" Adeena bit her lip and looked down, and Eluned immediately felt sorry for what he said. She asked for him to follow her up the mountain pass, and he did.

"You're right," She agreed. "But I don't just let my walls down for anyone." In Eluned's favorite spot on the mountain, the moonlight bathed the rock face in silver light. Adeena sat cross-legged and pulled out her dagger. Eluned cocked his head and sat beside her.

"I-I choose the life I have been given...and I want to heal." She said, softly. "I know I need to earn your trust, and affection. I *need* to heal...but I cannot do it alone." Eluned saw her blink away tears. He nodded, knowing what they were going to do.

He drew his sword, and gathered his long, black hair in his hand. Adeena let down hers and did the same. Eluned shut his eyes, gritted his teeth, and sliced his blade through his hair below the ears, and it fell to the ground.

Adeena had done the same.

Eluned exhaled, now feeling a giant weight had been lifted from his shoulder. Eluned laid his hand on Adeena's shoulder.

"Thank you," she said, her lower lip trembling. "I don't deserve this honor."

Eluned knew how she felt. They had performed the Elvish custom for grief...and she'd embraced her Elven blood.

"We...both need to heal in our own ways." He said, grinning.

"Well, aren't you going to fight Morem?" Adeena asked, quietly. "Isn't this goodbye?"

Eluned exhaled and looked at her.

"No," He exhaled. "I'm going back to Haven to protect my family... and I'm going to defend my home. I will not abandon these people—nor you, Adeena."

They stood and started to walk down the trail together in the moonlight.

"You seem like you'd be a good hunting partner." Adeena mentioned after a while. Eluned grinned. "Was that sarcasm?" He asked. Adeena walked ahead of him.

"Hey, if you take it as an insult that's on you." She shrugged. Eluned ran to catch up with her.

"Adeena," He quietly started. Adeena put a finger to his lips. "I know." She said gently. "But please...call me Addy." And for the first time, Adeena smiled. She punched his shoulder.

"Bet I'm faster than you!" She taunted. "Snail spawn!" Eluned laughed. "You can dream!" He cried, and took off down the pass to Haven, where he would dwell for many, many years to come.

THE PROTECTOR'S GUARDIAN

Ben Berwick

The drawbridge fell with a sharp clatter. Gasps from all around him echoed along the cold stone walls.

"We are breached!" One portly fellow yelled, dropping his golden goblet and spilling the rich red wine all over the uneven cobbles beneath him.

"Get the Lord out of here!" a second gruff voice commanded. He shot the lone figure standing in front of the gate a firm gaze. "Sir Carmichael, did you lower the drawbridge?" the man asked.

Carmichael shook his head. "No, but—" he gestured to his sword, dripping scarlet. "I have dispatched the cad who did." At Carmichael's feet lay the body of a young man, dressed in a dirty, torn shirt and ragged trousers. His eyes held the glassy look of death, and blood pooled underneath him.

The man met Carmichael's eyes and nodded in grim understanding. "I take it we cannot raise the drawbridge now?"

"No, Sir Brace, we cannot. This—boy," Carmichael briefly closed his eyes, "cut the ropes. He may be dressed as one of the servants, but his hair is too clean, and his hands too soft, he must have been sent as a saboteur."

Brace saw the dread in the other man's bright blue eyes. "If he has done this now, it must mean—"

Carmichael tilted his head. "Yes. It is time. Prepare your men, and man the battlements. Oh, and impress upon the Lord and his family that they must go."

The older man ran a hand over his bare scalp. "He will not want to leave his comfortable trappings."

"His *comfortable trappings* will be burned to the ground, with him among them, if he does not leave," Carmichael replied sternly. "You know that as well as I do, Sir Brace."

Brace ignored the sudden and sharp cold wind that billowed in through the gate and considered Carmichael's words for a moment. "Very well. I will go and have them prepare. How long do you think we have?"

"I would wager virtually no time, Sir Brace. We are fortunate their spy did not sabotage the gate as well, or we might already be under attack. As it is I—"

Carmichael was cut off by cries and exclamations from the battlements. His eyes snapped to Brace and both men understood.

"They are here. Grab your armour," Carmichael instructed. "And prepare for battle!"

Brace did not need to be told twice. He broke into a brisk jog and dodged several noblemen and women and their staffs as he headed for the Lord's chamber. His knuckles rapped the door twice and he did not wait to be invited in. Dirty boots pressed mud and grime into the expensive red carpet and the Lord shot him a repugnant glare, but Brace ignored it.

"Lord Whesk, we are under attack. The moment we feared is at hand and we must go."

Lord Whesk narrowed his aging grey eyes at the knight. "This is my home. I will not abandon it at the first sign of danger."

"My Lord, you know as well as I do if the enemy takes what they have come for, no one, anywhere, will ever be free again. They will slaughter everyone here to get their prize, including your children. You must go."

Whesk lovingly stared at the tapestries, paintings and golden trinkets, and fixed his longing gaze upon his old walnut wardrobe. "I will need provisions."

Brace drew upon all his discipline to avoid snapping. "My Lord, we have no time. I shall have the chef prepare some food for your journey, and the maids are getting your children ready, now get the Protector and get ready to leave!"

The lord scowled, and he stomped his bloated legs in the direction of his beautiful dresser. He reached for a small, battered wooden box and flipped it open.

Under the firelight, the red gem nestled upon velvet padding and cast a haunting glow. Brace caught the briefest of glimpses at the fist-sized jewel before it vanished into a straw bag.

"There, now let us see to the pantry, and then we can go."

After all this time does he still *not understand what he has?*

Brace nodded and led the way.

๛   ๛

Carmichael hated his armour, but he had to admit the chilly autumn air did not perturb him. His chainmail rattled and his breastplate warmed under the heat of the burning torches, and he tightly gripped the hilt of his broadsword as figures emerged from the tree line. At first all he could make out were a handful of armoured troops. He then caught glimpse of the unwelcome twin-dragon banner. His teeth gnashed together, and he suppressed the urge to spit, which would not prove wise in his helmet.

"At least they haven't brought ballistae or catapults," he muttered to himself. He drew his sword and held it in front of his face. "We march upon the fields, and we hold the line."

The frightened youthful faces that surrounded him did Carmichael's confidence no favours, but he gave them credit and a courteous nod as they strode forward with him, across the drawbridge and out into the dwindling sunlight. The green dragons on the banners became clearer.

"I wonder if Vorminside has sent their champion?" one scruffy man in loose chainmail asked aloud.

Carmichael did not look at him. "If they have, he will die here," he softly uttered. "Spread out and form ranks!" His voice rose to carry his orders, and he raised his sword high into the air. "Archers, ready!"

The enemy kept coming. They appeared to be holding for the perfect moment to charge forward, as though waiting – or goading – him into a rash action. Carmichael waited, as much as it annoyed him. Armour noisily clunked, stinging his ears. The foe's steel became all-too apparent.

"Ready!" he cried. The enemy had to have heard him, but their steady march remained unbroken.

"Loose!"

His sword swept downward. The first wave of arrows rained down towards the enemy. Carmichael wished he had been granted time to prepare more men; several arrows went astray, and he lacked the numbers as it was. Nonetheless several soldiers fell, but the remainder of the large force kept going, and then Carmichael heard the rich, arrogant voice of their commander.

"Break through!"

The hordes of Vorminside started to run, even as another wave of arrows sailed into their ranks. It pleased Carmichael to see the second salvo had more accuracy than the first, but they could not hope to get in a third round before the enemy reached his lines. Soldiers roared and others screamed as steel clashed against steel. Bodies pressed together in a sudden writhing throng of fear, aggression, and death.

Carmichael's gleaming blade grew stained with the rusty blood of any soul unfortunate enough to get close. Where his sword could not directly puncture armour it acted as a devastating club, smashing aside would-be killers. His nostrils filled with the stench of blood and sweat and the peaty earth around him, and as he brought his sword sharply across the face of a hapless soldier, Carmichael hoped he would survive long enough to know Brace and his charges had escaped.

⟳   ⟲

Brace held the reigns tightly and kept his horse heading away from the pained, angry cries coming from the castle. Had he not been escorting the Lord's carriage, he could have directed his beautiful jet-black Morgan horse into a powerful gallop, but he held her pace back.

"Easy girl," he patted her head. He felt her urge to unleash her power, and he knew all-too-well how perceptive horses could be of human emotions. "Easy Izzy, it's alright girl."

To his right and back came a mottled brown and white gypsy horse, complete with a magnificent white mane. The animal bore the weight of a pale young woman in an inconveniently long cream gown and several satchels of supplies. Brace smiled at the woman—girl really—with reassurance.

"Things will be alright, you'll see. With each second we move we become harder for Vorminside to track us."

His kindly voice did not appear to ease the girl's worry. She said nothing and kept her eyes on the road ahead.

Brace shot a look over his shoulder. The carriage came next, pulled by another, slightly bigger gypsy horse, that had flecks of black in his mane. He wondered what the Lord made of the rickety old servant's carriage. An image of the spoilt Lord being rattled like a pea in a pod brought a smile to his face.

He glanced to the sky. The sun had almost faded completely, and few torches up ahead had been lit. The thick trees on either side of the small road could hide a multitude of assassins, and they would never know until arrows and blades sliced their skin. Brace operated on protective instinct and had his horse drift slightly closer to the carriage.

"How long is this insufferable journey going to take?" Whesk's gruff voice whined over the clomping of hooves and the rattle of wooden wheels.

"As long as it takes, Sire." The guard within the carriage firmly answered. Brace smiled again.

"Well, I still don't see why my children and I couldn't travel in some form of comfort," Whesk huffed.

"Because, Sire, a bright golden carriage would attract all kinds of attention, the opposite of what we want." Brace made a note to reward the guard somehow, both for enduring travelling in the carriage and for his brisk answers.

He heard no further responses from Whesk, though Brace could not decide if that was a good thing. He left matters in the carriage alone and brought his horse back to the servant. The girl's round, plain face continued to hold fear, and he felt ashamed of himself for being unable to cure it.

"Where are we going?" she meekly asked. Her voice held a hind of awe.

"For the river. This escape was planned many months ago, in secret, so there should be a boat waiting for us."

The girl somehow managed to look even more concerned. "I do not do well on boats."

"Do not fear, it is a sturdy craft. What is your name?" Brace asked.

"Cristina," the girl replied. "I am Cristina."

"It is good to make your acquaintance, Christina. I am sorry you have been brought into this. Lord Whesk insisted upon your presence."

"It is quite alright," Cristina replied. She brushed a lock of brown hair from her eyes. "I would prefer to be here than at the castle right now."

Brace sagely nodded. "I understand."

৯   ৶

The castle's defenders fell back across the drawbridge, but Carmichael knew the reprieve was only temporary. Vorminside's ranks reasserted themselves and prepared to storm the narrow chokepoint, and he saw no means of slowing them, much less halting them.

"What do we do, sir?" A scrawny man, caked in earth and blood, asked. Carmichael wondered of his own appearance.

"We pray for an honourable and quick death." He knew his words would be cold comfort, but he owed his men honesty. "But not before we take as many of these bastards with us!" He defiantly cried. His exclamation was greeted with a roar of matching determination. *At least they have courage.*

"They have a catapult!" someone yelled from the battlements. "It approaches!"

Carmichael closed his eyes, suddenly aware of how tired he felt. His muscles ached and his soul hurt. "We will evacuate as many of the women and children as we can, as quickly as we can, but if they now bring catapults, the castle is most certainly lost."

The men around him exchanged nervous, uncertain stares. He saw their minds at work, as they considered abandoning everything they had sworn to protect.

"As long as the people of Clearwater remain together, what we are and what we stand for also remains." Carmichael said. "Though, I use *we* in a metaphorical sense. Those of us gathered here, we *will* buy our loved ones time. Now is the time to be fearless."

From outside the walls, they heard the cries and yells of men preparing to launch chunks of masonry. Carmichael gripped his sword tighter. "Prepare yourselves."

The first boulder smashed through the western-most battlement and Carmichael's world slowed. Pieces of masonry and woodwork sprayed in all directions. Shards pierced armour and flesh of the brave souls around him. His ears stung from their cries of pain.

He had no time to process the wanton destruction. Within moments Vorminside's swarms climbed through the rubble, stepping over the bodies of fallen archers. Carmichael snarled and led the race to meet them. His blade glinted under the torch lights, and he took a perverse pleasure in how it was the final sight for so many of the enemy's ranks. He took less joy at the sight of so many of his own, falling to the blades of the enemy. His ears and eyes kept him alert and moving and he swept beyond the reach of many a Vorminside sword, until his luck deserted him.

A heavy metal blade smashed against his breastplate and sent him sprawling onto the cold cobbles. He quickly brought his weapon back up, barely in time to prevent himself from being eviscerated. He flicked his sword to the left, sending his assailant to the side.

Carmichael quickly righted himself and snarled. He could not see the face of the other man behind the grill, but somehow he knew.

"Sir Marvin."

The fighting around them seemed to pull away, and pushed deeper into the castle, as though everyone had granted Carmichael space. He glanced at one of the purple tapestries on the wall to his left, then looked back to his opponent.

"Sir Carmichael." A rich, elegant voice responded. "I had hoped to find you alive."

Carmichael placed both hands upon the hilt of his blade. "So, you might have the pleasure of killing me yourself?"

"The thought had occurred to me." Marvin rotated his sword. "Though in truth, Sir Carmichael, I had hoped you could be persuaded to give up this foolish errand."

"I will never give up on what is right," Carmichael shot back.

"Still so firmly wedded to outdated concepts I see." Marvin's voice dripped with contempt. "These people have made you soft."

"You'll find out just how soft I am." Carmichael stepped forward and lunged. Marvin blocked with ease and swung his own sword for Carmichael's neck. Carmichael took a step back and watched the swipe slice through the old tapestry. He grabbed the torn fabric, pulled it down, and tossed it over Marvin. The dark knight yelled in annoyance. His cry was cut short by a hefty boot to the stomach, and he stumbled backward over the cobbles to land heavily on his back.

Carmichael moved to finish his foe off, but Marvin's instincts remained as honed as his own. The other knight's sword came up vertically, denying Carmichael's attempt at a decisive slice through the midriff. He grunted as Marvin's blade pushed him back and took a careful step backwards as Marvin threw off the ruined cloth and came for him once again.

"We are born to rule, to lead, not to cower in backwaters such as this. You are worthy of so much more," Marvin implored.

"You are worthy of nothing," Carmichael replied, "when you stand for nothing."

Marvin's response to the rebuke was to growl and launch a swift flurry of attacks that drove Carmichael towards the passageway behind them. One errant strike sliced through the torch where Carmichael's head had been, and he watched the flames as they licked the collection of dust and dirt on the cold floor. He could not shake the image of Lucifer moving towards him as Marvin pressed his assault. The sharp ping of metal upon stone hurt his ears as he retreated.

His blade clanged against Marvin's, and he pushed hard to grant himself a moment to grab at the bronze handle behind him. Carmichael yanked the ringed handle hard, and the heavy wooden door swung out. Right before Marvin could get back into range Carmichael entered the room beyond.

Behind Carmichael stood a large and long oak dining table. Beyond the smell of blood and fear, he smelled and almost tasted the hastily abandoned chicken, beef, and other foods he could not pin down. His stomach heaved and he suppressed the sudden and unpleasant sensation.

Marvin strode forward and glanced around the cavernous dining hall. He shook his head as he took in everything.

"So much gold and silver, so much opulence, and none of it is yours, when it should have been."

"Enough!" Carmichael fired back. "You treat your people as subjects to serve you, not as human beings. You were anointed to be a protector, not a tyrant!"

Marvin lowered his sword until the tip pointed at Carmichael's heart. "You serve a lord who genuinely believes his blood grants him the power—nay ability—to rule. He has stumbled and staggered through his reign and led his people to ruin. Why defend him?"

"I do not defend *him*. I defend his people. People you would slaughter as a casual afterthought if they do not pledge allegiance. We both know what you truly seek."

Marvin snorted through his helmet. "If I had the Protector, I would make this world safe. You have squandered its power."

Carmichael took his turn to sneer. "You would make this world safe for you, and terrible for everyone else."

Marvin's answer was to swing his sword down, aiming to cleave Carmichael down the middle. Carmichael swiped the incoming attack to one side and both knights watched the sword slice clean through the still-glistening suckling pig that sat on the table. Vegetables scattered everywhere and Carmichael felt tomatoes and carrots squish under his boots. He grimaced.

Marvin did not give him the time to consider his discomfort. His sword swung back. Carmichael easily deflected and pushed Marvin's weapon back upon the table. Fine silver and elaborate platters of fruit and smoked meats erupted from the table in protest. Carmichael stepped forward and drove his fist into Marvin's face. Armour clashed with armour. Carmichael took a grim satisfaction from Marvin's staggered step backwards.

He did not give his adversary time to recover. Another slash met Marvin's blade. Carmichael twisted from the hips and sent Marvin's weapon sliding across the stones. Another punch sent Marvin himself to the floor. Carmichael pressed his advantage. His hands brought his sword up and over Marvin's heart.

"Do it!" Marvin spat. "Or will you take the coward's way out, as always?"

Carmichael brought his body down to pin Marvin. "Damn you!" He closed his eyes and forced his sword down as hard as he could. He felt Marvin's armour buckle and he swore he felt the tip of his blade puncture flesh. Marvin grunted in pain and shock and Carmichael felt his foe's body spasm. Marvin let out a horrid wet cough and struggled to bring a hand to his visor.

Carmichael understood and brought his hand up to raise the visor. He gazed into the dark brown eyes of his vanquished opponent.

"Look at you," Marvin's voice sounded weak. "So determined, so noble, as always. Your spirit always did carry you beyond your ability."

"Ha, even now, you cannot resist a barb." Carmichael's eyes stung and he silently prayed his voice would not crack. His gloved hand somehow came to hold Marvin's. "You were my brother in arms. I loved you like a brother."

Marvin's grip slackened. "Somehow—our paths— were not meant to be entwined."

"Why did you do all this?" Carmichael asked, a note of pleading in his voice. "Why would you throw away what you stood for?"

"I—made—my choices. You made—yours. I would— get to the river—and quickly. You know—why." Blood seeped from Marvin's lips; his body trembled. Carmichael's ears rung from the eerie death rattle. Once he pushed his tears and his rage and his grief down, he took in the smoke and the cries and the fear as his castle burned all around him, and his people scattered. He gave himself precisely one second to take in what was happening, then sprinted for the rear exit.

"Wait!" Brace half-whispered his command and brought his horse to a halt. He heard Whesk's indignant voice pipe up, and silently thanked the guard for shutting him up. He watched Cristina's horse carry the servant behind the carriage and watched the lights in the distance near the water.

"This cannot be—" He muttered softly to himself. *At least in the darkness the fools have lit lanterns.*

The lights drifted up and down the riverbank and winked in and out of view as they crossed behind trees. That made counting their numbers difficult. Brace swore under his breath. He could eliminate some of them, but they would quickly notice as their numbers thinned.

I have no choice. Brace slowly, carefully moved through the trees, and took extra care to avoid branches and tripping hazards. His eyes scanned the scene before him, and he focused on the nearest enemy. The young man's black hair hung long, past his shoulders, and covered loose black leather armour. For a moment, Brace allowed himself to feel pride in his adversary, and pity. They had ditched their noisy, clunky armour for stealth, but that did not help them as Brace slipped his dagger from its hilt and sunk it between the man's shoulder blades. Brace's hand clamped around the man's mouth to subdue his gurgle of pain and shock, and he gently lowered his enemy to the ground below.

He dared not take the torch. It would reflect far too much light off his own armour. He parked it behind the closest tree and snaked his way through the woodland toward the next Vorminside agent. Brace dispatched two more guards in quick succession before his luck failed him.

"Eric is not at his post!" Someone shouted in a gruff accent. Brace froze and prayed no one would head in his direction. The carriage had disappeared from his sight, hidden by the frustratingly thick foliage. All Brace could do was keep himself out of sight and hope Whesk did nothing stupid.

"Someone is here! Search the woods, find them!" The original gruff voice shouted through the trees. Answers came back to the unseen voice, and Brace made his choice.

He swept from his position and felt like an avenging angel as he moved upon the nearest hapless Vorminside agent. The older man's eyes widened for an instant before Brace's sword cut through him, and his lantern fell to the ground. It shattered and burst into flames that lit up Brace's armour. He became a beacon to the remaining Vorminside party, who converged on his location.

Fire licked at the grass and the earth, and at every twig and leaf upon the ground. Smoke stung Brace's eyes and tried to get into his lungs. Wispy clouds of the burning ground started to rise. Four enemy soldiers attempted to surround him.

Brace felt oddly focused. He could not understand it, but as the first assailant charged, he felt as though everything happened in slow-motion. His feet smoothly moved and, despite the thickening smoke, his eyes saw everything in perfect clarity. He brought his sword up and deflected the first attack. He pushed it to one side, and a moment later the second enemy soldier looked at him as though he were a wraith, for Brace had batted aside his sweeping strike as though he had fought a child.

The third attacker stepped forward. Brace sliced his blade through the second and countered the attack. His peripheral vision saw the fourth assailant move to attack from his left. He knew the first attacker had righted himself, even though he could not see him through the thickening smoke.

Two quick parries kept Brace alive, and he slammed the hilt of his sword into someone's nose as they rushed him. Another swift deflection was followed up with a quick, deadly thrust through another man's chest. Brace dared not wonder how he had found such prowess, and his final enemy agent fell as his sword swept around and cleaved his head from his body.

Brace turned, spotted the lord's carriage, and yelped in sudden and furious agony. Pain blossomed in his thigh. He looked down to see an arrow embedded in his flesh.

He dropped to the ground as another arrow whooshed through the night air. A quick scan of the trees confirmed his sudden fear; the carriage was ablaze, shining brightly within the forest, and he could see no sign of Lord Whesk, his children, his guard, or Cristina.

Flashes of movement drew his attention. People moved towards the river. He grunted, stood, and tightly gripped his hilt.

"Over there!" someone cried in a thick Vorminside accent. "Kill him!"

Brace readied himself. He breathed deeply and tried to prepare his mind for death. Three fresh, armoured soldiers came for him, their swords drawn and pointed in his direction.

They drew near, and Brace snarled as he took a step back and assumed a fighting stance. Sharp pangs of pain shot through his thigh and his leg became wet as blood seeped from his wound. He prayed he could remain conscious long enough to kill at least one of them. His opponents spread out and sprinted toward him. Brace's unfathomable sense of focus returned anew. The pain in his thigh vanished. His body and sword moved as one fluid object. He pushed aside each strike or evaded them, and he retaliated with deadly force. Two of his foes fell to his blade; the third stepped back with wide, fearful eyes at Brace's unreal movements.

Brace suddenly understood what had happened. Behind his last remaining enemy he saw Cristina. She held the hands of Lord Whesk's two young children, and they moved as swiftly as they could for the river's edge. In Cristina's grip was the Protector, and it *glowed*. Its light served as a beacon and Brace could not imagine how no one had seen them move through the trees. Of Lord Whesk himself, there was no sign, and Brace feared for the worst.

Additional Vorminside reinforcements snaked their way through the foliage, but Brace did not *want* to call out and warn Cristina. With practiced skills he stepped forward and, after a few sharp swipes, his sword pierced his enemy's flesh.

The pain returned and Brace winced as he chased after Cristina. Each step produced a dull ache that grew worse as he ran.

"Over here!" More cries carried through the forest and Brace could not shake off his increasing lethargy. He came to a small clearing and once again prepared himself to die in the name of Clearwater and his people.

"Sir Brace!" A familiar voice shot through the sounds of the forest. Brace looked up and saw Carmichael smash through the nearest pair of Vorminside soldiers. The knight stood beside his comrade.

"Sir Carmichael," Brace said, weariness in his voice. "Lord Whesk is dead, but his children and their servant are headed for the river. You will not be able to miss them, they have the Protector, and it is—active."

Carmichael sagely nodded. "I felt as though my horse had never been faster as I raced to get here. The further we get—"

"The more vulnerable I will become. I know." Brace shot out his hand. "Please, go, and protect them. The enemy has no idea it's here, but that will not remain the case forever. They cannot find it, but I will buy you time."

Carmichael shook his head. "I will not leave a brother-in-arms to die alone."

Brace's arm dropped to his side. "Yes, you will. You have a duty to Clearwater, not to me. I do not need to explain this to you of all people."

Vorminside troops began to close in. "Please, Sir Carmichael, you have to help them."

Carmichael looked away, toward the river, and back to Brace. His eyes were clear. "Damn you, I will go. Should we both survive, I will find you again my friend." This time, as Brace offered his hand, Carmichael took it and firmly shook it. "Send these fiends to Hell."

Brace smiled. "As many as I can."

The small boat had been undisturbed, but Cristina clutched two frightened children in her arms, and neither would get into the craft. Julian's mop of dark brown hair obscured his reddened eyes, and Sophia had silently and uncontrollably sobbed. Cristina prayed that no unsavoury elements found them, but her terror threatened to overwhelm her.

In one hand she gripped the Protector. She had not understood why Lord Whesk had pressed the fist-sized ruby into her hands, but she had seen the look of urgency in his eyes and resolution as well. It had been hard to respect the pompous, pampered lord, but he had sacrificed himself for his children, and had saved her life as well. Tears stung her own eyes as all the events of the last few hours came back to her at full force.

Fresh shouts and angry cries brought her attention back to their current predicament. The children huddled closer, and she gripped so tight she feared she would hurt them, but they did not complain.

A twig snapped and her head jerked in the sound's direction. A figure stepped out from behind a thick tree, and Cristina felt the tension melt from her body.

"Sir Carmichael!" she blurted, louder than she had intended. "Where—where is Sir Brace?"

Carmichael's eyes darkened. "He gave his life to save ours."

Fresh tears threatened Cristina's eyes. "I did not know him, but he seemed—kind."

"He was." Carmichael's voice seemed to crack for an instant. "Where is Lord Whesk?"

Cristina shook her head. "He, too, gave his life, to protect his children, as did your guard."

"Today has seen so much sacrifice. I will not let anyone else die tonight. Let us get on the boat and get out of here."

A small round face peered up at the knight. "Will you keep us safe?" the boy asked.

Carmichael knelt down to meet the boy's eyes. "Yes, Lord Whesk. I know you are not yet ready for the title, but you *are* my lord, and I pledge my sword and my fidelity to you. Come, let us go." He scooped the frightened boy and gently placed him onto the rickety boat, whilst Cristina guided the sister aboard. She paused before she got on herself and looked squarely at Carmichael.

"Sir, this would be better in your care." She held her hand out and offered the Protector.

The burly knight stared at the glowing red gemstone. "It has responded to you, so you should keep it. It will keep you and the children safe."

"I—" Cristina glanced at the children, who had nestled close to one another at the bow of the small rowboat. "I do not know if I can do this."

"You can, and you will," Carmichael sternly replied. "I know this is asking so much of you, but I cannot wield the power of the Protector, and Vorminside forces will be hunting for me. Even with the Protector, if I expose you to constant danger, it will be the death of all of us."

"Please, Sir Carmichael, I cannot do this alone!" Cristina quietly pleaded. "Will you at least stay with us until we reach safety?"

He hesitated for a moment, then nodded. He gestured for Cristina to board the boat, eased the craft off the crumbling soil, and into the water. Before it could get too far Carmichael leapt in and grabbed the oars. He furiously rowed and prayed they would reach the other side of the river without being spotted. Their luck held, and Carmichael ushered everyone out of the boat as quickly as possible before he dragged it up the bank and out of sight.

"I will accompany you to Borostone where I have friends who will look after you. Keep the Protector out of sight; never reveal it. It cannot fall into the wrong hands."

Cristina appeared to have something to say but closed her mouth instead. She held the hands of the children and together the small group followed Carmichael into the darkness.

They walked for what felt like an eternity. Carmichael's feet grew heavy, and he ached in places he did not realise he had. The lord's children whimpered and occasionally whined of how tired they were, but he gave them credit for how they had handled themselves in such terrifying circumstances. Cristina did not speak but walked side-by-side with the youngsters whilst he stayed a few steps ahead. To his dismay he became aware of how much he needed to bathe, and he wondered if the others had picked up on his odour. At every rustle and every snapped twig his nerves jangled. He kept his hand on the hilt of his sword, ready to unleash it at every opportunity.

His heartbeat slowed when it became apparent no assassins would come hurtling out of the trees, and his nerves settled at the sight of a cobbled road. "That is the path to Borostone. Come," Carmichael reached out a hand to the new Lord Whesk. "The children have walked a great deal, let us carry them for a time."

With the children in their arms, Carmichael and Cristina made quick progress. They shared mutual glances of exhaustion and Carmichael knew the young woman's feet must have ached as much as his. The uneven cobbles offered a slight relief from the lumpy earth and pebbles, but he had to suppress wincing at every step.

He did not know how long they walked, until he spied the first reddened tinge in the night sky ahead of him. The stars faded, pushed away by the rising sun, but dawn did not bring relief to Carmichael's mood. A quick look at Lord Whesk's sleeping face soothed his soul a bit, and he offered a reassuring smile to Cristina as the road grew smoother and signs of civilization appeared on the horizon.

He saw villagers in the distance, but Carmichael could not tell how many. His instincts kicked in and his hand drifted automatically to the hilt of his blade. He recognized that the oncoming people held no weapons, he let his hand drift back to his side.

"Hello there!" A light southern-English accent came to him from one of the travelers ahead. "Welcome to Borostone! Are you from Clearwater?"

Cristina shot Carmichael a wary stare as they neared the villagers. Carmichael smiled softly at her before responding.

"We are survivors from Clearwater, yes. We seek shelter."

The group ahead resolved into two middle-aged men with deeply weather-worn faces that offered sympathy.

"Some of your people came here earlier, warning they were attacked by Vorminside. They are being tended to, and we will look after them. If you will follow us, we take you to your people."

Exhaustion threatened Carmichael but he kept himself upright and extended his hand. "Thank you. I cannot express our gratitude enough."

The other man took his hand and shook it firmly. "I am sorry for what has happened to your people. I pray that you may get your revenge."

Carmichael slowly shook his head. "I have had my fill of blood for now. All I desire is a warm bath and a place to rest my head."

"You shall have it, brave knight, as will your companions." The man and his friend fell into step beside the weary travelers and escorted them all the way to the castle town's gate. When they arrived, the men did not follow them inside.

"Why do you pause?" Carmichael asked.

"There may yet be other survivors from Clearwater. We will keep searching until all hope is lost."

"For this you have my thanks." Carmichael shook the man's hand again. "And I know you have the thanks of the—the new Lord Whesk here."

"You are welcome." The man patted him on the shoulder. "Go, get some rest."

The man and his companion headed back down the road towards the forest, leaving Carmichael to consider the kindness of strangers. He glanced at Cristina, and together they walked into the castle town of Borostone. Wooden and stone houses and shops lined the path and up ahead lay the beautiful, tall castle of Borostone itself. Seven spires shot skyward, and a phalanx of soldiers armed with long, gleaming sharp pikes marched past them without so much as a single look. The town opened up into the city square and the castle's wrought-iron gate waited, along with a surprise.

Carmichael had never met Lord Borostone, but the tall, gangly man in the puffy red and purple velvet jacket flanked by a pair of knights in beautifully polished armour *had* to be the lord.

"Sir knight, welcome to Borostone Castle." The lord's blue eyes seemed to shine. "Lord Whesk is not with you?"

Carmichael felt the boy stir in his arms. "Lord Whesk did not make it. His son Robert, he is Lord Whesk now."

Lord Borostone's face fell. "My cousin is dead?"

"I am afraid so my lord."

For a brief instance, Carmichael saw the tears that threatened Lord Borostone's eyes. The sorrow vanished and the lord's thin face hardened. "I had never imagined that Vorminside would be so bold as to attack my cousin's fiefdom. You have my word that this atrocity will not go unanswered."

The tired knight nodded. "You have my gratitude."

"Now, please, there are rooms prepared in the castle for those from Clearwater. Go, we will speak in more detail when you are ready."

ॐ   ॐ

Carmichael slept more deeply than he had imagined, for the firm mattress and soft pillow felt like the purest comfort. He did not recall his dreams and he thanked God for that small mercy as he threw his feet off the side of the bed and considered his opulent surroundings. Gold-framed paintings of past lords and ladies of Borostone served to remind him of his host's power, but Carmichael merely sniffed at them and pulled on his freshly-washed cotton shirt. Next came his trousers, likewise cleaned. He eased into them gently, for his muscles ached from his fights and exertions the night before. The full-length mirror allowed him to study his own face, and he pushed a lock of tired grey hair out from his eyes. An irritating stubbly shadow would have to be dealt with sooner rather than later, and the dark circles around his eyes made him look considerably older. *Even older than I feel.*

He stood and looked for his boots. One had somehow slipped under the bed and required him to awkwardly kneel on sore knees to retrieve it. The other had landed by the mirror.

Once booted, Carmichael took himself out of his room and into the spacious corridor that lay beyond. He noted with a poignant twinge in his heart the paintings of Lord Borostone with Lord Whesk, arm-in-arm as they showed off the deer they had hunted. *Evidently they were closer than I had thought.*

The grand hall had been elegantly prepared. Black cloth had been draped across the large oak table that cut through the middle of the room, as though the very castle itself was in mourning. Carmichael spied Robert, his sister, and Cristina at one end. They tucked into breads and jams, and he thought he saw bacon, too. He could certainly smell bacon, and a variety of other cooked meats. His hunger hit him with the force of a charging bull, and he quickly nodded in the direction of his companions from Clearwater before he slipped into a chair and dug in.

Roasted turkey and succulent pork loin was shoveled into his mouth without ceremony. He stopped when he noticed Cristina stand and bow her head, and Carmichael looked up to see Lord Borostone standing above him.

"My lord, thank you for your hospitality." He stood and bowed from the waist, masking his pain.

"It is the least we could do for the guardian of the Protector." Borostone answered. Something about his inflection raised hairs on Carmichael's neck. His eyes must have betrayed his concern, for Borostone raised a hand.

"Do not be concerned. I have no intention of taking it from you. In fact, I would request that you take it far from here, lest Vorminside cast their eyes on us."

Carmichael relaxed a little. "I had a similar plan, though I had considered it unwise to wield it myself. Vorminside will be looking for *me*, so I believed I could act as a diversion."

Lord Borostone appeared to chew over Carmichael's suggestion. "You are experienced in the field of combat, and I will defer to your thoughts, but something as powerful as the Protector, in the hands of a noble knight, would surely be a potent combination? You would keep it safe, and no one would ever be able to threaten you."

Carmichael slowly shook his head. "I fear I have too much darkness to wield the Protector properly, and even with its power, there would be too many enemies looking for me. Even if I survived to die of old age, someone would take it from my grave. No Sire, it cannot remain with me."

If Borostone was put out by the refusal Carmichael could read no sign of it on the lord's face.

"I understand." The Lord turned his gaze to the young Lord Whesk. "Nonetheless, I remain concerned that Vorminside— and others— will seek what we have here. I cannot bring ruin down upon my people."

Carmichael followed the Lord's gaze. "About that. I may have an idea."

ဇ   ಞ

Cristina sat very still. The simple servant's garment she had worn on her arrival had been replaced, and she barely recognised the woman that looked back at her in the mirror. The billowing blue and red gown she wore threatened to engulf her, and she had not mastered how to walk in it. Her hand fell to the satin pouch that blended into the belt wrapped around her waist. *I hope this is worth it.*

A gentle knock at the door drew her attention. She checked her hair one more time, made sure the bun was as secure as it could be, and answered the door. A woman not much older than her in the simple cream and brown outfit of a servant smiled warmly at her. "I am here to escort you to the hall, Milady."

She took a quick breath. "Lead the way."

The dining hall awaited her, and Cristina stopped short of Lord Borostone and Sir Carmichael, who stood side-by-side. Borostone's face was unreadable, but Cristina could see a note of sadness in the lines of Sir Carmichael's face.

"Cristina," Carmichael said, a tinge of concern in his voice, "what we are asking of you is not going to be easy. If you should wish to reconsider—"

Cristina raised her hand. "If this ensures the safety of Robert and Rose, so be it. I ask only that you tell me where I should go."

Borostone stepped forward. "Head for London. Within the city you will meet friends and allies of my family – the letter I will give you contains all the details you need. I will have a pair of guards in plain clothes escort you to the city."

"Tell no one of what you carry Cristina." Carmichael said softly. "Always keep it secret and safe."

"I will." Cristina flicked her eyes around the chamber. "I wish to say goodbye to Robert and Rose."

Another exchange of looks took place between Borostone and Carmichael.

"They remain asleep. I know how much they mean to you, but we cannot risk them knowing of our plan, it would put them and you in danger." Carmichael reached a hand out to Cristina. "I am sorry, but it is best to let them sleep."

Tears pricked her eyes but after a pause Cristina nodded. "I understand. Please tell them—tell them I love them."

"I will." Carmichael quietly answered.

"Your escorts and provisions await, Milady." Borostone added.

"Be safe, Cristina," Carmichael said. "And if God wills it, we will all meet again."

Cristina did not speak. She could not stop the tears from welling up and they spilled down her cheeks. Her hand took Carmichael's, squeezed it for a moment, and she was on her way out of the chamber and towards the stables.

~& &~

The sun faded towards the horizon and bathed the city of London in its pale red glow. Cristina looked over the sprawling array of wooden and stone buildings and watched the trail of carriages, horses, and people that moved in and out of the city. Her guards had wisely hung back, and lurked out of sight, ready to let her proceed but also prepared to intervene should danger loom. The passers-by that drifted in her direction gave her odd looks, and she knew why. An aristocrat lady on her own as night began to fall would invite trouble, but Cristina walked as smoothly and confidently as her emotions would allow. Like London, her future stretched out before her and it felt shrouded by darkness. The letter in her pouch would guide her to a stately home, where she would stay and hide. Her hand felt the cold hard form of the Protector, and she squeezed the stone for assurance. Like her, it would be hidden in the heart of London, buried among the riches of kings and queens. She would not speak of it, not to a soul, for the rest of her days.

THE STONE KNIGHT
Angel LaPoint

Brina looked down at her map, then back up at the seemingly unending lines of nearly identical trees.

"I should be there already," she groaned in frustration. "According to the map, the castle should be *right here*." She swept a hand through the air. "So where is it? Did I make a wrong turn." Brina dropped down onto a large boulder and hung her head. "I've been walking through these woods for nearly two days. I can't go back empty-handed. Papa and Lizzie are counting on me."

She heaved a heavy sigh. *It'll be dark again soon. Maybe I should just give up.* She shook away the thought. *Giving up is not an option.*

Brina set the map down beside her and took a swig from her water skin, thinking through her next steps. She glanced down. Something in the leaf-strewn ground caught her eye.

She frowned. "That doesn't look like an ordinary stone." She knelt on the ground and brushed aside leaves, sticks, and dirt. Her heart pounded and a hopeful smile tugged the corners of her mouth. "These stones were placed here intentionally. This is a path."

She clipped her water skin to her belt, grabbed the map, and carefully followed the path, clearing the way with the toe of her boot. She kept her eyes on the narrow strip of stones until she came upon a wall of resistance. She looked up, brow knit in confusion, and tilted her head to the side. She could not see anything directly in front of her, only a small gap between the trees. She reached out to touch the empty air, but something firm and solid stopped her hand. She pressed against it but could not get through. The harder she pushed against the invisible force, the more it pushed back against her.

"Come on!" She slammed her fists on the barrier, which hardened like a brick wall at her touch. "Let me through! I'm so close." She leaned forward, resting her head on the unseen wall. "Please." Brina thought back to her village, to her father and nephew and dying sister, all waiting on her to return. *Lizzie could already be dead.* Tears sprang into Brina's eyes. She squeezed them shut to keep the tears from escaping. *I can't think like that.*

The barrier gave under her head. Not much, but just enough to give Brina hope. She straightened and tentatively reached out a hand. Brina's fingers slipped through the barrier, disappearing from view.

Brina gasped and yanked her hand back. She wiggled her fingers, closely examining them.

"Well, they look alright, and I've come too far to turn back now." Brina took a deep breath and held it as she stepped through the invisible force.

The force offered some resistance, but not enough to stop Brina. It pressed against her, giving her the sensation of walking through thick mud. The effect lasted less than a second, like walking through a doorway. Brina emerged on the other side and took a moment to catch her breath. She tucked a few stray strands of her red hair back behind her ears.

"Now. Let's see where this took us." Brina took in her new surroundings.

The forest surrounding her did not look much different than the one she left. Gold and brown leaves clung to branches, dead leaves littered the ground, and small animals scurried through the trees. The main notable difference, however, was the large castle in the distance, its towers stretching above the tree line.

Brina laughed in relief. "There it is! It's real! That woman was right!" She surged forward through the trees, making sure to keep the castle in front of her.

Her pace slowed as she neared the large iron fence surrounding the castle grounds. The gate stretched several feet above her head and hung open. Overgrown vines wound through the bars and choked out the other plant life that tried to grow alongside them. Brina took her sword and cut aside the vines so she could pass.

She walked through an abandoned courtyard toward the castle. A large stone fountain, cracked and dry, sat to her left, and a tall, sturdy oak tree grew to the right. Broken statuary littered the courtyard. Weeds grew in patches of dirt that Brina imagined once contained colorful flowers.

I bet this place looked beautiful in its day.

She approached the doors of the castle and, expecting them to be bolted shut, pulled hard. The doors opened with a loud creak, but little resistance. Brina stumbled backward. Her foot caught a loose stone and she fell on her rear end.

"Ow! Good thing no one was around to see that." She stood and brushed herself off. "Now to get what I came here to find. It'll be harder to look once it gets dark, so I need to hurry."

Brina entered the castle. Her footsteps echoed through the wide, empty entrance hall as she took in her surroundings. A six-foot tall stone statue of a knight stood guard at the foot of a grand staircase. He faced the doorway and held his sword, blade pointed up toward the ceiling, with both hands. Unlike the other statues, the knight remained fully intact, though covered in a thin layer of dust. Brina stepped up to the statue.

"Why would they carve him in his uniform, rather than armor?" she wondered aloud. She tilted her head to the side and slowly reached out to touch the knight's cold, stone cheek. "Though, without a helmet, it does make it easier to see the detail in his face and beard. He looks so real, almost alive. And his hair –" Brina touched one of the stiff gray locks and frowned. She chuckled to herself. "I half expected it to move, like real hair."

She looked into the knight's intense, focused eyes; warmth flowed into her cheeks. "I wonder if he's based on a real person. If so, he was handsome."

She paused and shook her head. *It's a statue, Brina. Calm down.*

Her gaze drifted from the knight's face down his chest. In a cavity on the left side, right where his heart would be, sat a fist-sized ruby.

"It's real." Brina cried out in relief and stepped closer. "I'll finally be able to get help for Lizzie." She reached out a hand. "I can take care of my family." Her fingers inched closer to the ruby.

The statue came to life, grabbed Brina's wrist and wrenched it away from his chest cavity. Brina yelped, the sound more of surprise than pain.

"You didn't think it would be that easy, did you?" The knight looked down at Brina. His cold, stone eyes locked on to hers.

Brina gasped and leaned back; her wrist still trapped in the knight's firm hold. "I—I'm sorry. I didn't –"

"Didn't know I was alive?" the knight interrupted "Didn't know I would catch you?"

"Yes! I mean, no. I mean –" Brina tried to pull her arm out of the knight's grasp, but he did not loosen his grip. "Let me go!"

The knight leaned closer, his face inches away from hers. "Do you think it's acceptable to steal something just because you think no one is watching?"

"I wasn't trying to steal it!" Brina's words burst from her mouth in a flood. "I just needed a way to help my family. I didn't know you were alive. I'm sorry. A woman in the tavern told me about this place, about the ruby. I didn't know it belonged to you. She didn't say anything about you. Please. I don't want to steal anything. I just want to save my sister." A sob broke through on the word *sister.*

The knight released Brina's wrist, and she collapsed, weeping, at his feet. *I failed. I'm sorry, Lizzie. I'm sorry, Papa. I failed.*

The knight silently watched Brina for a long moment. He sheathed his sword, knelt beside her, and offered her his hand.

"I apologize," his expression softened. "I assumed you were like the others that came before you – a thief, only after my ruby for selfish reasons."

Brina looked up, into stone eyes that no longer appeared cold. Her heart skipped.

"My name is Jacob," continued the knight. "What is your name?"

"B –Brina."

"Are you hungry, Brina?"

She nodded and took his hand, allowing him to help her to her feet.

"Come with me." He turned and led Brina out of the entrance hall, toward the kitchen.

She followed him, admiring how easily he moved, despite being made of stone. *Was he always this way? What kind of enchantment is he under?*

They reached the kitchen and Jacob gestured to a wooden door. "The food in here is still fresh, the pantry untouched by time. Take what you will."

Brina stepped passed Jacob and opened the door. More food than Brina had ever seen in her life filled the room. It lined the wooden shelves, hung from the ceiling, and sat in barrels. Everything inside still looked and smelled fresh. Brina tore a chunk of bread from a nearby loaf and cautiously took a bite.

She turned to Jacob and smiled. "It tastes like it was baked yesterday. How is this possible?"

Jacob smiled at her in return. "I do not need food, but I knew others would come who did. This room is not the only one protected from the passage of time. It is easier to enchant a few rooms than an entire palace."

Brina nodded at his explanation. "I don't know much about magic, but that makes sense to me." She turned back to the pantry. "I feel guilty even looking at this much food when so many in my village are starving."

"Perhaps you can take some food back with you when you leave?"

Brina nodded again. "I would like that."

She looked through the pantry and gathered enough food to make a satisfying supper for herself. She sat down at the table to eat.

Jacob sat across from her. "You are welcome to stay here tonight. I've kept a spare bedroom ready, in case of a situation like this one. You may take as much food back as you'd like."

Brina looked up with a hopeful smile. "I don't suppose you'll let me take the ruby, too?"

Jacob covered the ruby with his hand and politely shook his head.

Brina glanced down at the table to hide her slight disappointment. "I didn't think so. Just thought I'd ask."

Jacob thoughtfully placed a hand on the table. "Brina, you mentioned a woman told you about this place. What exactly did she say?"

Brina chewed a bite of cheese as she thought. "She said she knew of a way I could save my sister, Lizzie. She's dying and we don't have enough money to get her the help she needs. The woman told me about a castle, hidden in the woods, containing a ruby the size of a man's hand. She said only someone with a pure heart could obtain the ruby, and she had a map to the castle. Well, actually, the map led me to the barrier hiding the castle." Brina paused. "I don't really consider myself to have a pure heart – I'm selfish at times, and I get angry and have thoughts my father considers *unbefitting of a young lady* – but I knew I had to do something. I couldn't just sit around and watch my sister –"

Tears threatened to surface. She took a deep breath and cleared her throat. "I have no brothers. My sister's husband died two years ago, and my nephew is still very young. My father works hard on our farm to support us. I knew it was up to me to do something, anything, to help. So, here I am." Brina held out both hands. "And, even though I can bring back some food for the village, I still can't help Lizzie."

"I'm afraid the woman who told you about this place was misinformed." Jacob touched the ruby. "This is no ordinary gemstone. It's what keeps me alive, it's my heart. Were it to leave my chest, the enchantment would end. I would die." He reached across the table and laid a gentle hand on Brina's arm, smooth stone, cold against her warm skin. "I am truly sorry. I wish I could help. I would offer you something else to help your sister, but everything of value in the castle is either gone or decayed, and the enchantment on the treasury can only be broken by royalty."

Brina nodded and offered Jacob a sad smile. She covered his hand with hers and rubbed her thumb against the back of his hand. "I understand. You've already been so kind to me. Thank you."

Jacob bowed his head in acknowledgment and offered her a kind smile in return. His eyes locked onto hers and a warm flutter filled Brina's stomach.

She finished her supper and followed Jacob to a small, simple room in the servants' wing.

"I'm sorry I can't offer you better quarters for the night," Jacob stood aside so Brina could enter, "but the room is safe and dry and there's wood for the fireplace."

"This is perfect." Brina stepped into the room and ran her hand along the woolen bedspread. She turned back to Jacob and smiled. "Thank you again."

Jacob nodded. "I will be at my post in the entrance hall if you need anything. Good night, Brina."

"Good night, Jacob."

Jacob paused in the doorway; lips slightly parted. Brina waited, heart loudly beating, in case he had more to say. He simply nodded again and backed out of the room, closing the door behind him. A soft, slightly disappointed sigh escaped

Brina's lips. She turned away from the door, started a small fire in the fireplace, and crawled into the warm bed.

৽   ৶

Sunlight streamed in through the window, warming Brina's face. She rubbed her eyes and sat up.

Morning. Time to go back home and face my family.

Brina met Jacob in the kitchen for a small, quick breakfast. The two made small conversation while she ate. Brina lingered at the table for as long as possible.

Why do I suddenly feel like I don't want to leave?

Jacob offered Brina two bags to add to her own, and she filled all three with as much food from the pantry as she could carry. Jacob escorted her to the barrier and the two paused to say their goodbyes.

"I pray you get home safe." Jacob smiled. "I would escort you the rest of the way, but the enchantment prevents me from passing through the barrier."

Brina tilted her head to one side. "I meant to ask about your enchantment. Were you always made of stone, and the enchantment brought you to life, or were you once a man? Why is there a barrier around the castle? Who put it in place, and who set the enchantment?"

Jacob chuckled. "There is no time for me to tell you the whole tale of how I came to be as I am now, but I will tell you that I was once flesh and blood, as you are." He lifted his hand to touch Brina's cheek but paused. Instead, he brushed aside a strand of hair from her face and tucked it behind her ear. "Perhaps one day, you'll have an opportunity to return, and I will tell you about the fall of a kingdom I swore to protect, and the one who still holds me to that vow."

Brina shivered at Jacob's touch, though her cheeks burned. A not altogether unpleasant sensation. *Now I know how Lizzie felt when she first met Daniel.* "You're saying I have permission to return?"

Jacob smiled. "Go. Take the food to your village. Be with your family. I hope you find a way to get help for your sister."

"Thank you. Goodbye, Jacob."

Brina turned away from the handsome stone knight with unexpected difficulty and approached the barrier. She held one hand out in front of her and stepped forward until the invisible force stopped her.

She looked over her shoulder. "I will see you again, Jacob."

He held up a hand in farewell. "I'll count the days."

Brina took a deep breath, ignored the sudden heaviness in her chest, and faced the barrier once more.

I will return someday, thought Brina as she stepped through the barrier. *As soon as Lizzie is safe and well, I will return.* Brina set her shoulders and started for home.

"I thought you said you could track her?"

"I can!"

"Coulda' fooled me!"

The sound of voices ahead of her stopped Brina in her tracks. She darted behind a tree and crept closer to get a better look. Five men, armed and angry, stood among the trees, arguing with each other.

The smallest of the men, the one who claimed to be a good tracker, spoke again. "She can't have gotten too far. She's just a silly girl."

"A silly girl with the map to *our* ruby!" said the man who first spoke, a grizzled man with gray hair.

Brina gasped and stepped back. Dry leaves crunched beneath her boots.

"Wait! I heard something!" The tracker looked toward Brina's hiding place.

"It better not be another rabbit or else *you'll* be the one I skin alive." A man with a twisted knife held the blade to the tracker's throat.

Brina froze, too afraid to even breathe. *He's right. I'm just a rabbit. Please go away.*

The largest man in the group glared at the others to silence them. A man with a large scar running down the length of his face stepped close to where Brina hid.

"Come on out, little bunny," said the scarred man. "We haven't had breakfast yet."

"If it were a real rabbit, it would have run out by now." The tracker kept a close eye on his companion's knife.

The scarred man looked over his shoulder. "Or you're just hearing things again."

The grizzled man let out a mirthless chuckle. "Wouldn't surprise me."

A man Brina had not noticed before dropped from a tree behind her. Brina yelped and turned to run. The man grabbed her tightly by the arm and dragged her toward the others. Brina struggled against him. Her heart wildly beat in her chest and tears filled her eyes.

I'm going to die.

"Kade was right. Look what I found." He threw Brina to the ground.

The other five men laughed; they formed a circle around her.

"Well, well," the tracker, Kade, looked at the others. "I told you I could find her." He grinned like a dog waiting for his master's approval.

"Shut up!" snapped the grizzled man.

Kade's grin faded, and he hung his head.

"Bad luck, girlie," the twisted knife turned in Brina's direction. "Now, hand over the map."

Brina quickly scrambled to her feet. She dropped her bags on the ground and brandished her sword, pointing it at the men in turn. They laughed again.

"Well, aren't you a feisty one," said the scarred man.

"I think we can have some fun with you," laughed Kade. "What do you think, Warin?"

The larger man stepped into the center of the circle. Brina turned to him, sword trembling. Warin loomed over Brina.

He bent over until he reached her eye level. "We're only here for the map. Give it to us, and we'll let you go."

Brina considered doing what Warin said. *There's no way I can fight six men at once, and it's unlikely they'll be able to get through the barrier, even if they do find it. Then again, there's a chance they could, and they won't hesitate to take the ruby from Jacob, or to kill me, whether I give them the map or not.*

"Well? What'll it be?" Warin asked again.

Brina tightened her grip on her sword. She looked past Warin. The other men gathered around him, leaving the space behind Brina open. *I can't fight them, but I might be able to outrun them.* With all her might, Brina threw her sword at the men. Without checking to see if she hit anyone, she grabbed her bag containing the map, abandoned the other two bags of food, and ran as fast as she could back toward the barrier.

The men roared in anger and gave chase. They were fast, but Brina was small and knew her destination. *All this food in my bag is slowing me down.* Brina dug through the bag until she found the map. She dropped the bag and raced on.

Searing pain shot through her left shoulder as she neared the barrier. She screamed and nearly stumbled. She reached behind her, and her fingers brushed the hilt of a knife. Another whizzed past her head, hit the barrier, and bounced off. Brina slowed to pass through, and another knife slashed at her right side. The barrier offered no resistance at all, and she easily slid through. The angry voices cut short as Brina's head emerged on the other side of the barrier. A final knife landed in her right calf.

Brina clenched her teeth and continued to the castle, dragging her right leg behind her. *I can't stop. Not yet. I have to warn Jacob.* The forest spun around her. She stumbled and landed hard on the ground. Spots flashed before her eyes. She tried, and failed, to get back to her feet.

"Jacob!" She called out in desperation, clawing forward with her good arm and leg. *I'm not going to make it.* "Jacob!" The pain grew more intense. Darkness filled the edges of her vision. "Please. Help me." She closed her eyes. "Jac—" Her voice trailed off as she faded into the welcoming black.

❧   ☙

Brina awoke back in the room where she spent the previous night. The places the knives hit her still hurt, but with less intensity. A fire burned in the fireplace and bandages covered her wounds. Jacob stood at the foot of the bed. Relief passed over his stone features when Brina's gaze fell on him.

He stepped closer and tenderly brushed a strand of hair from her face. "You're awake. What happened? I heard you call out my name and found you bleeding and unconscious in the forest."

Brina closed her eyes and smiled at his touch. "Bandits," her voice sounded hoarse and dry.

Jacob helped Brina sit up in the bed and drink from the cup of water he offered.

"There were bandits in the woods outside the barrier. Six of them." She leaned back against the pillows Jacob placed behind her. "It sounds like they'd been tracking me since I left my village. They were after the map, after your ruby. I knew I couldn't fight them off, so I took the map and ran. They chased me, but I made it through the barrier before they caught up to me."

"But not before they injured you."

Brina nodded. "The barrier will keep them out, right?" She looked up at Jacob, eyes pleading. "I doubt they're smart enough to figure out the secret."

Jacob sighed. "They wouldn't be the first thieves to get through, and if they saw you pass through, it may make them even more determined. There is a chance they'll eventually figure out a way inside, but if they do, I will take care of them. You don't need to concern yourself with anything other than recovery."

A wry chuckle escaped Brina's lips. "That's exactly what I told Lizzie before I left. I promised I'd only be gone a few days. Now, with my injuries and with those bandits outside, I likely won't make it home anytime soon. What if I don't make it back before she –" Tears filled Brina's eyes and she shook her head.

Jacob sat down on the edge of the bed and took her uninjured hand in his. "I know what it's like to watch the people you love suffer, and to feel powerless to help. I give you my word, I will do my best to help you heal as swiftly as possible and get you back home to your family." He wiped her tears with his thumb and left his hand resting against her cheek. "And though I cannot accompany you to your village, I promise, I will be here to comfort you should the worst occur."

Brina leaned into his touch, nodding in thanks. *How can cold stone feel so warm?*

"I've got some broth boiling in the kitchen for you. I need to check it. I'll be right back." Jacob helped Brina lay back down. "You rest. Let me take care of you."

Brina nodded again. "Thank you for saving me, Jacob. I knew you would."

Jacob lifted Brina's knuckles to his lips. "Always."

Brina closed her eyes again, unable to stay awake any longer.

The warm scent of vegetables and broth greeted Brina when she opened her eyes.

"That smells wonderful," she said, her voice still heavy with sleep.

Jacob smiled from his position at the foot of the bed. "Good. I can't smell or taste the broth, so I hope it turned out well. I did the best I could."

Brina frowned as Jacob helped her sit up. "You can't smell or taste?"

Jacob shook his head. "I have no stomach, and therefore no need for food. The enchantment left me with my sight and hearing, but my other senses were deemed unnecessary for my assignment." He picked up the bowl of broth he left warming near the fireplace and carried it over to Brina.

She brushed her fingers over his as she accepted the bowl. "So, you can't feel anything, either?"

A sad smile formed on Jacob's lips. "No," he traced a bent finger down Brina's cheek, "but I remember what touch felt like. I remember everything. I remember the softness of my sister's hair when she made me braid it for her, and the floral fragrance of my mother's perfume when she prepared for an event. I remember my father's deep, infectious laugh, and sparring with the prince." Jacob's eyes became distant with memory. "I remember everything, and I miss them."

"Will you tell me what happened?" asked Brina. "You promised you would."

"Indeed, I did." Jacob sat down on the edge of the bed. "This kingdom was once prosperous and fruitful, but when the king died, the entire kingdom fell into despair, especially the queen. She turned the kingdom over to her son, Darin, and left. No one knew where she went. The prince, my closest friend, did the best he could, but the combined stress of suddenly ruling the kingdom while still grieving the loss of his father and mother weighed heavily on him. I tried to support him, but he shut me out."

Jacob sighed. "He shut everyone out. He became withdrawn and sought counsel from others outside the court advisers. He allowed pain and anger to take the place of reason. I watched, helpless, as my best friend transformed from a kind, tender-hearted prince into a cruel tyrant."

Brina nodded. "I'd heard stories, reasons why we no longer have a king and queen. It's different to hear the story from someone who was there."

"One day, a woman appeared, out of thin air, in the throne room," continued Jacob. "She warned Darin that it was not too late for him to change his ways, and if he didn't, if he continued down his current path, it would lead to the destruction of his entire kingdom. The enchantress's words angered Darin, and he ordered us to attack her. The other knights obeyed without hesitation."

"But not you?"

Jacob shook his head. "When I took my vows, I swore to protect the kingdom and its inhabitants, not to blindly take orders I knew were unjust. Instead of attacking the woman, who only came to help, I turned to Darin. I begged him to consider her words, not just for the sake of the kingdom, but for his own sake as well. My cries fell on deaf ears. He attacked me."

Jacob fell silent. Brina set aside her empty broth bowl and took Jacob's hand, lacing her fingers between his.

"I can't even imagine how you must have felt," she whispered.

Jacob gently squeezed Brina's hand. "There are no words to describe it." They sat in silence for a moment longer before Jacob continued his story. "The enchantress saw that Darin would not change. With a wave of her hand, she translated the entire court, everyone inside the palace grounds, to the courtyard. She informed us that, as a consequence of Darin's choices, his kingdom would be taken from him. She would place a barrier around the grounds, trapping Darin, and any who remained, inside. The barrier would remain in place until Darin repented or until another heir, one just and righteous, arrived to take charge of the kingdom. She gave everyone until sundown to gather their belongings and take their leave. Then, she asked that someone, a single person, remain behind, to protect the barrier and offer Darin the continued opportunity to change his ways."

"You volunteered?"

Jacob nodded. "I did. The enchantress warned me that taking on this role meant I would remain until the kingdom was restored.

She told me exactly what the enchantment would entail, what it would mean for me to accept. If Darin went to his grave without changing, which he did, I would be alone, for as long as it took for a new ruler to arrive. My family begged me not to agree. They told me to leave with them, but I couldn't leave Darin alone. I knew him better than anyone else. I truly thought, given enough time with just him, I could convince him that who he had become was not who he was." Jacob closed his eyes and sighed. "I did try, for years, but he still refused to listen. He died less than five years after the barrier was put in place."

"And you've been alone ever since?"

"It wasn't as bad as it sounds, not for me. I can sort of sleep at my post, shutting out everything, including my perception of time, until someone arrives. Usually, it was bandits who raided the castle and tried to take my heart." Jacob turned to Brina and smiled. "Until you came along, that is. You've made all the centuries of waiting worth it."

Brina smiled. She let go of his hand and cupped his face. "I'm glad I found you."

Jacob leaned forward and pressed his forehead to hers. "I hope you don't find this too forward, but I love you, Brina."

She grinned. "I love you, too. I think I have from the moment I first saw you." She closed the short distance between them and pressed her lips to his, holding them there for a long moment before pulling back.

Jacob chuckled and tucked a strand of Brina's hair behind her ear. "I'm sorry for the stiffness. Stone lips must not be the most comfortable to kiss."

Brina shook her head. "I wouldn't know any different." She kissed him again. "They're softer than you think, and it has a lot to do with the person behind them."

Jacob smiled. "I'm glad."

❦

Days passed without incident. Jacob did his best to distract Brina from worrying about her family by telling her stories of his past and giving her a tour of the castle once she healed enough to leave the bed. It pained her leg to walk, so Jacob effortlessly carried her from room to room, describing how each looked centuries ago. Every night, after Brina fell asleep, Jacob walked to the barrier to look for any sign that the bandits made it through.

Jacob and Brina sat together in front of the fire, nearly a week after Brina first arrived at the castle. They sat on the floor, Brina wrapped in Jacob's arms.

"Do you think the bandits are still out there, trying to get in, or have they moved on by now?" asked Brina.

Jacob shook his head. "There's no way to tell without going back through the barrier."

"It hurts less to walk today than it did yesterday," Brina tilted her head to look up at Jacob. "Perhaps I should go check tomorrow. I'll leave the barrier far enough away from where I entered to spy on the bandits without them noticing me. I'll keep one hand on the barrier in case I need to escape."

"I would prefer you wait until you're fully healed," he softly smiled, "but I know you can't stay here forever."

She turned to face him better and touched his cheek. "Not yet. I do need to go home and check on my family, but I promise I'll return as soon as possible. I may even bring my family with me."

"I would love to meet them."

"I know they'll love you." Brina smiled. "And once I do return, I promise to never leave your side until the day I die." She kissed him then turned back around to lean against his chest. "But you're right. I should wait until I'm fully healed to leave. I won't do anyone any good if my wounds reopen in the middle of the woods."

Jacob wrapped his arms around Brina, tenderly holding her to his chest. They watched the flames dance in the fireplace.

જ   ৫

Brina woke late that night to a crash in the entrance hall. Brina sat straight up in bed. She looked at Jacob, standing guard in the doorway. He held a finger to his lips.

"Stay here," he whispered. "I will go investigate."

Brina nodded and pulled the blanket tight around herself. *It's the bandits,* she thought. *It has to be.*

Jacob quietly left the room. Silence stretched the seconds, Brina's hammering heart the only sound in the room. Screams of surprise echoed through the near empty halls of the castle.

"It's alive! That statue is alive!"

"Look! In its chest!"

"The ruby!"

"Get it!"

Brina recognized the voices of the bandits. The clink of metal against stone followed the shouts. *Jacob will be fine. He's a trained knight. He's fought off bandits before. He'll be fine.* Brina closed her eyes and imagined the battle in the other room. She pictured Jacob easily taking on all six of the cruel bandits and driving them from the castle. She could not bear to imagine any other outcome. The door to Brina's room creaked open. *I can still hear fighting. Who's –*

"Well, fancy seeing you again, girlie."

Brina opened her eyes at the bandit's voice. The twisted knife she hoped to never see again pointed straight at her neck. Brina screamed and moved as far back against the bed frame as possible.

"Brina!" Jacob shouted from the other room.

The bandit grabbed her by the left arm and yanked her from the bed. Pain shot through her shoulder as her still-healing wound tore open. Brina struggled in the bandit's tight grip. He spun her around, holding her against his chest, and pressed the twisted knife to her throat.

"I'd keep still, if I were you, girlie," he hissed in her ear. "My knife hasn't tasted human blood in weeks and it's starving." He dragged Brina to the entrance hall.

Jacob fought with the other five bandits. He tried to move toward the hall leading to Brina's room, but the bandits kept him in place. Sparks flew each time one of their metal swords came into contact with Jacob's stone blade.

"Look who I found!" The bandit holding Brina called out to his companions.

They all turned to look. Jacob took advantage of their distraction. He shoved past them and faced the bandit holding Brina.

"Release her," he narrowed his eyes. "Now."

I've never seen this much anger in his eyes before.

The bandit took half a step back but did not look away from Jacob. At the other end of the room, the scarred bandit moved to attack, but their leader silently held him back. He shook his head, indicating to the other bandits not to interfere.

"You're out numbered," said the bandit holding Brina.

"I've won against stronger opponents than the six of you." Jacob took a step closer. The bandit stepped back. "If you harm Brina, in any way. I swear, I will destroy you all. *Let her go.* I will not ask again." He punctuated his demand by leaning over the bandit.

The bandit swallowed hard. His knife wavered. He looked to his companions for help, but they remained in place. "G-give us the ruby, and we'll let her go."

Jacob glared at the bandit for a tense moment. His eyes flicked to Brina's and he held her gaze. "Get down."

Jacob grabbed the bandit's wrist and twisted, forcing the knife out of his hand. Brina ducked out of the way as the knight thrust his sword through the bandit's stomach. The other bandits glared at the scene. The bandit leader gave sharp nod to the others and the bandits moved as one to attack Jacob, throwing the fight back into full force.

"Stay behind me," Jacob ordered Brina. "I won't let them get to you again."

Jacob fought back against the bandits, keeping himself between them and Brina. The bandit who first captured Brina in the forest reached into a pouch on his leg and withdrew a knife, the same kind thrown at Brina when she escaped through the barrier.

"Jacob! Knives!" Brina called out.

"I see them."

The bandit threw the knife. The blade hit Jacob in the chest, bounced off his stone exterior, and fell uselessly to the ground.

Jacob looked down at the knife, then back up to the bandit. "Did that make you feel better?"

The bandit growled and threw another knife that Jacob knocked out of the air with his sword.

Time for me to go, I think. Brina stepped around the body of the fallen bandit and started for the hallway, intent on getting out of the way of the fight. *Jacob will be able to focus better if he's not worried about me.* The dead bandit's twisted knife caught Brina's eye. *I should have something to defend myself, just in case.* Brina paused to pick it up.

"Brina! Watch out!"

Brina turned at Jacob's warning, in time to see the knife wielding bandit jump from the staircase banister, headed right for her. Brina rolled out of the way. The bandit landed beside her, cutting her off from Jacob. The other bandits did not let up their attack. Jacob turned his attention to the knife wielding bandit and brought his sword down. The bandit jumped away. Brina scrambled to her feet, but the bandit pinned her down. Jacob swung his sword again, aiming the hilt at the bandit's back. He hit his mark, but not before the bandit thrust a knife into Brina's heart.

"You're fast," the bandit sneered at Jacob, "but I'm faster."

Brina cried out in pain and surprise. She looked down at the knife, buried up to the hilt in her chest. She looked at Jacob.

A furious roar tore from Jacob's throat. Brina flinched as Jacob picked up the bandit by the back of his shirt. He threw the bandit at the others, knocking them all backward.

Jacob dropped his sword and knelt beside a shuddering Brina. He scooped her into his arms, gently brushing the hair from her face. "Brina. I'm sorry. I failed to protect you."

Brina opened her mouth to speak, but nothing came out. *It's not your fault.* She reached up a trembling hand and touched his face. *I'm sorry. I didn't get out of the way fast enough.*

He held her hand to his cheek. "Stay with me. Please."

She nodded. *I'll try.* "I," she struggled to speak. *I have to tell him.* "I love you."

"I love you, too. I'll always love you." He held her close and pressed his lips to hers.

Brina closed her eyes and leaned into the kiss. *Goodbye my handsome stone knight.*

ൟ   ൰

Brina fell limp in Jacob's arms. "Goodbye, my love." He pressed a final, tender kiss to her forehead.

He heard the bandits get to their feet behind him. He gently laid Brina on the ground, reclaimed his sword, and stood to face them. One of the bandits, the one he threw at the others, the one who killed Brina, laid still on the ground, eyes glassy and vacant, neck bent at an unnatural angle.

Jacob's fingers tightened around his sword grip, hard enough to nearly crack the stone, even through the enchantment. He rushed at the remaining bandits. He fought with blind fury; unlike anything he had experienced before. He put the full strength of his stone form behind each swing. The only image in his mind was Brina. He would never again hear her laughter, never again gaze into her honey-colored eyes, never again hold her in his arms. *I wasn't strong enough to protect you. I wasn't fast enough. I failed. I'm sorry.*

The sound of battle silenced. Jacob blinked and shook his head, coming out of his trance. He looked around the entrance hall. The bodies of the other four bandits laid at his feet. Jacob dropped his sword and walked back over to Brina. He scooped her up in his arms and carried her to her room, laying her gently on the bed. He draped the blanket over her, covering her bloody chest, and tucked her hair behind her ear.

"There. You're just sleeping," he whispered. "I knew I would have to say goodbye to you, one day, but I thought we'd at least share several years together." Jacob looked down at his own chest, and the bright ruby in place of his heart. "Here. This has always been yours." He wrapped his fingers around the gemstone and pulled.

He gasped as pain, the first he'd felt in centuries, shot through his chest. Stiffness began in his feet and slowly moved up his legs. He placed the ruby heart on Brina's chest, using both her hand and his to hold it in place.

"Living forever matters nothing if you're not there. I will see you again, soon." Jacob leaned over Brina, cupping her face with his other hand, as his entire body froze into solid, non-living, stone.

❧   ☙

Brina winced. *My chest feels like it's on fire.* She paused. *Wait. I'm not dead? That bandit stabbed me. I should be dead.* She opened her eyes, but a weight on her chest prevented her from sitting up. She looked down. A man knelt, asleep, leaning over her. His head laid on her chest and his slow, steady breathing perfectly matched her own. She reached down and brushed aside a lock of his long, light brown hair.

Her breath caught in her throat. "Jacob?"

The man stirred at her voice. He slowly opened his eyes and lifted his head. Familiar gray eyes, though no longer stone, met hers. "Brina?"

She laughed, tears filling her eyes. "It's really you." She reached out and touched his cheek.

Jacob flinched at the touch and frowned. He covered her hand with his. "I can feel you."

Brina nodded. "You're not stone anymore." She took his other hand and held it up for him to see. "Look. You're flesh and blood again."

Jacob flexed his fingers. "I'm human. But how?" He turned his attention to Brina. "And how are you alive? I watched you die. I held you."

Brina shook her head. "I don't know. I was about to ask you the same question."

"It's impossible. Unless" Jacob paused. He put one hand over his own heart, and one over Brina's. He chuckled. "The ruby."

Brina tilted her head in confusion.

"When you died, I couldn't bear to live without you," explained Jacob. "I carried you in here and laid you in the bed. Then I pulled out the ruby, my heart, and gave it to you. I felt myself becoming stone, true stone. I thought it was the end." He laughed. "But somehow it brought us both back. Here." Jacob moved Brina's hands over their hearts. "Feel that? They're one."

Brina silently felt the two heartbeats, watched him breathe in sync with her. She even adjusted her breathing, which he matched without trying. She grinned and threw her arms around Jacob, pressing her lips to his in a passionate kiss.

Jacob pulled Brina as close as possible. When they broke apart, he leaned his forehead against hers. "You don't know how good it feels to *feel* again." He brushed a finger down her cheek. "To actually touch you without fingers made of cold stone."

Brina leaned against his chest. "You're so warm. I don't know how this happened, but at the moment, I don't really care."

Jacob chuckled. "Neither do I. Though I do have an idea."

Brina looked up at him, waiting for him to continue.

"I said the enchantment would only be broken by Darin changing his ways or another heir returned to take their rightful place. Darin never changed," Jacob smiled at Brina, "but I never considered the second part until now. Darin's mother, the queen, left the palace and no one heard from her again. We all assumed she died, but what if she didn't? What if she remarried and had another child? What if the royal line continued through her, but no one knew it?"

"Are you saying I could be a descendant of that queen?" Brina shook her head. "That's impossible. My family are farmers. We have been for generations."

Jacob stood and pulled Brina to her feet. Loose chunks of stone littered the ground around him. "Come with me."

Brina followed Jacob out of the room. They paused inside the empty entrance hall.

"What happened to the bandits?" asked Brina. She looked around. Everything looked just as it did the day she arrived, except for Jacob standing guard at the foot of the stairs.

Jacob shook his head. "I don't know. I left them right here, but now there's nothing, not even blood stains." He walked to the only other difference in the room, his sword - now steel instead of stone - propped against the stairs. He picked it up. "Even my blade is clean. I wonder if this is another effect of the enchantment being broken." He placed his sword into his scabbard and walked back over to Brina. "Come. This isn't what I wanted to show you."

Jacob led Brina to a large, ornate door with a strange lock. "This is the treasury. The enchantress said it could only be opened by someone with royal lineage, but she excluded Darin. If you can open the lock, then what I suspect is true. You are a descendant of the queen."

Brina stepped up to the lock. She paused and turned back around. "What if it doesn't work?"

"Then you and I go back to your village. You introduce me to your family, and I ask your father for your hand in marriage."

Brina smiled, then frowned. "What if it *does* work? I'm a farmer's daughter. I know nothing about running a kingdom."

Jacob put a hand on her shoulder. "Whatever happens, you are not alone. I will be with you."

Brina nodded and turned back to the door. She took a deep breath and touched the lock, unsure of what else to do. A loud click emanated from within the mechanisms and the lock dropped from the door. Brina gasped and backed away.

"You did it." Jacob's voice came out in a whisper of awe.

"I did it." Brina opened the door to the treasury and stepped inside. She took in the sight of countless chests of gold and gemstones, bundles of exquisite cloths, and barrels of exotic spices.

Jacob walked to a pedestal containing shining jewelry and picked up a silver tiara. He carried it over to Brina, placed it on her head, and knelt before her. "My princess."

Brina grabbed Jacob's hands and pulled him to his feet. "Don't do that. Please."

"As you wish." Jacob put a hand under Brina's chin and tilted her face up. "But you should keep the tiara. It suits you." He leaned down and pressed a gentle kiss to her mouth.

"Brina?"

"Brina, are you here?"

Brina quickly pulled away from Jacob and turned to the door. "Papa? Lizzie?" She ran out of the room, pulling Jacob behind her.

They ran to the entrance hall. Brina's father, sister, and nephew stood in the doorway, staring at the castle in awe. Brina ran and threw her arms around them all.

"You're here! All of you!" She pulled back and looked at her sister. "And you're well! How?"

"The day after you left, a woman came to the cottage," said Brina's father. "She told us not to worry about you, that your journey would take longer than expected, but we would see you again soon. Then she produced a vial of liquid and told me it would cure Elizabeth."

"I felt better almost immediately, but it still took me a few days to fully recover." Elizabeth took Brina's face in her hands. "But look at you. The woman told us that our ancestor was the missing queen. It seems she was right."

"She gave us a map and supplies and told us to travel to this castle to meet you," continued Brina's father.

"She was pretty!" added Lizzie's son.

Brina turned to Jacob. "I wonder if your enchantress, the woman who spoke to me in the tavern, and the woman who helped my family are one and the same."

"It would not surprise me," said Jacob.

"Papa, Lizzie, Danny, I want you to meet Jacob." Brina smiled. "He's the one who kept me safe."

Brina and Jacob together filled the others in on everything that happened over the past few days. At the end of their story, Jacob approached Brina's father. "Sir. Your daughter is unlike anyone I've ever met."

Brina's father held up a hand to stop Jacob. "I know what you're going to ask. You took care of my girl when I couldn't be there for her, and any fool could see how much you two love each other. So, you have my blessing to take her for your wife."

Jacob bowed his head in thanks while Brina jumped into her father's arms.

"Thank you, Papa."

"All I've ever wanted is for my girls to be happy." He took Lizzie and Brina by the hands.

"Me too, Granpa?" Danny looked up at the older man.

He chuckled and picked up the young boy. "Of course, you too." He turned back to Jacob and Brina. "It's this royalty thing that's got me stumped."

"Don't worry." All heads turned to the sound of the new voice. "I can help with that."

A dark-haired woman with kind eyes stood in the doorway.

Jacob lifted his chin. "You. You're the enchantress."

The woman bowed her head. "You've done well, Jacob. I'm sorry you had to be alone this whole time, but you needed to wait for the right person to come along, someone you would willingly give your heart to."

Jacob grabbed Brina's hand.

"Brina, you are destined to be a great queen, but you will not have to rule until you are ready," continued the woman. "I will remain a while longer, to help prepare you, and the rest of the kingdom." She gestured to Lizzie and their father. "Your family will be by your side and, so long as you rule with justice and kindness, your people will thrive."

"I'll do my best," promised Brina.

The woman smiled. "I know you will. I have waited a long time to see this day come to pass. As I'm sure Jacob will agree, it was worth the wait."

Jacob wrapped an arm around Brina and pulled her close. "Yes. I agree. She is worth it."

The woman nodded. "Today is the beginning of a new era."

THE HEART OF THE KING
Terri LaPoint

Sam noticed the darkness seconds before he heard the screams. He slipped behind a hay-filled wagon to hide and peered out at the chaotic scene in the courtyard. He followed the gaze of his terrified countrymen. A black, scaly dragon circled the sky, its huge wings blotting out the light of the sun as the beast descended.

Its massive tail smashed the tower in the center of the courtyard. The steeple toppled, and the dragon seized a ruby the size of a man's fist from its place of prominence within the tower. The beast roared in victory. The people below screamed in terror.

Sam's heart froze. The beast clutched the Heart of the King—his kingdom's most sacred treasure—in its filthy claws. It landed in the midst of the rubble with a ground-shaking thud. Dark clouds filled the sky, and gloom filled the atmosphere.

The people of Allandra, peasants and nobility alike, shrank back, but nobody ran away. They could not tear their eyes away from the horrifying scene unfolding before them.

Sam, a simple farmer with a golden mop of curls on his head, faded into the background behind the wagon and watched.

Hope arose in the crowd when Sir Octavius, the King's most trusted knight, marched into their midst. His white robe shimmered in what little light remained. His sword was drawn, and the ruby-red emblem on his shield reminded every friend and foe of the great power of the Heart of the King.

The priceless ruby had been in the kingdom of Allandra since time began, or so the legend went. It symbolized hope to the citizens, and it struck terror into the hearts of their enemies. From the time they suckled at their mother's breast, every child throughout the land heard the stories of the power of the Heart of the King.

It held supernatural power which protected the land and kept evil at bay. The gemstone linked to the lights in their homes, the prosperity of the people, and to the security of their borders. It also connected the people's hearts to each other in such a way that they often sensed what others felt.

How did this foul dragon manage to infiltrate the kingdom? Sam sensed the questions in all their minds. *How could it snatch the central power of Allandra?*

King Othniall had been away since the beginning of the month, attending the wedding festivities of a prince and princess in a faraway land. It was another week before his scheduled return, but no one had feared his absence. The king had placed Sir Octavius in charge. The knight was the champion of the people and the greatest servant of the king.

Sam felt hope stir in the hearts of the people around him when Sir Octavius appeared. Sam was not so confident. He stepped back deeper into the shadows. His stomach twisted into knots. He did not trust the White Knight.

The black dragon greeted the White Knight with its fiery breath. The stench of sulphur filled the air. The smoke from the beast's nostrils turned Sir Octavius's white cape to a dingy gray.

The knight brandished his sword at the dragon. The people cheered their hero. Sam saw it for what it was—a show, nothing more.

Octavius thrust and parried his sword at the dragon, and the beast ducked and spewed fire. The White Knight blocked the flames with his shield.

Suddenly, an unexpected sound rang out from behind the shield. Laughter. Not the White Knight's customary happy, victorious laughter Sam had heard so many times from the White Knight. This was wicked laughter—diabolical and terrifying.

That came from Sir Octavius.

A smoky fog surrounded the dragon, and the monster transformed before their very eyes into a man, dressed in knights' garb. The armor was identical to that of the White Knight, except his was as black as midnight.

Sam recognized the figure at once, as did everyone else in the courtyard—Sir Draegon, former knight of Allandra, banished decades before for high treason.

Draegon joined Octavius in his fiendish laughter, and the two knights embraced like long-lost brothers.

Sam shook his head. *That's how the dragon got in. Octavius has betrayed us all.*

"Welcome, old friend!" Octavius bellowed over the confused cries of the crowd. "I believe you have an announcement to make."

"Yes," Sir Draegon responded, and he turned to address the people of Allandra. "As you see, your kingdom is no longer protected. I now possess the Heart of the King. The light here will soon fade. There will be no provisions. Your king is gone. I have the jewel, and he cannot defeat me."

The despair in the atmosphere became almost palpable. Every ounce of hope the people felt moments before vanished as Draegon uttered his bewitching monologue. Their eyes glazed over, and their collective shoulders slumped.

Draegon continued his monotonous, almost hypnotic drone. "My battle is not with you, good people of Allandra. I have no quarrel with you. Sir Octavius and I have come to an agreement. He is now my second in command, and together we will protect you, under the Heart of the King. Gather your families and come to my castle just across the eastern river. You may not have noticed it before, but once the Heart of the King is in its place there, my castle will be more spectacular and glorious than Othniall'sss hall ever wasss." The serpentine knight hissed his last words.

The people nodded in zombie-like agreement, quietly turned, and made their way out of the courtyard. The Black Knight morphed back into dragon form. The White Knight climbed upon the beast's back, and the two traitors flew off toward the river.

Sam watched in disbelief as his friends and fellow Allandrians trudged by him. The light had vanished from their eyes. The lights in the courtyard and castle flickered out, one by one, as the people filed out of the gate. He stood, and he remembered the prophecy taught to him by his mother.

On that day so far away, betrayal comes from within. The serpent strikes, black as night, and all the people fear. They're led astray, bewitched, they say, by smooth and hissing words.

See through the lies; see through the glitter. The king alone must go, Save but one, the hidden one, the hidden champion. Golden rings and silver things—they hold the keys to free The precious thing: the Heart of the King That only royal eyes can see.

Was it somehow because of the prophecy the spell of the dragon had no effect on him? Sam wondered, but he could not be sure. He knew he must warn the king.

He squared his shoulders and joined the crowd exiting the courtyard. The Allandrians turned to the east as one body, like a hive of bees, toward Draegon's castle. Sam pushed and ducked, finally breaking free from the crowd. Alone, he trudged west—the direction of hope.

He heard a whinny and saw his best friend Franq approach on his chestnut brown mare. "Franq!"

"What is going on? I saw the smoke while on patrol." He looked at the crowd. "Where is Freya?"

Sam quickly described the events of the morning. "Freya is with the crowd heading to Sir Draegon's castle. I tried to call out to her, but her eyes were blank. I don't think she could hear me at all. She certainly didn't recognize me."

"We must go to her! The ruby may be the Heart of the King, but my heart belongs to my betrothed. I will not abandon Freya to whatever evil the Black Knight has planned."

"I cannot. I must find King Othniall!"

"Aye. Yes, my friend. You must."

"When you get to Sir Draegon's castle, try to stay hidden," Sam cautioned. "Trust no one. Sir Octavius is no longer our friend. Scout out the situation and be ready when we come. If we can get the Heart of the King, hopefully we can find a way to break the hold the serpent has over them."

"Be safe, my friend," Franq reached down and placed a comforting hand on Sam's shoulder. "Don't travel on the road. Keep by the edge of the woods. Remember we no longer have the security the Heart of the King provided. You are on your own. Do you want to take my horse? I can travel on foot."

"No. That won't be necessary. I am going home to get supplies, and I will get the pony. He is sturdy and well equipped for the journey." Sam had never before told anyone about the prophecy, but he confided it now to Franq. He never understood it before, but its meaning was clearer than it had ever been. At least parts of it were, and he hoped the words would bring courage to Franq's heart.

"Till our hearts meet again," Sam bade farewell to Franq with the traditional Allandrian benediction.

"Till our hearts meet again." Franq nudged his horse and rode away in search of his fiancé.

෧ ෬

Sam neared his farm twenty minutes later. His mother saw him and ran to meet him. "It's happened, hasn't it?" Nariah did not wait for an answer. She grabbed him by the hand and ran as fast as her arthritic legs could carry her to the old farmhouse where they lived.

Sam gathered bread, fruit, and other supplies as he described the events of the day to his mother. She helped him pack and listened, interrupting with a question every now and then.

"It's time, then. Time to tell you the rest of the story behind the prophesy." Nariah twisted a strand of her silver hair around her finger and studied her son. "Yes," she said after an intense pause. "You're ready. You have to be."

Sam did not understand. "What do you mean?"

"Help me move my bed." They moved her bed. She pried up a couple boards in the floor. He helped his petite mother lift out an ancient wooden chest from the hole.

"This cape will help to hide you should you need to be unseen." She shook out an old brownish-green cape with a golden clasp and handed it to her son.

He tried it on, surprised that it did not have any musty smell. It was almost like new.

"Where are you? Where did you go?" His mother's laughter rang out, her green eyes crinkled in amusement.

She stopped laughing and her eyes filled with tears as she looked down into the chest. She solemnly picked up a silver signet ring from the box and placed it in Sam's hand. It had a small ruby embedded in the silver, shaped like the Heart of the King, only smaller.

"What?" Sam exclaimed, confused. "Where did you get this? It must be worth a fortune. How do you have this?"

Nariah sat on the bed and patted the spot next to her. Sam sat obediently.

"You know the prophesy, but you don't know the rest of the story. Did you ever wonder why you have known the prophesy your whole life, but nobody else talks about it?"

"Yes, but you told me not to talk about it. I told it to Franq today, in hopes it would strengthen his heart with courage."

"That's good," she reassured him. "There's a reason others don't know it. It is for *you*. You have been hidden your entire life. We have been hidden. Even your father did not know the truth. I have been waiting, knowing one day this day would come."

"But why? What do I not know?"

"We had to stay hidden for your protection. My parents were warned about an attack that would come to the kingdom—a betrayal from within. Only someone from the royal bloodline would be able to see clearly." Nariah took her son's face in her hands and looked into his eyes. Sam felt she saw into his soul. "Only one with royal blood can see through the deception and save the kingdom. Don't you see? They couldn't know about you, or me."

Sam broke away and shook his head. "What does this have to do with us?"

"We are royal blood. You and me. The king's parents are my parents. He is my big brother. King Othniall is your uncle."

Sam fell to his knees and bowed his head to the ground. He knelt in stunned silence, then turned to sit on the floor. He looked at his mother. "The king is my uncle." He took a deep breath, trying to make this information seem real. "And you are, what? A princess?"

"Yes, yes. But that is not important. What is important is that, because you have royal blood, you can see through the deception of Sir Draegon. You did not fall under his hypnotic spell. It's why you were wary of Sir Octavius."

"Then why did the king trust him?"

"Oh, my sweet boy. Octavius was good at one time. The king—" She smiled. "My brother—saw the good in him, and he hoped the power of the Heart of the King would be enough to keep the White Knight on the straight and narrow. But Octavius let greed in his heart when Othniall went away. And now it is up to you to go to your uncle and help him recover what was lost."

"The signet ring. Will he recognize it?"

"Yes. When he sees it, he will know you are more than just a messenger. He will know you are family, and you have been hidden away until the right time." She stood, her voice strong and clear. "This is that day. Go, my son, and help bring back the Heart of the King!"

Sam loaded his provisions onto his pony. Nariah followed him out and pressed a very old-looking map into his hand. "Othniall may remember the hidden tunnel, but in case he has forgotten, take this. It will lead you to the old stables beside Draegon's castle."

He kissed his mother on the top of her head and rode away in search of the king, her words echoing in his heart.

He prayed his friend was able to rescue Freya, but he sensed things had gone wrong. The more he prayed, the more his heart grew troubled. *Oh, Franq. I fear you, and the rest of our people, are in more danger than we ever imagined possible.*

Sam's life had been turned upside down in the span of hours. His mind reeled from learning his true identity and his relationship to King Othniall. He suspected Franq's life had turned upside down as well, but in a vastly different way.

"Hurry," he spoke to his pony. "We must find the king. Our people are in trouble."

‌‌ಌ   ಌ

Franq had no difficulty tracking down the sea of Allandrians. They followed the well-worn road to the eastern river. By the time Franq caught up with them, they were almost to the bridge. Even from a distance, he felt their hopelessness swirling around them like a smoky blanket of doom.

He understood their despair. The Heart of the King was no longer in the center of their kingdom, protecting and providing for them. The king was gone. Their greatest knight no longer fought for them but had instead joined forces with their greatest enemy. Their only chance for survival was to follow the crown jewel to its new home in Sir Draegon's castle.

He spotted Freya, her countenance as blank as those around her. Franq tried to shake off the sense of foreboding, but his heart grew more faint with every step his horse took in the direction of the castle.

"Come," he whispered to his steed. He turned his horse away from the crowd of people and guided him to bank of the eastern river a few minutes ride north of the bridge. The water was shallow enough for him to cross. For a brief time, the music of the flowing river dispelled the despondency surrounding his heart.

He crested the hillside on the other side of the riverbank. An incredible sight met his eyes. A spectacular castle stood proudly in the valley below him, just past the forest. Brilliant banners streamed from the glistening ramparts. Sunlight glinted off the dazzling marble walls. *How have I never seen this before?*

Mesmerized, Franq coaxed his horse into a gallop. He had to find Freya. There was hope after all. He abandoned all pretense of stealth and rode into the crowd streaming toward the castle.

He spotted her ahead and urged his mount faster. She disappeared behind the gate. The crowd pressed around his horse, everyone pushing and shoving to get to the gate ahead of them. The sea of people carried Franq toward the gate. He was trapped and could not escape. It no longer mattered. He wanted the same thing they all did—to get inside the magnificently ornate entrance to the castle where, surely, more grandeur and opulence awaited them.

He no longer noticed the eerie stare in the people around him. Franq's eyes glassed over, blinded like the rest. He fell under Draegon's spell.

He crossed the threshold into the castle grounds. In an instant the glitter and glimmer faded. Terrified screams and the crack of whips filled the air. The stench of blood and sweat assaulted his nostrils. Darkness and gloom replaced the brilliant sunlight.

Cruel hands wrenched him down from his horse and threw him into a cage on a filthy wagon. The door of the cage clanged shut, and a padlock secured.

A near continuous cacophony of other cages clanging shut pounded like a drumbeat in his ears. Everyone who stepped inside the gate—ghastly from the inside view—was immediately seized and thrown into a cage.

Freya! Where is Freya?

He struggled to turn around in the tight cage and saw dozens of his fellow countrymen packed in similar cages like cattle. He spotted Freya about a hundred feet ahead of him on another wagon. Her hands gripped the bars of her cage, and she screamed in terror.

What have I done? Franq buried his head in his hands, and the wagons carted him and all the other Allandrians to a massive dungeon in the belly of the castle of deception. He remembered the prophesy Sam told him hours before, and he prayed it would be enough. "Hurry, Sam," he whispered. "It's worse than you can fathom. And I cannot help you."

๛ ๛

Sam slept fitfully under the branches of a mountain fir tree with his pack as a pillow. Images of frightened Allandrians in the clutches of the dark dragon haunted his dreams.

His pony nuzzled him awake at the first rays of sunlight. He shook off the lingering wisps of despair from his dreams. *It's a new day,* he told himself. *There is always hope with the dawn.*

After a quick breakfast of apples, the pair set off in search of King Othniall. He kept the road in view, riding a short distance inside the tree line, Franq's warning fresh on his mind.

Three hours into the morning's journey, he was forced to ride in the open across a vast meadow. A forest rose up in the distance before him. A group of horsemen and carriages emerged from the forest ahead of him. Sam stopped his pony and wished the wildflowers were a bit taller. He almost shouted in relief when the lead horseman's banner unfurled with its beautiful ruby red emblem—the Heart of the King—emblazoned upon it.

Sam rode to meet King Othniall and his entourage. The king's guards rode to meet Sam, and he quickly told them about the dragon. "I must talk to the king! Please."

The guards sensed no guile in the humble farmer. They escorted him to the king's carriage, and Sam told King Othniall and his guards about everything that happened at the courtyard.

"I had a sense something was wrong. That is why we took our leave early after the wedding festivities. I did not sleep well last night. I felt the kingdom's fear in my heart." The king gazed toward the east, as if by willing it, he might make things right again.

"There's more, isn't there?" the silver-haired king gently pressed. Sam looked into his uncle's green eyes. He had never been this close to him, so he never knew how much the king's eyes looked like his own.

"Yes. There is." He opened his bag and pulled out the silver signet ring his mother had given him.

King Othniall and his guards gasped in unison when Sam handed the ring to him.

"Golden rings and silver things—they hold the keys to free..." The king's whisper trailed off as he quoted the line to the prophesy. He met Sam's eyes. "So, you have the silver ring. The one which matches my gold one." He raised his hand to show Sam his golden signet ring. They were identical, except their metal.

"Who gave it to you?"

"My mother. She said she is—"

"My sister. Nariah." King Othniall finished Sam's sentence. "Indeed. I did not know if I would ever see her in this life."

The king let out a hearty laugh and embraced Sam in a big bear hug. "So, you are my nephew! Welcome!"

Sam breathed a sigh of relief and smiled, returning the hug. "Uncle! May I call you that?"

"Yes! Yes, of course. Uncle Othniall. I like the sound of that." He grasped his nephew's shoulders and gazed lovingly into his eyes before releasing him. His voice grew serious. "Now, the Heart of the King. We must get it back. I have always known deep inside that, when this day comes, I must go alone, '*save but one, the hidden one, the hidden champion.*' At one time, I considered the possibility Octavius might be by my side. He played the role of a champion, but there was nothing hidden about him, or his ego."

The guard behind the king tried to stifle a wry laugh.

"Could you be the '*hidden champion*,' Sam?" Othniall studied him. "You were certainly hidden from me."

Sam's eyes grew wide. In all the times he recited the prophecy with his mother, the thought he could be the hidden champion never crossed his mind. He simply thought his role was to give a message to the king when the time came.

"Only royal eyes can see," Sam muttered, comprehending. "Mother told me, *Only someone from the royal bloodline would be able to see clearly to see through the deception.* That is how I saw through Sir Octavius and how I did not come under the spell of Sir Draegon."

He looked up at his uncle, and determination filled his voice. "I don't know how to help or what to do. I am a simple farmer. But as my heart beats, I pledge to you, my king, that I will serve you and go with you to get back the Heart of the King." He knelt before King Othniall and bowed his head.

"And so, you shall, my son." The king raised his nephew to his feet and placed the silver ring on his finger. To his guards he shouted, "Make preparations! Make haste. Today we ride. Tomorrow, we take back the Heart of the King!"

Guards quickly loaded unnecessary gear into the carriages to be sent back to the castle. A young squire led two of the strongest royal horses to King Othniall and Sam.

Sam recognized the lad from the village. "What about my pony?"

"I will get him back safely to Nariah," he promised with a bow.

"Thank you," Sam and King Othniall replied in unison. The king added, "Tell my sister I shall see her soon."

King Othniall mounted his horse, signaling readiness to depart. "You will ride beside me, Hidden Champion."

Hope rose up in Sam's heart, and he climbed onto the royal steed next to his uncle.

The flag bearer led the entourage, unfurling the kingdom's banner in the wind. "For the Heart of the King!" he shouted.

"For the Heart of the King," the guards echoed.

They rode hard until the last light of the day faded.

King Othniall strategized his rescue and retrieval mission with his men around the campfire over supper. He did not want to risk his guards coming under the deception of the dragon and decided to station the men on the west side of the eastern river. They would wait there, ready when needed.

"Do you remember a hidden tunnel? Mother gave me this map before I left." Sam handed the old map to his uncle.

The king immediately recognized it and slapped his knee. "Oh, yes! I forgot about this! It's been so long. Draegon's father and I were friends when we were boys, long before darkness crept into his son's heart. We used to sneak into the stable and ride the horses into the north territory. Legends said there were dragons there; our parents did not want us anywhere near there."

Sam gasped.

"Oh, we never ran into anything. At least I didn't. I have to wonder now if that is what happened to darken Draegon's heart. What did he find?" King Othniall shuddered.

"Nonetheless, the tunnel may still be there. The entrance is likely covered up, somewhere in the forest just north of the main bridge. We can come across the smaller north bridge and come south. The tunnel comes out in the stables. I remember a secret passage from there into the castle, if it is still there. Once we are inside, I will search for the rogue knights, disarm them, and retrieve the ruby. I need you to find my people. Can you do that?"

"Of course. My friend Franq is supposed to be ready to assist when we get inside."

"Remember," the king cautioned, "he is likely under the same enchantment as the rest of the Allandrians. He may not be much help until we can break Draegon's power."

They slept soundly under the stars that night, strengthened by the closeness of family they never knew they had.

The sun shone high in the sky the next day when the royals split from the rest of the king's party. King Othniall and Sam rode to the north bridge, and the others journeyed to the main bridge to await what they prayed would be their king and kingdom's victory. They did not understand how they could win, but they took comfort in the words of the prophesy, recited to them by their king that morning at breakfast.

The door to the tunnel was in the side of a hill, exactly where King Othniall remembered. Like him, it evidenced the passing of the years. Vines and branches covered the entrance. Sam would not have noticed it if the king had not led him directly to it.

He helped his uncle clear away the foliage and shoved open the door. King Othniall fashioned torches for them from nearby branches. "It's been a long time since I've made my own torch," he chuckled as he handed one to Sam. "We will be thankful for these in a few minutes. I don't remember anything as dark as this passage gets."

"I hope it is not as dark as the black dragon. That is the greatest darkness I have ever felt."

"Of that I have no doubt," the king said with a sigh. "Let's go, Sam. Let us bring back the light of the Heart of the King." He led the way into the tunnel.

Other than the occasional spider web or scurry of a mouse, it looked as though the tunnel had not been disturbed since the king's last boyhood trek down its path many decades before. They walked in virtual silence for the better part of the next hour, each deep in his own thoughts and prayers for the people of Allandra.

They could not be certain which they became aware of first: the distant clanging sound, the foul smell, or the sense of despair in the atmosphere. "We must be getting close to something," Sam pointed out the obvious.

"Yes. It's not much further now." The tunnel turned sharply to the right and went up several stairs before ending with a rustic wooden door much like the one at the other end of the tunnel.

Sam put his ear to the door. "It sounds like a couple horses are there, but I don't hear any voices." He handed his torch to the king and gently pushed the door. It barely budged.

He shoved, much harder this time, and the door gave way, greatly offending a mare on the other side of the door. "Shhh," Sam quieted the horse and peered out of the stall. He turned to his uncle. "I don't see anyone here."

King Othniall doused the torches in the water trough and motioned to Sam, "This way to the passage to the castle. Let's hope it's still secret."

He led Sam to the harness room. "Draegon's soldiers don't care much about tidiness, do they?" Sam shook his head at the mess.

"It would seem not." The king strode past piles of livery, leather, and bolts scattered on the tables to a cabinet against the far wall. "Here. The entrance is hidden behind this."

Sam helped him slide the cabinet away from the wall. King Othniall bent down and disappeared into a large hole in the lower part of the wall. Sam climbed in after him and was relieved to find they had enough room to stand in the narrow passage.

Stealthily, they crept along the passageway into the castle for some distance, hearing only their own soft footsteps. They rounded a corner, and the king froze. Men's voices sounded like they were in the passage with them, but they were on the other side of the wall.

The king put a finger to his lips, and they tiptoed past the occupied room. They made another turn, then heard raucous carousing and laughter not far ahead of them.

"That is likely coming from the banquet hall," the king whispered. "We shall go right. If memory serves, the pantry underneath the kitchen is not far that way. It is probably the best place to slip in unobserved."

They found the hidden door the king remembered, but things had changed dramatically in the castle since his last visit. Othniall expected to see cheeses and onions hanging from the ceiling, and baskets of breads and vegetables on the shelves.

Sam stumbled into the room, almost on top of the king. Their eyes took a few moments to adjust to the dim light of the massive room. They gasped in unison.

"This is no pantry." The king's voice seethed in quiet rage.

"No," Sam echoed, his voice a ragged whisper. "This is a house of horrors."

Chains and whips hung from the ceiling. Instead of baskets on shelves, there were cages stacked on top of cages, as far as his eyes could see.

Those were people inside the cages. Allandrians. Men, women, and children. Old and young alike. Each in an individual cage. Sam slammed his hands over his mouth to keep from crying out.

He felt his uncle stiffen. He felt the rage rise up in the king's heart. He recognized it because it mirrored his own feelings. The ruby was suddenly the farthest thing from their minds.

The men in the cages next to them woke up when they heard the scuffle of Sam and Othniall's arrival. Their eyes pleaded for help, but they held up a finger to their lips and pointed to a table in the distance. Three guards sat sprawled around the table, their heads down, snoring among scattered playing cards and beer steins.

Sam heard a familiar voice whisper his name from a few feet away. He tasted bile in his throat. Franq was a prisoner in one of the cages. He hurried to him and grabbed the lock. It would not budge.

"I'm so sorry, Sam," Franq cried. "We are all here. We are all trapped. The castle—"

"It was so beautiful," a young man in the cage next to Franq explained. "Until we stepped through the gate." He could not have been more than sixteen years old.

"He had the Heart of the King, and we followed him," a woman in another cage whispered. Tears streaked her grimy face. "We fell for it, hook, line, and sinker."

"We can't get out," the despair in Franq's voice combined with guilt and shame.

The woman looked past Sam. Her eyes widened, and she bowed her head. "My king." All around them, Allandrians bowed their heads in reverence to their king.

The whispers around them grew louder and rippled throughout the room, as the people recognized King Othniall. "Please help us!"

Sam held up a finger to shush them. He remembered the cape his mother gave him and pulled it out of his bag. It was almost big enough to cover both him and his uncle.

"I don't think they will be waking up any time soon," an elderly man said. His cage was closer to the guards, and he saw how much they had to drink before they passed out. "But please hurry. Get us out of these cages."

"How?" asked a woman Sam recognized as the keeper of the library. "The guards with the keys left hours ago. The inebriated ones don't have keys."

King Othniall examined the heavy iron lock of the cage closest to him. There was an odd round indentation on the side of the lock. "What is this?" He motioned for Sam.

"It looks like— Could it be?" Sam pressed his signet ring into the indentation. The shape matched perfectly. He pulled on the lock, but nothing happened. "Maybe yours will work."

King Othniall's ring fit into the lock, but again, nothing happened. "Let's try both." Sam tried to find a place to put his ring on the other side of the padlock, but that did not budge the lock. He dropped the cape and tried the lock on the next cage, but his ring did not open that one either.

In a simultaneous motion, King Othniall and Sam bowed their heads against the locks in frustration as they each fought back tears.

Both locks clicked open. The two royals slowly turned to each other and whispered at the same time, "Golden rings and silver things—they hold the keys to free—"

Sam's mouth gaped open. The king pointed to Sam's golden curls. "Golden rings—ringlets. Your hair and my golden ring."

"And your silver hair. My silver ring! Silver things. We each have gold rings and silver things. It takes both of us!"

They each plucked a hair from their heads and went from cage to cage, setting the captives free. As soon as the hair touched the lock with the ring set in the indentation, the lock popped open. Hope rippled throughout the room.

Franq gathered the people as they quietly rejoiced and guided them to the door the king and Sam came in through. "Hurry, Franq." King Othniall instructed him to take the people through the hidden passage to the stable and told him where to find the hidden tunnel. "When you get to the other side, cross the north bridge and head south. You'll find my guards on the eastern side of the main bridge. Tell them to come." He grasped Franq's hand and solemnly charged him, "Get my people home."

The king and Sam maneuvered swiftly through the dungeon, awakening every captive and opening every cage, while the drunken guards slept.

The last lock clicked open. The last Allandrian climbed out of his cage and joined the crowd making their way to the secret passage. The aisles were still filled with hundreds of people when a door burst open.

Sir Draegon and Sir Octavius stormed into the room, followed by a handful of guards armed with swords and whips. One of the guards grabbed the escaped prisoner closest to him and held a sword to her throat.

"Freya!" Franq's voice rang out from the back of the room.

The people of Allandra steadily continued their exodus into the hidden passage, and the crowd quickly disappeared through the door.

King Othniall stepped forward. "Let her go!" he demanded. "Your quarrel is not with her. It is with me."

Draegon laughed, a wicked, condescending sound without an ounce of joy. "You. What are you now? You are nothing. I have the Heart of the King." The black knight proudly held up the ruby. "I have won!"

At that moment the last Allandrian disappeared into the passageway behind Franq.

Octavius stared in confused dismay at the rock Sir Draegon held proudly above his head. It was no longer brilliant ruby-red. It was not red at all. It was black. Cold. Lifeless and powerless. It looked like a huge lump of coal. "What is this? Where is the Heart of the King? What is that rock?"

The guards and Draegon stared at the rock in confusion. The guard holding Freya dropped his sword and turned around in disgust. Freya ran to Franq, and they vanished into the tunnel.

" W—w—wait! It was—it was red," Draegon stammered. Octavius and the other guards glared at him.

"This was all just another deception?" Octavius roared. "Was any of this real? Did you ever actually have the Heart of the King?"

Before Draegon could manufacture an excuse, King Othniall stepped forward. "Don't you see? It's the people. The Heart of the King has always been the people. It was never about the gemstone. The ruby has always been a symbol of the real power, which is the people whom I love. *They* are the Heart of the King. My heart."

Sam looked at his king in bewilderment. "The lights? When they went out in the courtyard?" His eyes grew wide as he struggled to understand. "Then it—it was not because Sir Draegon seized the ruby. It was because the people left?"

"Yes. When they lost hope and believed Draegon's deception, they left Allandra. The true power of the kingdom left with them. Now that they know the truth, the light of Allandra has returned. We don't need the ruby. The true Heart of the King is going back home."

At that moment, King Othniall's guards came through the door. The king pointed to the traitorous knights. "Take them away."

He put his arm around Sam. "Let's go home. I will send for Nariah, and we will celebrate with feasting and dancing. The Heart of the King has been restored!"

Sam grinned as his uncle tousled his golden curls. "So it has, Uncle. So it has!"

Malevolent Queen
Jennifer King

Chapter 1 ~ Northland

Arrows struck the ornate carriage. Horses reared. Knights pulled out swords and banged shields. Men stalked out of the forest, hunger in their eyes. Emerald and sapphires glinted midmorning light off the wagon.

"Guards! Surround the carriage!" Anola donned in silver plated armor propelled her sword into the air. The golden ride pulled by invisible beasts. Five knights committed to their given order.

The transport halted in snowy tracks and a tall man stepped out wrapped in a midnight blue velvet robe. His short black locks laid neatly to his ivory complexion. Heated magic swirled in his eyes.

A few men rushed the sorcerer. The man's deep green eyes flicked in the forest thief's direction. The land echoed with cracked timber. The pelted vibrations pulled the earth apart and swallowed them whole. Scavengers inhaled fear scrambled in despair returned to the woods.

Anola sheathed her blade and walked to the sorcerer.

"Master Morlain I'm Captain Anola of Vair. I apologize for not meeting up with you sooner. My knights and I are here to escort you to Northland Castle."

"Appears so." Morlain sealed the door.

The carriage proceeded forward, no beast print left in the frosted path. Anola mounted her mare. She collected white petals in her gloved hand. Winter.

Winter brought risks upon the land of Teirson. The awaking of Fathom Woods. A three-weeks ride from Northland Kingdom. The Fathom Woods inspired desperate individuals to risk everything for fabled fortune. In the frost the wood's living trees riled awake. Leaves transformed into lethal ice daggers.

"Captain!" Varin called out in his deep voice.

Anola turned to the knight. "Master Morlain would like a word with you."

"Interesting, Varin switch with me."

Anola trotted next to the porcelain carriage. "Master Morlain, what can I assist you with?"

"How well do you know the Fathom Woods?"

"Fathom Woods is filled with dangerous wildlife and beasts."

"Yes, I understand that but how well do you know the land itself."

"Well enough to get myself out if I find myself in there."

Morlain exhaled, "Very well."

"Master Morlain if I might ask..."

"You can return to your duty Captain. I shall speak to the King first upon arrival."

"Very well Master Morlain."

Anola rode up ahead of the carriage. "Varin, what do you know of Master Morlain?"

"Captain, he is known as the most renowned sorcerer in Westland. Not much is known about him personally other than he is a descendant of one the scholars who were sent to imprison the Malevolent Queen. Morlain's deeds have been spread throughout all of Teirson. He's defeated dragons, saved crops, and cured the rich of sickness. The magic man's feats equal the costs to his requests."

"I've heard some tales but why do you think King Vard has brought him to Northland?"

"Our King has reigned for three-years, but he is wise. There have been whispers of an attack coming from Eastland. Maybe our Northland King is preparing for the future."

"Possibly."
"One last thing Captain, his prices aren't always in gold."

᷆   ᷇

Midday market shoppers canvased the streets and halted at the sight of the enchanted carriage. Children and adults marveled. Large thick golden wheels moved freely; iridescent pearls adorned every edge of the ride. Bystanders peered off roof tops and staircases in hopes of catching a glimpse at the sorcerer.

"Raise the gate!"

Footsteps pounded along the top of the castle's gated wall. Northland Castle bridge hovered over blackened waters and welcomed all. The carriage stopped. Tiered staircases led to the grand entryway.

Morlain stepped onto gravel, the light crunch of ground pulled at Anola's gut. His movements coasted silence against uneven ground. Morlain, encased in deep emerald attire embroidered with rubies, glanced at the castle.

A pristine stronghold for over four centuries. The courtyard, half-moon shaped, filled with green and vibrant garden untouched by winters approach.

"Master Morlain, please come this way. Northland King Vard awaits your arrival." Bowed a puffed sleeved servant.

Morlain strode past the help his focus on the entrance. Anola kept her pace complementary to Morlain's tenacity. Doors whisked open. Ivory walls embossed with whimsical designs canvased the entryway. Tapestry threads danced woven stories. Carpets swirled white and blue metallic liquid ripples with every footstep. Pearl sconces guided the path to the King's thrown room.

Morlain slightly raised his brow amused by the magical creations in Northland kingdom. Westland considered itself the most prestigious magical land in Terison. Any magic outside of their territory is considered below quality.

Morlain cascaded past two heavy redwood doors. King Vard surrounded by counselors stared at the invited guest. Morlain presented himself with a slighted bow. Anola stifled a laugh; she considered such a gesture would cause Morlain internal pain.

"Northland King Vard, I've arrived at your personal, request."

"Welcome Master Morlain, I've anticipated your arrival. All leave the room we have many things to discuss. Captain Anola, I need you to stay. This will involve you."

"Yes your Highness."

King Vard led them to an extended room. Rows of panel-less windows floated in sunlight. A table drenched with aged maps and scattered charcoal bits stationed in the middle of the chamber.

"Captain Anola you might have heard the Eastland territory plans to attack my kingdom after winter ends. I've asked Master Morlain here to assist us with acquiring a magical object to help defend the kingdom. The Scarlet Heart."

Steel edge words sank into the room, the air churned colder, and Anola stiffened at the king's idea.

"King Vard, Fathom Woods lays as Queen's Tower guard. No one has ever returned."

"Hence why Master Morlain will accompany you and your knights to collect the source of her power. My research describes it as a massive crimson jewel holding the Malevolent Queen's power. With that I will be able to protect our lands and defeat any enemies that attempt to invade." King Vard gripped the table, his knuckles intense white, eyes focused on the maps deleterious destination.

"Your Highness, the dangers to the Malevolent Queen's Tower intensifies during winter."

"I said. Master Morlain will keep you and your company safe. Keep him guarded, all of you are important pieces to keeping this kingdom safe."

Anola's spine ached at having to drive good men into a fateful forest that never released its victims. Anola turned to Morlain, his stature poised and focused on loose paper scrips.

"Master Morlain there are terrors and horrors that occur in the Fathom Woods and who knows what guards the Queen's Tower."

"Captain Anola those concerns have been considered and addressed. The safety of the party will be fine. Now trust in your King."

Anola's stomach churned. "Your Highness, we will do as you bid."

Anola bowed and turned on her heel to leave.

"Captain." King Vard called, his focus on inked parchments.

Anola held her burden breath and turned toward the king.

"Tonight, we are holding a feast in honor of Master Morlain's arrival. Have you and your knights dress in your finest. All of you will be guests at the party."

"Thank you my King, I will inform my fellow knights."

Chapter 2 ~ Invitation

Anola's steps trudged toward the knight's barracks. Icy pricks of winter filled the halls. Maidens rushed to light fires to stave off winter sickness.

The last time Anola walked in Fathom Woods was ten years ago. The day her adopted father, Ahar, found her among the burgundy trees. A young girl with forgotten memories, bare feet, and a pendant.

Ahar passed Captain to Anola and choose to retire in the countryside he earned in service. She trained day and night to express gratitude for the life Ahar provided. Anola's unknowing past never presented a problem for her father. Ahar told Anola, "The future is where we are made. The present calls on our skills, and the past is where we can never walk again."

Anola squinted her dark amber eyes at the high risen sun. Aged memories filtered through the barracks cedar door. She flew the entrance open.

"Stand!" Varin shouted.

Five strong and trusted knights stood before Anola. Varin, Anola's fathers trusted friend, now her adviser. Bash and Luke trained with her since youth. Kendrick, the new and youngest recruit. Then there is Rynn, quiet and deadliest with a war hammer.

"Excellent work today knights. Yet our duty to safeguard Master Morlain is extended. Tomorrow at sunrise we leave for the Fathom Woods."

"Captain, those woods..."

"Kendrick, you pledged your allegiance to the kingdom and our king. Trust that he knows what is best for us. Our quest, is to collect the Queen's Scarlet Heart."

The room vibrated with conflicted emotions, old stories and cautions seeped into each mind. Varin stepped forward to end the silent rain of unease.

"Captain we will follow you where our King sends us."

"Thank you Varin. Now knights as part of our new arrivals presence the King has extended us all an invitation to tonight's dinner. Present yourself in your best."

Anola exited the barracks and walked home. She focused her mind on the upcoming travel. The Fathom Woods built nightmares into children. The woods quilted tales of beasts, size of mountains with teeth that slice at mere touch. Trees awoke at the chill to twist, crush, and confuse its lost victims. Frozen waters cried out for freedom would entice wanderers, hoping to escape its cold prison. Only to drag their victims into a suffocated watery death.

Anola gazed at herself in the tarnished mirror, green corseted dress tied in pale yellow cord felt inadequate compared to her armor. Battle on the field gained experience and honor. Ahar raised Anola to serve and become an example to the people they protected. Yet dinner at the king's table is a mix of elaborate words and prestige Anola knew little about. Dancing and dining with nobles was the farthest interest from her mind.

Anola touched the gem on her necklace. White mist flowed within the pendant's confined walls. Anola hoped the jewel would reveal a secret of her birth land. She tucked the pendent into her corset. She wrapped a red-wine wool cloak close to her body and stepped into the brisk chill of nightfall.

Chapter 3 ~ Disgusted Dance

The dining hall cascaded daylight from protruded goblet fixtures. Heavy drapes in hues of beryl blue and embroidered silver plastered on the walls. Clusters of guests filled every inch of the canvased corridors. Anola stepped into the whimsical evening. She dared to hope it would end soon.

Anola caught sight of Bash and Luke. She weaved around guests and servers. Anola stepped past hurdles of sophisticated dancers. Blocked. Master Morlain cut in front of Anola. Bash snickered and turned toward the youngest knight.

Morlain dressed in violet velvet outline in gold with bits of obsidian speckled into the lining. Ruffled cuffs protruded out of Morlain's sleeves in shades of golden foil matched darken boots.

"May I have this dance."

"I feel you would find my steps clumsy and out of place Master Morlain."

"I'm sure I can manage." Morlain laid out his hand, rejection not an option.

Anola felt the hum in her arm, refusal would lead to an awkward journey. Anola placed disdained fingertips into Morlain's gloved hand. Morlain led her onto the lively dance floor.

"Thank you for assisting me earlier today."

Anola tilted her head and narrowed her gaze to meet his. "You're welcome."

"The journey will be difficult, but I assure you and your men's lives have been calculated for everything."

"Sir, I may not have been captain long, but I assure you my knights and I are skilled to handle all matters. Those woods, are not meant to be entered. The trees and beasts guard that castle."

"I'm aware of the history of those woods, Captain Anola. I've taken precautions. And it is good to know, your skilled in all matters."

Anola felt the sway of dancing mix with Morlain's mischievous words and grin. Desired trust and lies mingled in the air. Morlain spun Anola into a darkened corner of the ballroom. Morlain pressed Anola against a view obstructed by drapes.

"Captain I promise you that I will find what the king has requested. Guard and guide me to the Queen's Scarlet Heart and all will be well."

"Master Morlain I believe this dance has ended." Anola pushed Morlain arm's length away. The light speckled against the gem on Anola necklace, Morlain's gaze landed on the mesmeric pattern.

"I do apologize for my rudeness milady. I do hope you allow me to make amends." Morlain stepped back into the crowd, swallowed within a purple mist.

Anola wiped her palms against her dress, the warmth of Morlain's grasp lingered.

"You enjoy your dance there, Captain?" Bash laughed as Anola slipped into her seat.

"As much as I enjoy drinking your home-made brew."

"Oh, my heart you have pained. That is a family recipe."

"And I'm glad that is where it will stay."

The table jostled with laughter. The rest of the night mingled with food and talk of old adventures.

Morlain walked into his study from a lavender mist doorway. Small circular room, carved in bookcases and desks tops saturated with ink and piles of drawings. Candles melted to wicks piled next to papers and colorful bottles mixed together in heaps.

Morlain searched an aged dark redwood bookcase with a glass door and timber handle. Thick worn books of darken shades of once brilliant colors lined row after row. Morlain edged his fingertips along the books and halted on a single red volume. He pulled the book out and flipped through pages. He stopped on an image of a single darken spire. The Malevolent Queen's Castle. Obsidian fortress led to the sky. At the top the Queen's throne room.

An image of a chest and next to it The Scarlet Heart. The container frozen on a pillar protected by two stone guardians. A small hollowed round orb locked crested along the edge of the box. A passage scribbled next to the drawing, mist and rock collided as one but beware unleashing what is contained it will bring back the ordained.

❧ ❧

Anola curled into bed; wisps of late-night drink mingled with faint excitement. Heated remnants of Morlain's touch rolled shivers into tense muscles. Anola's vision raced to find slumber. Darkness poured into dreams; dreams crashed into memories.

Anola's steps wove through wine-colored woods. Clear small footprints trailed behind. Young Anola's bare toes matched shadowed violet hues of snow. Her amber eyes transfixed on mirrored snowflakes; laughter echoed in wonder. She reached out to grab frigged petals.

Breath stilled, captured in frozen ground shakes. The trees rumbled, twisted branches shook bullets of frozen knives. Harden ice sliced into Anola's limbs.

Anola screamed, awaken by pain. Sweat slid down her face. She looked at her arms, needle pricks lingered. Anola threw off the covers. She crunched her toes against wooden panels.

Ahar told Anola that nightmares can haunt her outside of her dreams if she dragged them out with her. Fresh air spilled into the room. Anola gripped the window shutters, early morn brisk calmed her senses.

Chapter 4 ~ Fire Tales

The sun burst forth from the distance snow cap mountains. Anola's peace consumed by ignited nightmares. Vivid distant memories mixed with firm determination to return to the Fathom Woods. She adjusted the bit on her mare.

"Men, as you know the king has selected us to retrieve a powerful object, the Scarlet Heart. Our destination will lead us through a place filled with fearsome beasts and wildlife. Yet we, are the King's Knights. We have overcome fears and trials. Master Morlain will guide us through the woods which has not been accomplished in centuries. We will succeed where others have fallen. Let's head out!"

Cheers and farewells filled the crisp morning. Master Morlain pulled a dark red book from his bag. The pages worn and gray etched with charcoal images and words. Morlain flipped through pages and stopped halfway through the book. Inhaled breath blew dust off the pages.

The ash pieces danced in the air, battled into shape in a rhythmic dance. The ashes molded into a small bird. Air as mortar against continuous, rotated, unconnected charcoal specks.

A sparrow, the closest likeness Anola could compare to the fidgety being. The bird glided up and around finally settled onto Morlain's outstretch hand.

"Our guide." Morlain pulled himself onto his soot-colored horse.

Hooves marched past the entry way of the kingdom onto frosted covered ground. Anola rode next to Morlain and watched the bird flap its instinctive wings.

Three weeks passed by in a blur, Anola stared at the tree line of the Fathom Woods. She felt ice crystals attempt to peck between slits in her armor plating. Mountainous burgundy trunk trees reflected a gated fortress. The sleek line of trees went miles in either direction. White bristle leaves interlocked into one another prevented light into the woods. The trees thick and alive ruffled disdain for the visitors.

The ashen swallow dove back and forth along the edge of the Fathom Woods. Anola certain if it could sing it would have chirped out a tune of excitement. Anola disembarked from her horse. "We will make camp here tonight men, I do not want to start our trek in there at night."

Morlain rode next to Anola. "I understand you are weary to press on, but you shouldn't prevent completion of this task posthaste."

"Master Morlain your arrival to the destination is under my command. We will find the Scarlet Heart and return it to the king."

"Captain, the Scarlet Heart will have life altering effects on your kingdom."

"Master Morlain the only lives I'm concerned with are my men and yours. We will proceed at the break of dawn and those woods are not to be considered anything less than dangerous."

Morlain narrowed his eyes and dismounted disgruntled steps paced to the fire. The sorcerer weaved light blue ribbons of magic and collected dirt to form a reclined seat. Morlain dove into his book and ignored all around. Crackled bits of wood nipped at the icy wind.

"Master Morlain!" Bash called out with liquid curiosity.

Morlain eyes glazed in Bash's direction waited for next part of the conversation.

Bash grinned with his wine glossed eyes, "What are we supposed to...uh be aware of at this castle? The Malevolent Queen has been gone for over 400 years!"

Morlain closed his book move close to the fire. He waved figures into the flames. Thick vines with knife tipped spikes encircled the tower. The vines moved in serpentine fashion; movement never ceased in the smoky cloud they resided. Morlain moved his fur lined glove and highlighted the single massive window with an arched top.

"The Malevolent Queen observed all from her throne room. Her control widespread, sank into every crevice of ancient Teirson's history. The Malevolent Queen's reign silent and unprovoked."

"Aye Master Morlain,...hic... we have heard the tells from youth. What are we to face." Bash belched.

Morlain ignored the question and pressed on with his tale. Morlain waved his other hand, and the ashen bird flew to the tower. The bird nestled itself on the top of the flame silhouetted tower. Comfortable. Eerie.

"The Malevolent Queen would slip into the dreams of rulers and use them as pawns, sinking her ideas and curved paths to form her great reign. Those of the Collected Order, my ancestry, formed together to protect the land from her terror. They pulled together and stormed into her castle going up living stairs and monsters that would..."

Bash fell over passed out from drink and boredom.

"Looks like old tales sent poor Bash to sleep." Luke laughed among the knights.

Morlain rolled his eyes and whipped his hand back from fire. Anola observed Morlain whisper to the wind and a leaf edged door frame grew from the ground.

"Knock before we leave."

Morlain closed the door. Huddled knights slept next to the fire. Anola pulled the smoky fur blanket close and drifted off to asleep.

Anola young again, wondered in the Fathom Woods her focus anchored to the ground. Her footsteps moved forward but the ground shifted back. Large burgundy bark tree surrounded her. She braced her hands against the thick trunks and began to climb. Anola broke through the canopy. Miles and miles of black tree filled her view into the endless horizon. In the distance shadows rumbled and clawed together to form the Queen's Tower. She peered at the slender tall arched shaped window; a single pane framed in ebony.

Anola narrowed her view and gazed at sole figure; it moved in the window. She cupped her hands close to her eyes. Her focus on the silhouette. It turned around. The eyes debuted, clear icy blue and hollow night. They gripped Anola from treetop. Anola gasped as the stare pulled her breath out of her body. Anola lost her balance and smacked against the ground. Her vision went black.

Chapter 5 ~ Fathom Woods

Anola stared at the crisp lines of dawn. Chills of new nightmares sunk deep into Anola's soul. She shook prickled sensations off her limbs.

"Captain Anola, having vivid dreams?"

Anola pulled the blanket close. Morlain deteriorated the door. His eyes narrowed beyond Anola.

Anola felt layers peeled back expose hidden secrets. Thick slices of memory cut down to reveal terrors. "Master Morlain. If you want to know something, ask me. I do not give you permission for you to interfere in my thoughts."

"Pardon me milady, I do not mean to offended." Morlain's eyes widen as he vacated Anola's mental abode. "Captain Anola, I do apologize for crossing the line. I only wanted to ensure your well-being. We must all be mental prepared to enter the Fathom Woods."

Anola fixed her armor and blade to her side. "We are."

"Knights break camp and let's go."

Breakfast barley barely made it down as the company awaited before the woods. Anola pulled herself into the saddle.

"Do not give this place an inch of fear for it will surely bring death. Master Morlain I hope you know what you're doing."

"With absolution." Morlain hummed. The swallow fluttered its wings and landed on the sorcerer's arm. Morlain whispered to the bird. The ashen bird gargled and molded into larger narrow bird with claws and strong wings. Bits of purple hue meshed with the mortar air and pilling ash.

"Lead the way." Morlain propelled the newly formed guide into the air.

"The falcon will guide us on the safest path through this wood. Some trees like to remain asleep, while others want to let their rage drive them. We will avoid the disturbed woken ones in their madness, but we still need to tread cautiously."

Morlain wove illuminated daffodil glow orbs around the party. They crossed the threshold. The bird trailed amethyst dust against motionless trees. Branches vibrated anger released ice shards.

Varies sizes of pencil thin to barrel size trees scatted within the forest. Silver threaded lines curved into the rigid burgundy bark, to entice travelers underneath their branches.

Anola breathed in crisp frigged air; tiny icicles attempted to cut her from the inside but melted too fast to make a mark. The ashen falcon curved left and filed them all in a single line. Crack. The horses yanked their reigns. The mounts jerked and stamped in place. Bits of ground nipped at Rynn's horse.

Rynn squeezed and pulled on the reigns. The large steed rejected control and violently tossed back and forth. Rynn flew to the ground.

"Rynn get your horse under control!" Varin shouted.

Clumps of dirt and leaves crawled up the legs of Rynn's steed. Jingles of ice rung with excitement. Rynn rolled and jumped up. Hammer held tightly against him. The horse ran off the path. The mount bucked and flew against trees. The branches twisted propelled icicles till the steed neighed no more. Poppy red painted the ground.

Anola looked back at the knights held in firm formation. "Rynn you'll have to keep up with us. If you tire Kendrick can switch with you." Rynn pulled his dropped bag from the ground and tucked it to his side.

Morlain motioned for the ashen falcon to continue. The birds body ignited ribbons of violet and lavender. The fowl ruffled its wings and continued into the woods.

ఇ ಆ

Hours poured like days as they treaded surrounded in darkness. The path opened to a small clearing. The falcon froze in place. All stopped and gripped their weapons close. Bash dismounted. He pointed his blade into darkness. Mirrored snowflakes reflected off the sword.

"Captain, there is movement."

Morlain whistled low. The bird weaved a scarlet border around dormant trees.

"Stay within the crimson seam. It is the safest area from the trees."

The knights dismounted. Blade in hand the knights steady their shields. Rynn held his hammer stance firmly against stillness of pitch black.

"Morlain, can you see anything." Anola narrowed her vision.

Morlain pressed thumb, middle and fore finger together to create a diamond. The other digits wove minted green wisps into the hollow opening. He peered through the diamond vision gate; he moved across the trees.

"We are surrounded, there are three beasts. Fathom Wolves."

Kendrick pipped up, "We can take them."

"Do not underestimate these beasts. They are frost white and half the size of a house. Do not let them sink their teeth into you. They'll drag you off and we will not find a single bone." Anola ordered.

"Do these beasts have any weaknesses?"

Morlain's silent breath response sunk in the air. Heavy steps encircled. Ice shards hit the ground. Bristled fur flew between Bash and Kendrick. A wall of fur whipped at the young knight.

Kendrick hit the ground. He gasped for breath. Kendrick's shield lay next to him. Shredded in two. The large wolf arched its tail. Sharp rigid polar ice spears ribbed down its back. The wolf growled deep in its belly. Long knives glisten at its claws. The beast leapt back into cover of darkness.

"Circle around Morlain!" Anola order echoed.

The knights pulled together and pressed Morlain to the center.

"More light Morlain!"

"Give me some room to work!"

Morlain called forth the ashen falcon. He rolled his hands in a rapid circle. A lava lit orb took shape. Morlain commanded the falcon to open its charcoal beak. The sorcerer slid the small inferno light into the magical fowl. It rolled down the bird's throat and widen in its belly.

"Up!"

The ashen falcon flew up and hovered over the center of the party. Light casted over the battle ground. Snow pummeled steps multiplied into a whirlwind stampede. Crunch. Crunch. Silence.

Anola held her shield tight. Stillness of breath coated the moment. A Fathom wolf leaped forward. Claws aimed at Kendrick. Spears sliced through flesh. Fresh stench of iron coated the atmosphere. Flood of blood enthralled the burgundy trees. Trunks reverberated with expectation.

Kendrick fell to the ground. He gripped his leg. Bash clutched the young knight's shoulder and pulled him back. Luke wove bandage around the wound.

Ice white fur blended into the snow marred only by crimson. Rynn swung his thick monstrous spiked hammer at the beast. Hammer smashed against ground. The wolf sidestepped. Charcoal eyes fixated on its prey.

Luke picked up his tempered blade. Thick footsteps ran at the whimsical beast. The wolf howled and dashed at its opponent. Teeth mashed through armor. Luke released his sword. Wolf daggers lunged off the land and returned to darkness. Screams muffled by sounds of snapped tree trunks.

Anola swung into the empty air. "NO! Morlain do something!"

Rynn pulled back into the circle. Heavy rapid breath pulsed anger. Knights banged their shields.

"Lift your weapons!" Morlain commanded.

They slung their blades into the air. Morlain blew metallic dust. Their weapons radiated with braided rope enchantment of blood orange and yolk.

"This will cause fires to ignite when it touches the beasts. I suggest you hurry we won't last much longer."

"Bash, Varin get them to come toward you. Rynn be ready to smash them in half."

The mother of the beasts snarled as she moved between in the clearing. She surveyed her prey. Her obsidian eyes locked onto Anola. Black tunnel gaze pulled at Anola.

Crunch. Crunch.

Anola's mare dashed at the mother wolf. The wolf clashed paw to ribs. The horse wrestled for freedom. Anola charged. Varin yanked her back.

"Morlain where are the other two coming from!" Varin shouted.

"There!"

The smallest wolf bolted toward Bash. Bash slid. Varin descended down, blade in grasp. The blow sliced between the eyes of the beast. Orange liquid stained the ground. The beast lay still. Mother wolf howled. The beast in the woods trailed in the distance. The massive wolf dragged the mare into the woods. The mother wolf's eyes locked on Anola.

Chapter 6 ~ Promises

Anola scrambled to Kendrick's side, "Morlain heal him."

Morlain knelt next to the young knight. He unraveled the bandages. Morlain hovered his hands over exposed bone and flesh. Kendrick's wound rigid and dark violet.

"He has lost a lot of blood."

"Do what you can."

Hues of rosebud pink and sandy white beach misted wrapped Kendrick's leg. Morlain hummed over the peeled flesh. The wound stitched together left a white seared mark. Kendrick inhaled cries shifted to heavy slumbered breaths.

"He will rest till tomorrow; we won't know much until he awakens."

"Varin, Rynn place him on his horse."

Anola pulled Morlain to the outer portion of the barrier. The ashen falcon flapped without fail. "Exactly what just happened!"

"Those beasts are here to prevent us from reaching the Queen's castle. They guard what we are here to find."

"Morlain, Luke is dead, and Kendrick is barely alive. We all need to make it out alive. Can you guarantee the safety beyond this point?"

Morlain lowered his voice. "Anola, your king chose you because your men are expendable. My commission is to collect the Scarlet Heart first and protect you second. After that, all else is insignificant. Now let's put this aside. We have more to worry about. Have your men collect the wolf's blood it will help us for what we face next"

"My men are not insignificant, and I do not trust your word. If you want to go home safe, keep the rest of us alive." Anola shoved Morlain back. She stopped at the dead wolf. Vibrant blood painted the ground. Anola brows furrowed and grip tighten on her hilt. Morlain pulled out several corked topped vials from his satchel.

"Finish gathering, we leave now." Anola grabbed Luke's horse.

Morlain waved down the ashen bird. He gently pulled out the ball of molten light from its belly. The ashen falcon ruffled its feathers sank into weighted relief.

Anola firmly gripped the reins of Luke's horse. She traveled in silence focused on blurred thoughts. King Vard took reign after his father passed three years ago. Anola believed in what Ahar ingrained in her. A king stood on the trust and strength of their knights. Anola formed herself to be strong and forthright symbol for the kingdom. She needed to know if what Morlain spoke of rang true and if he deserved her trust.

The Fathom woods broke out into a curved clearing. A thick mist barricaded around the castle. Wisps of smoke broke from the top revealed clips of movement. The Queen's Castle a rigid and icy tower. A single window viewed the Northern Mountains.

"The Queen's Castle." Morlain exhaled.

Anola dismounted. "We will set up camp and tend to Kendrick. Morlain we have more to discuss."

"As you desire milady."

Rynn and Bash carefully lifted Kendrick and propped him against bags. Varin ignited the fire. Morlain followed Anola.

"You say the king has discarded us what proof do you have?"

Morlain tugged at his red velvet jacket revealed a thin scroll.

"Your king's words and seal."

Anola hovered her hand over the parchment. She took the scroll. She ran her fingertips over the seal. Copper wax held the king's ring imprint. The letter revealed all Morlain disclosed earlier. Anola handed it back to the sorcerer. Morlain took Anola's hand.

"I will do my best to get everyone else out."

"Keep your word wizard."

"I need something in return."

"What is that?"

"Tell me about yourself."

"I don't understand what do you have to gain from this?"

"Simply know I've become interested in you."

Anola felt hurt and uncertainty flood into throughout her being. Her gut cringed danger. She went against her natural instincts.

"The former Captain Ahar is my adopted father. He found me...inside the Fathom Woods ten winters ago. He saved me from the trees. This pendent is the only trace I have of my past. Furthermore, I have no memories before Ahar found me."

Anola armor gleamed in the moonlight as she walked away. Morlain grinned as he followed her to camp. Anola settled next to Bash. She grabbed a portion of Varin's mashed stew.

Anola watched the knights nosily fall into slumber. Morlain slid next her. Anola tightened the cloth around herself. Morlain held his palms toward the fire.

"Anola I know I haven't made a good impression. I will do my best to keep everyone alive."

"Why?"

Morlain drew his silver green eyes into Anola's. "I've researched and witness kingdoms and treachery. Yet from your strength I can tell you shouldn't be led by a king who would willing use you as pawn for power. King Vard's power is great he doesn't need the Queen's Heart. I will take it to the scholars for safe keeping."

"Morlain thank you for your honesty, but I will continue the mission and return with the Queen's Heart. I will see for myself what kind of king I risk my life for."

"I shall return with you. We don't know what will happen with power he could gain."

Anola stared into the fire, "What is in the mist?"

Morlain pulled the ashen book form his satchel. The sorcerer gently turned worn pages and stopped on ancient writings. Ink plots and written words swirled. Living images moved at Morlain's words on the pages.

"The mist contains living vines of thorns which crave blood. This is where the Fathom wolf's blood will come into play. Once we enter into the Queen's Castle we will have to be weary. I've studied what happened to the Queen that day. One of my descendant's is one of the scholars who besieged the Malevolent Queen's Castle. He wrote in elaborate detail what occurred. In an intense moment when they were sealing her power she disappeared."

The images on the pages moved from the Queen's throne room configured into explosion of ink smudges

"The books reveal creatures that live in the walls. They will do anything to prevent entry into the Queen's throne room. Once we get to the top there will be two stone guards they protect the contents of the chest. The Scarlet Heart is imbued with the Queen's abilities. It will provide dark wondrous power to anyone who welds it."

Anola twisted her pendant between nervous fingers. The misted waves in the gem reflected specks of moonlight.

"May I see?"

"I don't ever take it off, ever."

"You can keep it on."

Morlain reached close to Anola's neck and held the gem loosely in fingertip grip. His eyes glazed over with grayish tone. Morlain released the gem and gently coasted his hand along Anola's jawline as he pulled back.

"This is quite a pendant you wear. I do believe it will lead you to a great outcome."

"After all this is over you can enlighten me about what you know."

"Of course, milady. Get some rest we will need it tomorrow."

Morlain waved together a frame of taupe and mauve. A door arose from the dirt. Morlain stepped into the entry way. Anola peered into the room. Drawings of a chiseled chests and the

Queen's tower scattered along the walls. Firm rigid figures built of black soot and resin plastered along desks. The door closed.

Chapter 7 ~ Watch Out For That Vine

Slits of light crawled through the clouds. Anola stirred from sleep. Her eyes sunken. She stretched out tension. Gray mist wisped in the air flaunted motion beneath the cloudy wake.

"It won't be easy." Morlain walked out the earthen door. Morlain tailor together in velvet black jacket with silver lining, flat diamond buttons, and deep midnight bottoms.

"Not seeing where we will be going will be the most difficult. I do have a solution."

"Does it involve the vials of blood we collected?" Varin stared at the bottles.

"It does."

Anola winkled her nose and gazed at the open bag of sunburst morning orange blood vials. Kendrick laid up against a rock. His hand clutched his leg, and he inhaled heavy at the river of pain.

"Captain." Varin called out. "Can I have a word for a moment."

Anola nodded as she tightened her armor to her form. Varin a head taller with lines of wisdom creased his face. Varin's placed his gauntlet hand on Anola's shoulder.

"Captain I've known you since Ahar found you. You've proved yourself over and over. I would follow you as I have done with your father. That sorcerer over there...he is not one to be trusted. Yet he does appear as someone who may have earned your trust?"

"Varin, thank you for bringing your concerns. I agree something does not settle right with Morlain, but he has guaranteed our safety. After we return home I need to discuss some concerns. I don't have the full picture, but I will soon."

"Anola, you're family. Do what you deem best."

Anola forced a smiled, unease sunk into every step back to the fire.

"Knights, Morlain has a plan to get us through the vine field and into the tower."

Morlain stepped forward, "Those vials collected will serve as distractions. The vines in the mist are constantly searching for a feast. The blood will draw them away from our path. From there we will be at the Queen's door. I should be able to unlock it."

"You should?" Bash choked out.

"Yes should, not many of the books in my possession tell of how to open that door."

Anola stared past the top of the mist. A large, framed door engraved with magical symbols boasted of never being unlocked. Beveled bricks outlined the entryway dared those to cross the mist to find wonders or death.

"We will cross the mist. Throw the vials where Morlain tells you too. Kendrick you'll stay here. Call out if you see anything strange. Varin, Bash, Rynn keep tight, Morlain and I will take the lead. Let's go."

Morlain motion the ashen falcon above the mist. Threads of red and orange danced in the body of charcoal bird. The falcon flew high and above the cloudy barricade. The bird returned and perched on Morlain's shoulder it nudged its beak against his ear.

Morlain pointed to the northwestern area and tossed a vial. Rips of mist railed up as vines collied against the ground enticed by the smell and feel of blood. Anola tensed as viper vines patterned with massive thorns whipped out of the fog.

"Forward." Morlain commanded low and tense.

They walked slowly; the mist parted where Morlain stepped. The air radiated hunger as the vines searched for a feast. Varin tossed several vials in the direction Morlain silently commanded. Rynn kept a close eye on the mist as it closed off behind him. Rynn waved to Kendrick as the smoke wall closed with a pearl glint off in the distance.

Chills crawled over Anola; each step drew closer to the Queen's Castle. Morlain pointed east, Bash threw more vials. Anger and hunger snapped around broken shards. Rynn peered into this bag only a handful of vials left. Morlain motioned to the ashen bird. The falcon wove cords above to veer to the left. Bash signaled to Varin. Blood vines went silent.

The land shifted at Anola's feet. Dirt rumbled and vines smacked ruthlessly. Horses stampeded toward them. The hungry vines whaled out from the mist and clamped onto the steeds. A vine tightened around a gray mount; bones broke. Vines slashed for prey knocked Rynn down. Vials broke on impact.

Vines snaked underground and propelled out the surface and entangled in Rynn's legs. The vines yanked Rynn into the fog as he welded his hammer. Vines snaked along the terrain. Bash ran with blade in rage. Metallic air sent the vines into a frenzy.

"Morlain!" Anola cried as she sliced onslaught of blood vines.

Morlain weaved ebony strands and launched them into the ground. The braided flow of magic spiraled, land caved open and split. Anola narrowed in on the exposed Queen's gate. Each step she slashed her blade and drove back rapid hungry vines.

"There! Move!" Morlain dashed to the door.

Bash, Varin and Anola battled the vines as Morlain pressed his bare hands against the door. Carved emblems glowed in tangent. Dust sprayed as the door open. The entryway hissed and exposed access to the Queen's Castle. Anola pushed Bash and Varin through the door. She cut into the thorny vines. Morlain wrapped his arm around Anola and pulled her inside as the doors forced shut. Both crashed to the ground. Anola pushed Morlain away as his grinned sobered to a grimace.

"Your welcome milady."

"Morlain!" Anola pushed Morlain into the wall.

"You promised I would not lose another!"

"I promise I would do my best to keep them safe. Dangers have risks. Yours are the same as mine."

Anola released Morlain from her grip circled the massive open room.

"The king has sent us on quest of death." Anola lashed out.

Bash and Varin pointed their swords at Morlain.

"Stand your ground. Morlain is the one who showed me proof. I still want to hear it from our king. In the letter the King only wants the Queen's heart beyond anything else. We will complete our mission, return to the Northland and discover what this all about."

"This man may be in league our king but where does his loyalty really lie?" Bash growled.

"My allegiance is to myself, but my word is firmly planted with Anola. I will do my best to get us all back to your kingdom."

Varin eyes narrowed on Morlain, "As I said before Anola I will stand by you." Bash agreed with a firm nod.

Chapter 8 ~ Queen's Castle

Anola surveyed the entry room, the ceiling an endless view. Cold slate frosted stones decorated the interior with two mirrored staircases tiered along the back wall. Thick flaky vines grew up the railing.

The air stale, heavy, and undisturbed in centuries. Anola picked upped a round navy and black orb; dozens scattered the floor. Hollow cries broke out where Anola touched.

"The Queen had a unique style." Morlain marveled. "The books described how she never had to leave her tower. She entered into people's dreams, changing them from the inside to complete her will."

"What did she want?" Anola set the trinket down.

"That is the unsolved question I have yet to discover."

"Let's keep going, Varin, Bash take the stairs to the right. Morlain and I will go left."

Dark frosted staircase veered along the walls curled into two opposing corridors. Each flight of stairs led to thick metallic portals. Anola tapped the reflective doorway with the tip of her blade. Mirrored metal waves rippled outward reflected Morlain and Anola. Anola peered at her gem in the reflection it glowed. She casted her gaze at the pendent. The same frosted mist swirled inside the clear gem. Anola looked at Morlain who pressed his palm into the portal. His hand disappeared. Morlain nodded and entered the liquid doorway. Anola casted a final glance around the room. Barren and empty, she stepped through sword first.

The portal cool, transported Anola into a large room covered from ceiling to floor in volcanic red tapestries. Gold embodied thread curved into poetic details. Three colored matched sofas with dark burgundy wood trim circled around a sea green glass table. Two black goblets, thin in stem and wide bowl placed neatly on the table. Each filled to the brim with tinted azure liquid with specks of gold. Anola sidestepped; blade held out. She made her way to the center of the room.

"Morlain?" Anola whispered as she bobbed between translucent crimson fabric.

Morlain stepped out from a thick curtain and slid onto one of the silk sofas. Anola kept her blade ready.

"What exactly is this place?"

Morlain's smile sent chills down Anola's spine. "I believe in order to gain access to the Queen's Throne room we have to have a drink."

"I'm not drinking that."

"I don't think we have a choice."

Morlain pointed at the wall. Thick black sludge oozed between cracks. The dregs dropped to the floor and pulled together. Rigid legs formed and the body elevated into a grotesque abdomen. Anola stepped toward Morlain, her focus on the built form. Sounds of cascaded alluvium dripped off the walls flooded the chamber.

"I don't think they will stop even if we defeat them. The castle's ingrained magic will continuously make these creatures."

Anola turned as a partially formed creature clawed at her armor. The entity knocked Anola to the ground. It's head only half formed pillowed to completion. Continuous rivets of ooze rolled through the body of the monster. Thorned claws and barked legs.

Anola pushed herself up and cut through the arm of the being; the lobbed off claw dropped to the ground. It absorbed back into its owner's body. Morlain pulled Anola near him. He casted a barrier of tartar and ash chains. Creatures pelted on the shield.

"Anola we have to drink them. The Queen's tests us. She loved to play games. No matter how evil the results. Even though she disappeared doesn't mean her powers aren't still here."

Anola watched as more oozing creatures banged on the protective border. Morlain picked up the goblets handed one to Anola. She peered into the calm liquid and took the goblet from

Morlain as he drank his. His goblet clanged to the floor. The magic barrier began to fade. Anola inhaled the beverage; a burning sensation gripped the back of her throat. Stands of ivory blacked out her vision.

୨୦   ୧୨

"Dad! I can't do this! I'm not cut out to be a knight." Young Anola threw her wooden sword to the ground.

Ahar walked to a frustrated young Anola and knelt next to her.

"My daughter you have many abilities but building a skill will take time not all things will come easily."

"Dad why am I different?"

"What do you mean my daughter?"

"The other kids play all day, but I train. Am I not a kid too?"

Ahar laughed, "Daughter you have a gift and time will only tell how you will use it."

"Gift?"

୨୦   ୧୨

Anola landed on cold stones soaked in sweat and visions. Morlain offered her his hand. She took his hand. The Queen's throne room. Smaller than the entry way, rowed columns lead to the throne. A single window splashed in morning light.

"Are you two alright?" Anola looked at her knights.

Varin nodded with newly formed bruises on his face and Bash's left arm armorer gone. Morlain eyes widen in excitement. The pedestal between two stone figures held a large Fathom Woods burgundy chest with obsidian tree branches carved design.

Chapter 9 ~ Malevolent Queen

The Queen's thrown room. A circular room, two rows of columns led to the Queen's seat. Thick black metallic vines with sharp thorns wrapped around the seat of power. Each guardian held a sword in unmovable vows. Anola peered through the window. The Northern Mountains sunrise peaked in the distance.

Morlain cautiously moved in front of the chest. Anola close behind. Bash and Varin encircled behind the locked box.

"I don't know what may happen when I touch this." Morlain nimble hands moved.

"Hopefully those guards are only made of stone. Bash, Varian be ready." Anola stared passed Morlain at the engraved guards. Their helmets covered with curved designs matched the curtains from the previous room.

"Sto..." Anola's warning fell silent.

Morlain placed his gloved hands on the chest. A small flash of teal waved through the guardians. The stone guards cracked. Living mirror-like liquid bubbled out and shaped into movable armor.

"Move Morlain!"

Anola shoved Morlain away as one of the guardians slashed down on the sorcerer. Varin rammed the guardian to the ground. The guardian picked itself up and swung its blade. Varin braced. The blow thundered as Varin flew across the room.

Bash cried out in explosive anger. He brandished his blade. The knight drove his blade into the other guardian. The sword absorbed into the metallic guard.

Anola sliced through Varin's target guardian. Anola pulled Varin up. Varin gripped Anola's shoulder.

"Anola I don't know what was in that liquid we drank but I saw memories."

"Memories?"

"Of your father of when he first found you and discovered you have a gift."

"I saw memories as well, what is this gift he mentioned?"

"Anola, when your father first found you in the Fathom Woods. He didn't save you, you saved yourself. The Fathom trees were broken all around you and not a single wound on you."

"What?"

"Your father always said you had a gift but other than that day he never saw you display it again."

Morlain unleashed emerald and tang whips at the guardians. Vibrant vines thrashed the guardians against the wall. Bash slammed into a guardian; he held it in place. Varin squeezed Anola's forearm and nodded, he ran and pinned the other guardian.

"Get the chest!" Morlain cried out.

Anola approached the chest. Her pendent began to glow pale pulsing yellow. Anola lifted the gem from her collar. She held it before the box. Her hands moved of their own accord. The key fit. Click.

"Anola!!!" Varin yelled. One of the guardians broke free. The metallic keeper picked up Bash and hurled him at Anola. Both chest and Anola flew against the wall. Her vision blurred.

Morlain struggled to hold the one guardian in place. Varin and Bash clashed blades with the other keeper.

The guard rained down jabs at Bash and Varin. Anola pulled herself to her knees. She looked at the opened chest. Red pulsed rhythmic lights protruded from the massive ruby. The Queen's Scarlet Heart.

Anola inhaled; her eyes memorized at the eerie call within. She gripped the gem. Morlain turned to see Anola. His eyes widen. Anola pushed the Scarlet Heart into her chest.

Anola screamed. A rush of ruby and onyx ribbons encased her. Rapid waves of magic swirled and pulsed around the room. The guardians froze.

The cocoon dissolved. Heavy charcoal dust floated to the ground.

"Anola?" Varin whispered.

The figured turned. The Queen. Her eyes filled with icy blue hues and black threads. Dressed in glamorous onyx form fitted sheath dress with threaded designs poured onto the floor. A high collar of black thorns stretched to the ceiling.

"The Malevolent Queen." Varin gasped.

The Malevolent Queen looked directly at Varin. Her sly grin poured fear into the room. She flicked her fingers, Varin burst into ashen flakes. Bash barreled toward the Queen with Varin's sword. Blade held high. His steps landed into a pool of metallic ooze. He sank.

"Ano..!" Words choked out as Bash disappeared.

The Queen walked to her window. She gazed at the Northern Mountains. She observed the land below. Kendrick lay on the ground. The Queen waved her hand at the Fathom wolves.

The wolves pulled Kendrick into a pit. The mother of wolves looked at Queen and bowed. The wolves returned to the burgundy brush.

The Queen callously laughed as she ran fingertips along the frame of the window. A blast of ash rippled through the room. The room settled; diamonds littered the floor.

The Malevolent Queen glided to her thrown. Her raven hair continued to grow past her waist. The thorns slid out or her seat. The Queen took her position of power. The ashen falcon landed at the base of the throne. The bird ruffled its feathers and transformed into a peacock. The bird's laid a berth of feathers at the Queen's feet.

"You may step out sorcerer." Queen's voice low and calm.

Morlain stepped from behind a pillar. He strode toward the Queen. He knelt.

"My Queen, I have been awaiting your arrival."

The Malevolent Queen held out her hand. Morlain took it willingly and pressed his lips gently to her hand.

"You have served me well Morlain, as you will continue to serve me further."

Morlain slid next to the Queen's side.

"As my adoptive father said, I have a great gift. Time to use it and complete my vision."

Malevolent Queen

The Eternal Rose

Ruth Hamre

Summer in Scotland with her brother wasn't turning out to be quite as exciting as Aoife had hoped. They had spent most of it on the shores and boats of Loch Ness without catching so much as a glimpse of the infamous monster. Which was why she was slogging through the moors, actually hoping Jenny Green-teeth would show up. Her eyes, a lighter shade of gray than the water surrounding her, scanned constantly for ripples that might show her where the creature lurked.

When she felt the monster's malice and hunger, her first instinct was to freeze, but that would have warned the creature that she was aware of it, so she kept going, despite her brother's growing apprehension. Sir Finn was fully capable of dealing with anything that would come after her, and she wasn't helpless herself. Aside from the heavy branch she was using to test each step, she had a kunai hidden in each sleeve. None in her boots, this time, not with the brackish water coming up to her knees.

She pulled her foot free with a bit more effort on the next step. Had Jenny Green-teeth made a grab for her or was it just mud? Maybe it was time to turn back. Monsters weren't always the most dangerous thing around.

Just as she turned, a green-skinned hag burst out of the water, reaching for her with hands ending in long, claw-like nails. Aoife swung the branch at the creature and stepped to the side. A moment later, the corpse splashed into the water with her brother's crossbow bolt through its chest. Grinning, Aoife pulled the bolt out and made her way back to solid ground as quickly as she dared.

She reached the shore, and Finn hugged her. "I gotta admit, you had me worried, going out so far."

She hugged him back. "I know."

"Of course, you do. So why do you keep scaring me?"

"I knew we could handle it. And we did." Aoife pulled out of the hug to look back at the moor. "Almost too quickly."

"Are you suggesting that you're getting bored with spending the summer with your favorite brother?"

She lightly smacked his shoulder. "You're my only brother! Unless there's something Mom hasn't told me."

Finn's phone buzzed, and he pulled it out to check the message. "Looks like you won't have to be bored much longer. We've got another job."

Aoife grinned. "Let's go."

഻ ഻

The next day, they arrived at the castle. "It's smaller than I expected," Aoife admitted as they pulled up to the gate, rain pelting the roof of the car.

Finn shrugged. "That's only because skyscrapers are a thing now. Back in the day, this would have been huge."

As they rushed through the rain to the door, Aoife caught movement from the corner of her eye. She turned in time to see a cat's black tail disappear into a hedge. Probably nothing to worry about, but she had learned not to assume anything when hunting monsters. Finn used the iron knocker, the sound dulled by the rain. Aoife giggled as the door swung open. "Could you spare a cup of water?"

"Well, more than a cup!" the bald, powerfully built man at the door laughed. "Come on in before ye get soaked, although I suppose it's a bit late for that." They entered and hung their rain jackets on a coat rack by the door. "I'm afraid I've sent most of the staff away. It seemed safer. Allow me to introduce myself.

I'm Lord George McDonald. I take it the two of ye are from the Knights of Silene."

"Yes sir, I'm Sir Finn, and this is my sister, Ee-fa," he over enunciated her name, used to people getting it wrong.

"You're American? Pardon me, I was expecting someone more local."

"I'm stationed at Loch Ness, Aoife's interning with me for the summer. I suppose they sent us so she can get some experience."

The Lord nodded. "Fair enough. I suppose where ye come from does nae affect how good ye are at yer job."

"I was top of my class last year." Aoife said.

Finn rolled his eyes. "You've been top of your class since kindergarten!"

"My, that is impressive!"

"Hopefully, I can keep it that way till I graduate next year. I'd hate to trip at the finish line."

"Don't forget, training doesn't end with graduation. You've still got a long way to go." Finn turned to Lord McDonald. "Now if you don't mind getting to business, what makes you think you have a faerie problem?"

"Oh, we've always had a few incidents here and there. The place is supposed to be haunted, after all."

"Ghosts aren't exactly our thing," Aoife pointed out.

"No, and normally I would nae bother with that. A few footsteps down an empty hall now and then give the old place some character, and she's caused no real problems. Lately, however, there have been other things. Objects inexplicably moving, especially old valuable things, even furniture sometimes, but no one is ever around to see it. And then there's that cat. It may be a coincidence, but a strange cat started hanging around here about the same time the trouble started. The cook tried leaving out some milk, but that does nae seem to have helped."

Finn frowned. "That probably encouraged it to stick around."

"Oh, nobody expected that to get rid of it. We just thought it might calm things down a bit."

The Lord led them through the castle and pointed out the places where things had been moved. They came to the library, and a portrait hanging between two bookshelves immediately drew Aoife's attention. The picture depicted a young woman with blond hair and piercing blue eyes holding a huge rose. "Who is that?"

"That is Lady Katherine McDonald. She lived here in the Middle Ages. They say her ghost still does."

"Why would she be trapped here?"

"Well, according to the stories, she was accused of witchcraft, and, well, ye know how that would have turned out."

Aoife nodded, glad she hadn't been born into that era when her red hair, and even her freckles, could have been used as evidence against her. She studied the portrait a moment and pointed to the object the woman in the portrait held. "That's not a real flower, is it?"

"Supposedly, it was a ruby cut to look like one. Apparently, that was her dowry. They called it the Eternal Rose. Before ye ask I've nae idea where it is now. They say it disappeared around the time she was accused. Some think it was stolen, maybe by her accusers. Some say she hid it herself to keep them from getting it. There's nae telling what the truth is now."

"I'm surprised they left her portrait up, if they executed her for witchcraft," Finn said.

"Oh, it's been taken down a few times over the years. Whenever it comes down, the ghost kicks up a fuss. That's how I knew it wasn't her causing the latest trouble. I have thought about taking it down myself, just to see if the stories were true, but I decided I didn't want to find out they're not. Sometimes it's better not to have all the answers."

"I don't know about that. I think I'd like to get as many answers as I can," Aoife said.

"Not all though! Take Nessie. Once someone actually catches the beastie, people will lose interest. At that point it's nae a monster anymore, just another animal. The mystery is what keeps people interested. As long as those scientists keep comin' up with nothing' and sayin' it's nae there, people will keep believing in it and come looking."

"Of course, if it does get caught, I'm sure at least a few people will find a reason to say, *that's not it*," Finn said.

Lord McDonald laughed, "That's true enough!"

The tour ended at their guest rooms. "I'll leave ye to get settled, and rest. I expect ye will want to stay up tonight, trying to catch the faerie."

"It would be hard to catch it if we're sleeping when it shows up," Aoife said.

Finn laid a hand on her shoulder. "We'll just do reconnaissance tonight, find out what exactly we're up against before we actually take it on."

Aoife nodded, but if she saw a chance to take this thing down, she would.

Aoife was not sure whether she was naturally a night owl or if she had simply adjusted to the mostly nocturnal schedule necessary for fighting monsters. Either way, staying up late isn't the problem, it's the boredom. Surveillance may have been a vital task on any mission, but that did not change the fact that it bored her. She couldn't pull out her phone and play games as she sat in the dim room watching the monitors to see if a faerie showed up. The only reason she had her phone on her at all was so she and Finn, who was outside patrolling the grounds, could contact each other if something happened. So far it had been quiet, which should have been good news, but hurry up and wait got real old real fast. This could be nothing but a waste of time. Maybe whatever was causing the trouble had already gotten what it had come for. Maybe it had noticed that there were knights at the castle and would stay away. Of course, it could always come back after they left.

She stared at the monitors and a black cat stalked across one of the screens. Where had that come from? It could just be an ordinary cat that had found its way in, but considering why they were here, that seemed unlikely. Should she call Finn? She didn't want to distract him with something trivial, but she couldn't let it slide if this was it. Her gut told her this was no ordinary cat.

As the cat began wondering around a sitting room, Aoife stood and headed for the room as quickly and quietly as she could. This time, besides the kunai in her sleeves, she had one in each boot and a belt ringed with them, plus the two katanas on her back. She was ready for anything.

Aoife reached the door to the sitting room and flattened herself against the wall. She tilted her head and peered into the room without revealing herself. Impatience and frustration came from a presence in the room; not the sort of emotions she expected from an exploring cat. It was not her brother; he was still outside. She knew the feel of his emotions like the sound of his voice. It could be Lord McDonald, but he had gone to bed hours ago, and she didn't think she was close enough to pick up on him. That left the cat. That meant it wasn't a real cat.

She leaned around the door frame and saw the black form slip out from under an armchair. Bright green eyes fixed on her before she could react. The beast shimmered and, a moment later, a man about three feet tall stood where the cat had been. His skin was slightly lighter than the black velvet clothes he wore, contrasting with his startlingly white boots. His pointed ears removed any doubts that he was a faerie. "What are you doing?" He sprang out of the way as a kunai struck the chair. "Aoife! Watch it! You'll put someone's eye out!"

She froze a kunai in her hand. "How do you know my name?"

He stared at her, then slapped himself on the forehead. "Stupid, out of sync timelines!"

Aoife threw the kunai. He dodged. What was that nonsense about timelines? The most logical explanation was that he had heard Finn say her name and came up with the most absurd excuse he could to distract her, but his reaction had seemed genuine. There was no time to waste sorting it out. She had a job to do. She pulled another kunai.

"Not that this isn't fun, but I'm getting out of here. I'll tell Libby you said hi." He took a step and vanished.

Aoife's kunai passed through empty space. "Who the heck is Libby?"

ॐ ॐ

Finn's forest green eyes glared down at Aoife. "What were you thinking?"

She stared back up at him, unfazed. "I was thinking that if I waited, it would get away."

"It *did* get away! And we still don't know what it's after!"

"Who cares what it's after? It's a faerie, it's causing trouble. We're here to deal with it. At least we know it's a Cat Sith now."

"You could have figured that out from watching the monitors, like you were supposed to!"

"The whole point of this internship is to get experience in the field. How am I supposed to do that if I never actually do anything?"

"You should have at least let me know you were going to investigate!"

"You would have told me not to!"

"If you know that, you should have known not to go!" Finn took a deep breath before he continued. "The bottom line is that you left your post. What if there had been another one, and you didn't see it? It could have snuck-up on you and-"

Aoife scoffed. "And what? I don't think you understand how hard it is to take me by surprise. I get that the empathic thing isn't that common, and it freaks people out, but it comes in handy."

"Can you tell where they are? Or how close?"

"You know it doesn't work like that, but it gives me enough of a heads-up to react sooner than anyone would expect."

"It's not fool-proof. Certain faeries might be able to block you."

"They would have to know to do that, and I don't see how they could find out. Most of the people who know like to pretend they don't."

"Overconfidence is going to get you into trouble. The internship is about getting experience with someone here to help you. I can't do that if you keep going rogue! Not to mention that now we have to explain to Lord McDonald why there are holes in his antique chair."

"It's not like I missed! He just dodged!"

"Exactly! No matter how good you are, no matter how much experience you have, there's always a chance that the other guy will be better! That's why we never do this alone!"

"Okay." Aoife tried to control her tone, but she knew her brother knew she just wanted to end the lecture. "I'm sorry."

Finn sighed. "Look, just don't forget how dangerous this is. You never know when your next mission might be your last."

"I know," she whispered. That was one thing he didn't have to remind her of.

The next night, Aoife sat staring at the monitors again. Hopefully, they would catch the thing, and this could be their last night here. As she watched that same cat began making its way through the rooms. This time it went to the library.

Aoife snatched her cell phone and texted Finn. She told him the cat was in the library and she would meet him there. She left the phone, not waiting for his reply.

As she approached the room, she could sense the same impatience and frustration she had noticed from the Cat Sith the night before. There was something else this time; a sense of worry and urgency from someone she could not identify. Aoife carefully peered into the room. The only person she saw was the dwarf, standing in front of the portrait of Lady Kathrine. She reached for a kunai. She stopped as the dwarf pried at the portrait's frame. Surely, he didn't think there was a safe hidden behind it.

He did not find anything, stepped back, and stared up at the portrait. He turned his back to the door and looked between the portrait and the bookcase directly across from it. He crossed the room examined the shelf and returned to the portrait. He pulled it back from the wall again and reached up. He pressed a stone in the wall, the bookcase swung out to reveal a doorway. The man returned to cat shape and dashed across the room through the door. Aoife followed.

The cat was out of sight when she entered the dark and dusty passage. Maybe she should have brought her cell phone after all, for the flashlight. She wasn't about to go back for it now. She reached the end of the passage and stopped at the doorway to a small room. The dwarf stood in the middle of the space, holding a glowing stone. Shelves held several old chests and small boxes and glowed in bright white light. The little man climbed on top of one chest and scaled the shelves. He reached for one of the smaller boxes. Outstretched fingers grazed and shifted the container. It lipped the edged, tumbled, and crashed to the floor, bursting open. A blue cloth unfurled, and a ruby the size of a fist cut into the shape of a rose rolled free.

Aoife fully entered the room and drew her katanas. The dwarf jumped down from the shelves. She tapped the ruby with the toe of her boot. "I would ask what you want with this, but it's a giant freaking ruby, so the answer seems kind of obvious."

The little man shrugged. "Fair assumption, but the right answer isn't always so obvious."

"Aoife!" Finn ran in, claymore broadsword in his hands.

The dwarf glanced between them, then down at the ruby, sighed, and vanished.

"What were you thinking, coming in here alone?" Finn demanded.

"I was thinking about getting the job done! At least we know what he's after now." Aoife picked up the ruby. She looked up at her brother and gasped. A woman stood behind him, a faint red glow around her.

"What are you staring at?" Aoife handed him the ruby, and the woman disappeared. "What?"

"Turn around."

Finn did and jumped. "Where did she come from?"

"I think she's been here the whole time. I think she's the ghost. The Eternal Rose. Not just a rose that would last forever, but one that gives you a glimpse of eternity."

"Okay." Finn picked up the cloth from the floor and wrapped the ruby in it. "I'll have to see what Lord McDonald wants to do with this. You go back to your room and stay there."

"What? We should be planning! We could use that thing as bait-"

"Do you really think a Cat Sith would be stupid enough to fall for that, knowing that we know what it's after?"

"I seriously doubt it's going to let something like this go without a fight. It's gone to this much trouble to find it, it will not want to risk us sending it to a museum or something."

"As good of a point as that is, you have been reckless on this mission, and I have to seriously consider whether to allow you to continue participating in it."

"I'm just trying to do my job! If I hadn't followed him in here, he could have gotten away with that ruby, and we never would have known it!"

"You didn't know where that passage led, or if the door would close behind you, and you didn't even bring your phone with you so you could call for help if you got trapped, or if something else went wrong. Right now, your job is to learn, and as far as I can tell, you are refusing to do that!"

"You can't just...ground me! You aren't my dad! You aren't even really my brother!" Too far. She instantly knew it, but it was too late.

Finn took a deep, slow breath before he responded. "Genetics aside, as long as you are here, I am responsible for you. Now go to your room. I'll let you know what Lord McDonald and I decide to do later."

Aoife left without another word.

The next night, Aoife sat in front of the monitors waiting out Finn's instructions. "What do you do if something happens?"

"Call you and wait for instructions." As if he hadn't given her enough of those.

"You say that, but will you do it?"

"Yes."

Finn sighed. "I wish I could be sure of that. Honestly, the only reason I'm giving you the chance is because I don't think the thief is going to try again so soon."

"And as soon as they can send you some backup, you'll have me locked in my room during the real action."

"Not if you prove to me that I can trust you."

"How am I supposed to do that if nothing happens?"

"By following instructions for once. You'll get plenty of chances to take down monsters, but for now, you are still learning. You have to trust the people with more experience." His voice softened. "I understand that the rumors about your mother have you eager to prove yourself. I just don't want you to get yourself killed before you get the chance."

"You don't think they're true, do you?"

"I wish I could tell you they aren't, but I don't know. All I know is that they brought back your father's body and didn't find her one way or the other. I don't know why people were so quick to believe the worst. All I can tell you is that Aunt Tabitha always seemed nice to me. It's hard to believe she could do something like that. Of course, I was still a kid myself. There may be more to it than I know."

Aoife nodded. "All I know is that she promised she would come home, and she didn't."

Finn laid a hand on her shoulder. "I just want to make sure you get home-preferably breathing and in one piece."

"I know."

"Good." He left.

ço   ෬

The night dragged on as Aoife sat and watched the monitors. Nothing happened. She resisted the urge to play a game on her phone. She knew as soon as she did, she would miss something. *Or I would just run down the battery and wouldn't have it when I needed it.* She put her elbows on the desk, rested her chin in her palms and stared at the monitor. she perked up when the cat made his way toward the library. She reached for her phone.

"Oh no you don't."

Aoife jumped out of her chair and whirled around. A young man, about the same age as her brother, stood in the doorway, a sword in his hand. Her empathy should have alerted her that someone lurked nearby. She stared at him but could not sense his presence. "Who are you? How did you get in without-?"

"Talent. As for who I am, you'll find out. Eventually." He dragged the last word out in a way that would have been funny if the situation hadn't been so unnerving.

Aoife threw a kunai at him. He deflected it with a flick of the sword. "Easy there, Spitfire, I'm not gonna hurt you. I'm just here to keep you busy for a minute." His eyes flicked to the monitors behind her.

She took advantage of the distraction and threw another kunai at him. Again, he deflected it.

"I take it the Cat Sith that's been pestering Lord McDonald is a friend of yours?"

"More like an in-law, actually. I won't bore you with the whole family tree. It's a bit mangled. I chopped off a few limbs myself."

Aoife drew both katanas and charged at him. He dodged one and blocked the other. She pressed her attack with a triple swipe with her right and a lunge with her left. He easily blocked them. Steely eyes looked down at her across the blades. She realized she could not beat him and backed away.

He grinned. "Don't worry, it's not that you're bad. I'm just better." He glanced at the monitors again and ran from the room.

Aoife ran after him, then stopped. She sheathed one of her katanas, picked up her phone, and called Finn.

"Got something?"

"The Cat Sith is in the library and there's someone else here. I'm not sure what he is, but he could block my empathy, so he's definitely something, and I think he's heading for the library."

"I'll meet you there."

Aoife made it to the library at the same time as her brother. The Cat Sith held the ruby and stared up at the tall stranger. "Okay, let's go." A crossbow bolt knocked the ruby from his hand.

Aoife ran for the ruby. Finn reloaded his crossbow. The little man became a cat and ran at his leg; keeping him off-balance and unable to fire. The taller man reached the ruby at the same time as Aoife. They both grabbed it.

The world turned red, and Aoife no longer saw the castle library. She gazed at an alley where a teenage boy stood, panting. A man approached him with a sword in his hand. It had been over a decade since she had seen him, but Aoife immediately knew the man was her father. She saw no signs but knew the boy must have been a monster for her father to stalk him. The boy backed away with his hands up. Her father raised his sword. The point of a sword burst through her father's chest. Astonishment and anguish filled his face. He fell to the ground. Her mother stood behind him, bloody sword in her hands.

The ruby clattered to the stone floor. Aoife and the stranger both backed away from it. She saw fear and astonishment on his face, even without her empathy. His face grew pale, his eyes wide and dilated. "You could have warned me!"

"I didn't know that was going to happen! I don't even know *what* happened!"

Finn and the Cat Sith stopped fighting, concerned with their companion's well-being. Lord McDonald stood behind them wearing a dressing gown. Aoife glanced at them, took a deep breath and picked up the stone. She saw the ghost of Lady Kathrine, standing in the center of the room. "This was yours, wasn't it?"

Yes. It was strange. Aoife couldn't hear her, but she knew what the ghost was saying.

"What do *you* want?"

It does not belong in this world. These men have said they will take it to a place more suitable for such things.

Aoife looked at the two men. "What exactly do you guys want with this thing?"

They looked at each other. The Cat Sith spoke. "We have a friend, Libby, who has a place to store magical books and artifacts, to preserve them and make them available for anyone who needs them, she sent us to find it. Once I explained that to Lady Kathrine, she told me where to find it."

"Let them have it," Lord McDonald said. "I won't miss something I never had in the first place, and it sounds like it will do more good with this friend of theirs than gathering dust in a museum that won't even know what they've really got."

Aoife hesitated. She did not trust them. Usually, her empathy would have helped her decide how sincere they were, but with the taller man blocking that she couldn't be sure. It was even possible that Lady Kathrine really had been a witch and had other reasons for wanting these men to take it. At the very least, they admitted they were taking it to a place where it would be available for people to use, and she couldn't imagine a good use for something that clearly involved some kind of necromancy. The ruby belonged to Lord McDonald, and he was the one who had asked them to come. It was his call. *Besides, if these two cause trouble later, we can deal with them then.*

Aoife tossed the ruby to the taller man. He caught it and raised an eyebrow. "Won't you get in trouble?"

Finn shrugged. "Our job was to stop the disturbance. We can always tell them you got away with it before we caught up to you."

The little man stood next to his friend. "I guess we'll be seeing you then."

The taller man grinned. "But you'll see us first." The dwarf shook his head, and they disappeared. Aoife could not see Lady Kathrine's ghost without the ruby, but felt her emotions settle into contentment. Perhaps she could finally rest. The thought made Aoife feel better about giving up the ruby.

"I take it ye will be leaving tomorrow?" Lord McDonald asked.

"If you don't mind us staying the rest of the night," Finn said.

"Ye are welcome to stay longer than that, but fer now, I'm goin' back to bed," he waved and left the room.

Finn turned to Aoife. "Are you okay?"

"Yeah, I think so."

"What happened when you both had the ruby?"

She hesitated. Part of her didn't want to tell him, but she had to. "I saw my mo-I saw Tabitha kill my dad."

"Oh. That doesn't mean that's really what happened. Magic is unpredictable, that's what makes it so dangerous. It could have been pulling images out of your own head to get the reaction it wanted. Do you think he saw the same thing?"

"I don't know. Whatever he saw, he wasn't any happier about it than I was."

Finn nodded. "Even if that is what happened, we still don't know the whole story."

"Do you think we ever will?"

"I don't know. I hope so." He hugged her. "I bet you're hoping the rest of the summer won't be quite so exciting now."

"I don't know about that. I'd still like to see the Loch Ness monster for myself!"

"Well, you better go get some rest so we can get back out there, then."

"On my way." Aoife stopped in the doorway and looked back. "You're my favorite brother."

Finn smiled. "You're my favorite sister."

Read another anthology from

JUMPMASTER PRESS™

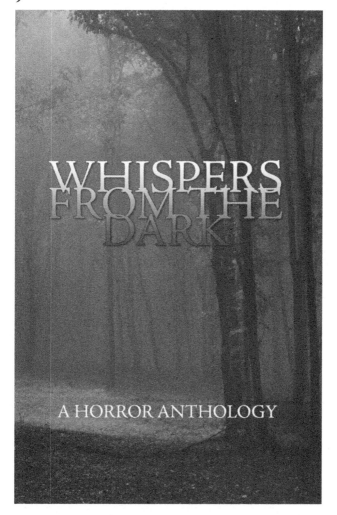

More exciting titles from

JUMPMASTER PRESS™

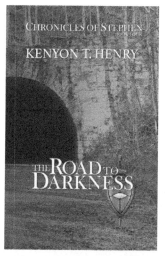

Made in United States
Orlando, FL
01 December 2023